NO PRAYERS FOR THE DYING

DALE M. NELSON

Severn River Publishing
www.SevernRiverBooks.com

78-1-64875-608-5 (Paperback)

ALSO BY DALE M. NELSON

The Gage Files

No Prayers for the Dying

One Bullet Away

With Andrew Watts

Agent of Influence

A Future Spy

Tournament of Shadows

All Secrets Die

Never miss a new release!

Sign up to receive exclusive updates from author Dale M. Nelson.

severnriverbooks.com

This one's for you, Pop. I think you would have liked it.

"It's hard to find a black cat in a dark room. Especially if he's not there."
- Chinese Proverb

"If you are far from the enemy, make him believe you are near."
- Sun Tzu

1

I dragged myself into the Santa Monica tiki bar that served as my office at the crack of noon, bleary eyed and in desperate need of coffee.

It'd been a long and late night.

I'd been looking into rumors that a pair of LA City Council members were granting lucrative contracts to minority-owned businesses. Seemed noble on the surface, until you peeled that dirty onion back and realized they were doing that at the expense of a different group of minority-owned businesses. All this to secure their positions on the council as protecting their base.

Unfortunately for me, one of the council members in question also had a handful of LAPD officers on their payroll. As I was meeting with my source, one of those cops showed up and tried to make trouble for us. It was never a good sign when you were doing escape-and-evasion techniques from the police in your own country. The evening started out that way and went downhill from there.

Upside, I wasn't in jail, and I was able to secure evidence for my client, an investigative journalist.

All in all, a success.

My name is Matt Gage, and I'm a private detective.

Sort of.

I'm an ex-spook. According to the CIA's HR people, they fired me. I maintain it was the other way around.

Who are you going to believe? They hire people to lie for a living.

When it was all over, I settled in Santa Monica, which was as far from Langley as I could get without a passport. Los Angeles was a place where there was an equal measure of discretionary money and quiet problems a lot of people would pay to keep from getting loud.

Ask me how I got into this and, honestly I'd just sort of fallen into it. When I got out of the Agency, I had a hard time finding work. I had a feeling they went out of their way to poison some wells on my behalf. Still, there were plenty of private security companies that would hire someone like me. In fact, they sought out people like me. Ex-spooks with an axe to grind, the kinds of people who didn't mind getting their hands dirty for a nice payout.

That wasn't me.

Though, in my darker moments, I was scared to admit … it almost was.

Jennie Burkhardt had saved me. Jennie was a college friend. We were very close, dated off and on, mostly because we got bored. Eventually decided we were better off as friends. We stayed in touch throughout my career in the "State Department"—which, to her credit, she *never* believed. When I got out and was looking for a place to land, she said, "Come out to LA. It's got all the fun of a third-world shitshow, but with 5G."

Well, Jennie also said, "I've got a place for you to crash".

I'd thought she meant *her* room. She meant the guest room.

The first night was a little awkward. Her boyfriend made it a little more awkward.

It took me a little longer to puzzle out that Jennie was really talking about a job opportunity. Jennie worked for an international investigative body called "the Orpheus Foundation." She'd become famous about ten years ago as part of the team who broke the Panama Papers. Orpheus was a figure in Greek mythology, a minstrel who journeyed into the underworld to save his love, Eurydice. He made a bargain with Hades to take her back, on the condition that he would not look back when traveling on the River Styx. Curiosity got the better of him, and Orpheus looked back. Hades revoked the bargain, and Orpheus lost Eurydice forever. The organization chose that legend for their inspiration because of the three-part lesson in having the courage to uncover the darkest secrets, to investigate them without looking back, and to always temper curiosity with sound judgment.

I was really good at one of those and tended to ignore the other two. I'll let you decide which.

Orpheus often employed freelance investigators to run leads down or dig into issues on behalf of the journalists working on a story. Sometimes that meant going into dangerous places and picking up some information they could get in trouble for sharing. Or it meant providing security so that someone like Jennie could meet with a source.

You know, ex-spook stuff.

Unfortunately, it wasn't always steady work and rarely did it pay well, so I had the bright idea of filling the extra time as a private detective. I've seen *Magnum*—how hard could it be?

And, anyway, here I am.

As I said, my office is the back booth of a Santa Monica tiki bar called Cosmic Ray's, a surfer dive on the beach. I did some work for the owner once, and he now allowed me use of one of the two upstairs offices. Occasionally, I took him up on it, but I'd found that if someone was going to hire me after meeting me at a surfer dive bar, they probably weren't picky about the accommodation and didn't need to be impressed by two folding metal chairs and a desk from the '60s. Ray had been a pro back in the '80s, and most of the vets who hung around knew him from the circuit back in the day.

I stepped into the bar's dark confines, lit only by the Christmas lights over the bar, some green mood lighting along the wall, and whatever crawled in from the beach. Half of the bar was opened to the beach-facing side with outdoor seating beneath a grass-thatched roof.

There were a couple of tourists at my usual table, and I asked them to kindly move, because it was working hours. One of the gomers gave me a confused look behind a Mai Tai that was way too big for him. "I'm working," I said flatly. "And you're sitting in my office."

"Matt, they're paying customers," said Vicky, Cosmic Ray's manager. Vicky was a semi-pro surfer who'd never quite broken through. If the surf was good, she bookended her shifts on the water. Ray's helped her make rent.

"So am I," I said with righteous indignation.

Vicky's tone dropped several octaves so only I could hear. "You haven't paid your tab in three weeks. We can't keep floating you, Matt."

"I always pay for my coffee."

"It's two bucks, and you get unlimited refills."

"I'm meeting a prospective client today. I'll settle up in a couple days."

Vicky left to set up a new table for the gomers.

I stood, arms folded, until the gomers moved out of my spot. They couldn't quite figure out why I wouldn't just move to one of the numerous open tables, and I couldn't figure why *they* wouldn't just move to one of the numerous open tables, so I just stared at them until it became uncomfortable. Vicky retrieved them, pointing to their new table, and offered to comp an appetizer. I sat down, ready to begin my workday. Vicky brought me my coffee, informed me that I was an asshole, but she said it kind of smiling, so I knew we were all good.

I had a few minutes, so I opened my laptop and acted like I was doing something while I sipped coffee and listened to the ambient music. At night, Ray piped in what you'd expect to hear in a tiki surfer bar. During the day, though, it was the '80s and '90s rock and mostly surf-circuit veterans. Until happy hour, this place was basically a casting call for *Point Break.*

So, it was to the power-sludge opening riff of Soundgarden's "Outshined" that Elizabeth Zhou walked into my life.

She was tall and slender, moving with an athletic grace that spoke of some sport she'd mastered early in life and likely kept up. She wore a navy skirt, white blouse, and navy jacket. I did some background before our meet. She'd grown up in Palo Alto, though she was born in Beijing, and her parents immigrated to the US when she was five. Stanford undergrad and UCLA law school and now an attorney with West Coast Media Associates, one of LA's largest and most powerful entertainment law firms. WCMA's client list included most of the studios as well as much of their talent. They had most of California's professional sports teams and that ninja show that was really just rebranded American Gladiators without the fighting. I really wanted an in at WCMA. These were the kinds of people who kept people like me on retainer to make sure their clients stayed out of trouble. Or, when they inevitably did, to make sure no one found out about it.

I caught Ms. Zhou's eye and gave her a quick nod to let her know I was the person she was here to meet. Though, considering the only other people in the place were sullen tourists sitting behind neon volcano drinks and aging surfers, she might have figured that out herself in time. I stood as she neared the table and offered my hand, which she took. She had a nice, guarded smile.

"Mr. Gage?"

"It's a pleasure to meet you, Ms. Zhou. Call me, Matt."

I motioned for us to sit, and Vicky appeared, asking if she'd like anything. I told Ms. Zhou the coffee was quite good. She indicated that she was fine. Vicky left her a water and me a sour look.

"This is an interesting...office," she said.

"My first job, I asked my boss why I was in a cubicle that wouldn't stand up against a harsh breeze or strong language. He told me if I had a nice office, I'd never leave it. My job was on the street. I took that to heart."

Zhou gave a wan smile and said, "I guess that's good advice for someone in your line of work."

It was. I left out that the office was in Cairo and the job was dodging the Mukhabarat.

"So, Ms. Zhou, how can I help you?"

"Elizabeth, please." Her voice was heavy, and I could see something behind her eyes, sorrow, maybe even despair. She was a woman who carried heavy things. Thoughts of a movie star who needed me to erase a mistake before it became a scandal disappeared. Whatever her situation, it was likely personal. A person can give away dozens of nonverbal cues in the span of a short conversation. Being able to quickly assess and interpret them is an invaluable and potentially life-saving skill for an intelligence officer. The direction of eye movement in a conversation can indicate possible deception, and a hand twitch might be an unconscious tell about a concealed weapon on their person.

"I'm not really sure what do to here, or if you can help. I was just told that, maybe, well..." Her eyes went to the wall behind me, as if the words she were looking for could be found there. "A family friend, someone I trust, said I should talk to you."

"Why don't you tell me what's wrong?"

"My father died a week ago."

"I'm very sorry to hear that." When she didn't say anything else, I asked her, "Was that what you wanted to see me about?"

"Yes. The police are calling his death a suicide. They tell me the detectives can often make this determination early but to leave it to the medical examiner for final confirmation. I haven't heard anything from the medical examiner, yet. Everyone is saying they can't tell me anything because it's an ongoing investigation. They've sealed off my father's house, calling it a crime scene."

While I'm not a police officer, that didn't seem right to me. Once they'd determined the cause of death was self-inflicted, my understanding was that the authorities turned it over to the next of kin.

"You don't think he committed suicide," I said in a way that wasn't a question. There was no doubt in her mind, I could tell that much already.

"No, Mr. Gage, I don't. My father wouldn't kill himself," she said with conviction. "The police, they won't even release the body so we can bury him. They're saying the investigation is 'ongoing.' Whenever I call the detective, he just keeps repeating that line and tells me to be patient."

I'd been on her side of the rope and knew how it felt—when you wish anyone in the system would give a shit just enough to push the gears for you.

"What does your mother say about all this?"

"My mother died several years ago. She had cancer."

"I'm sorry. I didn't mean to pry, I'm just trying to understand the situation."

"It's not your fault, Mr. Gage, you couldn't have known," she said. Her eyes were damp, but not yet ready to relieve themselves of their burden. "We'd grown distant after my mother died. It wasn't anything he said or did, he was just so sad. It was like he was broken. Eventually, I felt like I couldn't carry his grief along with my own. I feel so awful admitting that."

I knew how she felt, though I didn't say it because I didn't want it to sound trite. I understood what it was like to lose a parent and to have to spread the pain around.

"We reconnected in the last couple of months. I don't want you to think that I'd abandoned him or anything like that. I just didn't call as often, didn't go back home to see him as much. The emotional distance was there, though." She paused to take a few long breaths. "I went up to see him for a weekend, to check in. He said he needed to see me. I'd never seen him like that, before."

"How was he different?"

"Almost manic. He didn't sleep much, and when he did it, was fitful. He drank. He paced all the time."

Elizabeth was describing the classic signs of someone who bore the brunt of too many secrets. I certainly didn't know enough to say whether I agreed with her, but whatever was going on in her father's final days, it troubled him greatly, and he had nowhere to go with it. I could see those lines etched into Elizabeth's face as well. She'd carry that cross for the rest of her life.

"Did he ever open up to you about what was bothering him?" I asked.

"My father became erratic in the last few months. Nervous. The last time I saw him, he told me he believed someone was following him."

I had some idea already, because of the backgrounding I'd done, but asked her, "What did your father do for a living?"

"He was a venture capitalist. He was co-owner of an investment firm in Silicon Valley. My father ran their internet and security portfolio. I think they had fifty million under management."

Quite a lot of money, though perhaps not by valley standards.

I asked her the obvious but necessary questions about her father's business. Was he on good terms with his partners? Was he in debt? Was the business healthy? She gave me a pretty rosy outlook on all of it. In his early sixties, Johnnie Zhou had easily made enough to live very well for the rest of his days and still leave his only daughter a solid legacy. He didn't retire because he didn't know what else to do with his time now when he'd become a widower.

I circled back to their relationship.

"Is it okay if I ask you some personal questions?"

"Mr. Gage, there is nothing more personal than a girl's relationship with her father. His death doesn't change that. Ask away. If it's too close, I'll tell you."

"When you last saw him, you thought he was being erratic. He'd been agitated for some time, but this was worse, yes?"

"That's correct."

"He'd never spoken about taking his life? Not even after your mother died?"

"Never."

"Did you ever have reason to believe he wasn't stable?"

"No."

"But your mother's death affected him deeply. Could it be that he didn't tell you? Maybe he was embarrassed, ashamed to admit it?"

"No, I don't think so."

"People have a curious relationship with fear, Ms. Zhou. They don't often like to admit it."

She smiled grimly. "Speaking as an attorney, you'd be great in a courtroom."

For a glorious host of reasons, let's hope it never comes to that.

"Mr. Gage, my father was a flamboyant, larger-than-life personality. He was gregarious. I think there is always a certain amount of...bullshit, I guess you'd say, in his line of work. But he was always honest with me. Particularly after my mother died. I think that's why the change from bombastic glad-hander to cloistered widower shocked me so much. I can't know if anyone *was* following him, but I certainly believe he believed someone was."

"Who was the last person to see your father alive?"

"You mean other than the person who killed him?"

Touché.

She said, "I was. I'd gone up to visit him. He was sad and wanted to see me. He'd been drinking a little, and we had a fight. The kind where it was about that, the drinking, but *not* about that, you know? He admitted he thought someone was following him. I told him he needed to go to the police. He refused. Said he didn't trust them."

"Why not?"

"Because he grew up in communist China. The police were a weapon of the state. My father was at Tiananmen Square in 1989. He never felt safe with authority after that. Even here, he didn't necessarily trust the police."

"Okay," I said. "How did he die?"

"A gunshot to the head."

Luckily for me, I had extensive training on how to avoid showing my thoughts in my expression. If the police said he'd died by a gunshot wound to the head, that was probably what happened. There would be forensic evidence on his hand, gunpowder residue.

"Elizabeth, I'm sure the police explained how this works. They'll have told you there is evidence on his hands showing he pulled the trigger. That's easily proven."

"Can't that be faked?"

"I mean, I suppose it's possible," I said, hedging. Actually, it was entirely possible. I knew because I'd done it. Though I had resources at my disposal, most people would not. "It would require specialized expertise, which is hard to come by. The police are pretty good at figuring out this sort of thing. A suicide is hard to fake. Elizabeth, I'm going to be perfectly frank you with. I don't feel right taking your money."

"I think someone murdered my father, and I want you to prove it. If, however, you come to the same conclusion as the police when you're done with your investigation, I'll accept that. I trust you. I don't trust them any more than my father did."

"You don't?"

"The first time my father told me he thought someone was following him was a few months ago. I convinced him to go to the police even back then. He did, many times, and they told him it was probably nothing. He eventually talked to a detective who said crimes against Asian Americans were up and my father should consider a self-defense class." She shook her head. The corners of her mouth were pulled back in an angry grimace. "They wouldn't even listen to him. And my dad was sixty-two. Who was he going to fight?"

When you peeled away the gadgets and the codenames and the embassy parties, an intelligence officer's job ultimately came down to convincing people to unburden their secrets. Most people couldn't wait to tell you what they knew. They didn't like the weight of secrets. They wanted someone to share the load. Elizabeth told me a lot, but she hadn't told me everything.

"Look, I don't know exactly what you do, Mr. Gage, but I'm convinced my father was murdered. I don't know if he had enemies. I like to think he didn't, but I know from my line of work what some people will do for money. What I need is for someone to investigate my father's death with the thoroughness he deserves. I want the truth, and I want someone to be punished, if it turns out my father indeed has been murdered. I will pay you a lot to find that out."

I wanted to press my eyes tight and make the world go away for a while. I was friends with a few cops here in LA, and some of my Agency buddies ended up in law enforcement over the years. We'd talk shop. Suicide cases were mostly simple, even if the motives were not. They called them "casket jobs." Open and shut. Elizabeth was clearly in pain and looked like she was trying to buy her way out of some guilt. I didn't want any part of that.

I also had about six weeks before I was out on the street if I couldn't make rent.

"Here's what I can do for you. I will look around and ask some questions. I may be able to find out why the police aren't sharing much with you. I've also got some connections in the journalism community who might open a couple doors for me. I'll present you with what I find, and if you want me to keep going, I will. Is that fair?"

"It is."

"What if, in the end, I find that your father actually did kill himself?"

"I'll have to learn to live with it."

"Before I start, I have two questions for you. The first is how did you hear about me? Who referred you?"

"Nate McKellar. Nate and my father were close. He's kind of my godfather, I suppose. In my culture, we'd just call him 'uncle.'"

That changed things.

Nate McKellar had been my boss and mentor in the Agency. I knew Nate was living in San Jose now, though I hadn't looked him—or anyone—up since I'd gotten out. The kind of relationship Elizabeth was describing meant they must have gone back a long ways, certainly more than the couple of years he'd been in San Jose. Nate was an old hand from the Far East Division, and he'd done several tours in China.

A lot of questions popped to the surface, like air bubbles in a dark bog.

Why would he send her to me?

And how would he know to?

"Once the police gave me that bullshit about my father's death being a probable suicide, I talked to Nate and asked him what I should do. He told me my only real option was to hire a private detective. We have people the firm uses, but I wanted to keep this separate. He told me an old colleague was now helping people out, that I should look you up. You said there was a second question?"

"Well, I guess it's more of a caveat than a question. I'm not a licensed private investigator. I want to make sure you're comfortable with that."

"I don't care what you call yourself. I care that you can get me answers. Nate said that's what you're good at."

"Fair enough."

I'd tried to go the legit route, but I found that the FBI had made sure I could never get a PI license in any state. A little spiteful scorched earth on their part as I walked out the door.

I told Elizabeth Zhou that I'd be in touch in the next couple of days on whether I could take the case. I gave her the rates for my time, and she didn't blink.

Once she'd left, I walked home and stared at my phone for a very long time.

Eventually, I worked up the nerve and called Nate McKellar.

"It's good to hear your voice, Matt," he said.

"You probably know why I'm calling," I said.

"Maybe we should talk in person."

That was always a good sign.

2
———

I caught a five o'clock flight out of LAX to San Jose and took a cab to Nate's. I knew if I didn't go straight there, I'd find a reason not to. While I waited for my flight, I secured a hotel room near the airport for the night. The cab dropped me at Nate's door about eight. He lived in a small community called Los Altos in the foothills on the western edge of Silicon Valley. Looking at it from the street, you couldn't get a sense of how big the place was because of the dense landscaping. All you could tell was that it was a single-story home, but the dimensions were otherwise undetectable. There were also no windows facing the street. A wry smile hit my lips. Good tradecraft, even with his real-estate tastes.

Nate had semi-retired four or five years ago and was already out here when the Agency punched my ticket, so we hadn't actually seen each other in a few years. They tapped him to run an investment firm that targeted technologies of interest to the intelligence community, and more specifically, the ones we feared foreign powers were targeting. It was like In-Q-Tel, but covert. When I'd left the Agency, Nate had called me to say he heard what happened and didn't believe what they'd accused me of and fired me for. Still, I could admit I was more nervous walking up to his door than I thought I'd be.

After a heavy inhale, I knocked, and anxious seconds later, my old boss appeared.

Nate McKellar looked more like a neatly groomed Gandalf than he did "Wild Bill" Donovan. Nate was about six-two with a neatly trimmed white beard and shining eyes over a broad smile. He'd put on a few pounds since I'd seen him last, but he carried it well. Nate wore tan pants and a collared shirt with a subtle grid pattern. He was dressed much more DC than he was Silicon Valley.

"It's good to see you, Matt," Nate said, and with that mighty bear hug, my trepidation was gone.

"You too, boss," I said, my words loaded and tense. He welcomed me into his home, which was much larger than it appeared from the street. His wife of thirty-five years, Patricia, was in the kitchen, finishing up the dinner dishes. She put the pan she was working with down and walked over to give me a hug.

"Hello, Matthew," she said. "I won't ask if you're staying out of trouble."

Lot of ways I could take that.

"Hi, Pat," I said.

I stayed in the kitchen and chatted with Pat for a few minutes while Nate fixed drinks. His Manhattans were legendary. I asked Pat if she was enjoying California, and she told me she was but missed her family, although the eldest daughter lived in Colorado and was at least close. I'd worked for Nate three times and had become very close to Pat over the years. She had a habit of adopting the single officers at the station, making sure we had a welcoming place to go for the typical family holidays. She found out when our birthdays were and did something special for us. An overseas assignment could be isolating, and Pat knew how to take the edge off. Being on Nate's team always made it feel like being in a family.

Nate returned with two tumblers and a cocktail shaker. He poured the contents into the glass and shaved a pair of orange peels on a cutting board, which he dropped into the drink before handing it to me. Nate then guided me outside to his patio and a couch beneath a wood pergola. He dialed up some jazz on his phone, and smooth piano that I didn't recognize appeared all around us.

I sipped my drink. It was as good as ever.

"I hope you don't dress like that at the office," I said. "If you don't have a black hoodie, they're gonna know you're a spy."

Nate laughed and told me about the job. It was a kind of reward for his long career in the Agency. He had no desire to run a fusion center or one of the new "mission centers" they'd created over the past few years. Instead, they'd offered him something most of the career-minded senior intelligence officers wouldn't want—to covertly run a tech investment business, place some smart bets on interesting companies, and pay attention to what foreign activities are looking at. For Nate, it was a perfect way to ease out of the spy business and pay his wife back for a lifetime of following him all over the world, doing work he could never tell her about.

"I wished you'd come to see me sooner, kid," Nate finally told me.

I shrugged. "I wasn't sure how you felt."

"You know how I felt. What they did was bullshit, and I told you as much."

"Thank you. That means a lot." I felt a little more at ease.

"That doesn't mean it wasn't your fault."

That stung.

Nate wasn't known for pulling punches and I appreciated that about him. Though perhaps not right now.

On my last assignment, I made a mistake, and someone got killed.

I loved her very much.

Nate came from the "hard truth" school of mentoring, and I suspected this was a conversation he'd wanted to have for some time. I did not.

"What can you tell me about Johnnie Zhou?"

"Johnnie is an old friend."

"You meet him in Beijing?"

"Very good. You did your homework."

I knew Nate had been posted at Beijing Station early in his career. At the time, it was considered something of a backwater assignment. Certainly, it didn't carry the prestige of Moscow, Vienna, or Berlin. In the early '90s, the Chinese were scary but reserved it for their own citizens.

"We were trying to cultivate contacts through the local dissident community. We learned he'd been in the Tiananmen protests. Turns out, he was there but not politically active. He was an engineer. Had a young family," Nate shook his head, and his eyes went distant. "He wasn't going to risk that on riots that weren't going to move the needle. We got to be friends though. They moved to the States a few years later. I'd kept in touch and looked him up when he got settled here. We stayed close."

"Must have," I said. "Elizabeth said you were like her uncle."

"I may have greased a few skids to get them here. It wasn't safe for them after the riots. The Ministry of State Security wasn't what it is today; in some ways, it was worse. They took every page they could out of the old KGB playbooks. Ol' Mao loved him a purge, and so do his heirs."

Nate seemed like he wanted to say more, so I sipped my drink in silence for a time and waited for him to continue the thread. When he didn't, I changed the subject to current events. "Elizabeth is convinced someone murdered her father. I have to tell you, Nate, I don't know. You and I both know that even a gunshot can be fixed to look like a suicide with a little effort. And it would probably be enough to fool some local cop, but that assumes someone with that kind of skill would want to kill him."

"Be careful with your assumptions, Matt. You haven't lived in the US longer than a stretch of months basically since college. Your definition of a 'local cop' is fairly skewed. Law enforcement is big business. Hell, major police departments have some of the same analytic tools we had in the Agency."

"Fair enough," I said.

"Johnnie and I had drinks a few weeks ago. He'd really taken a slide when his wife passed. I was worried about him. Anyway, he told me he thought someone was following him."

"Yeah, Elizabeth said the same thing. Do you think there was anything to it?"

"Hard to say. Johnnie was always a cagey guy. I'd like to think he wouldn't make that sort of thing up. He was flamboyant, a little over the top, and he might stretch the truth, I've never known him to make something up."

"A bullshitter rather than a liar?"

"Exactly."

That was two datapoints. Or at least, Zhou told the same thing to two people he trusted.

"How would he know to look?" I asked.

"For a tail?" Nate said. "Well, he grew up in a surveillance state. The way Johnnie tells it, you just assumed someone was always watching you. That sort of thing never leaves you."

"What can you tell me about Zhou's business?"

"His first venture was called the Pinnacle Fund. He started it in 2003 after a dot com windfall. He made a lot of money early and got out before the bubble burst. It wasn't life-changing money; he still had to work. But he invested it smartly. He started Pinnacle with a guy named Benjamin Blake. They're still together. They had a third partner, Rakesh Davy. Davy was a kind of wunderkind investor. He'd put this deal together to have Andree-son-Horowitz buy Pinnacle, and when it fell through, he couldn't handle it. The way Johnnie tells it, it was the first time in the guy's life he'd failed at something. There's more to it than that, though it's not relevant. Took a dive off a bridge. So, his wife gets a third of the company. She was in marketing or something, had an iPhone and one of the first Twitter accounts, and thought that made her an expert. Within a year, she'd run Rakesh's port-folio into the dirt, cost the company millions. She also refused to let Johnnie and Ben buy her out. Eventually, Johnnie and Ben had enough and created a new firm, which they called Apex."

"That's literally the same thing."

"That was the point. They moved all their business over to Apex and let Rakesh's wife keep whatever was left of Pinnacle. They gave her a decent amount of money too—more than the partnership agreement called for. She sued them anyway, but the judge looked at her track record of invest-ment and suggested she needed a new line of work."

"Do you think Johnnie could've been mixed up in something? Did he give any indication that his life was in danger?"

"If he did, I'd have led with that. Matt, you and I know better than anyone about the masks people wear and the lengths they'll go to conceal things from even their closest relationships. I'd known Johnnie over thirty years. I don't have any reason to think he was involved in something illegal or immoral, but I don't *know*. I've never seen his books, and I only knew what he told me about his business. I know his daughter thinks something happened. The police seem to have written Johnnie off, and I don't like that. They're calling his home a crime scene and not telling his daughter why. The detective says it's a suicide, but they haven't ruled anything official. That strikes me as strange."

"So, why me, Nate? I don't have any law enforcement experience."

"Elizabeth needs closure. I don't think she's going to get that through official channels. The police have made such a mess of this, I can't think she'll trust the outcome no matter what it is. An independent eye may uncover something the police haven't. Even if you only validate what the police determine, it's worth it. And I agree with her, something about this feels off to me. I kept tabs on you. I know you're helping people who need help and that you sometimes work for that reporter outfit. The fact you do that and haven't spilled the Agency's dirty laundry all over the internet shows me I can still trust you. As for *why you*? You need this, Matt. As much as Elizabeth Zhou, maybe more."

"I need?"

"Yes, you do. I was serious when I said your situation was your own doing. This will be tough, but you need to hear it. It was your poor judgement that put you in that situation and got that woman killed. Yes, you were put there by a headquarters desk manager who demanded an ill-conceived, dangerous operation, and I don't fault you for not putting your people at risk. You shouldn't have gotten involved with someone in a place like Managua."

"That's not—" I started, and Nate cut me off with a hand.

"Either way, the CIA shouldn't have shit-canned you like that, even if the situation that forced it was your fault. What wasn't your fault was the Bureau trying to string you up to cover for their own mistakes. You need some redemption, and maybe this is the way you get it. I also think you're more of a detective than you realize. You spent nearly twenty years figuring out the deepest, darkest things people wanted to hide. If there's something here, *you* can find it. If there's nothing there, you bring a grieving daughter some closure. That is also worthy."

I nodded and leaned forward in my chair. My mind was moving now.

"How would you start?" I asked.

"You're a case officer, Matt. If you were trying to recruit Johnnie Zhou, how would you do it?"

"Start when he's alive," I said. The lines on Nate's brow told me I thought that was funnier than he did. "First, I'd build a profile. I'd learn everything I could about his business and his associates. Look for a gap in the armor. I'd understand what the patterns were so I could see if there was a deviation I could exploit. I'd find out what he wanted and see if there was a way I could help him get it."

For many years, the Agency taught that there were four basic motivations to someone betraying their country on America's behalf—for money, for ideology, because they were coerced, or for the thrill of it. I was trained on that. Nate, and a few others, believed that kind of thinking was reductive. Nate always preached it was more nuanced. A handler/agent relationship was intimate, based on trust and mutual benefit. Certainly, that could mean money, but it was often much deeper.

"Since I can't ask Johnnie directly, I'd need to widen that circle. See if there was someone in his orbit I could convince to talk to me about him. Johnnie may not have confided in you or even his daughter, but he must have talked to someone."

"Your logic is sound," Nate said.

"Tell me, did Johnnie know you were CIA? He knew your real name. Elizabeth led me to believe she didn't know you by anything else."

"I gave him the standard line that I was a diplomat and it was common for us to use different names overseas for security reasons."

It appeared I'd learned everything I was going to that night, and our conversation moved onto other topics as we finished the last of our drinks. We caught up on colleagues, friends, and enemies. Who'd risen and who'd fallen.

I stayed for another thirty minutes or so.

We embraced as I left, and I told him I'd be in touch. I wasn't sure I was going to take the job yet, but I promised to let him know one way or another.

"What's stopping you?"

"Elizabeth. I'm not going to do this unless I'm certain I can answer the question for her, one way or another. I need to think this through."

"I appreciate that, Matt. I really do. So will she. Remember what I said about there being value in uncovering the truth, either way."

3

The next morning, I decided to stick around for a few days to see what I could uncover. I extended my hotel stay and got a rental car, which the company would drop off in the hotel parking lot.

I called Elizabeth. Nine a.m. is basically dawn in Los Angeles, unless you have to drive anywhere, though I assumed she was already up and around.

"Apologies for calling so early. I wanted to run something by you and also make sure you were comfortable with me digging around for a couple days."

"It's not a problem, and yes, I am."

"Great. I wanted to see if I could get a look at the house. I know they're calling it a crime scene, but those things are usually wrapped up within forty-eight hours. You think a power of attorney would work?"

She barked out a sharp laugh that was both musical and cynical. "Matt, I'm an entertainment lawyer. I took one criminal class in law school and decided it wasn't for me. It's worth a shot though. WCMA doesn't have a criminal practice, obviously, but the connections are inevitable. Especially with our athletes. I can talk to someone. I can probably get one written up in a few hours."

"I don't know if it'll work," I said. "Worth a shot."

Elizabeth said she'd get on it and would fax a copy to the hotel.

My next call was the Los Altos Police Department. Los Altos is an idyl-lic, tree-lined community in the Santa Cruz foothills. They had a small PD with a single squad of detectives. They mostly dealt with property crime, so a violent death would take them by surprise. I managed to get the detective who'd handled Johnnie Zhou's case on the phone, and he didn't appreciate talking to a reporter (or an unlicensed private detective pretending to *be* a reporter so that he'd take my call). He was savvy enough to handle it profes-sionally.

"I took one look at that office and knew it was out of our scope," he said.

"That was Mr. Zhou's home office?"

"That's right. He died at home. We don't have a forensics lab in our department and would have to outsource it. I'd been trying to kick this upstairs when they told me the state cops were taking it over. We don't have the resources for...whatever this is. I'll tell you, I wasn't sorry to see it go."

"Detective Hanley, in your opinion, did Johnnie Zhou commit suicide or did someone kill him?"

"Above my pay grade," he said. I'd always hated that phrase. It was a complete cop-out. Somehow, it symbolized to me everything wrong about bureaucracies—*not my problem* and *I'm not paid enough to care.*

"Well, imagine if it was your pay grade. Could Zhou have been murdered?"

"Go to hell," the cop told me. "I'm not going to give you a wild-ass guess and have you put that in some paper. I'd lose my job."

Interesting. He went defensive fast.

"Detective, can I level with you?"

"I don't have time for this shit."

"Just one question. Please. It's important."

"You've got thirty seconds."

"Johnnie Zhou's daughter spoke to me. The state cops aren't telling her anything." I'd just learned from him that state cops were involved, so I figured I'd run with it.

"So she goes to the press? That's typical. That's why this country is going to hell, man. People get an answer they don't like and—"

I snapped. "Detective. She's an only child and just lost her last remaining parent. Maybe a little empathy, huh? You said you were going to your superiors to ask for help when they told you the state police were taking the case over. Why would they do that for a suicide?"

"There weren't any obvious signs of forced entry, okay? But when I was looking around, I saw some scratch marks on one of the doors."

Like the lock had been picked.

I asked, "What did the state police do with that information?" He didn't immediately answer. I followed up with, "Was anything taken from the home?"

The small-town detective, used to dealing with traffic accidents and petty theft, had apparently just realized his temper had backed him into a corner, and now he couldn't think fast enough to see his way out of it. He did what I expected him to do—he hung up on me.

Damn it.

I made a note to call on him when he cooled off a little. He was really eager to get rid of this thing, which was valuable to know. His department seemed to have felt the same way. The fact that when he was going to ask his superiors for help, they'd told him the state police had already contacted them was the biggest lead so far. Marks on the door though... That was something else.

An hour later, the rental car company dropped the car at the hotel. I signed for it and then got a text from Elizabeth, asking for the hotel's fax number. I replied with the number and asked if a faxed POA had the same legal weight as an originally signed one. She replied with a wink emoji and said it did. I went to the manager and got the fax, wondering if hotels were the last places that even had fax machines.

A few minutes later, I had a limited power of attorney signed for me, granting me access to the home. I asked the manager if they had any colored paper, and he quizzically replied that they did. He gave me a piece of light-blue paper they used for fliers. Borrowing a stapler, I attached the blue paper to the POA print out, as I'd seen done before. Then I tri-folded it, so it looked extra official.

My next call was to Apex to see if I could connect with Benjamin Blake. Elizabeth had his personal number, but I didn't want to use that just yet. If I pissed him off, he'd just block me anyway. I called and left a message with his personal assistant, saying I was a journalist and wanted to ask him a few questions for a story. I gave my contact info, and she said he'd return the call as soon as able.

It was time to check out the Zhou home and test the limits of my questionable strategy.

I hopped into my rental and drove to the address Elizabeth had provided.

She'd told me what the place was worth. Between Washington DC and Southern California, I knew there were homes that looked like six-million-dollar homes and were—just because of the zip code. Then, there were the places that looked like six-million-dollar homes because that was what they were actually worth. Zhou's house was somewhere in between. I grew up in a small Florida beach town. I hadn't known what six million dollars was until I had something like that in cash to buy off of an Afghan warlord on behalf of the United States government.

Zhou's home was in a small neighborhood set above the Foothills Expressway. Gnarled black oaks and lordly cypresses ringed the property and created a natural fence between neighbors. This was the kind of community that used landscaping on the property lines instead of fences, which were considered gauche. The house was a two-story Tuscan-style, set back from the street among the trees. There was a Los Altos PD squad car parked at an angle in the driveway.

I rolled past the house and parked along the street. The POA document was folded in my jacket pocket, which I removed well before I was within sight of the cop, since reaching into a jacket in front of the police was currently inadvisable. Approaching the house, I held the folded paper to my side but clearly visible. The cop in the prowl car was looking at his dash-mounted laptop when I approached, but he heard me once my heels hit the flagstone driveway. Even sitting down, I could see this guy was thick and didn't skip leg day. He'd shaved his head to stubble and had a chin like a wrecking ball.

"How can I help you, sir?" His tone was friendly, but as his eyes flicked to the paper in my hands, I could practically see the questions turning in his mind. Obviously, I wasn't there to ask directions.

"Hi, officer. My name is Matt Gage, and I represent Elizabeth Zhou, the deceased's sole surviving family member and heir. I have here a power of attorney, which entitles me to access the home and property on her behalf." I helpfully extended the folded document so he didn't have to exert himself. He didn't touch it. Instead, he tilted his head just enough to speak into the radio on his shoulder.

"Sir, I'm going to have to ask you to leave the premises."

"Officer, respectfully, this says I have a right to be here."

"I don't care what that says. Now, I need you to leave the premises, immediately. This is a crime scene."

I looked past the car to the door. There was still yellow-and-black tape across the front door.

Now, I had a few choices. I could do as he asked, which was not what my client was paying for. Or I could go full Karen and ask to talk to his supervisor. Neither would get me the result I was after.

"My understanding, officer, is that the investigating officials have determined the cause of death was a suicide. I'm here to take an inventory of the deceased's personal effects so that his daughter can begin settling the estate. I know you have your job to do, as do I. So, perhaps we can make some sort of accommodation? How about you go in with me?"

"I'm not asking you again, pal. You're trespassing, and I don't care what that paper says."

I took a step back. "I'm opening my jacket to place this fully executed *power of attorney* in my jacket pocket." The cop didn't react to my emphasis of the document. Once it was safely tucked away, I thanked him for his time, then left the scene.

The POA was a gamble—and one I really hadn't expected to work. Still, it was helpful for the other side to know they have competition. I'd gotten what I needed out of the encounter, which was confirmation that the house was still critical to their investigation. The police were freaked out and on edge about something there. That was worth knowing.

It confirmed something was going on beneath the surface.

I returned to my hotel and checked out. There was a flight to LA in about ninety minutes that I could just make if traffic wasn't full Thunderdome.

4

I was back in LA by late afternoon and home an hour after that.

Having spent most of the last two decades in third-world countries, I had no realistic appreciation for what things cost in the US. So, I'd rented a criminally small, overpriced, single-family home that some enterprising asshole split in half and turned into a duplex. I had the slightly larger half and the garage, for which I suitably compensated the owner the monthly price of a replacement kidney. Still, it was a block from the beach, and the garage meant I could store my two bicycles (mountain and road), kayak, and paddleboard. I really wanted to take up surfing, but Cosmic Ray told me I was too old and too angry. I owned a surfboard, and the staff at Ray's kindly asked me not to bring it by.

Needing to clear my head, I opted for the kayak. I loaded it onto my Land Rover's roof rack and drove to the beach. I paddled through the burnt-orange sunlight of early evening and tried to work the stress out of the last few days. Seeing the sky darken, I guided the kayak back to shore and went home to get cleaned up.

My half of the Craftsman was on the bottom, which meant I also got the back deck and the owner's supplied propane grill. To be neighborly, I shared that with the upstairs tenants, who were currently cool. I marinated and grilled some flank steak, sliced it paper thin, and made tacos. I diced an avocado I found on the counter and dropped that on top. Once that was done, I poured a few fingers of Oban and went out to the front porch to watch the sunset and think about what to do next.

My mind kept going back to the central question of who benefits from Johnnie Zhou's death. He owned half of Apex, so presumably whatever value he'd acquired would go to his daughter. However, seeing as she'd hired me to prove her father was murdered and my conclusions carried no legal weight, I reasoned that could safely rule her out as a suspect. Johnnie Zhou and Benjamin Blake had been in business together twenty years, and there had been no apparent signs of discontent there. Elizabeth told me the company was worth about fifty mil. That was a hell of a lot of money in anyone's book. Could Blake be trying some maneuver to take it all? That was top of my list. It seemed a little obvious, though Occam's Razor is a thing for a reason.

The other part of this I remained uncomfortable with was the police stance. It felt off to me. If they'd already determined it was a suicide, why tie up the home as a crime scene? Why not let Elizabeth get in there and start settling her father's estate? If it was a legitimate crime scene, then why weren't they telling her there was a suspect in his murder? It didn't add up.

By the time the sun and a second scotch went down, I was no closer to an answer. I called Jennie.

"Not interrupting anything, am I?" I asked when she answered.

"Just a glass of cab. I can multitask," she said.

"Cool. I need you to talk me out of something." That was a line from our college days and was how I started most of our phone calls. It usually meant what you'd expect.

"This'll be good," she said in her usual droll tone.

"I've got a line on a case, and I think it's got some legs."

"The case or the client," she said.

"Jen."

"Okay, the *case* has some legs, and you're not sure if you should take it. Because you're neck deep in my city council investigation."

"I can multitask," I said. *And I need to make rent.*

"Seriously, if you're not sure you should do something, there's usually a good reason why."

"This has some complications, for sure. Seems like the right thing to do though."

"Then what are you hemming about?"

I laid it out for her, keeping names out, but framing the basic details. I shared my concerns about the police playing games with the facts, if not outright obfuscating them. All the things I'd just debated with myself over two glasses of scotch. It took about fifteen minutes to work it all out, and by the time I'd finished, the sky had faded to a muted indigo.

"I guess I'm looking for your instincts as a journalist. If this were you and you had this as a lead, would you follow the story?"

"Matty, the case itself isn't the thing I worry about. From what you describe, it sounds to me like something is up. Someone isn't telling this woman the full truth, for sure. What I worry about is how it came to you."

"I trust my friend," I said.

"But should you? After what these people did to you?"

"That wasn't him," I said.

"Doesn't it matter? He's part of that system. What if this is just some way to cover up something illegal?"

Jennie never had a great love for the Agency, and the torture revelations or civilian casualties from drone strikes just eroded it further. She wasn't surprised at all to learn that machine had ground me up and spat me out when I was no further use than a scapegoat might be.

"He wouldn't do that to me. And anyway, he's not involved in this. He just teed the client up for me."

"Is this about helping this girl, or is it about proving to the Agency that you're better than they thought you were?"

"How does solving this case accomplish that?" I asked.

"It doesn't," she said firmly. "I just want to make sure that's clear in your mind."

"Whatever is happening, I don't think this woman is getting the full story about how her father died. She deserves answers."

"And you don't like it when the authorities flex over people."

"I do not," I said.

"Listen, you called asking for advice, so here it is. My gut is...something's up. At least enough to look into it. So, there's that. Based on what you got me last night—thank you for that, by the way—I don't think I need you for a few weeks. The fact that the source confirmed they had cops moonlighting as security and then your account of the police chasing you and the source? That's huge. This could be a massive public corruption story." Jennie paused to let the dregs of those thoughts settle into the glass. "Now, this thing with your client's father and the police withholding information? This could *also* be a public corruption story. If it is, I'd like first go at it."

"I don't know, Jen. I've got a feeling the client might want to keep this one quiet."

"Well, anything changes, let me know."

I wasn't aware I'd gone silent until Jennie prompted me. "What is it, Matt?"

"Nothing, I just ..." I didn't want to put it into words for fear of how it'd make me look. I wasn't blind to the fact that Elizabeth could be a springboard into an entirely different stratosphere of clientele. I was sure her firm had troubleshooters on retainer, people who made the problems go away. I could quickly go from refreshing my contacts list to see who had a spare couch to making serious money.

All that hinged on my delivering for her.

And there being something to deliver at all.

"Just a question, Jen, I suppose," I said eventually. It was a riff on what I'd asked her earlier. Just through a different lens.

"Shoot."

"If it were you, would you take this case?"

Without hesitation, Jennie said firmly, "No way in hell."

"Why?"

"It requires you to disprove the police's conclusion, and you'll have no legal access to evidence. It requires you to get information from people who either already told everything they had to the police and are, therefore, disinclined to talk to you. Or you'll need to find people the police could not. Which seems unlikely. That's not why I wouldn't do it. I wouldn't go anywhere near this thing because something about it stinks, and I don't trust the people you used to work for. Neither should you. If this comes down to needing a fall guy, you are tailor made for the part."

I called Elizabeth and asked if we could speak in person. I wanted to share what I'd learned and see how she took it. Her reaction was an important barometer for me.

We agreed to meet after work the next day to discuss it. Elizabeth told me to bring dinner.

I showed up wearing my only blazer, carrying Korean BBQ, and a zinfandel from Napa. Elizabeth owned a two-bedroom condo in Brentwood. She greeted me with forced smile, wearing a loose, cream-colored sweater over black leggings. The lines around her eyes betrayed late and restless nights. I followed her into her place, a steaming bag of Korean barbecue in tow. She'd converted a one bedroom on the main floor to an office, and the bedroom was at the top of a metal spiral staircase I wouldn't want to walk down after three drinks. The living room faced north, with a steepled, triangular ceiling that went up to the second floor. The walls and floor were white with walnut accents, and she decorated in bright colors. There were a lot of blues and reds that reminded me, a little too much, of police lights.

There was a small patio off the living room. Her unit was on the fourth floor, so we had a wonderful view of the sunset and the western edge of the Hollywood Hills.

I uncorked the wine and poured while she distributed the food.

This was a working dinner, and I didn't want to waste her time. Nor did I want to insult her by asking if she was doing okay. We ate, and I eased into it, asking about her father's associates, both business and personal. She said he hadn't had many friends, but a lot of acquaintances. Her parents had been members of country clubs in Palo Alto and in Los Altos, though after her mother died, her father cancelled both. As far as Elizabeth knew, Johnnie's business was thriving. In fact, his portfolio had grown, and she believed he had the majority of the firm's revenue under management. That was worth digging into.

One of the things they teach you at the Farm is how to memorize the key details of a conversation. A case officer was rarely in a position to take notes when meeting with an asset, so we learned how to commit those things to memory using a variety of mnemonic techniques. Writing notes in front of someone was a new experience for me—and oddly uncomfortable. Like my privacy was being invaded somehow. It was mostly for her benefit. I was afraid she wouldn't think I was taking this seriously if I didn't take notes.

Elizabeth told me about her childhood, what it was like to grow up in an immigrant family and how her father decided to move to venture capital. We talked about his business, but there wasn't anything I hadn't already learned from the internet, my conversation with Nate, or her when we'd first met.

We finished dinner, and she asked if I minded going inside. I cleaned up and met her in the living room, where she'd refreshed the wineglasses. She took up a position on a long, white couch. I sat on a chair opposite. Elizabeth pulled her legs in and then wrapped her arms around them.

I don't have much direct experience with murder, only its outcomes. Sure, I'd had an asset get discovered by his nation's security service, and that ended badly. Outside of counterterrorism, the Agency didn't often move through the dark alleys of the world, offing the enemies of democracy with silenced pistols. We had bureaucrats with drones for that. I knew murder in the abstract—the actions of genocidal dictators and sociopathic security services.

But a human taking another human's life beyond the circumstances of war ...well, that I'd only seen once firsthand.

Sometimes I still woke up shaking.

And that wasn't my crime to solve.

"I spoke with the Los Altos detective who was in charge of the case. He told me two things that I found curious. First, once he'd assessed the scene at your father's house, he went in to get additional support from his bosses, and they told him the state police would be taking over. I think I know the answer to this, but has anyone from the state contacted you?"

"No. I haven't heard a thing."

"The other thing the detective said was they found scratch marks on the door to the house, like maybe the lock had been picked. I put that next to your father telling you that he thought someone was following him. He told Nate McKellar the same thing, by the way. We also have the situation with the home. I brought the POA there, and the cop out front practically bounced me like I was a frat boy at last call. He was immediately aggressive. The Los Altos detective I talked to over the phone was also confrontational."

Elizabeth shook her head slowly. "They never said anything about signs of entry."

"What kind of security did he have?"

"Not as much as you might think. Dad lived modestly. For Silicon Valley," she added. "I mean, the house is nice, but some of those places, they've got motion detectors, night vision cameras. A kind of radar that can see into the ground ..."

"Lidar," I said.

"Yeah. Dad had none of that. He spent money on good locks and solid windows. I finally got him to install a security system, but it's not active anymore."

"Why so little security?"

"Dad was weird about tech. He bought and sold it all day, every day. He lived and breathed the stuff, but on a personal level, it didn't interest him. He didn't need the latest whatever it was. He was kind of an anachronism, I guess you'd say. That's what makes this so frustrating. He knew better."

As I thought through the questions I wanted to ask, I began to understand why Nate had set her up with me. The difference between field-collected intelligence and evidence was mostly semantic. Just like the police, we tried to find information that would let us head off bad things from happening as much as we'd use it to attribute culpability to bad things that occurred. My mind immediately went to all the things I'd look for. The first thing the police would do is grab his computer, phone, and any physical files he'd have. If they were smart, they'd look for patterns. Still, if they'd taken all that already, why keep the house locked down? The ballistics work would have been done within the first forty-eight hours.

"I'd like to ask you some questions that I assume the police have already covered. It'll be helpful for me to know what they know. That may give me some insight into why they're keeping things from you."

"Okay," she said.

We covered Johnnie Zhou's friends and his business partner to the best of Elizabeth's knowledge.

"Did your father have any enemies? Someone who might want to hurt him? Did he ever mention a business deal that went south?"

"We didn't talk about it much, to be honest. It's not right to say that I didn't care, but I'm just not that into tech. Dad was always going on about secure VPNs and tunnels and guarded satcom and whatever. I don't know what any of that means."

I laughed. "So, to your knowledge, there wasn't a deal that fell apart or a company he invested in that didn't make it? Someone that might have felt wronged by him?"

"Nothing that comes to mind. I wish my mom was here to ask. Dad confided more of that kind of thing to her," Elizabeth said, though mostly to herself.

"When was the last time you've spoken to the police?"

"I called again today, explaining that I need to settle his affairs, and they gave me the same old story." Her frustration was palpable, I could practically wring it out of a towel.

I'd been studying her reactions to my questions and statements. Everything checked as genuine to me. She was troubled and had received no answers from the one institution that should be reassuring her they were moving mountains.

If they couldn't or wouldn't solve this, I would.

I stood to leave.

"Elizabeth, I think I've got enough to keep going. Too many things don't add up for me."

"Thank you," she said in a small voice.

"I'm going to relocate to San Jose in the morning. I'll keep you posted."

"Okay. I need to finish up some work for a client, and then I'll be going up there myself. Hopefully, by then I can get into the house. I need to start settling my father's estate. I can't even have a funeral until they release him to me." She was on the verge of tears.

We covered a few minor logistical details before I left, and I asked her to download the Signal app so we could communicate securely.

If there really was something going on with law enforcement, I didn't want them confiscating our phones to read our messages.

I headed home to pack.

I truly believed this situation was off its axis and the authorities weren't telling Elizabeth why. By now, I'd convinced myself I was doing this to get her answers and not because I was one last missed rent payment from being on the street.

Jennie's words, though, hung over my shoulder, the ever-vigilant specter. If someone was looking for a setup, I was straight out of central casting. Could be her fear and distrust of my former employer. Or it could be some damned sage advice. There was only one way to figure that out.

5

The 10 runs into the sea about a mile from my house, so I picked that up to the 405 and headed north. I drove a matte black '93 Land Rover Defender that I bought when I left the Agency. I then paid a small fortune to have one of SoCal's many custom car builders restomod it for me. In addition to all the modern amenities, the Defender had multiple secure lockboxes where I could stash gear, like my laptop. Two of those boxes were concealed and even the police wouldn't find them unless they put some hardware behind it. My Glock 34, the same model I'd used with the Agency, typically went in one box located in the driver's side door. The truck was a hell of a lot more secure than my condo. Miguel, the guy who built her for me, had offered to make it an electric conversion. Apparently, that was all the rage now. I turned him down. Unfortunately, in California, driving a 1990s-era, 10 miles-per-gallon SUV basically makes me a war criminal.

I made San Jose by lunchtime and found a room at the Cupertino Hotel.

Since Benjamin Blake still hadn't returned my calls, I decided to stake out the office. Apex had a suite on the second floor of a two-story glass building in a brand new Mountain View office park. I knew what Blake looked like from the company's webpage, so I parked at the back of the lot where I had a good line of sight to the reserved spots in front of the build-ing. My money was on the Lucid Air parked a few steps from the front door.

Sure enough, he emerged at five from the office, slid into his six-figure electric vehicle, and rolled home at an astonishing speed with minimal environmental impact.

The next morning, I was back at the office park at eight forty-five armed with a coffee and the expectation to wait. I'd have put hard cash on no arrival before ten, but he surprised me and Vegas by being in his spot when I arrived. I waited until nine and then went in. They had an impressive front desk defending their suite from casual traffic and companies that weren't worth their time. However, it was still early and whomever manned this thing during the day wasn't here yet. I tried the door, found it open, and went inside. Locating the boss's office wasn't hard.

Apex was a relatively small fund with just a few employees. Johnnie Zhou and Benjamin Blake had kept it simple, with them actively involved in its operations and investments. Elizabeth said they had a team of four portfolio managers supported by a small admin and analytical staff. Blake's door was open, and I spotted him, eyes on his screen. The office was other-wise empty. His executive assistant intercepted me before I could make the door.

"May I help you?" she asked in a passively-aggressive tone that suggested she had no intention of being helpful.

"There was no one out front," I said.

"That means you should wait until someone is."

"There was no one out there to tell me to wait." Satisfied that my mental judo had pinned her to the mat, I said, "I'm here to see Mr. Blake."

"You don't have an appointment," she dutifully informed me.

"You're good. You're not even looking at his calendar."

"We have QBRs today, so I know it's booked for internal meetings."

She said the acronym as if I'd understand what it was.

"I'll just be a minute," I said, raising my voice just slightly. Not rudely, mind you, just elevating it in volume to get Blake's attention.

"Grace? Everything all right?" Blake asked from his office.

"This...gentlemen...says he's here to see you, but he doesn't have an appointment."

"It's fine, Grace. I have a few minutes, though I doubt I'll need it."

I gave Grace a satisfied smile and walked to his door. "May I come in?"

Blake stood.

Hardly anyone wore suits outside of government anymore, but he still managed a four-figure outfit even without a jacket.

"Good morning, Mister..."

"Matt Gage," I said.

He sized me up and ran through some sort of mental cross-check that he must have honed through years of weeding through bullshit.

"Mr. Gage, I'm guessing you're not here to tell me about some app you want me to invest in."

"No. I'm working for Elizabeth Zhou," I said.

"Are you an attorney?"

"Not exactly."

"Well, then what's this about?"

"I'm trying to understand a little more about Mr. Zhou's side of the business. Do you know of anyone who'd felt wronged by Zhou? Maybe a company he invested in that failed...or perhaps someone he chose not to invest in? Anyone that might have felt cheated or held a grudge?"

"What exactly are you doing for Elizabeth?"

"Asking questions," I said. "Ones that don't seem to have been asked."

"So, she's hired a private detective, then?" Blake walked back around to his desk and picked up his smart phone. I watched him unlock it. "I think I know where this is going," he said, still tapping and swiping on his phone. Clearly, my time wasn't worth more to him than whatever he was multitasking, and he wanted me to know it.

"And where is that, Mr. Blake?"

"Elizabeth is understandably upset, and she's acting out."

I didn't like that. My client was a grieving orphan, not a petulant child. She had a right to straight answers.

"Mr. Gage, I've already spoken with the police, and you can rest assured, I'll be speaking with them again."

"I've been threatened with police in countries a lot scarier than this one, so that's unlikely to keep me up at night. One more question, Mr. Blake."

"I've indulged this nonsense as much as I have the patience to." He tapped something on his phone.

Time to make this personal, see how he reacts. "With Johnnie dead, who gets controlling interest of the company? Do you, or do you have to split it with Elizabeth?"

"I assume you already know the answer to that, which is why we're having this conversation."

"Humor me," I said.

"Haven't I been doing that already?"

The look I gave him in response melted his self-satisfied mask, just enough.

"Fine. Johnnie and I had an agreement. They're not uncommon in our business, where the partners own the entire operation. Normally, in the event of a partner's untimely death, say from cancer, their interest would go to their surviving heirs. Typically with an illness, we know it's coming and can make arrangements. But, sometimes, the partners don't trust each other, or perhaps they don't trust their next of kin. I'm not saying that was the case with Johnnie and me. It wasn't. But we had a partner in a previous company who took his own life, and his wife got a third stake in the business."

"Rakesh Davy," I said.

"That's right. Then you know what happened, and you can probably appreciate why Johnnie and I made that arrangement. Now, Johnnie wanted to make sure his beloved daughter would be taken care of, and she will get her due."

"Let me see if I have this right. You've got a suicide clause in your business arrangement?"

"That's right," Blake said.

"But not one for murder?"

"No," he said. If his tone were an EKG, the patient's chances wouldn't be good. "Do you know what the statistics are for death by murder, Mr. Gage?"

It occurred to me that in this line of work, that was actually something I *should* be able to rattle off the top of my head.

"I don't."

"Well, we'll just say they're a touch lower than suicide."

I hated it when assholes went out of their way to sound snide.

"They're here, Ben," Grace said from behind us. I looked over my shoulder and saw a pair of uniformed rent-a-cops.

"That's funny," I said.

"I don't get the joke," Blake said.

"You wouldn't."

Picking up on the contextual clues, I decided it was time for me to leave.

I thanked Benjamin Blake for his time, and I had a suspicion it wouldn't be the last lie I told today. Clapping one of the rent-a-cops on the shoulder as I passed him, I said, "You want me to make you look good in front of the boss?"

He seemed very confused, so I just left the building.

So. That was...interesting. Zhou's business partner now had a financial interest in not overturning the police's initial determination of death.

I'd barely made it to my Land Rover when my phone rang. I answered with an amiable "hello." *Never let 'em hear you sweat, right?*

"Mr. Gage, my name is Arnie McWhorter. I represent Benjamin Blake." That was fast. I was puzzling out how this guy got my phone number because I hadn't left it with him, but then I remembered giving it to Blake's assistant the day before. "We'll keep this short. I'll be sending a cease-and-desist order to your offices, directing you to refrain from further contact with any employees, clients current, former or prospective, or officers of Apex Investments. This is a very difficult time for Mr. Blake and the company, as I'm sure you can appreciate."

"You don't think that Johnnie Zhou's death is worth looking into? What if he was murdered?"

"He wasn't."

"The police haven't made that determination yet," I told him.

"My understanding is that they have. Listen, Mr. Gage, I don't want to speak ill of the dead, but toward the end of his life, Johnnie was quite troubled. His wife's death had affected him terribly. I understand he was never the same. I'm not surprised he took his own life. You need to do Elizabeth a kindness and wrap this up so she can move on. So they can all move on."

"They?"

"Yes, they. Mr. Blake and his employees."

"So, that makes you Mr. Blake's personal attorney. You're not Apex's general council?"

"What does that have to do with anything?" he asked, and I could tell he was struggling to understand what difference it made. So, I hit him with it.

"Tell me, Arnie, how much does Ben stand to make off of Johnnie's part of the company?"

"That's confidential information."

"But it is in your client's personal financial interest for me to give up and go home, right?"

"That's not how I would put it."

"It wouldn't be. But it's also not wrong, is it?"

Silence on the other end.

"You still there, Arnie?"

"Elizabeth Zhou would profit significantly by her father's death being ruled anything other than suicide. I can hardly call your motivations here *pure*. Tell me, how much of a finder's fee do you get if Elizabeth were to get her father's stake in Apex?"

"None, actually. I just learned about the suicide clause about ten minutes ago."

"Then, you're clearly out of your depth. Wrap this up quickly, for her sake as well as yours, Mr. Gage." He paused to let me tremble a little. "Before we go, could you share your California private detective's license number with me? I'd like to include that in my records. In case I need to file a complaint with the state board for professional misconduct."

Shit.

Remember what I'd said earlier about lawyers asking questions that they already had the answer to?

"I'm an investigative journalist. Somebody is lying, Arnie, and they're going to great lengths to cover it up. I don't know that your client is trying to cheat Elizabeth out of what's rightly hers, but no one is playing straight with her—not you, your client, or the police. If, when I'm done poking around, I don't like what I hear, I go public."

"I would strongly advise against that. Good day, Mr. Gage. You'll expect to receive my cease-and-desist presently."

He hung up. I almost wished I could be there when some buttoned-up process server stepped into Cosmic Ray's to hand me a piece of paper.

As a rule, I didn't like getting news that I should otherwise have known. This thing about the suicide clause should've come from my client, not Benjamin Blake and reinforced by his attorney. The fact that the latter made such a point about it, though, was also interesting. In the way that smoke is related to fire.

I went back to the hotel and thought about my next move. After debating with myself over it for a while, I messaged Elizabeth through Signal and asked her why I was just now learning about the clause. When she didn't immediately write back to me, I figured she was either busy or trying to come up with an answer. Avenues of insight into Johnnie Zhou were quickly getting closed off. His daughter didn't actually know any of the man's associations, and his business partner just threatened legal action within ten minutes of meeting me. That had to be some kind of record.

Several threads didn't add up, which only convinced me something was going on behind the scenes. The police ruled it a suicide, though they were keeping the house a crime scene. Why? Zhou had an arrangement with his business partner that transferred the business to him in the event of Zhou's suicide. Blake was rich, powerful and well connected. Could he put weight on the scale, influence a small-town police department to call a murder something else?

Then we have Elizabeth. She gets half the business if her father was murdered.

There is a clear motive on both sides for the ruling to come down one way or the other. A completely objective person would look at Elizabeth's hiring of a private investigator and wonder if that was why.

The other irony, though, was this case was in real danger of stalling out, and I'd barely started. No one wanted to talk, and I'd managed to alienate the two people outside the family with direct knowledge of Johnnie Zhou's death. The detective didn't want to talk to me because he thought I was the press and he had no reason to. Blake gave me the brush because he had something to lose.

Before I left LA, I used a generative AI research assistant called Look-ingGlass to aggregate all of the articles on Johnnie Zhou that it could find.

Most of the afternoon burned away skimming those. The majority were fluff pieces or corporate PR bits. His wife had been active in their community, volunteered and served on several committees. There was a little more there. I opened up a mind-mapping app on my MacBook that I'd coopted to conduct link analysis. Man, I was really missing my Agency tool suite right now. I understood why we'd automated this.

There was one article I keyed in on, though I wasn't sure what I wanted to do with it yet. There was a piece in the *San Jose Mercury-News* about Johnnie Zhou's suicide. It was less a profile than it was an examination of a suicide with strange circumstances. The author seemed to have come to much the same conclusion that I had—that it was strange for the police to have kept the house locked down as a crime scene for so long after the subject's death. He speculated it could have been the result of a small-town police department being ill-equipped to handle a such a case, but then answered his own question by saying the matter had been referred to the state's investigative bureau. And rhetorically adding, "If it's a suicide, why is it a crime?"

I'd also tracked down Rakesh Davy's widow, Amanda, getting her phone number from an internet white pages site for a couple of bucks. Calling her probably wouldn't net me anything useful, but I filed the number away. If nothing else, it'd get back to Blake and freak him out. Anything I could do to pay him back for the cease-and-desist would be worth it.

By four thirty, I'd had enough reading and went back to the bar I'd visited the night before. The bartender recognized me. I ordered a Back in Black from 21st Amendment and pondered the menu, settling on a cheeseburger and anger. The place was dark and quiet, which fit my mood. I ate in silence and chased it with another beer.

While I was working on my second beer, Elizabeth messaged me back: *I didn't want you to think that's why I was doing this.*

Several follow up questions came to mind, but I couldn't ask any of them over chat. I needed to see her reaction.

Instead, I'd said that we could talk about it later.

Then I texted: *Did you speak to a San Jose reporter named Glenn Byrne?*

She responded with: *IDK. I've gotten calls from a few papers but haven't talked to anyone. Didn't want to.*

She paused for a few beats and then added:

Ben said I shouldn't talk to press. Said Apex PR would handle it.

Interesting.

Finished the beer and paid up, leaving the bartender a good tip. She smiled and thanked me. I headed back to the hotel, unsure of how I was going to spend my evening. That question was answered for me, in part, when a suit peeled itself off a car door it had been leaning against and moved to intercept me before I could enter the hotel. He was shorter than me by a couple inches, and I'm five eleven. He had close-cropped hair with too much product and an off-the-rack suit. That would make him a detective. Movement in the corner of my eye confirmed his partner had flanked me.

"Mr. Gage, my name is Special Agent Jack Nugent of the California Bureau of Investigations. We'd like to ask you some questions."

6

_____

Two guesses as to who set this up, but my money was on Artie McWhorter. He wanted me to know how much traction he had and with whom. The kind of guy who could sick a couple of state police investigators on me within a few hours.

I put Nugent in his late thirties. He introduced his partner as Agent Montoya, who was about five-five and had the thick musculature of an ex-gymnast. She had short hair pulled into a tight tail. Both wore sunglasses. Badges were proffered for my perusal and then disappeared into their jackets. California has a few state-level law enforcement agencies. The highway patrol had merged with the state police in the '90s and now had jurisdiction over the entire state, not just the roadways. The Bureau of Investigation reported to the state's AG and covered many of the kinds of crimes that the FBI did.

"What's your interest in Johnnie Zhou, Mr. Gage?" Nugent asked.

"I find it interesting that a man kills himself, and his home is turned into a crime scene for two weeks," I said. Then added, "Allegedly."

"Why are you here?" Montoya asked.

No "good cop," then. Guess that's out of fashion.

"His daughter hired me. She doesn't think she's getting straight answers from the authorities and wanted an independent look at it. I have to tell you, from what I've seen so far, I can't say that I blame her."

"The Los Altos PD detective that brought us in—"

"Hanley," I said.

"Hanley, right," Nugent said.

That was bullshit. Hanley hadn't brought them in, but I didn't press him on it yet.

Nugent continued. "He told us you called him and asked a bunch of questions."

"Reporters do that sort of thing."

Montoya cut in. "Thing is, Gage, you're not a reporter. And you're not a PI, either. So, what the hell are you, and why are you nosing around?"

"What do you want from me? It's a hard job. Investigations take time. I'm sure you can appreciate that."

"Paper thin," she said. "Maybe you convinced Ms. Zhou that you were a real detective and that you could help." Montoya turned her head to address her partner, keeping her eyes on me. "What I think we've got here is a charlatan bilking a grieving woman who just tragically lost her father."

"Fraud is one of the things our office specializes in, Mr. Gage. We just wanted that out in the open," Nugent said.

"What does it matter to you that I'm asking some questions? If Mr. Zhou did kill himself, then you've got nothing to hide and we help my client get some closure. She hired me because she thinks the police are hiding something from her. I didn't put that idea in her head. If Mr. Zhou didn't kill himself, then you've got some problems. Because now you've got a young woman who might be in danger, and you're not doing anything about it. No one is talking to her."

"What exactly do you think you can do here, Gage?" Nugent asked.

The words, *Well, your job, by the look of it*, were on the tip of my tongue. I decided against it.

"You should know that trying to bully me into leaving only convinces me there's something worth looking at. If there really was nothing to this, you'd show me what you have and convince me to convince my client she's got nothing to worry about. You could've solved this whole thing by saying,

'You're right. We should share what we know with her.' Instead, you take the hard road, try to throw your weight around and"—I threw a couple of eye daggers at Montoya—"accuse me of taking advantage of Ms. Zhou's grief. I could've been convinced to back off and walk away before now. Forget that."

"I'm literally quaking in my boots," Montoya said.

I looked down at her feet. "Those look like flats. You don't even know the difference between kinds of shoes, no wonder you can't figure out if Johnnie Zhou was murdered or not."

Nugent stepped in between his partner and me.

"Gage, attempting to be a private detective in the State of California without a license is illegal. That's the only warning you're going to get."

"I'm just asking questions on someone's behalf. That doesn't mean I'm posing as a PI"

"I think it's exactly what it means."

"*I* think the Los Altos police saw something in that house. Something like a murder someone fixed to look like a suicide. That's hard to do, but not impossible. I can tell you from experience. A skilled hit man could do it. Not a gangbanger or even one of the buttoned-up thugs that second-rate mobsters use. I'm talking about a cleaner. And those guys don't come cheap. The next question you have to ask yourself is, who benefits? And who can afford someone with those kinds of skills? Well, as I understand it, there's at least twenty-five million dollars on the line here. So far, Johnnie Zhou's business partner isn't guilty of anything more than being an asshole, but if *I* was looking for an intersection between motive and opportunity, I might start there."

"You've got a wild imagination," Nugent said after a few long breaths. He was stalling. My comment about the cleaner had landed.

Those kinds of people existed. I seriously doubted Benjamin Blake knew about them, let alone where to find one.

"It's interesting to me that within five minutes of talking to Ben Blake, his lawyer threatens me with legal action, and just a few hours later, a pair of state investigators try to scare me off. This all *screams* of someone with pull trying to get all eyes looking everywhere else."

Nugent and Montoya traded a look, which I only caught because the sun hit Nugent's shades at an angle where I could see through them. The glance might have meant, "Holy shit, Gage just figured all this out," or "Get a load of this asshole."

"You've got a lot of fantastic theories, Gage. I can see how you snowed a vulnerable woman into hiring you," Montoya said. "As a woman, that makes me sick. At best, you're a con man. At worst, you're a predator."

The Agency spends a lot of time teaching you to stay cool under pressure, and I'd sure been in situations with higher stakes than these, but the accusation that I was taking advantage of Elizabeth and running a con about sent me over the edge.

"Stay away from the house. We've got work to do there, and you showing up, trying to bulldoze a beat cop with a power of attorney is some weak sauce," Nugent said.

"Ahh yes, the not-quite crime scene. Detective Hanley sure seemed perplexed about that one. Couldn't tell why you've still got it locked up, given the cause of death. *Alleged* cause." He hadn't said that, but it was my word against his, and I needed some breathing room. Get these guys to second-guess themselves. I decided not to mention Hanley's comment about the scratches on the lock. "And don't hand me some bullshit about Hanley asking you to take the case over. He said he was going to ask for help and learned you guys had already swooped in and taken the case from him. You still don't have a solid explanation for why they haven't officially ruled it a suicide, other than that's the only reason you can keep the house locked up."

"Maybe we're doing our goddamn jobs. You ever think of that? Maybe we've got an old man who killed himself, and we're trying to figure out why he did it so we can tell his family," Nugent said.

"That'd be a great story if it at all matched with what you actually told the family. Which is nothing."

"Gage, we're through here. And so are you. Back off. Go back to LA and give that woman whatever money she paid you because you haven't earned it, and you aren't going to. Forget about Johnnie Zhou."

No one spoke. The only sounds were the ambient city noise and the dull roar of freeway traffic beyond the hotel parking lot.

Someone was going through a lot of effort to scare me off.

And they weren't telling my client a damned thing.

That didn't add up.

The kicker, though, wasn't when Montoya called me a predator. It was when she closed with, "You're a fraud and if we catch you sticking your nose where it doesn't along, we're going to arrest you."

"You know what the Orpheus Foundation is?"

The cops exchanged a look. Nugent said, "no."

"It's a global collective of investigative journalists. They specialize in exposing government corruption. Remember the Panama Papers? That was them."

Montoya whistled and twirled her finger in a mocking gesture, but her partner was a little more wary. He was staring at a me intently.

"I work for them as a freelance investigator. Fact finding, due diligence. Some security work. I don't need a license for that sort of thing. The work I'm doing for Elizabeth Zhou was more of a favor. If, however, I find that someone—say a state law enforcement agency—was covering up evidence, or perhaps leaning a little too far in one direction because someone with connections in Sacramento benefited from it...well, that's the sort of thing Orpheus has made a career of."

"You threatening me, shitbird?" Montoya said. You could scrape the frost off her words with an ice chipper.

"I'm not threatening anyone. If the truth is threatening to you, you may want to lawyer up."

"Fuck you, Gage," she said.

"Let's go," Nugent said, guiding her back to their car. He paused and turned back to me. "You can rest assured I'll look into this foundation of yours and ask around. You'd better goddamned pray someone there knows you, because if they don't, I'm arresting you."

"In this conversation, you two have threatened arrest three times. Seems excessive." Technically, they'd only threatened to arrest me once, and the other two were just poorly camouflaged warnings about how they could if they wanted. That sort of conversational recordkeeping didn't seem like it would impress them, though.

Nugent said, "I don't want to see you again."

I watched the investigators leave and then got back into the Defender. I drove around until I found a liquor store and bought a bottle of Lagavulin.

Back at the room, I poured two fingers and stewed. The room had a large, plush club chair, which I sank into with my drink and thought through my next steps.

The house was the key. Something had happened there, and it wasn't just a gunshot.

More than that, I didn't like getting pushed around by cops. They were abusing their authority because they could get away with it. It wasn't the first time I'd experienced this, and it boiled my blood.

I wouldn't find answers unless I looked. The police made it very clear they didn't want anyone knowing what had happened.

That really left one option.

I was going to have to break into Johnnie Zhou's house and see for myself.

7

Nate McKellar had recognized that the Agency had overcorrected on counterterrorism and moved too far away from core intelligence work, from street craft. He'd picked the best of us and built a specialized covert action group. We went after the worst of humanity. The kinds of scumbags that slipped through the cracks in the Global War on Terror because they didn't wear keffiyehs. War criminals and arms dealers. Human traffickers. Narcoterrorists. We also disrupted our biggest rivals' most secretive operations. We didn't learn that the Iranians infiltrated our country's critical infrastructure solely through digital forensics. Part of the training for that was a graduate level education in defeating security systems. I'd walked unseen through the Russian Embassy in Vienna, so the locks on a tech exec's house weren't going to be much more than a speed bump.

I waited until the next night to enter.

I messaged Elizabeth via Signal and asked her to stay by her phone in case I needed anything today but didn't elaborate. She'd responded with an okay.

One of the things I loved about California was the abundance of privacy enthusiasts.

For example, if you knew where to look, you could rent a car more or less anonymously. The idea came out of the hacker community. People who needed a car but didn't want the leave a digital record of it. The intent wasn't to enable crimes; the intent was to have a short-term vehicle without a digital footprint at a rental agency. Why someone would want that, I could not tell you, other than "because...California."

Since I had a power of attorney granting me authorization to be in the house, I felt I'd satisfied the part about not committing crimes. My way into the house left that up for some debate.

The PD still had a squad car parked in the driveway, and the front lights of the house were on, but they'd kept the back patio dark. After doing a pass by the front, where I'd verified the police were still on scene and not paying a hell of a lot of attention, I parked my rental on the street behind the house. The neighborhoods in the area were terraced, climbing up the foothills, with just enough room for one street and a row of homes. I found a house on the terrace below Zhou's backyard that looked like they were hosting a party, so I parked among the cars lined up around it. The street was not lit, and I easily slid into the darkness beneath the trees. I wore dark clothes—jeans and a gray tee, loose enough for mobility but wouldn't rub and make noise. I wore a jacket from a company that made "mission ready" gear favored by people in my line of work, and people who wanted to look like they were in my line of work.

I'd found the house and padded across the grass, keeping to the right side of the yard. The shadows were deeper there. Most of the backyard was converted to patio with a large pool in the center. There were clusters of chairs stationed at each corner and a wide, wooden ramada over a table. I detached myself from the shadows and slid past an outdoor kitchen that was nicer than the indoor one in my house. There was no moon tonight, but just enough ambient light that I could make out the individual shapes on the patio.

The back of the house was mostly glass. There was a covered seating area beneath a large section of roof, big enough to be a room on its own. There were two sliding glass doors, one on the left and one deeper to the front. Both had closed vertical blinds. *Leave it to them to choose the loudest possible window treatments.*

Trusting that Elizabeth was right about her father's security setup, I glided up to the sliding glass door on my left and crouched, pulling a pair of booties over my shoes. They'd make some soft crinkling noises inside but not enough that the cop outside would hear it. Obviously, I had gloves on.

I removed the ballistic nylon sleeve where I kept my lock picks and set to work. First, I inserted the tension wrench and then the actual pick, maneuvering both to select the individual pins, lifting them into place. The door opened in thirty seconds. Elizabeth had been correct; it was a high-quality lock and probably would've spoofed most cat burglars, though it was far from "secure". I maneuvered the door just enough for me to slink through, bracing the blinds so they didn't clack. Once I was inside, I softly closed the door. There was an alarm system—I could see the sensors attached to the door—but it was deactivated. That made sense as the police were likely in and out.

I stood in the dead man's office.

A wave of sadness washed over me then. This was where it had happened. By all accounts, Johnnie Zhou had been a good man, a good husband and father. He was an eccentric, gregarious, larger than life personality. And he was gone. Even though I'd never met him, I could feel his absence from the world in this room.

I removed a small pen light from my jacket and activated it, shining the beam over the space in a practiced pattern.

You never got used to violent death.

I'd never killed anyone, though I'd seen the outcome often enough. It stayed with you.

I'd spare the details here because they were ugly, and because some-how, describing the rust-colored image of the moment after Johnnie Zhou's death lessened his life. I didn't want to reduce him to forensic details.

Instead, I focused on assessing the room for intelligence collection.

Zhou's office was a long, rectangular shape with sliding glass doors on two sides. His desk faced the covered part of the patio. It was a blond wood, though heavily stained and splattered. Zhou had two monitors on the desk with cords dangling like loose appendages. They'd taken his computer.

Zhou had a wall safe, which sat half open. It was concealed behind the third of three paintings hanging on the wall behind his desk. A quick flash of the pen light showed the safe had been cleaned out as well. I turned to the desk. The drawers were taped shut, but I peeled the tape off and opened them. Those were empty as well.

Nate told me to work this like a case, so I'd been thinking through how I would manipulate Zhou into being an asset. What levers would I pull to get him to steal secrets for me? Those led me to three theories on how he'd died. One, Zhou had made an enemy (rightly or wrongly) in his business dealings, and this was a revenge killing. Two, Zhou's business partner had him killed, probably to take over the business. Three, Zhou knew something or possessed something, and it was worth enough to someone else to kill him for it.

I left the office and investigated the rest of the ground floor. There was a large living room to the right and a short hallway to the left that ultimately led to the garage. The kitchen was in front of me. I went left, walking down the angled hallway.

I had no doubts that the state investigators had been over this place thoroughly, and if there was evidence to find, they'd have gotten it. Anything that was in plain sight. The thing I'd been taught to look for was where a man hid his secrets.

Training for Nate's black ops unit wasn't just picking locks, advanced surveillance, and combat driving. We spent a lot of time with the Agency's psychologists, breaking down human behavior. One of the things we'd learned was that people tended to hide things in the places where they felt safest. By this, I don't meant the obvious places like the safe in his office. The challenging part of this, the thing that would chew clock, was that I didn't know Zhou well enough to know where that might be.

The angled hallway had cupboards on both sides and doubled as a pantry and laundry area. Working quickly but methodically, I tested each of the cupboards, looking for false bottoms or backs. It took twenty minutes. Now conscious that I'd spent a half hour inside the house, I knew I had to pick it up. It didn't seem like the local police were running checks inside the home, but I also didn't *know*, and that made it risky for me. There was nothing here. I killed the light and decided to move upstairs.

The kitchen was located in the interior of the house without any windows, so I walked through it to the front room. The curtains were drawn closed, which was good, but there were three small windows above the front door, which faced the wide, curving staircase that led to the second floor. Hugging the interior of the curve to mask my movements from outside view, I slid upstairs. A quick scan of the hallway revealed three bedrooms on this level, with the master suite facing the front and side of the house. Ambient light illuminated the doorway, and I realized just in time that the curtains were pulled back. The crime scene investigators likely had opened them to let more natural light in and didn't think to close them. Or, since Zhou had died in his office, he might not have been up to the bedroom that last night.

Luckily for me, the second floor was set back some distance from the house's front, so if I kept low, the cop in the squad car wouldn't have a direct line of sight into the room. Doubtful he'd be able to see me anyway without a backlight to give him contrast, but I wasn't going to take the chance. I crab-walked over to the walk-in closet, where I could stand again and started my search there. After closing the closet door to shield the light from view, I twisted the flashlight on and quickly searched. The carpet showed signs of being pulled up, so I gave it a cursory inspection. If there was something there, it'd have been found. Next, I moved anything pushed up against the walls, looking for a hidden safe. It was a large closet, but I cleared it quickly. Zhou hadn't kept any of his wife's things after she passed, and he'd barely made use of the remaining half. I turned off the flash and returned to the bedroom on hands and knees.

A quick glance at my watch told me I'd been in the house forty-five minutes. Every second was one that might overlap with a cop deciding he needed to check on the place.

I needed to wrap this up.

I also knew there had to be something here, some clue the police hadn't uncovered yet. Why else would they keep the home sealed up like this and keep Elizabeth at arm's length? They couldn't find "it," so they'd keep this locked up until they did.

Scanning the room, left to right, taking it in, I tried to put myself in his head, think about where Johnnie Zhou might have chosen a hiding place. It was here, in this room. There was a throw rug at the foot of the bed. Why? You didn't get out of bed at the foot. Normally, that was where someone would put a bench or a trunk. I pulled the rug away and ran my fingers along the floor, which was wood paneling rather than carpet.

There it was.

I felt a seam in the floorboards underneath the bed. The rug obscured part of it. I'd seen panels like these before. They reminded me of those "magic eye" puzzles, where your brain thinks it's seeing something else. You look at them in daylight, and you probably just see the floorboards. If you touch it though, you can feel the seam. I pressed down and released the panel, and it flipped up on the long side, revealing a two- by one-foot space. We'd seen these used for stashing small arms, cash, passports, thumb drives, or a stolen copy of Iran's nuclear strategy—admittedly, a highly specific example. It was a smart location. If it'd been under a trunk or some other large object, the police would've clued in on it right away. A throw rug was easily moved and moved back. It faded into the visual background, easily forgotten.

Whatever elation I felt at the discovery quickly dissolved as I saw the safe beneath it. Unlike the one downstairs, this one was electronic.

I powered on my phone. The location services were all disabled, and I'd shut off the cellular function, but I'd need that connection now. If the police ever matched me with this phone, they'd see that it came up on whatever cell tower serviced this location. It wouldn't take a master detective to pinpoint that I was near the house—though I could probably make the case that I'd just been driving by. That was cripplingly thin and wouldn't wash if they knew someone had been in here.

I messaged Elizabeth:

What is your birthday and your parent's anniversary?

Her first reply was "???" Then she sent me her birthday but said she needed time to figure out what year her parents were married. It occurred to me that I couldn't easily answer that question about my own parents either.

I entered her digits into the keypad, and it flashed red. Most systems gave you three strikes.

While I waited for Elizabeth to write back to me with the anniversary, I tried to review everything I'd learned about Johnnie Zhou's life. Especially those things that might translate to numbers.

If he was smart, it'd be a series of random numbers that he'd commit to memory.

That would also be impossible to guess.

I thought through what I'd known about his life. Birthdays, anniversaries...both of those were bad. They tended to be security challenge questions for online accounts, most of which were easily hacked. His citizenship date was another possibility. That wouldn't come up in standard questions. Nor would the date they'd first moved to the U.S.

Nate said Zhou had been a protestor at the Tiananmen Square Massacre. I was in grade school when it happened, and while I certainly remember it from the news, I only had a vague recollection of when. Risking another network ping, I used a private browser to look up the date. June 4^t, 1989.

I tapped "0-6-0-4-8-9" on the keypad, and it flashed red. Probably one try left. This time, I did "6-4-1-9-8-9," and the light flashed green, followed by a click that sounded like thunder in the silent house. I opened the safe.

Well, my instinct that the house was the key to this was right.

I just didn't know what in the hell "this" was.

All I knew, looking in that safe, was that Johnnie Zhou had some secrets.

8

I removed the safe's contents and set them on the floor so I could create a mental inventory.

Taking anything with me would be removing evidence from a crime scene. However I justified getting in here, even I knew what I could get away with was limited. It also risked the police taking them from me, which would certainly expose how I'd gotten them.

Seeing this, I was sure there was something here that would give this case the life it needed. And I'd bet that I was the only one who knew about it.

Zhou had made excellent use of the small space and planned it carefully. First, I found a pair of small Moleskine notebooks. Next, I found a pocket torch, like you'd use to light cigars. Then, a small black pouch made of a heavy, thick fabric. There was a phone inside. I guessed the bag was a faraday pouch. Finally, there was a small plastic case, holding a single key.

Before doing anything else, I crept over to the window and looked out over the driveway. The car was still there, and I could see the blue-white glow of a screen through the back window. Reasoning the cop wasn't going anywhere, I removed the notebooks and crawled over to the closet, again closing the door behind me. Then, I removed some clothes from a drawer in the closet. They felt like sweaters. I rolled them up and placed them at the door's base, covering the gap between it and the floor, then turned on the light. I examined the notebooks, one red and one black. Unfortunately, both were written in Chinese.

Starting with the black one, I took a picture of the cover and then snapped a shot of every page. There were only twenty or so with writing on them. The last two pages stopped me cold—they were names. A quick scan showed they were all Chinese Americans, with mostly Anglicized first names and Chinese surnames. Robert Li, Joseph Gao, Charles Zheng, Ethan Jian. There were fifteen names total.

I repeated the process with the red one. That had more the look of a journal—entries with what looked like dates and some numbers. I snapped probably double the amount of photos for this notebook. There was a lot of information here to parse, and I couldn't do it in a dead man's closet.

I returned the clothes to their drawer, flicked off the light, and gave my eyes a minute to adjust. I crawled over to the safe and returned the items the way I'd found them, then closed it and returned the floor panel. Before vanishing, I did a quick equipment inventory, making sure I didn't leave any of my gear behind. Satisfied, I crept over to the door and then slinked down the stairs, hugging the wall. I peeked my head around the corner to check the driveway before proceeding. Seeing no movement from the police car, I slid deeper into the house and out the way I'd come, taking care to lock Zhou's office door as I left.

I paused again on the patio, listening for any signs of detection.

Then I disappeared into the night.

⸻

I dropped the car at the rental place and walked to find a cab. It was close to eleven. Forty-five minutes later, I was back in my hotel room and working out the translation problem. I picked up a few languages in the Agency, and none of them were Mandarin. That school was two years long. There were plenty of apps that could translate text from a photo; however, many of them retained that data on their servers. Not only did that create a trail of digital breadcrumbs connecting me with Zhou, if there was anything illegal or dangerous in those notes, it could trip some alarms. And because I couldn't read the native text, I couldn't know this in advance. For the same reasons, I couldn't just take them to a translation service.

I didn't want to involve Elizabeth. She'd not mentioned being fluent in Mandarin. And if there was something illegal in those notes, I wanted to know it first so Elizabeth could get legal protection. I didn't want her learning about whatever it might be via her translating it.

First, I transferred the files to an encrypted partition on my hard drive that was not connected to the internet. Then I used a VPN favored by the privacy-inclined that didn't track my moves and would obfuscate my online presence. I accessed a web-based photo-translation app. I avoided Google's because I knew they'd scrape whatever I uploaded, but a smaller company might not. I started with the images from the black notebook. The translations appeared to be gibberish or nonsensical, just random strings of words. The idea hit me, however, that this could be a code. If that was the case, I had some people that I might be able to call.

Some of them might even answer.

I moved on to the names. Each had a string of numbers next to it, which I could tell immediately was an IP address. There was another string of Chinese characters after those, which the translation app showed to be several words. Next to the entry for the top name, "Robert Li," the translation app returned, "branch glare sound eagle masonry purple". I smiled. It was a passphrase. *Now we're getting somewhere.* The question, of course, was: a passphrase to what?

I navigated to Robert Li's IP address.

It was password protected. I entered the phrases after his name as they appeared on the page and...nothing. It was late and had been a long day, I was adrenaline-crashing from the entry into Zhou's home and probably not thinking clearly. I tried the phrases again but put a dash in between the words.

Working through the list, I translated the passphrase and created a separate document, saved on the partitioned drive, for easier reference. All the sites were the same as Robert Li's-- a digital drop box—and all of them were empty. This brought me to one in the morning, and I decided to call it a night.

The next morning, I called an old Agency friend, an analyst assigned to the Asia Division and was now in CIA's new China Mission Center. Not surprisingly, the call went straight to voicemail. Agency employees couldn't bring their personal phones into the building. Kim was fluent in Mandarin, and she'd worked at the State Department's intel division before going to Langley. If anyone could make sense of what that text was, she could. Fifty-fifty shot I'd hear back from her.

Agency leadership scorched me with the rank-and-file. They made an "example" of me to hide a senior leader's fuckup. Some of my old colleagues knew it for what it was and still kept their distance out of a sense of self-preservation.

Of course, once I went to work for a group of investigative journalists, that pretty much burned me with the rest of them. The CIA had a curious relationship with the press. They were generally supportive of the Fourth Estate—especially in other countries. Intelligence work and journalism had a lot in common. The Agency just doesn't like anyone airing its secrets, and newspapers had a tendency to do that.

I knew that many former colleagues thought I'd gone to work for Orpheus as a way of getting back at the Agency, air some dirty laundry, expose my enemies, maybe write a book.

In truth, my aims were far less grandiose. I just wanted to make rent and be able to look myself in the mirror.

After a quick breakfast and a coffee to clear my head, I was back at it.

I decided to take another look at the names, IP addresses, and code phrases. See if maybe I'd missed something the night before. A six-word code phrase was long, even by professional standards. Most password crackers couldn't handle five. It could be that whatever Zhou was trying to hide, he wanted to make absolutely certain it couldn't be found. No security system was impenetrable, but the more characters and phrases, the harder it became. I reread each name, IP, and passphrase combos on the doc I'd created, looking for patterns. Seeing them in a cleartext document, rather than individually on a translator, one thing struck out. The last word of each phrase was a color. Purple, black, blue, orange, violet, and down the line, all fifteen. There were no dashes in between the phases on the page, but I'd had to include the dashes to access the cloud drive.

Looking back at the original list, the character representing the color was spaced farther out than the others.

"Holy shit, it's a cipher," I said.

I tried the first IP/passphrase combo again, including the dashes but leaving out the color.

It worked.

My suspicions from the previous night were confirmed, this was a digital drop box on a private cloud server. There was nothing in it. I worked through the rest of the list, and it was the same. The boxes were empty. Still, that was something. Zhou had gone through the trouble of creating anonymous virtual storage sites and was storing the logon info in a hidden safe.

"What were you hiding?" I asked his ghost.

The colors appeared to be a cipher, but keying in to what? The translator app created a text file of its output, so I copied those into a doc on my machine. Then I searched for each of the colors. Nothing.

I hadn't yet translated the pictures from the red notebook, so I set the colors aside and went to those pictures. Repeating the same process as last night, I entered the pics into the translator and dropped the results into a text file.

The answer came almost immediately.

Each of the colors matched up to a physical address that was listed on a line in the red notebook. There was no name associated—that was in the black book with the IP address. It was a great system, assuming no one person had both books.

Which, apparently, I did.

Still, this was a kind of air gapping, and it told me something else. Whatever Zhou wanted to keep secret, he didn't trust putting it online. Not even in an encrypted file. That spoke volumes about who he was hiding from, though I still didn't know *what.*

I created a separate file on the partitioned drive linking the names and addresses so I had an easy reference. Then I started looking them up on my TOR browser.

Of the fifteen, eight were located here in the Bay Area. Three were in Los Angeles, one in San Diego, two in Seattle, and one in Vancouver.

Over the next few hours, I used various open source tools to compile the phone numbers associated with each of the names. Unfortunately, this was all perfectly legal, and most people didn't realize how much "data" was in the public domain. Because cell phone numbers had been portable between carriers for at least twenty years, many of them tended to outlast physical addresses. It had become one of the easiest ways to triangulate an individual in a sea of data. By noon, I had what I believed to be the phone numbers for each of the fifteen names.

My phone beeped, and I peered at the text on the screen. It was from Kim.

Hey Matt, sorry I missed your call, you know how it is. Hope you're doing well.

I responded with, *Hanging in. I'm sort of a PI now in Cali. Would you mind taking a look at something for me, it's for a case. Need help translating something in Chinese. Might be code.*

The waving ellipses appeared indicating she was typing a response. It vanished, appeared again, and vanished again. Whatever she was trying to say, she'd thought better of it a few times.

After about a minute, Kim finally responded:

I can't help. Sorry. Good luck.

Can't or won't? In the end, what's the difference?

I texted her a few of the pictures anyway, with a note:

Just in case you change your mind.

She didn't respond.

But I knew how her mind worked, and she obsessed over puzzles. For her, everything was a mystery to unravel. She'd look at that photo and translate it and then start thinking about what it meant. Eventually, the question would worm its way into her mind, and she wouldn't be able to resist it.

Or she'd delete the message from me instantly because she'd been told to.

Returning to my list of names, I started researching them. I wanted to build a profile of each. That would give me insight into who Johnnie Zhou was. Who were these people to him and why were their names in a notebook in a floor safe, protected by a cipher? Right now, the common thread was their heritage—all appeared to be Chinese Americans. Or, at least, had

Chinese surnames. I knew from work in the region that could actually mean one of a dozen countries.

Within a few hours, a pattern emerged. There were searchable public records databases one could subscribe to. I had an account already with one that I knew was popular with private eyes. It compiled public records, court filings, and employment data. Thirteen of them were between the ages of fifty and seventy-five. Nine were journalists (two were retired), one was a college professor, and two looked to be some kind of software engineer. Eleven of the fifteen were men.

Now that I had several datapoints on each one, I ran internet searches against their names. Most came up blank. There were a few community-related pieces. The nine journalists, however, returned a trove of articles, which I saved on my machine to review later. I also searched the usual social media sites and LinkedIn, which didn't return much. It appeared most of these people maintained a minimal online presence. The searching took the remainder of the afternoon. There were two curious returns, however. Kevin Wei, fifty six, of Richmond, had died in a car accident two months ago. Ryan Tan, thirty six, a software engineer right here in Cupertino, had been found dead in his apartment three weeks ago. The cause of death wasn't listed, at least nowhere I could find online. His obituary listed it as "accidental."

Tan had died a week before Johnnie Zhou.

I needed to speak with one of these people and find out what they knew about Zhou, how they knew him. And why he kept their names in a notebook in a safe.

I started with Jason Ming, because he was retired.

No answer, so I moved on to the next name, Samuel Wu.

Wu was the college professor, located in LA and with a PhD in economics.

"Hello?"

"Professor Wu?"

"That's correct, whom am I speaking with?"

"My names is Chuck Thomas. I'm a reporter investigating the death of a Johnnie Zhou. A source told me you were acquainted."

Wu immediately said, "I'm sorry, but I'm due in class. I'm sorry." He hung up. I called back, but it didn't even go to voicemail. He must have blocked my number.

Well, that was something.

I tried two more names and no dice. Both went straight to voicemail.

I wasn't going to call each of these people at random, especially considering the reaction I'd gotten from Wu. If they all knew each other, they would certainly alert the others that someone was taking about Zhou. Wu's reaction was telling. His flight instinct had triggered immediately. He didn't deny that he knew Johnnie Zhou, which someone with training might have done. He just wanted to get out of the situation as quickly as possible. Was he afraid of his association with Zhou? Did Zhou have something on him?

Switching tactics, I went back through the names and chose Robert Li. Starting with people outside the local area was a mistake. I couldn't see if my contacting them forced an action. I hadn't expected them to shut it down so fast. He was on the top of the list—perhaps that was random or perhaps there was a reason he was listed first. He also lived here in San Jose, maybe twenty minutes from my hotel.

I'd worked through lunch and was now famished, so I grabbed an early dinner. That gave me time to plan out my next move. First, I'd establish surveillance on the house and then use an old counterintelligence trick to flush the subject out so I could follow him. The idea was to dangle a bit of bait and get him to bite. Given how Professor Wu had reacted, I had a notion of what that bait should be.

An hour later, I was parked down the street from Li's house. He lived on Tenth Street, in the heart of San Jose's Asian community, on the edge of Japantown and several blocks north of Little Saigon. It was a small single-family home with a carport. The lawn looked well maintained and conservatively landscaped. The one splash of color was a pink rosebush. A large oak provided shade over the house and cast a long, evening shadow over the lawn.

Shades covered the single front-facing windows, but I saw the glow of light behind them. There was a silver Prius in the driveway, plugged into an outlet. From what I could determine online, Li wasn't married. There were some indications he was a widower, but I wasn't certain about that.

If he were an intelligence target, this process would typically take weeks if not months. I'd have become an expert in Robert Li. I'd understand, deeply, that one thing he desperately needed. Sometimes it was money, though most often, that was for logistics. When recruiting in repressive governments, it was almost always an opportunity to do some good, to strike back at a regime that terrorized its people. There were some that did it for personal gain. I'd run an army officer in Gabon once who was just looking for a way to advance through the ranks and was happy to sell out anyone in his government to do it. Those people were less common than you might think. One thing working in the Agency had taught me was there were a lot of good people in the world who will stick their necks out given the right incentive.

Unfortunately, I didn't have that kind of time.

Not only did I have to show results to my client, I had to do it faster than the police could. Given what I'd seen so far, they might close this thing and not offer Elizabeth anything that amounted to closure. It could be as half-assed as ruling it a suicide so the case would go away, or it could be something more. Either way, I needed to find out before they did.

My brief call with Wu was insightful in that I could intuit that some, if not all, of those names on the list knew Johnnie Zhou. More importantly, the nature of that relationship was something they wanted to keep quiet.

I called Robert Li.

He sent the call to voicemail.

I waited three agonizing minutes and called back. Some robo-dialers will do that but most were programmed to try again immediately.

This time, he answered.

"I don't need an extended warranty for my—"

"Mr. Li, please don't hang up," I said.

"Who is this?"

I decided to avoid the subterfuge this time and just tell him what I wanted. "I'd like to speak to you about Johnnie Zhou. I understand you were acquainted. If it's not too much trouble, could I have a few moments of your time?"

"This isn't a good...I'm sorry, I can't help you."

"Could I call back at a better time, sir?"

"No, I don't think so." And he hung up.

I was staring at Li's house from half a block away, when I saw the front light go out. The man hurriedly emerged from his house, disconnected the Prius, and pulled out onto the street. He drove past me, heading south on Tenth. I waited until he'd gone a block and then turned around to follow him. I'd gambled that my calling and mentioning Johnnie Zhou would flush him out. He'd leave to make a phone call, meet up with someone, anything he didn't want connected to his home.

Looks like I was right.

We rode Tenth straight for ten, maybe fifteen blocks, past San Jose State and onto the 280 interchange. Single car vehicular surveillance was one of the hardest things to do without assistance. Tailing someone in a car usually involved multiple chase vehicles, all coordinated by radio and, ideally, augmented by electro/optical surveillance.

I actually kept Apple AirTags with magnetic sheaths in my kit, which I'd used on occasion to surveil a target (yes, I know the State of California's opinion on the matter, but it works). While the outcome had always been to get Li to move, I wasn't about to try and put a bug on his car in broad daylight. I also didn't think I should push this out another day.

I'd become impatient, and after multiple days of setbacks, I'd forced the action.

This was one of the dangers of working by yourself. There was no one to point out the blind spots in the operations plan.

Thankfully, a Prius was easy to catch. The hardest part was actually making sure I had the right one.

We were in the thick of the evening rush, and traffic had slowed to a crawl not long after we got on 280. The upside, though, meant that with no one overtaking, I could hang out a car or two behind Li and he'd think nothing of it. We trudged forward in an agonizing march around Silicon Valley for the next hour. Something sure had spooked him for him to be willing to sit through this shit.

Li worked his way over to the right and took the Skyline Drive offramp, across from San Andreas Lake. I followed. Unfortunately, I was the only other car taking that exit. The sprawling SFO complex unfolded to my right, across a narrow valley. I let Li get some lengths ahead of me and followed him through a twisting series of turns through residential neighborhoods for about two miles, taking us back under 280 and then doubling back south.

Then our destination became clear. He was heading to Junipero Sierra Park.

Li drove into the park, ignoring the admonishment to pay six dollars to enter.

I followed at a distance and also kept my six bucks. It was September, and the park would only be open another thirty minutes or so. The sky was a blazing burnt orange, but the land was dark with long, indigo shadows, deepened by the trees. It took a few minutes of searching, but I spotted Li's car and parked in the next row. He was already out of the car and walking quickly. He was wearing a lightweight blue jacket and chinos. I got out and followed.

Li moved fast for an older man and was in good shape. He picked up a trail leading into the woods. I didn't have any choice but to follow him, but if he checked his six, ever, he'd see me easily. The phone reception wasn't good here, and I was having trouble downloading a park map. So, with no better options, I gave him a head start and followed. The trail immediately hooked to the left and then wended its way back, gradually going uphill. I lost sight of him, but that would mean he couldn't see me either.

When I saw a sign for the Buckeye Picnic Area, I picked up my pace a little. If I ran into him, I could just fake needing to ask for directions and use that as a way into a conversation with him. The trail was easy to follow, and I caught sight of his blue jacket as it disappeared around a corner. The gnarled, claw-like oaks made for a dark tunnel, and it was getting difficult to see.

I finally emerged from the trail to catch Li bolting across the picnic area. He made for the line of trees on the far side, which gave a commanding view of San Francisco International and the bay beyond it. He disappeared over the hill then emerged from the woods, walking toward a small BBQ grill.

I made fast steps to the grill.

Li was about to burn something. Whatever it was, it was a good bet it'd been hidden up here.

Okay. My mind was working now, connections forming. Johnnie Zhou had a list of names, and one of them maintained a dead drop.

"Excuse me, Robert Li?" I said as I got closer.

Li pretended not to hear me. Instead, he fumbled with a lighter, nervous hands trying to get the flint to strike. If he'd had a butane lighter like Zhou, whatever it was would be on fire by now.

"Mr. Li? I'd like a word, sir," I said, realizing only too late that I must have sounded exactly like a cop. *Well, let that work for me for a change.* "Mr. Li, I need you to put the lighter down and step away from the grill, sir."

9

Li's lighter caught, and arm quaking, he shoved it at the papers bunched in his hand.

Whatever that was, it was tied to Johnnie Zhou, and I needed to see it before it went up. That might be my only chance to figure out what in the actual hell was going on here.

"Stop," I said, commandingly. "Don't burn that."

He ignored me.

"I'm just trying to learn who killed Johnnie Zhou."

Robert Li put both his hands on the edges of the cold grill, as if bracing himself. He exhaled heavily and looked like he'd just lost a race. His head dropped almost between his shoulders.

The papers continued to burn at the corners.

"Mr. Li, I need to speak with you. I'm not the police, and you're not in trouble."

"You can't know that," he said.

"What do you mean?" I said, walking up to him. I reached into the grill and grabbed the bunched-up papers. He didn't stop me. I dropped them onto the ground and stepped on the burning edges, extinguishing the flames.

"That won't do you any good," he said.

"I hear that a lot," I said, picking up the crumpled wad of papers.

"Are you the one who called about Johnnie?"

First names. That was something.

"I am," I admitted. "My name is Matt Gage."

Li stepped back from the grill and turned to face me. He stuffed his hands into his jacket pockets, and I could see they were balled fists. I knew from my backgrounding that Li was fifty-eight. He was a dual citizen. Li had a lean build and was slightly stooped. His hair was more salt than pepper, and there were deep lines creased on his face.

"Well, if you're not the police, who are you? Reporter?"

"I'm working for Zhou's daughter," I said. "She wants answers that she's not getting from the police. I want to make sure she's not also in danger."

Robert adjusted his posture as he looked up at me in the growing twilight. The way people carried themselves can tell you volumes about them if you know how to look. Robert Li had a quiet dignity and a resolve that his earlier actions seemed to mask.

I didn't know, yet, the nature of Li's connection to Zhou or why Johnnie had this man's name in a hidden, ciphered notebook among fourteen others. I could guess why a phone call from me got him to race up here and burn something he'd hidden in the park. I suspected that reason was the same one that would have everyone else on that list running for cover when I called them. Now I just had to coax it out of him.

"Mr. Li, can I buy you a cup of coffee?"

"It's Robert, and I think we're going to need a little something stronger than that. I know a place."

Li looked down at the singed papers and held his hand out. "First, you need to let me burn those."

"Tell me what they are."

"In due time. That's the price."

I handed them over, and Li set them alight. He watched them burn in silence, the fire light reflecting in his eyes. They were wet, but maybe that was from the smoke.

When it was done, he said, "We can go now."

I followed him down the hill to the parking lot.

Li didn't speak on the way down, and I let him have his silence. When we reached the cars, he said, "You already know how to follow me, so I won't bother with directions." And he was off.

I followed him to a restaurant just outside the airport called Harry's By the Bay. It was the kind of gritty, local place that had been in business for years and was fiercely popular with the locals. It was a single-story building facing the water. We walked in, and Robert told the server we'd take a table on the patio. She said for us to help ourselves. It was already starting to get brisk, so there wasn't a lot of competition for seating, and the nearly constant roar of planes overhead made eavesdropping almost impossible.

Apart from not spotting a tail, Robert Li's tradecraft wasn't bad.

I ordered an Anchor Steam. I'd heard they were going out of business, and figured I should have one while I could still get it. Robert did the same.

"So, you're working for Johnnie's daughter. Did you know him as well?"

I shook a negative. "I did not. I only just met her."

"How'd she find you?" Robert asked.

"I'm in the book," I said in a way that told him that line of inquiry was a dead end.

"You're, what, a private detective?"

"Something like that." Robert was sizing me up, an animal circling in the wild, trying to decide if I was a predator or not.

"What's your relationship with Johnnie Zhou?" I asked him. Our beers arrived. A plane took off. The air was thick and funky with salt and marine life. The server loudly asked us if we wanted food. I ordered a basket of fries to make her happy.

"Johnnie and I were friends. We'd known each other a long, long time." Li lifted his beer, considered something, and then drank. He didn't speak until he set the beer back down. "Johnnie's daughter hired you because she thinks someone killed him?"

"That's right," I said, wondering how long we were going to dance. "She thinks he was murdered and that either the police think that too and aren't telling her, or they're just trying to wipe this under the rug for some other reason. Either way, they aren't giving her the truth. At least, not all of it."

"I never met Elizabeth, but Johnnie talked about her a lot. He was really proud of her." Li took another drink, then gazed into his beer.

"Do you think there's anything to it? Could someone have murdered him?" I asked.

Li shrugged. "I don't know."

His hesitation spoke volumes. He didn't want to commit to the idea, didn't want to put words to it, but he couldn't deny it either. I sensed he was being cryptic because he didn't trust me enough to share the truth. We didn't have that kind of time. My involvement, asking questions, poking around, had spurred some people to action. It would either be Blake's lawyer or the state cops. Maybe it'd be both.

"Robert, what are we doing here?"

"So, you probably know that I'm a journalist. I've written for the *Chronicle*, the *China Times*, and the *South China Morning Post*. I'm freelance now. I also run a blog and contribute to some underground papers, websites, using pen names. I mostly cover the Chinese Communist Party, with a focus on exposing corruption." A bitter laugh issued from his mouth. "It's steady work. I can never go home again. If I stepped foot in China, I'd be arrested immediately. More on that in a bit. I've got an ailing father; he's in his nineties. I know I'll never see him again. That's a hard pill to swallow."

He exhaled, took another drink, then continued. "Johnnie and I met during the Tiananmen protests. He was a graduate engineering student at the time. I was covering them for a regional paper. It was Tank Man, though, who got me involved. Watching him stand there, refusing to move. When I saw that kind of courage, I knew I couldn't just 'report' news. I had to expose the government for what it was. So, I started writing. It was easier then. They didn't have the surveillance technology that they do now. Eventually, I moved my family to Hong Kong in 1995 and continued to cover the government from there. Once the transition happened, though, things changed. It got dangerous. I received a letter from Johnnie, who said he was living out here, and my wife and I emigrated in 2002.

"We moved to San Francisco, got involved in the local Chinese-American community, ran into some old friends. We raised a family. I found work as a journalist covering Asia. It was a good life." The weight he put on the word "was" was unmistakably sad. His voice cracked when he'd said it, almost imperceptibly, but it was there.

"A few years ago, Johnnie approached me," he went on. "I hadn't seen him in a long time. We both saw what was happening back home and wanted to do something about it. He asked me if I was still writing about the corruption. I was, though not with the same 'counterrevolutionary fervor' of my youth." He favored the latter with a grim smile. "My wife died recently, and I was looking for a cause, I guess. I agreed to help. Johnnie always had these grand ideas. You've heard the old joke, how do you eat an elephant?"

"Yeah," I said. "One bite at a time."

"Right, so Johnnie didn't know anything about that," Robert said, a smile lighting his face. For the first time, there was genuine humor in his eyes. "We have this myth about a snake called *Bashe* that swallowed an elephant whole. That's Johnnie. He wanted to run dedicated campaigns to undermine the government in Beijing. Educate the world about what was happening and help the organizations back home fighting for change. He used his company to invest in technology that could be repurposed to beat the surveillance state. You have to understand, the CCP controls the media; they control the tech industry. Any app that gets built, any platform that's launched, they all have to be sanctioned by the party. And those companies have to turn their data over to the government. WeChat, which nearly everyone uses for communication, banking, social media, shopping...it's monitored constantly."

I cut in. "I know a little bit about how he managed his tech business. You've mentioned it, and I've also spoken with his business partner. Some of the companies he invested in over the years developed tech that could be repurposed to undermine CCP surveillance. Did any those companies know it?" I'd begun to wonder if, maybe, someone didn't like their tech being used for subversion.

Robert shook his head. "I don't know all the particulars of his business. I do know Johnnie was careful about how he used the tech, though. He always got a company's permission first. Last thing he needed was a lawsuit. Anyway, Johnnie created this whole network of dissident journalists. People like me who were trying to shine some lights into some very dark places. He paid us for our time. I don't know how, and it wasn't much. Never asked. We set up websites and ran a pro-democracy online newspaper. He figured out a way to get it through the Chinese government's firewalls."

"Do you know any of the other journalists he worked with?" I asked.

"No."

"Did you ever know anyone named Kevin Wei?" Wei was one of the names on Zhou's list, who'd died in a car accident two months before Johnnie's "suicide."

Li held up both hands, shaking his head. "I don't, and I don't want to. Please don't ask me that again."

"Okay, I won't. I apologize," I said. His reaction there and earlier when I'd said Elizabeth thought Johnnie had been murdered told me Li believed that to be true. It also told me he was scared. "Robert, I know this is a difficult subject for you. I want to be respectful of that. If anything I ask is out of line, just tell me. Fair?" He nodded; I continued. "I asked this before and you said you didn't know. I want to try again. Do you think someone killed Johnnie?"

Li got quiet again, considering his next words carefully.

"The Chinese government has always cracked down on dissidents, but they've stepped up efforts on a global scale under President Xi. He's turned the country into an apex predator with no natural enemies. While America was fighting in Iraq and Afghanistan for twenty years, China invested heavily in Europe, Asia, Africa, building up its power base. They expanded their reach in the UN, gaining leadership on committees to influence global technology standards that favored Chinese ones rather than American. The goal was to make China ubiquitous."

"I don't see what that has to do with killing dissidents."

"If they're the world's superpower, who is going to stop them? Watching the Saudis get away with murdering a *Washington Post* reporter was a watershed moment for Xi. Once that happened, he knew he could do whatever he wanted as long as he had enough influence."

"But I don't understand why *now*? Relations between the US and China are as tense as they've ever been. Why risk an operation on foreign soil like that?"

"Grain," Li said flatly.

"Grain," I replied, incredulous.

"Or, more precisely, the lack of it. The Chinese wheat crop has been devastated these last two years. It's nearly famine levels. They used to be a net exporter of winter wheat throughout Asia, which was a major economic driver. Those crops are gone. Now, not only is the Chinese economy in trouble, there isn't enough food to go around, and they can't import enough. Turns out, feeding one point four billion people is a logistical challenge," Robert gave a grim smile and reached for his drink. "Hungry people get angry, and angry people topple governments. Or at least they try. The CCP is worried that if enough dissident networks latch onto the narrative that China can't feed its own people, it'll catch fire. Internationally, it undermines their position as a superpower. Domestically, it might just encourage people to rise up."

Li drained his beer, and the server appeared with a fresh pair after getting a slight nod from me. Li waited until the server was back inside before he picked the thread back up. "Those papers you saw me burning?"

"Yeah," I said.

"That was my latest reporting. A lead. It was something I wanted to get into the network's hands before I published anything. To protect them. Also, I wasn't sure if I should. I didn't even want it in my house, so instead of putting something on a computer file and hiding it online, which Johnnie taught me how to do, I just wrote it down and hid it here. When you called, asking about him, I wasn't sure if it was a trap or not. I also wasn't sure that Johnnie had gotten the report before he died. Hell, I don't know if that's why he was killed."

"What was the report about?"

"There are these...call them 'community outreach centers' that are appearing in major cities worldwide. Mostly in Europe. Ostensibly, these are to help Chinese citizens abroad with passport or immigration issues. All of my reporting was in those notes, including sources. I don't know if it would do any good or not, but I thought by burning them, I'd sever a link between that information and our network."

I didn't exactly follow Li's logic. It was also possible he was not totally honest about what he'd burned. We'd just met, and he had no reason to trust me. I decided not to press it for now.

"Immigration and passport problems... Isn't that what a consulate is for?"

"Exactly right," he said. "Seems like a great way to collect intelligence on the community, doesn't it? I've been working with some colleagues, fellow journalists in Europe, and we started piecing this together. There's a very curious correlation between the location of these 'community centers' and the disappearances of noted dissidents."

My mind immediately went to the two names from Johnnie's notebook, Ryan Tan and Kevin Wei. Both had died within the last month.

"How did you find out about it?" I asked.

"They contacted me from the local community center. I'm a dual citizen, and they said there was a problem with my Chinese citizenship and that I should come in and talk to them." A curt, slightly cynical laugh issued from his mouth. "As you might imagine, I did not want to do this. It seemed wrong to me, so I started looking into this community center. I can't find any references to its existence or creation. One day it wasn't there, and the next day it was. My best estimation is that it had opened in the last six months."

"Did Johnnie ever say anything to you about being followed?"

"Once. I think it was a few weeks ago. I didn't know if he was being paranoid or if, maybe, there was something to it. Johnnie could be a little hyperbolic. When he kept at it, we agreed it was best not to keep anything about the community centers on a computer."

An old graybeard at the Agency used to talk about a "sixth sense," what most people would call a gut instinct. It was just this feeling you got— about the rhythm of the street, the way a collection target behaved, or the way you know an asset was lying to you. Or how you knew that of all the people involved, you knew the least.

That was how I felt at that moment.

Johnnie Zhou had talked an old friend of his, Robert Li, into helping him expose Chinese corruption. Given what I'd learned about the backgrounds of the other names on that list, I could assume Zhou had a similar relationship with them. That was smart. No one on the list knew who any of the others were. Then Zhou turned up dead, and my old CIA boss suggested to the man's daughter that she ask *me*, of all people, to look into it.

I could begin to see why state police investigators would now roll in and take this over. What made less sense was for them not to say something to Elizabeth to assure her there was a broader investigation underway.

No assumptions. No half measures. That was something a grizzled old case officer had once told me. Guessing based on half the facts led to sloppy intelligence and incorrect conclusions.

I didn't have enough facts for a decision yet, and I cautioned myself against making any. Though I suspected someone had more information than I did.

"Robert, you've just given me a really important lead to track down. I want to find out who's responsible and expose them. Hopefully, that will force the police to act. If it doesn't, I have other means at my disposal."

Li gave a half-laugh. "That sounds sinister."

"I work as a freelance investigator for a privately funded journalistic foundation. You'd love them. They do a lot of the same kind of work that you're doing on your own. I think they'd be very interested to speak to you about these 'community centers,' if you'd be amenable to it. Regarding Johnnie's killer, the foundation is my other lever. Of course, I'd need to clear this with Elizabeth first. Understandably, she wants to keep things quiet. However, if the police won't do anything, the foundation can light this up with a megawatt bulb. Will you help me?"

"Let me think on it," he said.

"Fair enough. Have you spoken with the police regarding Johnnie? Do they know about your connection to him?"

"I haven't spoken with them. As far as I know, they don't know who I am. I'd like to keep it that way, if it's all the same to you."

"I understand. I'll call you in a few days."

He smiled softly. "You've already got my number."

"Thank you. For your time and for the work you do."

He responded with a quizzical look.

I said, "Let's just say I used to be in a line of work where I greatly appreciated that sort of thing. You and I have a lot more in common than you might think."

I paid the check on the way out.

Then I drove to Nate McKellar's house.

10

Los Altos is one of the northern communities on Silicon Valley's west side and close to the Burlingame bar we'd been at. I didn't like dropping in on Nate unannounced, but there was no possible way Johnnie Zhou and he were close friends and Nate—a career intelligence officer—didn't know Zhou was running a network of dissident journalists out of his home. The fact that Nate hadn't told me at the outset pissed me off. Knowing this from the jump would have changed my entire approach to the case. There were about a hundred new rocks to look under now.

This revelation didn't mean I was letting Benjamin Blake off the hook. In fact, both things could be true. Blake had twenty-five million reasons to benefit from Zhou's death. And he'd also come at me with a pretty big stick, which said something.

However, the fact that Zhou was running his own ring of anti-communist agitators against the world's foremost oppressive regime and surveillance state changed the case on a fundamental level. It also meant I needed to consider an opposition more dedicated, more ruthless than some state cops.

Two totally independent, unrelated events, and one just forced exposure of the other.

I called Nate when I was ten minutes from his home and told him I'd be there shortly, that we needed to speak in person. Nate sounded a little put out that I was showing up on short notice and so late at night. He asked if this could wait until morning. I told him it could not.

Nate greeted me coolly, though it seemed the sentiment derived more from being tired than irritated. It was almost nine when I arrived. He showed me in and guided me straight back to his office, where he did not offer me a drink.

The office was in the back corner of this house overlooking the lawn. He had a large desk with a bookcase behind it, half filled with books—many of which were CIA memoirs written by friends of his. There were a lot of mementos from his intelligence career, though they were more subtle. If you didn't know him, looking at this you'd think Nate was someone who'd simply traveled widely and experienced much.

The desk dominated the space, but he had a pair of brown-leather Manhattan chairs at an angle toward one another beneath a tattered map of Afghanistan on the wall. He pointed at one of the chairs.

He closed the door and sat down. Before he had a chance to speak, I said, "Why didn't you tell me Zhou was running a ring of dissident journalists in his spare time? I can't imagine that slipped your notice."

Nate got pin-drop quiet.

Without saying anything else, he stood and walked over to a side table where he had a crystal decanter and four glasses. We'd given him that, once Nate's time as our team leader was done. As with the other artifacts in the room, there was nothing tying him to the Agency, that unit, or our time there. Just an innocuous quote etched on the side of the decanter, meaningless to anyone else: *Now you're all under arrest.* Cary Grant's line in "Gunga Din" when he's completely surrounded by the enemy. It was our unofficial motto.

Nate poured two bourbons, handing me one on the way back to his chair.

"How'd you figure that out?"

"My first thought was part of the reason you hired me was to see if I could. That'd give you a read on whether the secret was safe or not."

"Fair enough."

After the pair of beers I'd had earlier, I wasn't interested in the whiskey. I left it on the occasional table between the two chairs.

"I first met Johnnie in 1989, when I was stationed in Beijing. That part you knew already," Nate said. "It wasn't exactly a backwater post, but it wasn't Moscow or Vienna by any stretch. We didn't consider China a pacing threat in those days, and it would be another decade until we really started taking them seriously. We still thought they were a wedge to use against the Soviets. The riots took everyone by surprise. The protests started because a pro-reform CCP general secretary died in office, and the youth movement feared the hardliners would take control and reverse the reforms. Which they did. The students revolted. We wanted to get into the movement and see if there were any levers to pull. There was a moment there when I think we might have been able to accelerate a push to democracy. Or at least capitalism."

Nate considered the glass in his hand. I watched the lines on his face lengthen and deepen as subtle tics worked themselves out almost in time with his mind stepping through its gears. "I don't believe serious thinkers ever considered China would democratize. I do think there have been windows in history where they could've taken the approach Vietnam did in the eighties—vote out the old guard and reform. Vietnam remained notionally socialist, but for all intents and purposes, they're a developing, market-based economy. Anyway, we'd hoped the Chinese would do the same and wanted to nudge them in that direction. Part of the plan to was get involved with the student movement and cultivate that. We wanted to show the party leaders this was a fire that wasn't going to go out unless they adopted some reforms. And there was always the possibility that yesterday's agitators would become tomorrow's leaders. We wanted an early in on that."

Nate reclined in his seat and stretched his long legs out in front of him.

"Now that we've got the realpolitik behind us, on to Johnnie. Like I told you, I met him during the student uprising. The part I didn't tell you was that I recruited him."

"Zhou was an asset?" I let the words out slowly.

That, I had not expected.

"He sure was, and a damned good one. Johnnie knew everybody. He had a dozen sub-sources, and they were all good collectors. By 1993, I was getting ready to rotate to another assignment, and we thought the particular window for motivating reform was shut tight. We were getting rumblings that they might try some shit with Taiwan"—Nate rolled his free hand—"Which turned into the Taiwan Strait Crisis of 1995. I liked Johnnie. He was free with the information he could get and was doing it because he loved his country and wanted to see it get better. I transferred him to a case officer I trusted, and I went on to my next assignment.

"In '95, I'd heard from his new case officer that Johnnie was looking to emigrate. He had a young family and was worried about being in the China with the stain of having participated in the protest movement. The case officer asked me what I thought. I told him Johnnie had helped us out, provided good intel, and was a good guy. He was a computer engineer, and as long as he passed all the counterintelligence screening, we should bring him over. I greased some skids with the State Department guys I knew and got him and his family back here. They settled in San Francisco, and Johnnie got a job with one of the early internet startups. Some of his work informed IPv3, if you can believe it."

Nate stared straight ahead as he spoke, a wistful expression on his face.

"We were trying to penetrate the student movement so we could understand how to covertly support it. Johnnie was a grad student and had a family, so he wasn't as involved as some of the others. What I recognized about him was that he was charismatic and a natural organizer. He could get others to do things. He'd get small pockets of people together and have them start protests of their own, write and distribute underground newspapers, stuff like that. Once I turned him over to the new case officer, that activity kind of died down, mostly because he didn't want to stick his neck out and risk his family."

That wasn't a full answer, but I knew Nate well enough that he wasn't going to offer anything else.

What I was looking for was an angle, some insight into Johnnie's past that might explain why he was killed. Had he made an enemy back then, someone with a long memory?

"Was he still involved when he got here?" I asked, hesitantly, unsure of how deeply I should probe this.

Johnnie's involvement in the local community might also be relevant. Not only did the Ministry of State Security maintain a vigorous collection program, particularly here in California, but they also tacitly worked with the Chinese criminal gangs for a variety of nefarious ends. The Triads typically preyed on their own community. That might be something worth investigating further.

"No. He retired from service when he moved here. The Agency closed his file. Johnnie had the serendipitous luck to be a computer engineer at the dawn of the internet boom. He made a lot of money quickly. Not enough to retire, but enough that he could decide what he was going to do with that money. He founded his businesses, which we've already covered."

"So, let's skip to the part where he's organizing networks of activists," I said.

"Well, I wasn't involved in that. I can tell you it's something that's always been in Johnnie's blood. He organizes, he motivates, he—"

"When did you tell him your real name?" I asked. Case officers *never* revealed their true names to assets. Eventually in the recruitment process, we had to acknowledge we were CIA and explicitly ask them if they would collect intelligence on our behalf. But we never told them our real names. That would mean a connection could be made between a real person and the Agency. It was dangerous. For Nate to do so, even long after Johnnie Zhou was "retired" as an asset, was a grave breach of security, of protocol, of every ounce of training we poured into young intelligence officers. Espionage was a gray business. Right or wrong, there were a lot of things you could justify in the field. This was not one. I'd never seen this side of Nate McKellar.

I'd never seen him make a mistake before.

No, this wasn't a mistake. This was a sin of commission.

Nate gave a short, terse laugh.

"One of the reasons I took you under my wing, Matthew, was that we're cut from the same cloth. I don't like the rules any more than you do; I'm just better at navigating them." Nate sipped his bourbon. "I'd been to his home. I'd met his parents, when I was still 'Frank from the State Department.' Elizabeth won't remember this, but I held her on my knee when she was a baby. Johnnie took a poly every year that he was my asset. He passed a full

CI investigation to get here. He was safe, and I knew he was safe. I told him my real name around 2003. He'd been retired as an agent for eight years at that point and had become an American citizen. It was no big deal in the grand scheme."

Just a foundational security violation, but yeah.

"Did he organize these dissident groups the whole time?"

I studied Nate's face as he spoke, hunting for tells. Most people would inadvertently show you when they were lying. I knew all the things to look for. I just had the disadvantage of trying that trick with someone who knew the game better than I did.

Nate nodded. "He did. These sorts of thing have a lifecycle to them, an ebb and flow. I spent half my career doing political covert action. You spin groups up, and if they're effective, they might last for a few years until they either get caught or lose steam. Some endure, most don't. Anyway, Johnnie had been organizing groups for years. He asked me for help, advice on how to set it up. He actually had an instinctive sense of tradecraft. Of course, there were things I'd taught him when he was an asset, but he had a talent for it."

My mind immediately went to following Robert Li to a dead drop earlier that night.

Or the floor safe in Zhou's bedroom.

"Johnnie lived frugally. He's got a nice home, but conservative by the standards of the tech industry and certainly less than he could afford. Elizabeth went to Stanford, but they paid mostly cash for that. He spent a lot of what he'd made on funding these networks, and he invested in technologies to enable them to penetrate the digital walls the Chinese government set up."

I held my hands up. This whole thing had to stop.

"Nate, have you spoken with CI about this?"

An agent, even a retired one, learning a case officer's true identity was a major security breach and a potential counterintelligence landmine. How could Nate be certain that over the last thirty years, Zhou hadn't inadvertently leaked that name to someone? All it would take is one slip. God knew the Chinese intelligence services were all over Silicon Valley.

"I didn't and I don't need to. Johnnie was retired."

"That's not good enough, Nate," I said. "You've got to cover yourself. If you haven't spoken to CI, you need to get a lawyer."

"A lawyer? And what exactly am I going to tell them?"

"If it gets out that you told an agent your true..." My voice trailed off as it hit me.

That was why he hired me. I was here to see if Nate was exposed as much as I was to see if Johnnie Zhou had been murdered.

Nate finished his drink in one go and refilled it. I still hadn't touched mine.

When he spoke again, his voice was calmer. "I'm sorry I didn't tell you about Johnnie being an asset. I'd like to keep that quiet, for obvious reasons. I brought you into this because I trust you and you're a damned good case officer...when your mouth doesn't get in the way."

Nate's face broke into a broad, slightly sad smile.

He added, "Someone killed my friend, Matt. I want to know who and why."

We weren't probing any deeper into Johnnie Zhou that night. The question was, what was my responsibility with that knowledge? How did this change the case?

"Do you know anything about the people he was working with?" I asked.

"No," Nate replied, slowly shaking his head. "I didn't want to."

"Any reason to believe Chinese intelligence penetrated his network?"

"Not that I know of. Though I can't say for certain. But, again, I stayed well clear of that and made sure Johnnie knew I couldn't be involved. Are you worried that someone knew he was a retired agent?"

"Two people in Johnnie's network died in the last couple months. One was a car accident, the other was just listed as an 'accidental death.' Both of those things could've been intentional. Then Johnnie's death. If the Chinese did turn one of them, the rest of the group could be in danger."

"You think they did?"

"I've gotten some information about what the network was working on. Seems like they stumbled on what could be a Chinese covert intel operation here."

Nate's brow creased. "How'd you find that out?"

I shook my head. "I'm going to keep that to myself for now. Sources and methods."

"You don't get to pull that shit with me, Matt. You need to follow the law here."

"I'm not breaking the law," I said. At least, not *all* of it. "I'm going to keep some parts of this to myself for now."

"You need to tell me."

"No, actually I don't, Nate. You're not my client. Elizabeth is. If and when I uncover something that I think is a legitimate national security risk, I'll tell you."

"You're being petty."

"You told an agent your real name and then got me hired to find out if you were exposed."

I needed to take this down a notch. We were both on the defensive, and that wouldn't help anyone.

Spies were at their best when they lied to everyone else, just not each other.

"Nate, learning that Johnnie was your agent is something I think you should have told me from the beginning. I would have approached this case differently. I think I understand why you did it this way, though I don't agree with it. Now, I need you to be objective, and I need your advice, because I may have uncovered something bigger than just a murder. I'll share more with you once I'm certain of it. Fair?"

"Fair," he said.

I'd keep Robert Li's identity secret for now.

I would also keep my suspicions about Elizabeth hiring me to protect her inheritance to myself. Nate might not be objective about her, And like the community centers, I had to run it down before I came forward.

Nate said, "If you give me the names, I can have one of our counterintelligence guys look into this. They can make some inquiries without raising any suspicion."

"If you give me a minute to get my computer, I can get them for you."

That would give me time to consider whether I felt comfortable releasing them.

"I'll give you a secure spot you can drop them," he said. Then, "How'd you find the names?"

I held up a hand. "You hired me for a reason, Nate. Let's not ask messy details about the *how*."

Nate stood and went over to his desk. He took a piece of note paper and wrote something on it, folded it and handed it to me. I looked at it—an IP address.

"Sorry I got up on my hind legs," I said.

Nate shook his head, letting me know all was forgotten. We shook hands, and I left, though it felt different this time.

Back at the hotel, I typed up everything that had transpired with Nate and stored it on the encrypted drive. Then I connected to a VPN and navigated to the IP address Nate had given me.

Despite what happened earlier, I'd need to trust him if this was going to work. And if those people were in danger, we needed to protect them. I copied the names and addresses from the file and put them on the drive, minus Robert Li's. Then I texted Nate through Signal to tell him they were available. He said he'd grab them right away and clear the server.

I put the lights out and fell into a deep, dreamless sleep.

11

I was up early. There was a lot to do.

For the first time since taking this case, I knew I was onto something. I jogged a few miles around Cupertino to clear my head and then got to work. First, I used my AI information aggregator to set alerts for each of the names on Zhou's list. If they appeared anywhere on online media, I'd know about it.

The case now had two angles, both wildly separate. The first had to do with Zhou's business, his partner, and the manner in which his shares of it would transfer ownership in the event of his death. Solid grounds to suspect a murder—or a motive to create enough questions to overturn a suicide determination. I almost prayed Zhou's death was related to espionage because this first angle took me down some pretty dark paths.

People did horrible things for money.

The second angle came from the revelations of the previous evening. That Johnnie Zhou ran a network of anticommunist agitators and the possibility that Chinese government killed him for it.

I'd left things ambiguous with Robert Li, but I couldn't make much progress without him. I looked his number up on Signal and found he was already on the platform. I messaged him, along with a picture of myself to prove it was me. I suggested we meet for coffee and discuss the next steps regarding investigating the community center. He said he was free that afternoon and suggested a coffee shop near his home.

Elizabeth called me.

"Good morning," I said.

"Hey. I'm on my way up to my dad's place," she said. I could hear the car noise in the background. "I figured if I was up there, they might be forced to deal with me, you know? Maybe I can at least get dad buried." The pain in her voice was clear, but she did an admirable job trying to mask it. "How are things going on your end?"

"We should probably talk in person."

"That bad?"

"No, it's just...well, I think it's better we do this sort of thing face to face. I'm a stickler for security. Old habits."

"Okay. That's fair. You've got some updates though?"

"I do. I've made a lot of progress in the last couple of days. There are several things I need to bring you up to speed on. I was actually going to call you this morning and see if you wanted me to fly down."

"Great. Well, I got an early start, wanted to beat the traffic getting out of LA. So, I should be there a little after lunchtime. I'm going to check into my hotel and have a late lunch with a college friend. Maybe we can meet for a drink later and you can fill me in?"

"That's perfect. I'll see you this evening," I said and hung up.

I left to go meet Robert and arrived to see him already sitting on a bench out front.

"I got you a coffee," Robert said and handed me a to-go cup. "Hope black is okay."

"That's perfect, thank you," I said, accepting the cup. My hand passed underneath the bottom, and I felt something taped there. I looked over at Robert, and he winked at me.

Well played.

"Thank you for helping me," I said.

"Let's not get ahead of ourselves. I haven't decided that I'm going to yet. My friend stuck his neck out, and he's dead." A grim shadow passed over Robert's face.

A slight nod, and I said, "I understand. I don't want to make you uncomfortable or push you into something you're not ready for."

"I can't stay, sorry. Deadlines. Call me in a day or two, and I'll have an answer for you," he said and headed off down the street.

I palmed the paper slip taped to the bottom and looked at it. An address in San Francisco. Looked like I had my afternoon's work cut out for me. Coffee in hand, I hopped in the Defender and drove into the city. I took the 101, driving along the coast and watched the sprawling, once majestic city unfold in front of me. The marine layer burned away, and now the sunlight exposed the cracks, the things the shadows couldn't hide.

It had been a long time since I'd been to San Francisco, other than transiting the airport. Almost my entire Agency career I'd spent overseas. The last time I'd been here, it was in the mid-2000s, the early days of the tech boom. It was vibrant, powerful and vital, pulsing with life and culture that seemed to ride roughshod over the darker undercurrents. To see the city now was heartbreaking, like it was being eaten alive from the inside. San Francisco looked like a robber baron dying of cancer.

The city shared LA's homelessness problem, but it seemed so much worse here because LA was a sprawling megalopolis, whereas San Francisco was a fraction of the size and hemmed in on three sides by water. There were whole encampments of homeless in the Tenderloin District; they'd pretty much taken it over. Drugs were everywhere. I could see rows of tents, lean-tos and tarps covering entire sidewalks on my drive in. Traffic was steady, a slow, congested sluice, but it did move. It gave me time to look around. One of the things that always struck me about San Francisco was how they would put a home on any conceivable surface. If there was an inch of horizontal surface, someone would put a house there. These people had a suicidal disposition toward risk.

The address Li gave me was in Chinatown, which was in the city's northeastern quadrant, with the Financial District to the south and the piers wrapping their way around to North Beach on the far side. The 101 took me all the way into downtown, and if I stayed on it, would eventually wrap around to the Golden Gate and the greener pastures of Marin County to the north. I exited on California Street and drove east toward the bay. I found a parking garage on Stockton, which would hold my car at rates other cities would consider usurious. Before getting out, I grabbed a ball cap from the back.

This was a piece of gear that I conveniently forgot to turn back into Agency logistics. The cap had a mesh lining that would scramble electro-optical surveillance, what lay people called "cameras." While you could buy a version of these caps on the open market, I knew how well this one worked, and it fit well. I wore aviator sunglasses, because the lenses covered a large portion of my face and made visual recognition harder.

Once I was out of the parking garage and back on the street, I felt right again. This was where I belonged. It was about three blocks to the location, and even though I knew nobody was looking for me, I improvised a surveillance detection route anyway. An SDR was exactly what it sounded like—a series of loop backs, what we called stair-steps (up a block and over two, or vice versa) and seemingly random turns, all designed to see if you were being followed. You normally planned them days or weeks in advance and had backup routes in the event of unforeseen obstructions like accidents or construction. In a place like Moscow or Beijing, where you had aggressive and pervasive opposition, an SDR might take ten or more hours. All for a meeting that might last five minutes.

I spent the next forty-five minutes walking my improvised SDR. I missed the street. I'd pick a person out at random and see how close I could get before they'd notice me, whether I could slip by them without them noticing. This was shadowboxing for ex-spooks.

Of course, these days, in some parts of the world, it was pretty easy to spot the tail. They were the ones whose faces weren't buried in their phones.

No one was following me, but I'd just felt the need to flex some old muscles.

Eventually, I made my way to Grant Avenue, between Washington and Jackson. I stopped across the street to contemplate the menu of the Jade Palace Restaurant, studying the community center's front in the window reflection. It was a nondescript storefront in the center of the block. A single door advertised the center, I assumed—the writing was all in Mandarin. The front window was frosted over, so I couldn't see inside. It was clear up top, though there was more writing across that. It looked to me like it was the same as on the door. The block was one large, four-story building subdivided into smaller units. The community center was in the middle. I took a couple of tourist selfies, thumbs-upping my foray into Chinatown. A quick scan of the photos showed I'd captured the storefront and the writing, which Robert could translate for me.

It occurred to me that he could certainly decipher what I'd found in Johnnie's safe, though I wasn't sure I wanted him to yet. If this went badly somehow, that might implicate him in the break-in, and I didn't want to do that.

I didn't see any cameras directly over the door, so I looked up, and sure enough, there were two on the roof. In days past, I'd also look for other surveillance indicators on the roof, such as concealed satellite antennas. That would still be worthwhile if I could get up there, though they were just as likely to use secured, encrypted VPNs to communicate with home station.

I walked to the end of the block, hung a left and kept going along the side of the building until I came to the back alley. There a few white signs with red lettering over doorways. Just about every door had an iron gate in front of it. I did see the telltale black hemisphere that said "electric eye," and it was in the right spot.

I didn't have objectives in coming here, other than to put eyes on the place. Nothing was a giveaway, though the cameras were certainly an indicator. The next step was to get inside.

Satisfied that I'd learned enough for now, I killed the next thirty minutes on an SDR back to the Land Rover. Since I had no operational or practical experience in the city, learning the surrounding streets was a useful investment in time.

Elizabeth messaged me around five and suggested a wine bar in Palo Alto, seven o'clock. I put on my one blazer, a white oxford, and pair of dark jeans and met her there. She was in jeans, a red blouse, and a black leather jacket, and her hair fell on the left side. She looked good. She set her phone down, and smiled as I entered. The bar was an old single-story, mission-style home in downtown. We took a couch and a chair in the front corner, next to an open window.

"Hi," I said. "Did you have a nice dinner?"

She gave me a pale smile that looked like work. "I did. Nice to catch up with an old friend."

"If this is out of line, forgive me. I don't want to overstep, but you're dealing with a lot, and our conversations are never going to be easy. That's the nature of it. Before we get started, I want to make sure you're doing okay."

"As well as can be, I suppose. And it's not out of line. It's kind of you to ask. I appreciate it. LA is very fake, and it can be isolating. Most people don't care about you, they just pretend to so they can get something out of it." Elizabeth opened the menu and closed the subject. "I just realized I never asked you if you even drank wine."

"I do. I spent some time in Argentina. They've got an incredible wine country."

"I've heard."

"I am fairly unsophisticated, so why don't you order for us?"

"Have you been to Napa before?" She asked.

"Yeah. I went up for a few days when I first moved to LA, kind of to clear my head. I didn't really have an agenda. I looked up places that seemed interesting and went," I said. "It was nice."

"A whole weekend of drinking alone. You must've been pretty wound up," she said playfully, but also asking a question.

I had been saying goodbye to someone I loved, some *thing* I loved. I think I mumbled a "yeah," and she picked up that I didn't want to talk about it.

"My dad collected wine," she said as she scanned the menu. "The Chinese have this weird obsession with French wine. I think half of the Bordeaux sold in the world actually ends up there. Once we moved here and my dad started making money, he'd go up to Napa and Sonoma all the time, like one weekend a month and come back with cases of stuff. He's got an impressive wine cellar in the house."

I didn't find that when I was "visiting," though there were a few rooms on the first floor that I'd skipped for time. Knowing that now, however...it might be worthwhile to check it out, once Elizabeth and I could get into the house.

The server returned, and she ordered a bottle of a Napa cabernet from a winery called Ghost Block.

"My parents were like Asian parents in all the stereotypical ways. They pushed me hard in school. I had to excel at everything, and they were just a little disappointed when I decided to go to law school instead of into medicine. But there was this undercurrent of Americanism. They let me drink at home, only wine though, and just on Saturday night. That was our big family dinner night. Sunday was a school night, so that was out." She smiled at the memory.

The server returned with the bottle, made a showing of it, opened it, and proceeded with the ritualized presentation of the cork. Once Elizabeth judged it free from rot, the server poured a splash into Elizabeth's glass for the second trial. Upon smiling and saying, "That's good," the server returned a knowing smile, poured our glasses, and withdrew to other tables.

"As you can imagine, some of my clients have some pretty expensive collections. Having a little bit of knowledge helps," she said. She took a sip, savored it, and set her glass down. "Well, it's not a tiki bar, but hopefully this is okay."

"Touché," I said.

"Is that a gag, or is your office really at Cosmic Ray's?"

"It really is at Cosmic Ray's," I admitted. "Look, I did some work for Ray a while back, and he lets me hang out there. He's got a second office upstairs that he never uses, and I can take if I need it. Like I said when we first met, you don't want a hire a guy with a nice office. You want to hire a guy who's going to go beat feet."

"You aren't worried that people won't take you seriously?"

I shrugged. "I don't really care how people take me. Most of my work comes from a foundation anyway, and they don't care where I hang my hat. It's mostly virtual. If someone is going to be impressed by an office, they're probably not my type of client. If they get offended that they have to meet me in a tiki bar, they're definitely not my type of client. And Ray is a good dude. Plus, I spent most of my adult life in some really shitty places doing things I can't talk about and wouldn't even if I could. There are worse things than listening to a half-baked stoner philosophize while making lava drinks all day."

Elizabeth laughed, and it was a beautiful, musical sound. "So, I know that you and Nate worked together, but he didn't give me a lot of details. How long have you known him?"

Nate never told me what he'd told *her*. Johnnie would've known Nate was CIA, but he hopefully did not share that with his family.

"I've known him almost twenty years," I said. "About half of that, I was working directly for him."

"Do you miss it? The CIA, I mean."

I lifted an eyebrow. "So, he told you," I said in the way that wasn't a question.

"Well, I had an idea that's what Nate did before he retired. Then, when I asked him why he thought you'd be the right person to hire, he told me you were with the Agency and your job was finding people who couldn't be found. That's how he put it."

"That's about right. Though I wouldn't go spreading it around," I said. "Nate is a good man. I owe him a lot. I loved my job, and I like to think I did some good in the world."

"Why'd you leave? You must've been close to qualifying for a pension."

"That's a complicated answer," I said. I finally lifted the wineglass and took a long swallow. "CIA is a lot more political than people realize. What goes on in the field, where I spent almost all of my time, is really disconnected from headquarters. Admittedly, I didn't play the political game very well. I picked fights with people at Langley when I didn't get the support I felt I needed. There was a system, a way of getting things done, and I didn't want to follow it. I bulldozed obstacles when I should have been building bridges over them. That's not to say that I was always wrong though. You've got some really brave and intelligent people doing some of the hardest work imaginable. But something happens to some of them when they get into leadership positions. Maybe it's the proximity to real power...I don't know. Something goes wrong, and they're looking for someone to blame.

They have to show the next level up that there will be 'accountability.' No one in those senior levels ever goes, 'Maybe it was me. Maybe *I* gave an order that I shouldn't have.' Headquarters directed me to run an operation that I thought was hastily planned and poorly conceived. It failed and someone got hurt. They blamed me."

"That's incredibly vague," she said, a teasing lilt in her voice. In the short time I'd known her, Elizabeth had understandably sounded emotionally drained, distant. It was the first time I'd heard something resembling a happy emotion in her voice. I was glad to experience it. Small steps to healing.

I smiled. "It's as specific as I can get. I quit after that, though I could tell I was getting railroaded out anyway."

"No one stuck up for you?"

"Nate did. But, like I said, something went badly wrong, and they needed someone to blame. I was the closest expendable person. My problem was that I hated politics and didn't invest in building the relationships with senior leaders so that when I needed a favor, I had one in the bank. No one would tell you I did bad work. They would just tell you my elbows were too sharp and the hallways too narrow." I paused and drank, concentrating on the wine for a moment instead of my past.

So," I said, drawing the word out, "how about I bring you up to speed on your case." I proceeded to describe the last few days, leaving out the minor detail of breaking into her father's home. "I've spoken with the police, and they're very protective. They won't share anything, not that I would necessarily expect them to, but if they had solid evidence, I could see them telling me what it was so I would go away and stop asking questions."

"The detective still won't return my calls," she said.

"Have you spoke with the state Bureau of Investigation?"

"Nope," she said curtly.

"I have. The part of this that doesn't add up to me is, according to the Los Altos detective who first investigated this, he went to his superiors to ask for more resources and was told the California Bureau of Investigation was taking over. They completely preempted him. No one will tell me how they knew to do that."

"Did you press them?"

"I did. They dismissed my question and said one of the things their office handles is fraud investigations. Then they pivoted and threatened me."

"How?" Her concerned expression seemed genuine.

"Because I don't have a PI license."

"Can you get in trouble?"

"Probably."

"Matt, we don't have to do this. I mean, I don't want you to—"

"A PI license is a piece of paper so some bureaucrat in an office can feel like they did their job. It doesn't affect my ability to do mine. Or give me any cosmic powers to get answers on your behalf. I've closed twice as many cases as these clowns have, but they just didn't end in arrests." I lifted my wineglass. "You hired me because Nate McKellar told you I can find things out for you, and that's what I'm doing." I gave her my best rakish smile. "Besides, if I get into trouble, you work at a company full of lawyers. I'm sure someone can get me off the hook."

Someone told me once that I could convincingly pass for Cary Grant when I wanted to. It took me a long time to realize they didn't mean that as a compliment. Maybe if I'd have been sitting across the table from anyone else, I'd have remembered the warning.

On the subject of her father's extracurricular activism, I decided to approach that gingerly. I'd left out any mention of the list of names or my meeting with Robert Li. "Did your father ever talk about politics in China?"

"Like, all the time," she said.

"To the point of doing something about it, or was he just yelling into the wind?"

"What do you mean?"

"I think your dad got involved in the cause. I understand he was involved in the Tiananmen Square protests in 1989, and that it had a catalyzing effect on him." Elizabeth nodded in agreement but didn't say anything. "It seems that he stayed active in the Chinese pro-democracy movement, maybe even had some connections with the underground. Just wondering if he'd talked to you about it."

"That's not something I know much about, though it wouldn't surprise me."

From what I could tell, the Zhous had been a tight-knit group. A loving family, Elizabeth had a warm upbringing and wanted for little. She stayed close with her parents after college, save the usual distance adulthood brings. Yet, she didn't have direct knowledge into something central to her father's life. Interesting, to say the least.

I couldn't help but wonder what secrets my parents had kept from me.

"If it's not too personal, do you mind my asking why not?"

"Why what? Why I didn't know my dad was still an activist?"

"Yeah."

"Do *you* want to have political arguments with your parents?" When she put it like that, I could understand her reaction. "I always admired his fervor. Even though I was born there, I have no memories of China. I suppose if I had any kind of connection to the place, I might have cared more. To me, it's just this monolithic, incomprehensible thing, you know? And it's not my problem."

"Your father may have thought it was his."

"Yeah, he had a real Don Quixote complex about it. To be honest, I never understood it. It's an unsolvable problem."

Revolutions started with individuals. I knew that firsthand. Someone starts a fire, and maybe it catches. You get enough people starting enough fires, eventually it all goes up. "I think your dad believed he could make a difference. Anyway, I bring this up because I met a friend of his. For now, I'm going to keep names out of it, at the person's request. He's someone your father knew from the old days, from the Tiananmen movement. They were working together. I asked if they thought someone might try to kill your father. They talked a lot about the lengths the Chinese government is going through to silence dissidents. What we call, 'active measures,' in my line of work."

"Jesus," Elizabeth's voice dropped to a stage whisper, and there was shock and what sounded like deeper fear behind it. "You don't think the Chinese had anything to do with it, do you?"

"I don't know. It seems like a stretch to me. Still, it's a lead I need to pursue. Right now, I'm asking all the questions. Then I'll narrow it down to the facts."

"I understand."

"Don't let it worry you. The reception I got from Benjamin Blake was decidedly icier."

She laughed, and I could tell she was glad to change the subject. "I'm not surprised. I know him, of course. He and Dad were partners, but they were never really friends. The most they'd do was golf together, and that was all business anyway. We'd go to his house for parties and things, but as soon as I was old enough to get out of it, I would."

"You didn't like him?"

"I didn't like or dislike him. He just always struck me as someone too slick for their own good. Benjamin Blake is only interested in business. If you aren't relevant to his business interests, you aren't relevant to him. He and Dad got along fine, worked well together, were good partners, they just weren't friends. I didn't necessarily trust him. But as long as Dad did, I didn't care. Mom kind of liked him, though. It was nothing unethical or immoral. There just isn't a lot of space in the room for you, Ben Blake, and Blake's ego."

"Why'd your Mom tolerate him?"

"She was an expert compartmentalizer. As long as Benjamin was good at the business and treated Dad fairly, Mom didn't give a shit how obnoxious and self-absorbed he was."

"Did you know anything about their business, specifically about your father's partnership with Blake?" I'd asked a flavor of this question when she and I first met, but I'd learned enough since then that I needed to make another pass at it.

"Not really, why?"

This was a risky line of inquiry, and I knew I had to tread carefully. "Again, just checking boxes. Situations like this, one of the first questions you need to ask is, who benefits?"

"Now it's my turn for a complicated answer," she said. "My father's estate attorney spoke with me as soon as he died. I know about the agreement, and how I'm not supposed to get any of my father's interests if his death is ruled a suicide. I'll spare you the legalese, but the estate lawyer isn't sure this particular thing has been tested in court and may not hold up. I haven't spoken with Benjamin yet; it's all been too soon. I don't want any of the business. I know all about what happened before with their first partner. I watched it happen. I'd never do that. I'm only interested in whatever part of my father's estate is legally mine. Blake can keep the business, cash out dad's share, or whatever."

She'd certainly told me what I wanted to hear.

"Why didn't you tell me about the clause at the outset?"

"I didn't want you to think that I was doing this for the money," she said.

"You have to appreciate how this looks from my view, though. This feels like you're hiding something."

"Why would I? If you were worth anything as a detective, you'd figure this out right away. And you did. Think about where my head was at when I first spoke to you. I'm lucky I could tell you as much as I did. I'm not hiding anything from you."

How do women have the ability to take a perfectly reasonable question and twist it so that you feel guilty and wrong not just for having asked it, but for even generating the sentiment behind it.

"For the time being, I'd stay away from Blake. Let your attorney handle it. I think I scared him asking questions. He sicced *his* lawyers on me right away. Then a pair of state cops paid me a visit. Tried to shake me off."

"Oh, Matt," she said, but I held up a hand.

"Elizabeth, this is what you're paying me for. I ask questions on your behalf. Both the police and Blake tried shutting me down with a quickness that tells me there's something one or both don't want me to find."

"Just promise me you'll be careful."

I flashed her my best half-cocked smile. "I promise I'll be as careful as I get."

The heady subjects out of the way, we shifted gears to more friendly topics as we worked our way through the bottle of wine. We talked about the surreal nature of life in LA. She was very interested in how I'd come to set up shop at a back table in a tiki bar. I asked her about her practice and whether I'd know any of her clients. She told me I probably knew *all* of her clients and that she was professionally bound not to dish on them.

She did admit, however, "The ones you think are dicks...they are."

We had a pleasant evening, and I enjoyed her company very much. I walked her to her car and then found my own.

A thought continued to plague me as I walked.

The thing I hadn't drilled into yet, because I didn't have enough standing with her, was the last fight she and her father had. Tonight was as much about laying the groundwork to have that conversation as it was probing on her motivations.

The next morning, I got a call from Benjamin Blake.

Calls from this guy always seemed to have curious timing.

12

"I'd like to meet, if you're open to it," Benjamin Blake said. "We got off on the wrong foot, and maybe we can reset the relationship."

"Yeah, weird how having your attorney threaten me gives me the idea you don't like me. Super weird."

"Could you just hear me out, please?"

I tried to imagine what Blake would say to an investment pitch he wasn't interested in. "You have thirty seconds to convince me to keep listening," I said.

"In person."

"This better be good, Blake."

"I assure you it will be worth your time."

I'd already decided to meet with him. Maybe I thought he'd have new information for me. Maybe I just wanted to pick a fight. Still, I let him think I was deliberating. Then I said, "Fine, give me the address."

"Thank you, Mr. Gage. I'll text it to you."

Blake sent me the details and wanted to meet me at two. I didn't have a heavy agenda that day, other than reading the collected open source intel summaries that the AI aggregator retrieved for me. I'd finished that by midmorning and decided to go for a hike in Castle Rock State Park. The fresh air was a nice change, and the exercise helped clear my head. I used that time to prepare for the meeting with Blake.

The address was for the Founder's Club of Palo Alto. Their website showed only a stylized silhouette of the building and a description as Silicon Valley's premiere social organization for executives. Reading between the lines, this was the kind of place where the wealth of nations discreetly changed hands. I didn't bother with a jacket, knowing whatever I owned wouldn't be up to their standards. And I was running a little short on time, so I wasn't able to pick up a $500 dollar hoodie on the way over.

The club was a modern building of dark wood and blue-mirrored glass. The location is marked only by a single plaque, black with silver lettering, *The Founders Club of Palo Alto* and the address. A tall and very businesslike woman behind a desk greeted me curtly as I entered the dark and anti-septic reception area. I noted this was blocked off from any other part of the building She knew by sight that I wasn't a member. I wondered if their OJT involved memorizing tech bro mugshots.

"How may I help you, sir?"

"My name is Matt Gage. I'm a guest of Benjamin Blake."

She spent just enough time reviewing her computer screen to make it uncomfortable and then coolly said, "Of course. Right this way, Mr. Gage." As we walked, she told me a little of the history of the club. Apparently, someone with early Google money was at one of the country clubs in the area and got outed meeting with a rival firm. He sank a bunch of money into this place to create a safe space for tech execs to have discreet conversations. She didn't use any of those words, of course, but these lines weren't hard to read between. I got the gist. Membership was probably what most people spent on cars and came with layers of nondisclosure agreements. "Since you're not a member, Mr. Gage, your conduct here is Mr. Blake's responsibility. We trust that you will act with sovereign discretion."

Was that even a thing?

I told her I would.

When I saw Zuck arguing with someone in the background, I got what she meant.

She led me up to the rooftop patio where I found Benjamin Blake in light gray pants, an equally light blue shirt, and sockless loafers. He sat with practiced ease underneath a series of umbrellas. He was just starting into a tan-looking cocktail in a lowball glass.

"Afternoon, Blake," I said, once she'd escorted me to his couch.

"Thank you, Rebecca," he said.

"Of course, Mr. Blake." She asked me if I wanted anything to drink. I didn't. I wanted to be out of here already.

I don't mind meeting people on their terms; it's part of the job. I do mind being summoned, and this felt a lot like that. Blake was the kind of guy who had enough money that it no longer mattered to him anymore. It was just some abstraction. What he valued was time, and his alone. Likely, he'd met someone here already and was just daisy-chaining appointments so he didn't have to run anywhere else.

I sat, and he got the perfunctory statement out of the way, thanking me for coming.

Blake was nothing if not perceptive, and I made no secret of hiding my annoyance.

"Are you sure I can't offer you anything? The Bufala Negra is exceptional," he said, flipping an eye toward his drink.

"You wanted to see me, Blake. Here I am. Your time is valuable," then I added, "to you. So is mine. Why am I here?"

Blake exhaled and set his drink down. "I was aggressive when we first met, and I apologize for that. Elizabeth's hiring you took us all by surprise, I must admit. We didn't know how to take it."

"Who's 'we,' in this case?"

"Me and the rest of the executive leadership team."

"I see. And what does the general counsel have to say about it? I noticed you had your personal attorney call me, not the firm's."

"Again, I was aggressive. That was the wrong approach. However, you have to understand how this looked from our perspective. We assumed Elizabeth had an estate lawyer talking in her ear about how to get half the company. I simply wanted to prevent that."

I softened my tone, just a little. "You and I talked before about the situation with Rakesh's widow, and I understand where you're coming from. You spent twenty years building this business, and you don't want to lose it. I get that. What I was trying to explain at the time is that I'm not concerned with your business and neither is my client. She's got reason to believe someone murdered her father. She hired me to help her answer that question."

"Surely, you don't think I had anything to do with his death," Blake said. He was looking for reassurance and wasn't doing much to mask it.

"A minute ago, you asked me to see things your way. Now, how about you try to see things from mine? You made a big show of telling me about that suicide clause."

Blake held up is hands and said, "Your words."

"And your attorney's. In any case, if that stays in place, you retain ownership of the business and, by my math, about twenty-five million dollars. That seems like a pretty strong incentive to shut down any investigation I'm doing. Then, not five minutes after having me escorted out of your building, you have your lawyer give me the attack-dog routine. Got me a visit with some state police too."

"I didn't know anything about that," he said, and he might not have. A good lawyer made problems go away, and a great one made them disappear. "In any event, let me offer this. I have discussed this situation with my executive leadership team, and we all agree that what Johnnie would've wanted was for his daughter to be taken care of. He worked hard to build Apex into what it is. Elizabeth should get something for that."

There was something strange about the way he was edging around the topic, but I couldn't figure out what.

"We're not going to enforce the suicide clause," he said. "She'll get the equity value of his portion of the business, either in restricted stock or she can cash it out now for a slightly lower amount. It's the same deal we all get, and it's what I'd get if I left. In exchange, she agrees to relinquish any management stake in the business."

That was a pretty good deal, on the surface of it. I didn't know how much she stood to make, but it was probably fifteen million in cash if she took the direct payout now. That, on top of whatever other assets she'd have of her father's. If what she'd said about not wanting the business was true, she'd jump at that.

I had to assume that I'd rattled Blake's cage asking questions. He might've known that the clause wouldn't hold up in court. I didn't know if it would or not, though Elizabeth and Nate both seemed to think it could be challenged. This offer was a preemptive move to settle. Or at least, a way to avoid a costly and unnecessary trial that would net Blake and Apex nothing but bad publicity. There was no positive spin he could put on trying to deny Johnnie Zhou's only heir her legal inheritance.

It also wasn't lost on me that by hiring me, Elizabeth had likely increased her take by ten million dollars.

What had been so clear to me the night before was much muddier now.

"Perhaps you can convince Elizabeth it's in her best interest to take this deal," Blake said.

"Why not talk to her directly?"

"She'll listen to you. And it'll go faster if we get her to agree to this first, rather than work it through the lawyers."

Blake had been at least acquainted with Elizabeth since she was a child, so it was odd to me that he didn't want to reach out to her directly. Why? There was also the move to settle so soon after putting his attack dog on me. The abrupt reversal raised questions.

Mostly, what was he hiding?

It wasn't my concern, because that wasn't what I'd been hired for. Knowing he had something to hide might be useful to me, however.

"Listen, Blake, that's not my job. She hired me to find out if someone killed her father. If you want to make her an offer, you need to approach her yourself."

"You understand how crazy that is though, don't you? Why would anyone want to kill Johnnie?"

Aside from the money, there were a lot of reasons, and I discovered more of them with every stone I kicked over.

"Just talk to her, would you?"

I said, "It's a lot of money. I'm sure she'll give it serious thought."

"I hope she does, for her sake."

"That sounds like a threat."

"No, it sounds like good advice, Matt. Johnnie died broke and heavily in debt. He had a second mortgage on his house, burned his savings and even borrowed against his equity in the business."

"What?"

"Yes. If she doesn't know it now, she will as soon as the probate judge transfers all of Johnnie's assets over to her. I know he didn't gamble. He never talked about what the money was for. Several of us assumed he was moonlighting, running his own fund on businesses that we didn't agree to back. It didn't turn out well for him."

"You mind me asking you a personal question?"

"I don't like the premise. If I don't like your question, I'm not entitled to answer it, but I also don't want you to accuse me of being evasive."

"Fine."

"Then ask."

"How much is your business worth?"

"We have 200 million under management today. The equity valuation is substantially lower. You have to understand this business. We don't necessarily invest 100 percent of our firm's money; rather, we build coalitions of investors. If any partner were to cash out and leave the business, which is what we're offering Elizabeth, we would convert their equity stake to liquid capital and give them the lump sum. It's cleaner than retaining equity in the company, since we wouldn't want them to have influence on business decisions after departing. If she signed papers today, it would still be about ten million. I think the home was worth about six, but the lien would need to be satisfied. She can probably walk away with three, all told. That's back of the napkin stuff though. I don't know exactly how much he owed. "

Ten.

Blake was right. I didn't understand this business and had made a dangerous assumption about it. I was wrong by orders of magnitude, and the mistake made me look amateurish. Elizabeth had led me to believe she'd be getting about twenty-five million.

Blake didn't care about the dollars involved; he cared about equity and control of the business.

I also hadn't known the depth of Johnnie's debts. I wondered, then, if Elizabeth had and if that was part of the reason for hiring me. Did she want a larger settlement so she could satisfy those debts?

Zhou certainly funded his operations out of his own pocket, even acquired some tech on their behalf that they'd used to stay active. I could see how he'd run up so much debt. We'd done this sort of thing in the Agency. It wasn't cheap.

"I asked him if he needed help," Blake said. "Time away, counseling, whatever he needed, short of money. That seemed to be the source of his problems, and I didn't want to enable him by giving him more. We worked side by side for twenty years. I knew the man. Something was eating away at him, and he wasn't the same. I was not surprised when the police told me he'd killed himself." Blake's expression softened, and then it darkened. "It was the fastest road out."

Blake didn't seem like a murderer to me. There was "killer instinct" and "killer's instinct," and the two aren't the same. The question was whether Johnnie's debts and his erratic behavior had presented a fundamental risk to their business.

I didn't think so. There were any number of legal remedies Blake could employ to get control of the business, if he was truly worried about Johnnie's actions impacting it. I think there was more going on here than Blake was letting on. I just didn't believe murder was part of it.

"I appreciate you bringing me here to tell me this," I said. "You need to reach out to Elizabeth and make the offer. I won't do that for you. But I think it's a generous one and the right thing to do. If she asks my advice, I'll suggest she take it."

"Thank you, Matt."

I stood, and we shook hands. I hadn't wanted to Columbo the guy, but I did have one last question. "Before I leave, just one thing."

"Sure."

"I asked you this before, but I think we're on a different footing now. In the time you'd known Johnnie, can you think of anyone who'd felt wronged by him? Anyone who might want to seek revenge? Maybe a deal that went south? I understand your feelings about his death, but I'm not convinced that he killed himself."

"No one that I was aware of. I told the police the same thing."

"I'm honestly surprised they asked," I said.

"Really? Why?"

"They seemed to be in a hurry to close this as a suicide. That was part of the reason my hairs went up when you came at me so hard with your lawyer. It made it look like you had something to hide." Someone still suspecting him of murder might argue that Blake's offer was a way to make this go away quietly, to cover up what he'd done. I could tell when someone was hiding something, being evasive. When Blake told me he'd tried to help his partner, I believed him. He'd said it with a conviction not easily faked.

"Maybe they're in a rush to close it because they figured out what I already knew."

"What's that?"

"Johnnie was in a lot of pain. Something was eating that man's soul, and one night, he had enough."

I thanked Blake for his time and saw myself out. On the way to the stairs, a helpful employee materialized at my side to make sure I found my way to the front door by the most expeditious route.

Blake's words stayed with me as my feet hit the pavement outside the club. I think he may have unintentionally given me some crucial insight. Had something happened to Johnnie on the night in question? Had whatever was eating at Johnnie's soul pushed him to do something that forced his killer's hand? If I could answer that question, I might go a long way to finding out who'd killed him and why.

13

Instead of returning to my hotel and calling it a day, I decided to head into town. I wanted a second look at that community center. This time, I was going inside.

The drive gave me time to think about what Blake had said.

Did I think he killed Zhou? No. Blake might be a Machiavellian weasel, but he was no murderer. Did I think he would use Johnnie's death to his advantage? Given the opportunity, I did.

And there was still plenty that didn't add up for me.

The secrecy surrounding Zhou's cause of death remained a major red flag. The other part that didn't track for me was the state investigators. How did they know to contact the Los Altos Police? How did they get wind of this to take it over before that lone detective had even filed his request for more help?

That was where Blake and his machinations fit, in my head. I could see this guy—or his attorney—having connections in Sacramento and leveraging them to get Johnnie's death ruled a suicide. Now, if the police genuinely believed Zhou had been murdered, there was no amount of political pressure Blake or anyone else could apply to convince them otherwise. However, if there was doubt, he might just be able to apply some pressure for them to close it quickly.

Police agencies across the country were overworked and understaffed, and murders tended to suck all the oxygen out of a small detective bureau. I didn't want to believe they'd take the easy out to close the case, but I could also see it happening. If they were on the fence and had an offramp to call it a suicide, maybe that'd be enough to justify it in some overworked cop's mind. I'd seen that kind of thing in the Agency too. Overworked case officers might justify letting a potential collection target disappear because there weren't the resources to pursue it. When, in reality, they were just justifying not putting in the work.

If that was true, then Blake set this whole thing in motion and was, perhaps, obfuscating something darker, some deeper thread.

I didn't share any of that with Blake because it wasn't his business, and I didn't feel I owed him an explanation about how his partner really died.

Maybe his involvement ended with Elizabeth's payout.

Unless, of course, I could prove he tried to influence the police's decision.

I didn't like Blake. I'd convinced myself he wasn't a murderer, but it didn't mean he was free from culpability.

A warning light started blinking in the back of my mind.

I hoped I wasn't chasing ghosts of espionage. That I wasn't inventing a phantom spy ring because I didn't want to believe what I was involved in was some petty, cynical machinations for control of something.

Again.

I crawled up the interstate into San Francisco and navigated to Chinatown using a different path than the last time. Different parking garage. I wore a lightweight jacket, collared shirt, gray chinos, and my ball cap to scramble electrical surveillance. I also had a pair of eyeglasses with a coating on the lens that would mask my eyes on a camera. I walked over several blocks using Columbus Avenue, which cut a diagonal swath through Chinatown, then I looped back south on Beckett, then over to Grant. It was about four in the afternoon, and I realized this decision was going to cost me about two hours in the car trying to get out of the city.

I walked into the community center and a low rumble of sound and constant motion.

It had a short, stubby room that passed for a lobby and was packed to the walls. There was a row of folding chairs along the front window, all full. And another along the far wall, with several people standing, waiting for a place to sit. There was a nearly constant din of conversation, unintelligible to me. It was too hot by several degrees and stuffy from too many people breathing the same air. A low table had pamphlets and other papers, all of it in Mandarin. The walls had photos of China, but they looked fairly generic. I was the only white person.

I walked up to the counter, which had a sign-in sheet on a clipboard, also in Mandarin.

"Excuse me," I said to the man behind the counter.

He ignored me. So, I used the rationale perfected by Americans abroad. If the man couldn't understand me, it was clearly because I wasn't speaking loud enough.

Raising my voice slightly, I repeated, "Excuse me."

He looked up and rattled something off in Mandarin.

"I don't speak Chinese," I said.

He replied, again in Mandarin, and this time, he tapped the clipboard.

"Oh, I see," I said helpfully. I wrote "CARL LANIER" in block letters and handed him the clipboard, which he didn't take. I set it back down on the counter. "Can you answer some questions for me?"

He replied, again in Mandarin, and pointed at the chairs.

"I'm sorry, sir, but again, I don't speak Chinese. Is there someone here who speaks English?"

Some statements transcend language.

"He says for you to wait here," the woman said from behind me, motioning to the chairs, which were full. I thanked her and sat. "How long have you been waiting?" I asked her.

"Five hours."

They called her up about forty-five minutes later, and she disappeared into the back. While I waited, I scanned the stuffy waiting area. A camera inside a cyclopean black dome peered out from the corner of the room, giving it a view of whatever happened behind the desk and the lobby. There was a heavy door separating this room from the back offices. A short hallway with flickering lights to the left led to bathrooms and a cleaning closet. I doubt either got much attention. Gradually, the room thinned out, though more people entered, I was at least able to score a seat.

Someone new appeared up front and said, "Carl Lanier," in accented English. I stood, approached the counter and smiled. "Hi. Good afternoon. I was hoping you might be able to help me, I've been trying to reach someone in charge here for a few weeks. I'm with the city's Department of Building Codes. The city is planning some major construction on Grant Avenue here, and I was hoping that I might be able to have a peek at your records. We need to determine if you're responsible for the scaffolding that has to go out front, or if we are. Normally, this is something the city would have to pay for, but I guess your lease agreement is a little different. Is there someone I could speak to?"

As an (alleged) Chinese government functionary, this man would be well versed in confusing, overlapping regulations with unclear direction. I was appealing to that baser bureaucratic instinct to let me get a look at their records. My goal here was twofold. First, I wanted to find out who was paying for this office. That would tell me a lot about how it was organized. Second, I wanted to find out who was in charge so I could assess them for access.

"I'm sorry, I don't have access to that information," the man behind the counter said. "Perhaps if you made an appointment to come back later in the week, we could prepare what you require."

"I'm afraid that won't work. We really need to look at those records today. My office has sent four letters and made multiple attempts to contact you by phone. Surely you've seen those."

"I don't recall seeing any letters," he said, stammering.

"Well, they were sent. The last was certified mail. Are you in charge of this office, sir?" I kept my tone amiable and polite but authoritative. It wouldn't do to piss him off. What I needed was for them to fear the possibility of a governmental spotlight just enough that they'd get me what I needed and speed me on my way.

The man behind the counter picked up a phone, pressed a button, and spoke in hurried tones. This was in Mandarin, but I could guess by his inflection the gist of it.

A few moments of awkward silence passed, and the man made no attempt at small talk. The door behind him opened, and another man appeared. He wore a black suit of a not-particularly-impressive quality, white shirt, and dark gray tie.

"How may I help you, mister?"

"Carl Lanier. I'm with the city's Department of Building Codes. As I was explaining to your colleague here, the city is about to begin construction on Grant out front, and that's going to require us to put up some scaffolding to protect the sidewalk. In some cases, because of how the building codes are written, the tenant must pay for those. Which you would do through the tax office. Anyway, we've tried to call and sent several letters, and no one got back to us. If I could just look at your lease agreement."

"This is the first I'm hearing of it," he said brusquely.

"My office sent several letters."

"We've received no such letters."

"What's your name, sir?"

"Huang," he said. Then, "May I see some credentials?"

"We don't typically require credentials of our civil servants," I said with a hint of superiority in my smile. "Unless, of course, one is a CPA or something," I added.

"I see. Well, we've received no such communication from your office, Mr. Lanier. I think, perhaps, it would be best if you scheduled a time to come back in the future and perhaps brought a copy of this letter with you. I'm sure we can sort this out in time."

"I'm afraid, Mr. Huang, my office has been quite patient. We really do need to take a look at your lease agreement now."

"But we have no such documentation. The center is leased through our parent organization, the China-America Fellowship Institute. If you require access to records, I am afraid you'll need to contact them."

That sounded bogus to me. I could tell this guy wasn't going to budge, and he clearly felt insulated by this "fellowship institute," whatever that was.

"Can I make an appointment to speak with you later this week?"

"Mr. Chung can handle that for you. Good day, Mr. Lanier."

"Thank you for your time," I said and watched him disappear back through the door. I made a show of rejecting the first two appointments

Chung proposed, before selecting a lunchtime slot on Friday, which I had no intention of meeting. I felt the electric eyes on my back as I left the office.

It was after six by the time I got to my car and eight thirty when I finally got back to the hotel. I walked over to the shopping center my hotel shared a parking lot with, grabbed takeout, and went back to my room to figure out my next steps. It didn't take me long.

I'd been bouncing off invisible walls since I'd started this thing because I was approaching this case how I thought a private detective would. Instead, I should've followed Nate's advice, how would I have done it if I were still a case officer.

That community center was never going to let me inside.

But they'd take Robert Li in with open arms.

14

The next morning, I called Robert and told him I had an idea and asked if he could he meet for lunch. He said he was working on a story but could take a break, recommending a sandwich shop near his home. I called an order in and met him at his house with a pair of sandwiches and a six pack of Sierra Nevada. Robert set us up in his backyard at a small teak table beneath an acacia tree. We unfolded the butcher paper and dove into the food. I popped the caps on the beers and handed him one.

"How is your investigation going?"

"Well, the state police tried to scare me off of it, so I think I'm onto something. I've dug into Johnnie's business and his partner, Benjamin Blake. I think I can rule him out as a suspect." Then I added, "At least for the murder."

"What convinced you?"

"He was worried about Johnnie's erratic behavior and the possibility it'd blow back on their business. Blake wouldn't kill him to make that go away though. He had a few legal options for that. He didn't say it, but I got the impression he'd been ready to make a move. Maybe even buy Johnnie out, which he probably would've taken, given his financial straits. Blake would see Johnnie's death as an opportunity, and he might use some influence to get the police to rule it a suicide. But he didn't pull the trigger. Or order it done."

"I didn't realize Johnnie's work with us was interfering with his business."

I nodded behind my beer. "It seems your friend was pretty deep in the hole. I think he was funding his network out of his own pocket."

Robert exhaled heavily, and his head dropped as if it had suddenly become too heavy to hold up.

I gave him a few moments to process this new information and gave him some distance.

In time, Robert lifted his head. Whatever internal dialogue he'd had was over. Still, he waited for me to speak.

"Please don't blame yourself. Obviously, I didn't know the man, but everything I've learned about him tells me he believed strongly in what he was doing. If he cared about the money, or the debt, he cared about it far less than the work you all did."

Robert nodded solemnly. "Thank you for saying that."

"I checked out the outreach center yesterday," I said.

"Thought you might."

"No dice. Tried to get them to let me look at their records. I wanted to see who'd leased the building. If they'd been forthcoming, I might've been convinced everything was above board. Instead, I got a couple of hours in the lobby and a practiced brush-off from the manager. I did get a name—the China-America Fellowship Institute."

"That sounds made up."

"That was my thinking too. It's probably a shell corporation. I did a little cursory digging last night and couldn't find much." I'd also spoken with Jennie, since her group was familiar with how those operations work from unravelling the Panama Papers. Having worked with plenty of CIA front companies over the years, I suspected there was little behind the China-America Fellowship Institute than a name. It would just roll up to a succession of other, innocuous sounding businesses.

"The office head's name is Huang. At least, that's the name he gave me," I said. "I never asked before, so I apologize, but would you prefer that I call you by your given name?"

He smiled. "I appreciate the gesture, but I've been going by Robert for twenty years."

"Fair enough."

"So, what's this idea of yours?"

"I want to get a closer look at this community center."

"How do you aim to do that?"

Recruiting an agent for the Agency, as I'd mentioned, took months of work, sometimes years. We exhaustively researched and profiled our recruitment targets so that we understood them on a fundamental level, so we understand what levers we can pull to get them to steal secrets. That often required them putting their lives at risk, a responsibility case officers did not take lightly.

What we were doing here wasn't that different.

Instead of weeks, I had this one conversation.

If Robert's research and my gut were right, this was indeed a foreign intelligence operation run by an oppressive government. One that we'd suspected was already responsible for one murder and probably three.

"We need to get inside. See if we can look at their files, find out who they're targeting," I said. "Maybe we can connect them with Johnnie or the other two men who turned up dead. Or, if possible, find out what agency is pulling the strings. You could get Huang to talk to you. If you tell him you're a journalist, he'd view that as extending his reach in the community, getting access to people he doesn't know now. Establish a rapport—"

"Oh, I don't have to do all that," Robert said, cutting me off.

"You don't?"

"No. They tried to get me already."

"What?"

"When we first met, I told you that I got a phone call about two months ago claiming there was some problem with my citizenship status. That their group was set up by the Chinese government to help with that sort of thing. When I told him I'd check with the consulate to see if it was true, he got a little aggressive. I didn't think anything of it at the time, other than maybe it was a phishing scam. Then I got a call from a trusted contact about a local businessman named George Xie."

He worked his neck a little, then continued. "So, my contact put me in touch with Xie's wife. Mr. Xie was also a dual citizen. He'd written an article a few months ago for a business blog with tips for travelers going to China. Things like traveling with disposable technology and not having proprietary business information on your computer. He talked about the high degree of IP theft and cautioned people to be careful. Nothing controversial. This is all stuff on the State Department travel guidelines. The community center had contacted him and said there was a problem with his citizenship status, some minor bureaucratic hiccup, but it had to be corrected in Beijing. They offered to fly him home to fix it. George goes, thinking he gets a free trip out of it. He was arrested at the airport for 'incitement to subversion.' A 'trial' and a five-year prison sentence. He's in jail now. Once I learned about him, I started looking into others. That's what you saw me burning in the park—it was the names of all the people they made disappear. I thought at the time you might be a... What do you call it?"

"An agent," I finished for him.

"Right. That convinced me this was no community outreach activity." Robert sipped his beer in silence. "This is risky for me, Matt. I'm still not convinced I should do it."

"I know it is. If you don't think you can do it, I understand, and I'll never ask again."

"Maybe you should try again," he said. "I can help you this time. I don't think it'd work if I went, since they already know who I am."

"Actually, that's exactly why it'd work. You are already on their radar, and that gives us the in."

"I don't know. If I were to do this, I'd need something from you."

"Name it," I said.

"I want to expose them. You said you had connections with some reporters. I am just one person. I want to amplify this."

"I'll see what I can do."

"No. I need your word, or I can't go forward."

There are little lies and big lies in this business. The little ones grease the wheels and can get information moving. The big ones get people killed or jailed. I said, "Okay. I'll make it happen." And I truly hoped it was the former.

"And you think the information you talked about before, the names and things... that will just be lying around?"

"No, it will not. Which is why the first step is I need to teach you how to be a spy."

Okay, that might have been a bit of a stretch.

What I needed him to be able to do was confidently walk into that community center, ask questions, and gather some intelligence. Gain Huang's confidence enough that he'd be willing to meet outside of the center.

I also needed Robert to be able to get out of there and know whether someone was following him. That was a tall order, given the timeframe we had. However, as we began the basics, I found that he'd already picked up quite a lot from Johnnie. I could see Nate's hand in Johnnie's training, even after all these years.

Robert amounted to what we called a sub-source, which was an asset that a case officer's agent recruited to provide additional conduits of information. Some agents could run whole networks of sub-sources, and I was getting the impression Johnnie Zhou had done just that. It seemed he'd taken everything he'd learned working for Nate as an asset in Beijing and used that to create and run his own network.

"The first thing we have to do is talk about how we're going to get information from them. Remember they're talking to you because you have something they want. Either it's information on other dissidents or they want you specifically. Let's assume it's the former until we have evidence otherwise. Tell me how you would approach a conversation in the center. How would you act?"

He gave that a few seconds of thought, then, "First of all, I'd be very polite, courteous. In our culture, we're very respectful toward elders, which I can play to my advantage. We are also deferential to authority figures."

"That's perfect. You want to be friendly and respectful. Put them at ease. You want them to have enjoyed talking to you. Try to find a way to make a connection. Next, don't explicitly ask for information. Rather, let them come to you. I think this is something you already know how to do as a journalist, so I won't spend much time on it now. Just to say that it's the same thing. You have the information requirements in your head. Gently nudge the conversation in that direction."

"How do I open the conversation?" Robert asked.

"You've already got an in, right? They asked you to come in and talk about some irregularities with your citizenship, so start there. Try to probe that. What are the problems? Why do they exist? Look for holes in the story. As if it's common for dual citizens to have these kinds of issues. You want to see if you can trick him into revealing things."

If I'd still been a case officer, I'd have understood Robert's capabilities as a source—as well as or better than he did. By the time we'd developed a plan to send him into this community center, I would know whether he could be a collector, if I thought he could actually recruit sub-sources or even go undercover himself. There was a potential here that Robert could even become a double agent and work to unravel their operation from the inside. I didn't know if he was capable of that and wasn't putting him in the position to do so without a lot more work.

For now, I just wanted to see what they knew. I'd also decided against using electronic surveillance. If this were an Agency operation, the first thing I'd have Robert do was plant a bug in the community center. That was illegal without a warrant. Breaking into Zhou's house was as far as I was going to go. And, yes, that was a serious transgression, and I knew what I'd done was "wrong" in a legal sense. I'd been pissed off at being rail-roaded and lied to, frustrated the case wasn't going anywhere and for the police not answering my client's reasonable questions. But I also knew I couldn't push that any further.

Robert and I role-played for several hours, going through various scenarios and approaches he might use. At first, I'd stop him when he made a mistake so I could teach the correct action. Then, I made him play through it. He needed to learn how to recover from a tactical error. He needed to learn the difference between minor gaffes that could be recovered from and the big ones that signaled to get the hell out of there. We stopped for the night when I could tell he was exhausted. I ordered us a pizza, and we finished the beers I'd brought, talking about anything but

Chinese politics. Robert loved baseball and lectured me for thirty straight minutes on the Giants' bullpen problems.

The next morning, we rehearsed again. But this time, we reversed our roles so that Robert acted as the community center official. I wanted him to put himself in their shoes as I tried to get information from him. I wanted him to understand what it felt like having someone try to trick you into spilling secrets. I wanted him to think through how *he* would try to pick up on those subtle clues in conversation. That could help him avoid those pitfalls in practice. He had to learn how to think like the opposition. This was one of the most valuable skills a case officer could instill in their asset. No, he wouldn't do it in a single day's session, but it was a start.

Later that day, I instructed him on how to spot details in the room, to learn the things that we might need for later reference. Was there a safe? Did they use computers, and if so, what kind were they? What level of technology did they have? We didn't know what ministry actually ran this center, so I wanted him to look for clues that might answer that question. The Chinese government had multiple foreign intelligence activities—primarily the People's Liberation Army Intelligence and their foreign intelligence service, the Ministry of State Security. Doubtless, there were other activities operating abroad that we might not know about. Generally, Western intelligence services had poor penetration into China.

We also applied some COVCOM techniques. I didn't like using phones operationally. Hell, I didn't like using them in my private life. Too many people had eyes and ears on us now, but they'd become a mostly necessary evil. In covert communications—COVCOM—we gave our assets specific phrases to use when transmitting messages, which were usually buried in the body of the message. It's typically something like leaving the first word in a sentence uncapitalized, not using punctuation, or substituting a word for a synonym. These people should have no reason to think Robert was working with someone—or, truly, that he was "working" at all. We couldn't count on that, however. Most of this job was anticipating what could go wrong and having a backup plan. And if this community center truly was run by some Chinese government entity, it was better to assume they had some counterintelligence capacity. In the event Robert became compromised and they forced him to send a message to whomever he was working with in order to capture them, he was to work in the phrase "sidewalk." The all-clear signal was to send at least two sentences of text and ask to meet for coffee.

After three intense days, Li told me he was ready.

We'd barely scratched the surface of what I felt he needed. Though I could also admit there weren't better options.

"One last question," I said, as we were wrapping up. We were sitting in Robert's home office, a converted bedroom he'd turned into a kind of war room. He'd hung a corkboard on one wall, and it showed the clusters of datapoints he'd collected on these Chinese community centers worldwide and their correlation to disappeared political dissidents. The other wall had a well-used whiteboard, covered in the ghosts of notes and other markings, lines turned into ideas. Robert had a series of questions in the whiteboard's upper corner, many of which were the same we'd been asking over the previous three days. He'd done all this on his own. It was damned impressive work.

Robert lifted his eyebrows in response to my statement and said, "What's that?"

"Do you know the difference between fear and panic?"

"Of course," he said.

"I'm serious, because this could save your life. You should have fear when you walk into that place, because what I'm asking you to do is a scary thing. Controlled fear is healthy. It's a survival instinct. Panic is when fear becomes uncontrolled. Panic will get you killed. It will freeze out everything else."

"I understand."

"Do you, Robert? Because I don't want you going into that place unless you're absolutely certain you know the difference."

"Matt, I appreciate what you're trying to do."

"What's that?"

"You're giving me a way out, if I don't think I can do it. I thank you for that. Someone killed my friend. I was not sure at first, but now I am."

"What changed your mind?"

"Johnnie was deeply troubled these last two years. He was lost when Grace died. This...thing"— Robert made an abstract gesture with his hands

—"gave him purpose. He told me he thought someone was following him, and I didn't really believe him. Even though I knew better." He waved a hand at the corkboard. "After talking with you, though, I became convinced they had to have done this. Johnnie and I both believed the CCP is using this community center and others like it around the world to find the people who dare to speak out against them. He wouldn't leave that fight so callously."

Robert's expression darkened. "I wished I'd believed him when he came to me about these...I don't know what you call them. Shadows? Pursuers? Maybe we could've done something."

"He told the police. *They* didn't do anything," I said.

That was what angered me more than anything. Johnnie did what he was supposed to do. He'd reported the incidents and asked the authorities for help, but they ignored him. It was just as easy to blame the system as it was to use it to give authorities a pass. I didn't care if they were overworked and understaffed. They hadn't done their jobs, and a man died, and now they were trying to cover it...or *something* up.

This was why I did what I do. Because people like Johnnie Zhou trusted a system to help them, and it failed them.

I did this work because there was a time in my life when *I* needed someone like me. And there wasn't.

Finally, Robert said, "That's right. They didn't do anything, and my friend is dead because of it. Let's get some answers."

We wrapped up, and I went back to my hotel when the phone started blowing up. It was Vicky, the manager at Cosmic Ray's.

"Hey, Vic, is someone there to see me? I'm out of town for a bit."

"Matt, a state police detective just called here asking about you."

My blood iced over.

"What'd he say?"

"That it was illegal for you to call this place your office unless we were actually your employer. If it *is* your office, he said we're liable for whatever you do. What the fuck is going on, man? What you into?"

"I'm not 'into' anything. I'm asking questions that the state police should have, and it's making them nervous."

"Well, stop!"

"Vicky...this is my job."

"Well, you can't tell people you work out of Ray's, man. They said we could expect calls from the health inspector and probably the police for a 'random drug sweep.' Asshole thinks we're a bunch of burnouts."

"They're just trying to scare you. They're looking for ways to get to me."

"I don't care, Matt. Whatever you do, you're on your own. You cannot involve Ray. This place...man, this is all most of us have. No one else is going to let us balance the competition schedule with work. We're barely scraping by as it is."

"Okay, Vicky, okay. I'll take care of it. You won't see me until this is done."

"Matt, if we get one more call from the police, we'd better not hear from you ever."

15

So, Hanley and Montoya were going after Cosmic Ray's to get to me.

If that wasn't an abuse of power, I don't know what was.

I wanted to call Ray himself and talk this out, but he wasn't much for phones. Instead, I called Jennie, but she didn't pick up, so I texted and asked her to call me.

Though he didn't exactly admit it—and didn't deny it either—I still thought Blake or his lawyer had used their connections at the capital to get the state inspectors on the Zhou case. Maybe now that Blake seemed ready to settle, he would dial back from that. However, I didn't know that the police would. I couldn't help but wonder whether this was an attack dog that Blake couldn't get back on the leash.

The situation with Ray's wasn't a solvable problem right now, though it would need to be handled, and soon. It killed me to put that on the back burner. They were good people and didn't deserve collateral damage just for letting me hang out.

Everything was escalating quickly beyond my control. And I was about to send a barely prepared civilian into a possible foreign intelligence operation.

We also had no choice.

Robert's information on the community center was the only real lead we had and the one probable link to Johnnie's murder. Given how much misdirection I'd received from the police already, I knew we had to be the ones to crack this. If Nugent and Montoya got it first, I had no reason to believe Elizabeth would ever get the answers or closure she deserved.

The next morning, I drove Robert into the city. I dropped him off four blocks from the community center and then found a place to park. There was a small cafe about a block away on Waverly, so I made my way there, ordered a coffee, and tried to busy myself with the news. San Francisco's homeless problem was at endemic proportions. The city was overwhelmed and just didn't know what to do anymore. I milked the coffee and breakfast sandwich as long as I could, but angry stares from behind the counter told me I'd worn out my welcome. It was time to hit the bricks.

I left the cafe and started walking, maintaining an orbit of about two blocks around the community center. I wanted to be close if Robert called. My previous experience there told me this could take some time.

My phone rang as I was walking. Anxiously, I grabbed it and looked at the caller ID. It was not Robert. It was a 415 number, so I answered.

"Matt Gage," the caller said when I answered.

"Who's calling?"

"My name is David Hu, San Francisco Police. I'd like to speak to you. Can I get a few minutes of your time?"

"Sure. What's this about?"

"I understand you're asking around about Johnnie Zhou," he said.

Alarm bells started going off in my head. What was a San Francisco cop doing asking me about Zhou? Zhou lived and worked in Silicon Valley, which denoted the city's southern suburbs. I suppose some of the businesses he invested in could've been located here in the city, but that wouldn't matter. There was no part of this case that was in Hu's jurisdiction.

"Can I ask what your interest in this is, Officer Hu? And in me?"

"Let's talk in person. How quickly can you get into the city?"

"Actually, I'm here now."

"Great. There's a coffee shop on Jackson and Powell called the Bean Republic. It's across from the Chinatown branch of the public library. I'll meet you there in a half hour."

"Okay," I said.

I didn't like coincidences, mostly because I didn't believe in them.

Robert goes into this community center to get answers about Johnnie and then some cop calls me out of the blue and wants to talk to me. This just hours after I learned the state police were causing trouble at Cosmic Ray's to get to me.

The Bean Republic's logo took up its entire front window. It was a riff on the California state flag, but the bear was holding a mug of coffee. I stepped inside. Hu wasn't hard to spot.

Some people just look like cops.

He was six feet tall and weight-room big. He wore jeans, a graphic tee-shirt with an emblem I didn't recognize, and a black hoodie. Hu's hair was cut short, just north of stubble. He leaned across the counter, making small talk with the tattooed barista. He clocked me walking in, nodded, and finished up his conversation with the counter girl.

Hu sauntered over and asked if I wanted anything, pointing at me as he did with a finger that looked like it could hurl lightning.

"I'm good," I said.

"Cool," Hu said. He nodded to a booth that was, surprisingly, empty, and we sat.

"So, you're a San Francisco cop," I said after we'd exchanged greetings and first names. "You mind showing me some ID first?" An annoyed look passed over his face, like he wasn't used to being pressed. He dug into his pocket and removed a badge and his SFPD identification card. I picked the card up and turned it over, looking at it from a few angles. If it was fake, it was a good fake.

He scoffed at my inspection. "That's right."

I asked, "What do you do, exactly?"

"Community Violence Reduction Team," he said. "It's what used to be the Gang Task Force." I was nominally familiar. The Gang Task Force was created in the late seventies, about the same time LAPD stood up its own infamous anti-gang unit, known as CRASH. SFPD's chief of police recently announced the task force would be shut down and rebuilt. I still didn't see what this had to do with me, or Johnnie Zhou.

"You focus mostly on Triads, I take it?"

"Yeah, and the Tongs," he said. Chinese organized crime, often called "secret societies" in their culture, were quite different than the European criminal outfits, which all mostly resembled the corporate-like mafia structure. "I started as a beat cop here in Chinatown. Grew up here. CVRT was a chance to give back, do something, you know?"

"Admirable," I said. "So, what does a Chinatown gang cop want to do with me?"

Hu leaned back in his seat. "When a prominent member of our community is killed, it tends to make a splash. Mr. Zhou was a successful businessman, provided to a lot of charities... He was active. Did a lot of good. I'd like to know why you're asking questions."

"With respect, Officer Hu," I said.

"I'm a sergeant, but call me David."

"Right, David. With respect, what business is it of yours if I'm asking questions? Mr. Zhou didn't live in your jurisdiction. He didn't die there either," I added helpfully, just in case there was any questions where the boundaries were.

"Hey, that's fair, and I'm sure this seems a little weird, me asking you and all."

"It does. How'd you get my phone number?"

He gave me a withering look that telegraphed the unsaid: *Because I'm a cop.*

"You're what...a private eye or something?"

"Or something," I said. "Mr. Zhou's daughter doesn't believe he committed suicide. The local police and the state police aren't very forthcoming with information or answers. She's frustrated and angry. Understandably so, I think. He's been dead almost three weeks, and they've got the house locked up like a crime scene. They won't release the body for her to bury him. Ms. Zhou hired me to look into things on her behalf. Ask some questions."

Hu nodded. I got the impression he thought I was pitching him on something. Maybe that was what unquestioned authority got you these days.

"You're really looking to help?" But he'd said it in a way that was neither a question nor a fact. Just a statement. In the context of this conversation, it felt strange to me.

"I am," I said.

"So, I have a friend in the Los Altos PD," he said. "I live in South Bay, and all the cops around here know each other. We're all in the same softball leagues and shit. Anyway, my friend tells me he's heard that you're looking around, wanted to pass on some information you might find useful."

"Why?"

"Maybe it can help."

"Why not come to me directly?"

"Have you seen that department?" he asked, incredulous. "They've got about a hundred people. Someone leaks, they're gonna nail it down in a hot minute."

"So, he's afraid he'll get found out," I said, restating but looking for some visual confirmation. Hu nodded. As one of my instructors at the clandestine service school would say, "This is when your spidey sense should start tingling." I was wary of David Hu. Considering the treatment I'd received from law enforcement so far, how could you blame me? Still, it tracked that someone on the inside who was frustrated with the pace of the investigation, or that the state police had taken it from them, or that they were keeping the family in the dark, might try to contact me. My phone number was at the station. For a fleeting moment, I thought it might even be Detective Hanley, though I quickly dismissed that as too obvious.

Hu hadn't earned my trust yet, but I was interested enough to continue the conversation.

"Hanley send you?" I said.

"No, I don't know who that is."

Worth a shot.

"Does your friend think Zhou committed suicide?"

"He doesn't know," Hu said flatly. "State guys have the forensics data tied up. Said this thing stinks. There's some smoke-and-mirrors shit going on."

"That's my sense as well," I said. "Do you think he'd be willing to let me look at some case files?"

Hu held up his hands. "Let's crawl, then we walk. He's got to be careful."

"That's fair. I understand. But if he's not trying to help my investigation out, what's the point to our even talking? Why contact me?"

Police were some of the best assets you could have. In many of the countries we operated in, a good cop might be an invaluable ally against a tyrannical government. They could get you real-time street intelligence, handle logistics like IDs and weapons, or warn you if you were in danger.

I knew a little about how gang cops worked. Human intelligence— HUMINT— was a large part of what they did. Former case officers routinely lectured to law enforcement organizations, to police and sheriff's departments, teaching them the latest techniques in cultivating assets. The ones we could share, at any rate. So, Hu knew the game. He was acting as a cutout, a go-between. He'd know that I would need more information to proceed, to prove that his source was legitimate and that he could produce what Hu suggested he could.

Hu's brow furrowed, and he leaned in again. "He wants to help, but wants to know first that you're serious. Are you genuinely trying to solve this thing or just make a buck?"

"I am faithfully representing my client's interests," I said. "If your friend would like to know more, I need something to convince me he's on the up. Get me something tangible that convinces me your friend cares as much as you say he does, and I'll be willing to share what I know. The best case scenario, I'm in a position to point the official investigation in the right direction, prove that Johnnie Zhou was murdered." And show that the state police were trying to cover that up and abusing their power. I left that part out.

"Hey—that's not how this works," Hu said, gruffly.

"Maybe I've got reason not to trust cops right now. Maybe the state police are coming off a little heavy and that gets my hackles up."

"All right, all right," Hu said, backing down a little. Then he nodded, as if satisfying some internal conversation. "I'll see what I can do."

"Okay. I'll wait to hear from you."

I left the cafe. By now, I had a good sense for the neighborhood. I walked two blocks north to Broadway, the heart of Chinatown, and faded into the background. As crime and homelessness spiraled out of control in this city, tourism suffered, though Chinatown was always a popular and lively destination. It neighbored the Financial District and the piers and was swelled with the lunch rush. The sun was just now burning through the marine layer, and it was cool. The clouds hid the grime that suffused everything. I zigzagged my route between blocks, cutting back across my route several times, wanting to see if Hu was following.

There wasn't any sign of him, but my instincts told me something was off.

Not to say that his source wasn't legit, some cop looking to help—I could see those dominos lining up. I just didn't like Hu.

This could easily be a state police setup, and I wouldn't put it past them. They'd use Hu as a double agent to work his way into my confidence, maybe even share disposable evidence with me to bolster his credibility. They could use that to throw me off track, see how much I knew, and determine if I was a threat to whatever this operation was. As a law enforcement officer, Hu could testify as an undercover to whatever he'd seen. The most they could get me on was pretending to be a private eye or that catch-all, *obstruction of justice*. It'd kill my case and any hope Elizabeth Zhou would have of finding out the truth. If they really had something to hide, I could see that.

Which was why I'd given him a little pushback about the state, but not too much.

No, I'd be careful with David Hu.

Did I really need to burn time on a surveillance detection route with him? Probably not. Call it an abundance of caution. His calling me out of the blue at the exact moment Robert went into the community center gave me a queer feeling. I'd learned that lesson in Buenos Aires when a federal police officer tried to burn me by exposing one of my agents. My cover job was as a State Department officer with reason to be out in the community, meeting with local government officials. I got a call on my office line from this federal officer requesting a meeting. We had a feeling there was a leak, and the Argentine government—with whom we did not enjoy good relations—suspected which of the embassy staff were CIA. That meeting felt like a setup, and I didn't take it, I also terminated that case immediately. Though not a perfect analogy, this situation reminded me of that.

Maybe Hu was on the level and was trying to be the go-between. If so, he wouldn't be tailing me, and I just got a little exercise. If not, it was worth the time to know I was in the clear.

Satisfied that if Hu had followed me, I'd lost him, I returned to a group of streets near the community center.

No messages from Robert.

Chinatown was mostly low buildings, two or three stories, and tightly packed. The streets cut narrow canyons through their midst, with cars parked in every available space. There was little room to move and nowhere I could stand guard without looking obvious. The sidewalks here were tight strips of broken concrete and the local restaurants didn't use them for outdoor seating. The cafe across the street from the community center was a little too close for me. Without knowing the relationship between the shop owner and the community center, I chanced that the owner would tell Huang I'd been hanging out there for longer than a lunch.

Instead, I flitted between the shops and tea houses in a two block radius of the community center.

Two hours burned, and I was running out of places I could waste time in.

I still hadn't heard from Robert.

Elizabeth messaged me in Signal, asking for an update. I ignored that for now.

Robert's silence had been long enough I was starting to get worried.

We'd planned to meet at Sidney Walton Park, about six blocks outside of Chinatown and close to the water. As I made my way there, I passed a homeless camp on Broadway. With twenty or so tents pitched in an empty lot, the uncollected detritus of street life piled up around the edges and flowed out, a multicolored but dingy river of debris. Things I'd rather not inspect further crunched underfoot as I passed.

I'd walked alone down some dark streets in some pretty awful places in the world. Spots where you had good cause to fear for your life. This wasn't exactly that, more a sense of grim foreboding mixed with regret at what the city had become. My base instinct told me there was an unwritten but understood code that guided these streets—don't make yourself a target, and you'd probably be left alone. Step outside of the paint, though, and you were fair game.

There was a sense of gritty menace in the dark places around the low canyon of buildings around me.

As if punctuating that, an SFPD car raced by, heading back in the direction I'd just come, lights and sirens.

I reached the park, a small patch of land, about a block across and ringed with trees, some small sculptures. There was one tent and some homeless wandering about, though it was quiet, and people seemed to keep to themselves. A couple of kids played with a frisbee with a parent looking on.

I found a bench facing west so I could see Robert's approach. My heart raced in time with the pace of dark thoughts I fought to control, all the terrible things that might be happening to Robert right now. Yes, he was probably just sitting in an uncomfortable chair, reading the same magazine for eight hours. Or his name was on some list, and they'd pulled him into a back room to do unspeakable things.

It was an admittedly wide spectrum from the mundane to the horrible.

The protein bar I'd brought for sustenance had burned through a long time ago, so I walked over and found a food truck that was closing up shop after the late-afternoon crowd. I paid ten bucks for something in taco form and wolfed that down with a bottle of water.

Jennie called me and said it definitely sounded like the state police were harassing Ray's to get to me, that it was without question an abuse of power, and that the foundation could do nothing unless it related to a story they were working on. She also reminded me not to namedrop Orpheus.

I told her I hadn't.

That was technically true, though I had implied it.

Regardless, I was on my own.

There was still no word from Robert.

16

The sun was low in the sky, and I wrote Elizabeth back, telling her I'd have an update for her later but was in the middle of what I'd termed an "investigation activity."

She didn't reply.

At six, I walked to a nearby Starbucks for a coffee and then returned to the park.

The sky reddened, and shadows got longer. I noticed that the park's population increased as the afternoon faded to evening. Now I had an additional concern. Chinatown was experiencing a surge in crime as the homelessness got worse. People were getting mugged at alarming rates, and Robert was sixty-something years old. The most direct route here would take him right past that camp on Broadway.

I texted him again and asked if he was okay. I set a timer in Signal for the message to delete itself in an hour. If the Chinese had him, they had his phone, and they'd have access to his messaging apps.

At ten to eight, I got a ping in Signal, and I opened to find a message from Robert:

Sorry was held up, long meeting. Got time for a coffee?

The messaging was part of our COVCOM strategy. The message itself was throwaway text to embed the code phrase and writing in all lowercase meant he wasn't under duress. Asking for a coffee was the all-clear signal.

I wrote back to him immediately and gave him a bar on Columbus Avenue. It was a major street, well lit, and close to him. I left the park, taking Washington past the massive TransAmerica Pyramid. Trading speed for security, I took the most direct route I could. Ten minutes later, I was walking into the bar and saw Robert there, waiting for a seat.

I walked up to him and said, "We should put some distance between us and downtown."

He followed me out the back, and we walked a circuitous, improvised SDR to my Defender. Again, I'd cut this shorter than I normally might've, but I wanted to get him out of the city so we could debrief.

San Francisco was a hard city to get out of fast.

It was built on a peninsula with two bridges, one going north and the other east. Your other option was an interstate and a state highway going south. Like LA, rush hour never really seemed to end—there were just times when traffic was heavier than others. I took the 101 south out of the city to the Dumbarton Bridge that would cross the bay into Fremont.

Once we were moving, I periodically flipped my gaze to the rearview to check for tails. Spotting a pursuit in a car at night wasn't easy. It relied heavily on pattern recognition. You tried to memorize the shape of the headlights and see which ones stuck with you, who followed you off a turn. It was hard as hell, unless you were in a place like Moscow or Tehran, where they didn't care if you knew they were there.

I started the debrief.

I'd always preferred debriefing in cars. I liked the idea of being on the move and having options if I needed them.

"Walk me through it," I said.

"I told them I was coming in because they said there was a problem with my citizenship. They took me to a room in the back. They immediately asked for my passports—Chinese and American. When I said I didn't have them, the guy got angry and said he didn't think he could help me."

"Trying to confiscate them so they can coerce you," I said. "What did the back area look like? Try to remember everything you can. Details matter."

"It looked like a government office, honestly. There were no decorations. All the furniture looked cheap. It was pretty cramped. They had a small central area with a table and chairs. There was a counter with a sink, and I saw a hotplate with a teapot. Lots of filing cabinets with simple locks. There were some safes. They took me into an office, which had a desk and two chairs. I spotted a camera in the ceiling when I walked in, so I didn't look around the desk at all. Or take out my phone."

"That was a heads-up play," I said. "Smart."

"Thank you. After waiting about twenty minutes, a man walked in. Black suit, maybe late forties. He introduced himself as Weibo Chen." I asked him to describe the man's features, and he did in detail. Sounded like Chen looked exactly like I remembered Mr. "Huang."

Robert continued. "Mr. Weibo made small talk first. He asked how long I'd lived in the US, why I'd immigrated, and how often I made it home. My first clue was that he asked the questions in a way that indicated he already knew the answers. It's something I've done when researching stories with people who I don't think are being honest with me. It just clicked for me right away."

Robert seemed to have a natural aptitude for this, and the more I spoke with him, the more I was both impressed and not surprised he'd chosen to be an investigative journalist. He had good instincts too. That couldn't be taught.

"Did you try asking him any questions?"

"I did. His answers were short and practiced, and he steered the conversation back to me each time. He said he was from a small town about two hours east of Beijing."

Probably made up, I thought.

"When he said that he was glad I'd decided to come in, I knew the real questions were about to start. He said I should've brought my passports but that, hopefully, he could still help. That must've been about fifteen or twenty minutes into it. I tried taking the initiative, asking why *he* was speaking with me and not someone from the consulate. He repeated the line about it being a community outreach center to help people with visas and passports and the like. When I asked him why people couldn't just do that at the consulate, he said sometimes the government process was confusing or intimidating, and because people didn't want to go to the consulate, they acted as intermediaries. He also said, and I think this is an exact quote, 'Our government can be intimidating to some, so we try to act as a bridge.' I tried pressing him on how, if they were all volunteers, they had the authority to do anything. Weibo's answer was a little vague, just that they had 'full governmental support.' He started pressing me on why I'd left China, then he wanted to know about my work, who my employers were, and whether I still paid individual income tax in China."

"Dual citizens don't normally pay taxes in both places," I said. "Most countries, it's just the one they reside in."

"It's the same in China, which I mentioned. He said because my income was generated online, I was liable for anything derived from China-only newspapers. I told him I didn't write for any Chinese papers."

I could see the snare Weibo was carefully looping around Robert's feet and wondered if Robert had picked it up as well. By getting him to admit he didn't write for any "patriotic publications," they might be able to back into his being a dissident. The CCP had a real "you're with us or against us" mentality.

"He handed me a piece of paper and asked me to write down all the outlets I wrote for, so he could verify whether there would be a tax liability."

"Which ones did you list?"

"Just the American ones. I assumed he already knew about the regional publications, but I wasn't going to bring them up. My really salacious work, I save for the pen name. Then there was a knock on the door, someone walked in and handed him a file. I knew there was a problem when this person didn't leave the doorway, essentially blocking me in. Weibo looked over the file for a time."

"Did you notice if he did anything with his hands before the person came in? Like drop them below the desk?"

"I don't recall. I admit I was getting a little agitated."

"That was a timely entry with the file. It wouldn't shock me if Weibo had a way to signal someone outside the office."

"Weibo spent a lot of time looking through my file. Eventually, he told me that as a dual citizen, I needed to return to China every five years in order to maintain it. That if I didn't, they'd revoke my citizenship. I told him I wasn't planning to return, I was comfortable here. He said, 'Mr. Li, if you lose your Chinese citizenship, you lose your American citizenship as well. You could be deported if this isn't resolved.'"

I said, "I'm no immigration expert, but that cannot be true. If you lose citizenship in one country, it wouldn't have anything to do with the other."

"I thought that as well and said as much, but he was quite insistent. He got aggressive, telling me that if I didn't resolve this, I could even face criminal penalties here. That he didn't want to but would be required by a treaty with the American government to notify the authorities. When I asked what treaty, he couldn't immediately name it and asked why I was being difficult."

"Sounds like they aren't used to people pushing back," I said.

"You don't have much experience with the CCP, do you, Matt? Then I told him I'd just go to the consulate to resolve whatever problem there was, Weibo insisted this could only be solved if I returned to China."

Traffic was still heavy, but it was moving, and we were making good time. I picked up the 880 Freeway in Fremont and took that south to San Jose.

"In fact," Robert said, "they offered to put me on an Air China flight later this week, and I'd be back here within a few days. I said I had a speaking engagement at a local civic organization, and my absence would be conspicuous."

"That was smart," I said.

"I used those exact words."

"Did they mention Johnnie at all?"

"No," he said. I could sense the weariness in his voice. "After that first session, they left me in the room with some forms to fill out."

"Forms?"

"Yes, they were government documents. It looked mostly like demographic info, but they were pressing me to sign. Honestly, I just had the sense they wanted my signature on something."

"Did you sign them?"

"I didn't. That was part of what took so long, really. I just kept stalling them. Weibo got aggressive when I refused to sign and pressed him about what the forms were for. He kept assuring me it was routine. When I told him I'd never heard anything from the Chinese government about any citizenship issues, he asked me why I was being so difficult and repeated that he was just trying to help me."

Patterns began to form, and from what Robert told me, I could start piecing their operation together. They would approach their targets with fabricated charges or even benign issues that could only be resolved at home. Pressing Robert to get on a prearranged flight on the country's flag carrier only cemented that in my mind. I made a note to dig into it further to see if I could identify anyone who'd returned to China from another country only to be convicted of treason or whatever generic charge they'd made up. I'd heard "subversion" was popular these days.

Robert said, "They left me alone for about two hours. I didn't feel comfortable messaging you. Even when I was by myself, I knew they had a camera on me, and I was concerned they would see over my shoulder to read the message. When he came back in, he brought some water and asked if I wanted anything to eat. He had some food from a place across the street." A wave of relief washed over me at having not picked that place for an observation post. "He said that as a journalist, I must know many members of the Chinese-American community. He asked if I'd be willing to assist them in locating some people they were trying to help."

"To help?" I asked.

"Yes. People who were in a similar predicament as my own. He said the cooperation might aid me in resolving my situation."

"You have a 'situation' now? That was fast."

"I told them again that I had to leave, that I was expected somewhere. There was always a reason for me not to leave though. They said if I left, or I didn't sign the papers, or whatever it was they wanted me to do, it would show I didn't want to cooperate. Eventually, I think this was around seven, I got up to leave. They'd left me alone in the office again. Weibo intercepted me not five steps from that room, so I knew they were watching me on camera. He said we were almost done. I told him no, *I* was done. I reminded him that he had no legal authority to keep me there. He asked me if I was on WeChat, and I told him no."

WeChat was the so-called "everything app" in China. Nearly ubiquitous, Chinese citizens used it for cashless transactions, news, social media, travel, e-commerce, and even real estate. The Chinese government used it to keep track of everything their citizens did. Though built by a private company, the CCP oversaw all their operations by virtue of mandated "advisory" seats on the company's board, and Chinese law mandated the company turn any data collected over to the government. The government used that information to monitor every aspect of their citizens' lives.

"Weibo handed me a piece of paper with a QR code on it. I asked him what it was. He said they had an app that I could use to follow my case and that they could use to get in touch with me since I wasn't on WeChat. Then I was free to go. I scanned it, and he told me they'd be in touch."

"Did the app download?"

"I think so." Robert opened up his phone. "Looks like it."

"Your phone is compromised. They're already inside it. They've got your contacts, emails, phone records, search history. Everything."

I'd been watching a pair of headlights in my rearview for about a mile now. That all but confirmed for me that someone was following us.

"I didn't know what else to do. Weibo was blocking me from leaving. I thought if I just downloaded the thing, they'd let me leave."

Keeping my left hand on the wheel, I grabbed the phone with my right and powered it off. Then I dropped it in my center console.

I thought about our chats on Signal. As a matter of practice, I set those up to auto-delete upon being read or after a certain amount of time if they'd gone unread.

When I spoke next, I kept my voice low. "Robert, we may have picked up a tail. If I'm right, they're tracking your phone. I don't want to drop you anywhere near your house. I'm going to lose them and let you off downtown, somewhere with a lot of lights."

"Japantown," he said. "It's close enough to my house that I can walk home, and it'll still be busy this time of night."

"Okay. We're going do a rolling drop-off. I'm going to slow down, and you hop out. All right? We won't be going fast. It'll let me keep moving and put some distance between you and your phone."

"I understand."

It was possible they'd remotely activated the phone's microphone and listened in on our entire conversation. This was something we at the Agency had done time and again, though it wasn't easy to pull off. Still, with nearly every smartphone in the world being manufactured in China, they likely had resources we didn't. And it was possible to both track a phone and trigger the mic without turning it on. The phone had been in his pocket until I asked him about the app. Possibly, anything they might have overheard would be muffled and unintelligible. *Let's hope.*

"The phone's gone," I said. "I'm going to dispose of it for you. Get a new one tomorrow and restore it from an online backup that exists before today. That shouldn't be a problem because you wouldn't have been able to sync it."

"Okay."

I navigated the Defender through nighttime San Jose. Robert's house was a little over five blocks from Fifth and Jackson, where we decided I'd drop him. On the way, I tried a few tricks to confirm we were indeed being tailed. We were. As we neared the drop point, I accelerated to just above the speed limit, looking to put some distance between us and the tail. Since they were following electronically, I presumed, they wouldn't be as aggressive in following me. That was also why I didn't pick up a second car.

Robert was almost silent since he'd told me about the app. The guilt over a perceived failure leaked out of his pores. He'd gone up against some pros. They'd used authoritarian playbook shit to wear him down, convince him of their superiority and authority in order to get him to do what they wanted. Robert had held out, and it wasn't until the end that he acquiesced to one small thing to get out of a bad situation. That was how it started— one small hook.

Whoever this Weibo was, he was a pro.

I turned onto Fifth and accelerated. Spotting a parking lot with a second exit on the connecting street, I pulled into that, slowed the car to my best approximation of a walking pace, and said, "Okay, Robert, go. Call me as soon as you get a new phone."

"I will," he said and opened his door.

"Don't beat yourself up over this. These guys are professional. My guess is it's the MSS or one of the PLA's covert action groups. Get some sleep, and let's regroup tomorrow. You did good."

He said, "Okay," though without vigor. He stepped out of the Defender and disappeared into the dark parking lot.

I pulled out onto the far street and was gone.

Two blocks later, the tail picked me back up.

17

Keeping my eyes on the road, I pulled the phone out of the console, powered it back up, and dropped it back in.

Time to have some fun with these assholes.

I accelerated down Fourth Street, heading for the freeway. There were few traffic lights on this street, which worked out to my benefit. If you were being followed, the last thing you wanted was to be stationary. Contrary to what you saw in movies, to shake a tail you didn't blast through an intersection or stoplight. That was a great way to get into a dangerous and potentially fatal situation. Instead, the way you lose them is by blending in. If that wasn't an option, you simply out-drove them. Took the city streets and changed direction often. Doubled back. The objective was to put space between you and the pursuer so that you could get off the road and hide or ditch the vehicle. Which I obviously wasn't doing. And I had to assume they were following the phone.

It seemed like they'd decided they wanted to pick Robert up right now.

While I'd physically located most of Johnnie's people in short order using open-source tools, it was possible they didn't know where Robert's house was. Grabbing someone while they were moving between two points at night was a hell of a lot easier than breaking into their suburban home and kidnapping them.

Some distant part of my case officer's lizard brain reminded me I wasn't on the streets of Karachi or Cairo, but San Jose, California. My tail was a foreign intelligence service operating here illegally. I wondered if there was a way to alert local police—that would potentially solve a couple of my problems. At least, it would make things a lot harder for the opposition.

Then I remembered David Hu, and that opened up a whole new spectrum of complication.

What if that car following me was Hu, or Nugent and Montoya? I had no real proof it was the Chinese. That was just a guess based on timing and the assumption they'd hacked Robert's phone. You couldn't tell who was chasing you from a pair of headlights.

My first instinct when I met Hu was that he could be a plant the state investigators had put on me. Nothing about how he'd contacted me added up. If that car belonged to them, then they weren't after Robert—rather, they were after me. That absolutely changed how I approached ditching the tail. Nugent and Montoya would use any minor infraction as an excuse to nail me to the wall. I had no problem bumping a Chinese intel officer's drop car. I wasn't about to pull a hit-and-run with a state cop.

I hopped on the interstate going north, back toward the city.

This tracked entirely with the pattern of harassment the state detectives had started. They'd figured I had connections with Johnnie's people and couldn't figure out how to get access to them. So they'd tail me and have me do the legwork for them.

"Let's see how well you drive, Dave," I said.

I accelerated and weaved around some cars, though stayed below the speed limit and signaled. I wasn't going to give them a reason to pull me over.

At the last second, I ditched the interstate at the Saratoga Avenue offramp, heading into Santa Clara. The chase car had to cross two lanes of traffic to make the exit. So much for inconspicuous. I had half a mind to pull over and let them catch up to me, just so I could confront them.

The first block up, I made a left at a yellow light that was damn near orange and blasted down the block. I turned left again, this time into the parking lot of a strip mall that had several restaurants and a supermarket, all still open. There was a frontage road on the far side, which I took. The interstate onramp was on the left and clusters of apartment complexes on the right.

The chase car hadn't caught up yet.

There was only a thin median between the frontage road and the onramp, and it was mostly filled with trees. I spotted an open patch up ahead that also didn't have a metal guardrail on either side. Easy for a Land Rover, less so for a sedan.

I pulled a hard left over the dirt, punched the accelerator with dirt exploding behind the Defender. I cranked the wheel to avoid a car—*sorry, buddy*—and rode the shoulder until I'd picked up enough speed to merge with traffic.

I smirked as I had this image in my head of David Hu standing on the frontage road, shaking a fist hilariously at my taillights as I disappeared onto the interstate.

I took the next exit, which dropped me in Cupertino, next to the Apple campus. I circled that and pulled into the residential neighborhood on the opposite side. Once I was three streets deep, I pulled over and stopped. My hotel was only two miles from where I sat, but I didn't want to go there. First, I needed to dispose of Robert's phone. It was nearly impossible to truly wipe an electronic device without industrial tools. Intelligence agencies could also reconstruct the data on hard drives from almost nothing. Instead, I'd just improvise a Faraday cage to prevent anyone from tracking the phone and just dump it in a trash bin somewhere. That would shake off our friends at the community center, and I was confident I'd lost the police.

I turned about and drove toward Sunnyvale, looking for a convenience store so I could buy a roll of tin foil to make the Faraday cage.

I picked up El Camino Real and headed northwest. It was a three-lane road that cut a diagonal path across this part of Silicon Valley. It was close to nine, and I hadn't eaten a real meal in hours. Maybe if I'd been looking behind me and not for supper, I'd have seen a pair of headlights behind me. Instead, what I noticed was the black car next to me that wouldn't move over when I tried to change lanes. I accelerated, and so he matched speed. Same when I tried to slow. The guy behind me did the same, classic box-in technique.

Shit.

I was in the leftmost of the three lanes.

I hammered the brakes, downshifted, and cranked the wheel hard to the left, power sliding into the turn lane. Then I gunned it and blasted across three lanes in the opposite direction, aiming for the entrance to a parking lot on the far side.

Horns erupted on both sides of the street, aimed at me and the asshole following me as he tried to make the turn too.

No lights, no sirens.

I'd been wrong. These weren't cops.

The parking lot, a wedge shape in the corner between El Camino Real and the cross street, was mostly empty this time of night. I raced to the far side as my pursuer broke all of the traffic laws to get behind me. Looking ahead, I was perpendicular to the flow of traffic, making it very hard to time. Headlights bounced into the far end of the parking lot behind me. Ignoring the stop sign, I pulled out onto the three-lane road and turned right because that was my only option.

Unfortunately, I didn't make the light.

I was already two cars deep, and there was nowhere to move. Even if I could get over to the median to reverse direction, it was still a six-inch pile of concrete. Yes, the LR could do it...but it would not be fast, and it would get everyone's attention. Behind me, I saw the black car that had been tailing me pull out onto the road.

I willed the light to change as the car crept closer.

There were two cars between us.

Green lights, and I was...not going anywhere. A gap opened up next to me, so I hit it before another driver did. Pulling around the car that had been in front of me, I made the light and blasted through the intersection. I reached the far side, punched the accelerator, and the block vanished behind me. This part of town was a mix of apartments and businesses, with sporadic construction and renovation underway.

The black car ripped around the vehicles separating us, no longer concerned with hiding their pursuit.

I was nearing the end of the block and approaching another intersection. The chase car was right behind me now.

The light was still green.

It dissolved to yellow.

"Sorry, Miguel," I said to the mechanic who'd restored and modernized my Defender. I punched the brake and skidded to a screaming almost-stop as the black car rammed into my rear bumper. As soon as I felt the impact, I hit the gas again, and the truck's front end jumped. I'd slowed enough to force the crash but hadn't lost all my momentum yet. I made the intersection just as cars started turning.

I saw a pancaked car behind me creep forward. I turned left.

And there was another car in my lane, heading straight for me.

They'd meant to cut me off in the intersection and hadn't counted on me forcing the collision.

This guy wasn't turning.

Stupid. I was in a heavy SUV with brush guards and a reinforced front bumper. The most I'd get out of a head-on collision was an airbag deployment.

He kept heading straight for me.

At the last second, he ditched for a lot on my right. I turned my wheel to clip the back of his car.

Physics was a harsh mistress.

His trajectory turned violently in the other direction, and as I passed him, I saw the car spin halfway around before crashing into a fence.

I turned right at the end of the block. The other driver had pulled into a construction site. I wanted some goddamned answers. Plus, there was still the second car, and I knew they were tracking me by following Robert's phone. As long as I had that in my possession, they could find me. Rabbiting now would only get me so much.

I parked on the street alongside the construction fence, pulled my Glock out of the door, and got out. There was an entry to the construction site on this side street, so I took that and was maybe fifty feet from where the car had ended up. He'd crashed into some support beams, which dropped a load of scaffolding onto the roof.

The second car roared into the lot.

The car's headlights painted me, and the driver hit the accelerator.

No time to get a shot off, I lunged to the side, out of the way, and made a full on sprint across the dirt lot for the concrete skeleton beyond.

I was behind the beginnings of a wall when I heard doors slam and people shouting in Mandarin.

In about six months, this would probably be an office building. Creeping slowly and silently, I slid along the wall to a stairwell. I backed into that, keeping my pistol trained on the opening. There was almost no light, just the ghostly afterimages of streetlamps beyond the construction site. Though I didn't know what they were saying, one of them was clearly issuing orders.

My pursuers entered the building. I orbited around the wall and crouched, waiting.

They relied on their numerical superiority and didn't worry about stealth. Stupid, again.

The one coming up the stairs gave me all the warning I'd need. I holstered my weapon and waited for him to reach the top of the stairs. He exited the stairwell pistol first, and I grabbed his wrist and forearm with both hands. I brought his arm down hard on my knee. There wasn't enough force to break the bone, but I was sure I'd made that thing numb. He dropped the pistol, and I used my left hand to knuckle-punch him in the trachea. Then I grabbed his arm and, using my bodyweight as leverage, corked him out of the stairwell and threw him. The guy landed with a hard crash, sliding across the concrete.

Despite the hit to the throat, he closed the gap between us lightning fast and landed a kick to my thigh that I thought would break my leg. He stepped inside my reach and landed a punch on my temple. A galaxy of stars exploded across my eyes.

I threw a haymaker just to put some distance between us while I recovered. The punch didn't hit anything but air.

Then I punched low, hitting his kidneys, though it didn't do much thanks to his jacket. I launched an upward strike, hitting his chin with the heel of my left hand. His mouth cracked shut so hard I heard his teeth snap together. He made a sweeping motion with one arm, and I saw a glint of metal.

Knife.

Oh, it was worth noting that the building's design apparently called for an atrium because there was a large open space in the center. I slid forward, turned, and landed a sidekick right in the center of his chest.

The guy staggered backward, and there was just enough scattered light for me to catch the surprise on his face when his foot touched open air. A second later, he crashed to the ground, writhing in pain. I knew the fall wouldn't kill him, though he'd probably gotten a broken leg out of it. Maybe worse. I didn't care.

A dull thud snapped the air.

A gunshot had a way of reframing your thinking.

Suppressed pistols still made noise; they were just muffled and you didn't see the muzzle flash. Still, if you were close enough, you could hear it. He missed (obviously) and I put some distance between me and the stairwell.

"This building is surrounded," he said. I was surprised to hear a British accent.

While I wanted to tell him that it wasn't, I also didn't want to give my position away now that I was out of his line of sight.

I'd found a concrete pillar to hide behind when he said, "Give me Robert Li, and I will let you leave here."

"What do you want with him?" I asked, less concerned about my location now that I had cover.

"That's my business. He is a wanted man, and I am to ensure he's brought to trial."

I bet.

The pillar I used for cover was in the northwest corner of the structure and in complete darkness. The Chinese intelligence officer was at the center, not far from where I'd kicked his friend over the side. To get to me, he'd need to pass by three large cutouts that would one day be windows. Meaning, he'd have to pass from pure darkness to faded streetlight three times.

"Give me Robert," he said, stepping forward behind his pistol.

"He's not here. You've been following his phone, not him. He's somewhere safe, with my government."

The man chuckled. "I doubt that very much, my friend."

Just another couple of steps.

"Now, tell me where I can find him and you walk away."

He emerged from the inky dark into the gap of streetlight coming in from the window holes.

I orbited out from behind cover, still nearly invisible to him.

"Drop your weapon, put your hands in the air, and lace them behind your head. I have you covered. If you move, I will fire."

He twitched, his muscles an extension of the debate going on in his mind.

"It appears we have a standoff," he said. He was trying to force calm into his voice. It wasn't there.

"No, we don't. We have a rule in this country. If you go to the hospital with a gunshot wound, they're required to report it to the police. What do you think is going to happen when they figure out you're an unregistered foreign agent? You go to jail, just not the one you think. It's going to be a dark hole in the ground we don't really tell people about. And then you sit there until your government has something we want. Given the state of things, I bet that's a long goddamn time." Paused a beat. "Take your pick."

Silence and fast thoughts.

One hand went out slowly, palm up.

He knelt down glacially, not taking an eye off me and placed his gun on the ground. He stood up just as slowly. Arms went up behind his head.

Then I shot him in the leg anyway.

18

I'd never loved violence, and while I carried a pistol in the field my entire career, I'd never had cause to use it.

Shooting him had as much to do with possibly getting him arrested and exposed as a foreign agent as it did anything else. A long shot, perhaps, though maybe the right authorities would finally start paying attention now. Odds were better he'd get away and be patched up by a government medic at his consulate. Still, two enemies were off the board for a while.

I disappeared quickly.

Ten minutes later, I'd found a convenience store and left with a roll of aluminum foil. I used almost the entire roll to wrap Robert's phone and then found a dumpster behind a restaurant to drop it in. I might not have been able to completely destroy it, but I could at least make it impossible for them to find.

Satisfied that no one was watching me, I returned to my hotel, poured two fingers of scotch, and sipped it until my nerves calmed. That fight had been close. It was luck that I saw the knife. Had I not, he'd have stuck me at least once.

Sleep came eventually, but it was restless and filled with the kind of dreams you'd expect.

The next morning, I called Elizabeth and apologized for not being available. She wanted to see me right away for an update. We made plans to meet midmorning in Palo Alto. My first stop was to check on Robert. Normally a fast, short drive, but with the morning rush and my additional precautions against surveillance, it took about forty-five minutes to get to him. Which meant I'd be pushing it to meet Elizabeth on time.

Robert was awake and didn't seem too shaken, though he didn't yet know what had happened to me. I debated telling him but decided he deserved to know. After all, they'd been looking for him.

"We need to go to the police," he said.

My first thought was, *Which ones?*

The logical choice was to contact Nugent and Montoya. As state cops, they'd have connections with the FBI, which was responsible for domestic counterintelligence. That, in and of itself, would bring a host of additional problems, on top of bringing my case to a screaming halt.

"I understand why you feel that way," I said. "If you'd feel safer doing that, I don't blame you."

"You don't think I should. I can tell by your tone."

I explained the jurisdictional challenges as I saw them. The local police didn't have the resources or the training for this sort of thing, and involving them would waste more time than it would save. It might even tip off the opposition. The state police had given me enough reason not to trust them. There was only one lever I had to pull here, and that was Nate. I couldn't share that with Robert though. "There's the additional problem that I'm the one who actually saw them. You don't have anything to report. I don't want to involve the police, at least not yet. It's possible they know about the Chinese, and that's why they're so closed off. It's also possible they don't. If some local cops go bungling in, they could scare these guys off before we learn anything. They go to ground, and we lose the whole thing." I paused and let him offer a protest. He didn't. "Let's give It a day or two. See if you detect something suspicious, someone following you. In the meantime, are you getting a new phone?"

"I am. Maybe a disposable one."

"Just make sure you can get apps so we can communicate. In the meantime, do you know what an onion router is?"

Robert gave a slightly irritated glower and said, "What do you think?"

I gave him a disposable email address I used and said to let me know when he was back up with a phone.

Elizabeth suggested a cafe in Palo Alto near her hotel. I would have preferred somewhere more discreet, but I didn't want to alarm her. She was sitting at a round metal table underneath an umbrella when I arrived. She wore jeans and a lightweight sweatshirt, large sunglasses, and a Stanford ball cap. She looked like what a regular person assumed "inconspicuous" to be.

"May I sit," I asked as I approached the table. She nodded. Her mood was frosty, and I was anxious to understand why. "Have you made any more progress with your father's estate?"

"Matt, why am I getting threatening phone calls from the California Bureau of Investigation?"

Okay, so no small talk.

"What did they say?"

"That you were interfering with a police investigation and it constituted obstruction of justice. They said they'd charge *me* with it too, since I hired you."

"That just means they're scared. They're hiding something, and I'm getting close to finding out what it is."

"I don't care, Matt. I could be disbarred. I'll be ruined," she said.

"Listen, I know this sounds scary, but they're just trying to use their weight to convince you to quit."

"Why shouldn't I?"

"I don't think your father would want that."

"How in the hell would you know? You've never even met him."

"I've learned quite a lot in the last few days. Enough to know that he stayed in the fight. And, I think that's what got him killed."

"What fight? What the hell are you even talking about?"

I lowered my voice and did a quick scan of our surroundings, eyeing nearby patrons. I also didn't want a server coming by and possibly over-hearing what I had to say. "This might not be the best place for this conversation," I said.

Elizabeth's features, what I could see of them beneath the cap and the glasses, darkened.

"Fine." She balled her napkin and dropped it on the table, pushing her chair back with furious vigor. She left a ten on the table under her coffee mug. I stood and had to make fast strides to catch up with her.

"Before I talk to you about what I've learned about your father, I need to get something else out of the way. This is important context for what I have to tell you. Have you spoken with Benjamin Blake or his attorney?"

"He's left some messages, but I haven't returned them. You said it wasn't a good idea for me to speak to him, so I didn't."

"I met with him again. Blake is the one who sent the state police after me in the first place."

"What?"

"He's a rich man, and he employs a top-tier law firm. They've got traction. I'm sure your firm has similar pull in LA. He used his connections to get the state police to try to scare me off. They even called Ray's and said they'd make trouble for them. Blake thought you were going after his business, and if he could jam me up with the police, that would stop it. I convinced him you weren't, that you just want to know if someone killed your father." I paused to let her process that. I also wanted to hear her confirm it that what I'd said was actually true. Needed to hear that she wasn't in this for the money.

"Blake wants to offer you a deal," I said.

"What kind of deal?"

"He told me it was in the ballpark of fifteen million. They wanted me to convince you to take it."

"No, that's not right. That company is worth two hundred million. My father's share should be so much more than that."

"Blake and his people can walk you through the numbers better than I can. All I can tell you is when he explained it to me, I thought it made sense. It's nowhere near two hundred—that's what they have under management, not how much your father had invested. He also told me your father was broke."

"That's impossible."

"Do you have access to your father's assets? Can you verify it?"

"They're locked up in probate. They don't want to release anything until the cause of death is official," she said, and the frustration in her voice was as genuine as it was understandable.

"Blake told me your father had leveraged all his assets, even his house. He'd borrowed against his equity in the company, even gone to Blake for a personal loan once."

Elizabeth stopped and sat on a low brick wall next to the sidewalk, holding her head in her hands.

"That was the context I spoke about. This all tracks with what I've found out independently," I said.

"Which is what?"

"You probably know that back in China, when you were a baby, your father was active in some student protests of the communist government."

"A little. He didn't speak of it very much. I think I was twelve before he ever mentioned it to me."

"Well, he stayed active in the movement through the years. He was financing dissidents to run subversion campaigns against the communist party and the government. Most of the technologies he invested in were to help people communicate securely inside China, to evade government surveillance."

"I don't understand. Why would he do that?" Her tone spiked aggressively and fast, like forcing me to prove it rather than looking for an explanation.

"Because he wanted to expose the atrocities the Chinese government gets away with every day. He wanted to fight for the people who don't have a voice, and he thought he was in a position to do something about it. Revolutions aren't cheap though, and it bankrupted him." I sat next to her on the wall. "Blake thinks what he's offering is probably enough to satisfy your father's debts and still leave you with a lot of money."

"Does that mean Dad really did kill himself?"

I shook my head. "I don't think so. Part of his...network, I guess you'd call it, uncovered what they think is a covert intelligence operation run by the Chinese government. Right here in San Francisco. They're targeting political dissidents, agitators, people who are speaking out against the communist party. People like your father. They're trying to scare them into flying back to China to resolve made-up immigration or citizenship issues, most of which are contrived, and when they do, the state police arrest them."

"Oh my God," she said. I'd debated telling her about Robert's efforts with the community center, afraid that she'd panic. Or worse, think that someone might be out to get her.

"My theory is that's what got him killed. I think these agents, from one of China's intelligence services, found out about his network and murdered him. Making a murder look like a suicide is hard, though not for a pro."

Elizabeth hadn't said anything further. She just sat on that brick wall, staring at some spot across the street. I didn't push her. She had a lot of information to process. "We need to go to the police. This is way outside of what I signed up for."

What could I say? Outside of major metropolitan police forces like New York or Los Angeles, local law enforcement didn't have counterintelligence capabilities. These guys were not equipped to go up against a foreign spy agency. We'd need the FBI for that, which I also didn't want. The last thing we needed was the Bureau poking around into Johnnie Zhou and his associations, and then Nate's operation is probably blown up. That would not end well for him.

"Right now, what I have is a theory. Even if I trusted the police, what would we tell them? Remember, this is the reason you brought me in here." And, if I turned over what I'd learned, they'd want to know how I got it. Somehow, I didn't expect a fair treatment from Nugent and Montoya.

"How do I know you aren't just jumping at shadows, Matt? How do I know you aren't seeing spies in the woodwork because that's all you know?"

"So, what, I'm just a hammer looking for nails?"

"Aren't you? You really want to tell me that my father is wrapped up in some goddamn global spy game? That he knew something, and the Chinese government murdered him for it?"

"Well, two men jumped me last night after I went poking around."

"What are you talking about?"

"I was following your father's research, and it led to me to the place he thought they were operating out of. They didn't take too kindly to my asking questions and their guns were fairly convincing."

"Do you know how insane this sounds? First, you tell me we can't go to the police because...because I don't know why. Then you tell me my father was involved in international espionage? This is completely crazy."

"Elizabeth, *you* told me you thought the police were covering something up. Those state investigators who tried to scare you off? Nugent and Montoya? I told you they called Cosmic Ray's and threatened them because they're associated with me. Said they were going to send a narcotics unit in and poke around, dig into their books. Maybe have a health inspector come down. They're going after my friends because I'm asking questions. I've seen enough tin-pot dictatorships in this world to know that's what a coverup looks like. So, no, I don't think the police can be trusted. The only part I haven't answered yet is what they're covering up and how it relates to your father's death. Once I have enough evidence, I'd like to give this to a reporter friend. We'll blow this thing right up if the police don't tell us what's going on with your dad's death."

"Matt, I'd like you to send me an itemized list of expenses to date."

"We are close. We should not stop now."

"Listen to what you're saying," Elizabeth spoke in an even tone that seemed to barely contain roiling anger. "We can't trust the police because it's a coverup, and the whole town is crawling with Chinese spies."

That actually summed the situation up pretty well. It didn't seem like the right time to mention it though.

"I'll expect your final invoice, Matt."

Elizabeth turned on her heel so hard she could've ground a hole into the sidewalk, and off she stalked.

I watched my client walk away, and the case with it.

Something had changed her mind, and the speed with which it happened jarred me.

As I replayed our conversation, it was clear she'd come looking for a fight. Or a quick way to end the case without much explanation. The question was why. Even when I told her what went down last night, her attitude didn't change much. When I told her I'd been braced, she focused on anything but that.

I didn't want to believe that the only reason she'd hired me was to break the stalemate with Blake. Still, all evidence to the contrary, it was hard to argue it was anything other than that.

Eventually, I found my way back to the hotel and another takeout dinner. I needed some fresh air, so I took the bottle of scotch I'd bought and went to go sit next to the hotel pool, despite the multiple admonishments not to have glass on the deck. This wasn't the third world—I refused to drink scotch out of a plastic cup.

I drank in silence and tried to focus on the questions hammering my head like rain.

The fundamental one that drove this case always came to the fore. It was the one I'd first started asking about Johnnie Zhou's death and was just as relevant now that I'd been fired.

Who benefitted by shutting me down?

The police. They would get me out of their business, whatever that may be.

The Chinese government. If they were actually involved, Robert and I seemed to be the only ones who knew.

Benjamin Blake. This whole thing would get wrapped up quietly and cleanly, for him, and he would pay Elizabeth to go away. Also, quietly and cleanly.

Finally, I circled back to my client. I reviewed everything I knew about her. She was the last one to see her father alive—they had an argument. He was found dead the next morning. The police called it a suicide, which nullified the agreement Johnnie had with his business partners. One that Elizabeth claimed not to have known about. She contacted me a week after he died. Enough time to learn she wasn't getting any money. I didn't know whether what she told me about the probate angle was true. If not, and she actually did have access to his accounts immediately after his death, or he'd told her, Elizabeth would know that her father was in serious financial trouble. And that she'd be responsible for settling the estate. That added serious incentive to disprove the suicide, but they'd need the police to do that. Which was why I hadn't considered her a factor in the investigation.

Until now.

Now the answer to the question of "who benefitted" had a clear winner, and it was Elizabeth. With Blake willing to pay her off in exchange for not challenging the partnership agreement in court, she stood to make enough money to pay off her father's debts and have enough left to get a substantial nest egg. Blake wouldn't have offered her anything if I hadn't intervened, which added some weight to the argument as to why she'd hired me, as well as some salt to the wound.

She'd break even, maybe even clear a cold million.

I'd seen people sell their souls for far less.

Two glasses down, and I hadn't shaken that thought.

I also didn't have any reason to continue this investigation. Elizabeth made that fairly clear to me. In fact, if I did, I'd not only have the police coming after me, but she could unleash a legal storm that would bury me forever. Her firm knew how to protect a reputation and how to bury a problem. They could make me go away without breaking a sweat.

And here I thought the firm would be on my side if we needed it.

It was starting to get cold, so I collected the bottle and headed back to my room. I checked my phone, which I'd left in the room so I could have some peace. No messages from Robert, which was a little surprising because I thought he'd have gone to get his new phone today.

There was also nothing from Elizabeth.

I couldn't shake the conjectures I'd just made and wondered whether all of this was just a way to get Blake to the negotiating table. A way to build leverage. Win battles without firing a shot, all of that.

The sort of tactic you'd expect from someone whose firm's practice was about keeping celebrities out of unfortunate spotlights.

The other inescapable truth was that I'd been played.

Maybe I shouldn't care. I just hated the idea that Elizabeth had used me for something so base as increasing her payout from her father's business partner. If she'd have been up front about it, I could've said that wasn't for me. And if I'm being honest, my ego was taking a serious hit for not seeing this coming. *Way to go, master spy.*

I powered up my computer to check the email account I'd given Robert to see if he'd checked in. As soon as I did, my browser erupted with alerts from the news triggers I set.

Ethan Jian, one of the men in Johnnie's network, was dead.

19

There wasn't much on Jian yet, little more than a blotter entry.

Ethan Jian, 52, of Burlingame, died when his car veered off the road the night before. He was traveling northbound on Bayshore Boulevard, just outside SFO, when his vehicle lost control and crashed through the chain-link fence at a high rate of speed. The car, a Tesla Model 3, rolled down the hill and came to a stop at the railroad tracks that ran next to the 101 freeway. He was pronounced dead at the scene of a broken neck. Jian was survived by his wife and two children.

I stared at the screen for a very long time.

There was another inescapable truth, I realized.

My client may have hired me for less than noble reasons, but it didn't change the fact that I actually *had* uncovered an active-measures campaign to silence dissidents.

The questions was what would I do about it?

I already knew the answer to that. I had a habit of asking myself rhetorical questions when I didn't have the benefit of someone to talk me out of it. Elizabeth fired me, and that should be the end of it. I *should* be packing up and going home.

That was the last thing I was going to do.

Three people from Johnnie's list—including himself—were dead in the last four weeks. Someone had to protect the ones who were left, and it wasn't like I could just hand that list to the police and say, "Here, do your jobs".

And maybe, in all of this, I could convince Elizabeth there was still something worthy of answering.

The evidence said she was in this for the money. The problem was, those members of her father's network weren't. They fought for a cause, and if I walked away now, how did I know they'd be safe? I didn't, because they wouldn't. Someone had to act for them, before they became the dying.

The next morning, somewhat regretting the amount of scotch I'd had the night before, I called the California Highway Patrol's Golden Gate Division, identified myself as a reporter, and asked to speak with their traffic unit. For the next ten minutes, they played follow-the-bouncing-ball, juggling me between different extensions. Finally, I was connected to a human, a patrol sergeant. He informed me that Jian was traveling at nearly eighty miles an hour and couldn't make the turn. I'd already looked the spot up and saw it was a dogleg curve to the left.

"Were there any brake marks or other indications that he tried to stop?" I asked.

"No," the sergeant told me. "We won't know for a while yet, but he may have had his auto-drive activated and wasn't paying attention. We're seeing that more and more these days. Could be the car didn't sense the turn for some reason." He added, "I don't trust those things."

"Do you think someone hit him? Another driver, maybe? Any chance this was a hit-and-run?"

"We didn't see any indication of that," he said. "The damage on the car was consistent with the rollover situation I described."

This wasn't going any further. I thanked the sergeant for his time and hung up.

It *was* possible to bump another car and not damage it. Rolling rear-ends happened all the time. It was another story, however, to pull it off while moving. And if someone was pushing him from behind, Jian would most likely try to force the turn, which would result in a harder contact that would leave marks on his car. To pull that off, someone would basically have to be tailgating Jian until the last minute when they bumper-kissed him and floored it. It would need to be precisely timed to pull it off and would certainly look like a hit-and-run.

My phone pinged. It was a text from Elizabeth, a regular message, not in Signal:

When you get a chance, send the itemized bill. Thx.

I called her back immediately, and it went straight to voicemail.

I texted her and asked her to call me immediately.

"What is it, Matt?" she said in a tired voice. There was one chance left.

"Two nights ago, one of the men your father worked with died. That makes three, all of them under suspicious circumstances. Two of them in the weeks before your father."

"Matt, there is no *network*. I don't even know what you're talking about."

"Yes, Elizabeth, there is. Your father supported journalists, organizers, activists, and technologists in trying to undermine the Chinese Communist Party. That's what bankrupted him."

"That's insane. How do you even know that?"

"Because I *spoke* to one! I've met one of the men he worked with. Someone he'd been involved with since his student protest days in the '80s. This is real. It is absolutely real, and your father was part of it. I think he was rattling cages a little too loudly, and they killed him for it."

"Matt, it's over. Please send me an invoice, now, so I can pay you."

"Did you ever actually care how your father died, or were you just trying to force Blake's hand?"

"What did you just say to me?"

"It's a little funny to me that the day after Ben Blake offers to settle for the full amount, you decide to pull up stakes and let me go. I just told you that three people connected to your father are dead, and it doesn't even matter to you."

"Because it's not my fucking problem! My father spent my entire life lamenting over leaving home. He couldn't appreciate everything we had right here. Or that our life was infinitely better than it would've been in

China. He was so goddamned obsessed with fighting the communists, or whatever, that he either didn't know or didn't pay attention to my mother getting sick. Maybe if he'd have cared just a *little* bit more, they might've caught it in time. So, no, Matt, I don't give a shit about his work. Or who else was involved. Think what you want about why I hired you, though obviously that was a mistake. And it's over. Send me a bill or don't. But if you do anything else about any of this, I'm going to have to take action." She disconnected.

There were few sounds more final than the silence after a woman hung up on you.

I felt lost and alone and used.

Hard to argue against the logic now that Elizabeth had hired me to scare Blake into changing course. Nate admitted he didn't know anything about her own finances, and despite her considering him an uncle, he didn't exactly know her *that* well. I'd need to talk to him again, and soon.

I sent Jennie a text and said we needed to speak later. That I had a story for her. There was nothing to protect now.

By the time I talked to her, I'd have figured out how to steer her away from Nate. And, I suppose, Elizabeth. She'd given me an unambiguous "or else." Still, there was a way to get at the dissident ring without risking legal action from my client. Former client. Whatever.

Since Robert didn't have a phone yet, I decided to drop by and see him. He needed to know that Ethan Jian was dead. One of us had to talk to Jian's wife. Perhaps while he was doing that, I could look into the crash. Between my combat driving courses and black ops work, I had some ideas on how someone could force another car off the road without making it look like a hit-and-run. As the investigation was shifting now, I had to look into the deaths of the other two men, Wei and Tan. Both of those seemed suspicious and curiously timed when I'd first learned of them. Now it was a pattern.

I resolved myself that as soon as I spoke to Robert, I had to dedicate the rest of my time to notifying these people about the danger they were in. That would have to be in person.

Newly energized and angry, I got in the Defender and drove a straight line to Robert Li's house.

My newfound invigoration died immediately when I arrived.

There was police tape across the door, a crime scene unit in the driveway, and a prowl car parked out front.

20

I watched the house for long enough that I realized it was becoming conspicuous.

There was a crime scene van in the driveway with evidence techs periodically returning to the truck. It was the San Jose PD squad car parked on the street out front that got my attention, or rather, the other way around. I clocked the cop watching me watching the house. I nodded to him and got out of the Defender. The police vehicle was parked with the driver's side facing the house, so the officer got out as I approached.

"May I help you, sir?"

"Yes, officer. I'm a friend of Robert Li's. I was supposed to meet him this morning. Can you tell me what's going on?"

"Not unless you're family," he said.

"Can you at least tell me if Robert is okay?"

"Afraid not, sir. Like I said, family only."

"Is there anyone I can contact? Do you at least know what hospital he was taken to?"

"Sir, I cannot give you any information unless you are family," the cop said, and the irritation of having to repeat himself a second time edged in on anger.

"I understand, officer. Can you tell me the name of the detective in charge, at least?" I knew people, such as some unscrupulous reporters and ambulance-chasing attorneys, might try posing as family or a close friend to get information. I didn't blame the cop for being guarded, even though it made my job difficult now.

"Rivera," he said.

The officer's nameplate read, "Petrowski", and he had two stripes on his sleeve.

I went back to the Defender and looked up the closest hospital, San Jose Regional Medical Center. Not wanting to arouse any more suspicion from the cop, I drove around the corner so I could make a call. It took a more than a little waiting and number-pad navigation, but I finally got the patient registry and asked if they had a Robert Li admitted. The admin told me they had no one by that name registered. Could be that he was registered as a John Doe, especially if the police feared for his safety. This was San Jose, however. Unless the state investigators knew Robert was involved, and there was no reason to believe they did, it didn't seem plausible that the San Jose Police would connect that thread to a death across the valley almost three weeks before. I called the San Jose Police, got the detective bureau, and left a message for Rivera, indicating I had information on Robert Li. I didn't, really, but it was the only way I could probably get a callback. I returned to the hotel, intending to call the other hospitals in the valley, just in case they hadn't brought him to the closest one.

I didn't want to call the county morgue, even though that cold and dark feeling of an inescapable, nauseating hunch lingered in the back of my mind, creeping like a rat.

As I passed through the hotel lobby, the manager flagged me from behind the counter. "Mr. Gage, you've got a package. A courier dropped it off for you earlier this morning."

"What did the courier look like?"

"Sorry, I wasn't the one to take it."

"No worries, thank you," I said and walked over. It hadn't been a courier service; the package was a heavy-grade security envelope that you could buy at any drugstore. I tore the seal as I made fast steps back to my room. There was another envelope inside. Once I was in my room, I tore open the second envelope. Inside, there were two small stacks of paper. A hand-written note was attached to the top one with a paperclip.

Matt—I didn't want this lying around my house after what happened at the center. Some of this is new to me, and we are definitely onto something. I got a hotel room and a new phone, like you instructed. Phone number is the same. Talk soon, Robert

So, Robert had dropped it off, not a courier service like the desk manager said. Without knowing what actually happened at his house or when, I couldn't know if he'd dropped it off before or after.

Meaning I still had no way of knowing if he was safe.

I flipped through the documents he sent me. The first were Robert's translation of Johnnie's notes on the community center. Johnnie wrote that the community center contacted someone Johnnie knew—the text didn't stipulate if they were a member of his network or not—regarding irregularities with their immigration status. The staff said this person's green card could be revoked if the matter wasn't resolved and that it could only be done in China. The staff organized a flight to Beijing for them. Johnnie wrote that upon arriving in Beijing, this person was arrested, charged with "incitement to subversion," and quickly convicted.

This wasn't "new news," but it was further confirmation that the community center was targeting enemies of the state and coercing them to return to China in order to stand trial. I now had two independent data-points describing forced repatriation. And that was beyond them tailing me, thinking I was Robert. God only knew what they'd have done that night if it hadn't been me.

The second collection of papers, four in total, was interesting, though I couldn't yet determine the relevance. They were transcriptions of Johnnie Zhou's meetings with a person named Fang Yìchén. I went back to the list of documents I'd photographed in Johnnie's safe. Fang Yìchén, known by his Americanized name, Lawrence Fang, was a professor of Asian-American studies at Stanford. According to the transcripts, Johnnie and Fang met about once a month going back to February. Curiously, Zhou didn't note what the meetings were about, just that they'd happened.

That Johnnie Zhou, a successful Chinese-American entrepreneur and exile, would meet with a professor of Asian-American studies did not strike me as odd. That he created a paper trail documenting the date, time, and location of those meetings, but not the substance, did. I opened up a browser on my laptop, accessing the internet through my VPN, and navigated to a map application. I looked up each of the locations Johnnie documented. They were primarily restaurants, tea shops, and cafes located throughout Silicon Valley. The May and June meetings took place in local parks.

My first thought—this looked exactly like a record of someone meeting with a source.

Was Lawrence Fang an asset that Johnnie was trying to cultivate? It certainly looked that way.

Fang was listed separately in Johnnie's notebooks from the rest of his network. But why?

I tried Robert, but he didn't answer. Then I found Fang's number in Johnnie's notes and called. It went to voicemail, so I left him a message saying I wanted to speak to him about Johnnie.

It was a risk, for sure. If the police already knew about him, or if Elizabeth did, they'd warn him off, and I could find myself having some uncomfortable conversations.

While I was waiting to see if Fang would return my call, I had another agonizing call to make. Johnnie and three members of his network were dead. I didn't know if Robert was okay, but at a minimum his house had been broken into. Lives were at risk, and I was the only one who knew. Or, rather, the good guy.

More to the point, I'd found out their names by breaking into Johnnie Zhou's house and finding a pair of ciphered notebooks the police didn't even know about.

I could call each of them and warn them, though they'd have no reason to believe me, and I couldn't share *how* I knew they were in danger, only that they were.

Calling each of the individual police jurisdictions would be a waste of time. They wouldn't take me seriously without proof, which I couldn't provide.

The only people I could truly contact about this were the state investigators; they were the only ones with an inkling of the truth—although they didn't know the Chinese government may be involved. And they had no reason to believe me. Not without proof. If I shared my proof, they'd charge me with a slew of crimes, and I had no reason to believe they'd even act on the evidence.

But if I didn't do *something*, these people were going to get killed.

God help me, I called Nugent.

And it went straight to voicemail.

How the mighty have fallen. I'd once caused an actual coup, and now I'm getting ghosted by a state policeman.

I called him again and then texted.

After a few minutes, he called. "What do you want, Gage?"

"I got your message. You can leave my friends out of this," I said. *Let him think he's got the upper hand.*

"Be a damn shame if that place shuts down," he said, clearly having fun with it.

"Listen, I'd like to talk to you. Reset things. I'm no longer working for Elizabeth Zhou and was hoping I could turn some leads over to you. Maybe you can do something with it."

"I doubt that, shamus."

Gangster patter? He was really laying it on thick now.

"Look, I think Johnnie Zhou uncovered a Chinese espionage operation here in the Bay Area. I think that's what got him killed. Three other people he was connected to have also died in the last two months. I'm afraid more are at risk."

I couldn't hear anything on the other side except for Nugent breathing through his mouth.

"I think you got a wild imagination, Gage. I think you tried convincing a grieving daughter that her daddy was involved in a spy ring."

"That's not what this is, and I think you know it. Why else would you keep that house locked up?"

"Gage, I don't want to hear from you again. Go home, and I might just leave your friends alone. You stay in this, and everyone goes down for the trouble. You get me?"

"People are going to die, Nugent, and it's going to be on you," I said and immediately wished I hadn't.

"You threatening me, Gage?"

"You know damned well I'm not. I'm trying to get you off your ass and do your job."

"I'm going to do my job all right. Get a lawyer." And he hung up.

What I really needed was some advice. Nate was now the only person I could speak to. I texted him, asked if we could meet for a drink and that it was related to the case.

Three hours ticked by, and I didn't hear from anyone.

I called Robert again. There was nothing at any of the local hospitals, and the detective hadn't returned my call. I'd also struck out with the airport hotels. Robert would've told them not to give his name out or acknowledge he was staying there.

My phone rang, and it was a number I didn't recognize.

I took the call. "This is Matt."

"Mr. Gage, hello, this is Lawrence Fang, returning your call."

"Thank you for getting back to me, Professor Fang."

"You said you wanted to speak to me about Johnnie Zhou?"

There was no way to know if the Chinese already knew about Robert or if they found out by following us out of Chinatown that day. Regardless, I could still conclude that my pushing Robert into going to that community center had escalated this situation. I didn't know if he was alive or dead, just that his home had been burglarized and he wasn't returning calls now. I was rapidly running out of other options.

"Yes, would it be possible for me to come see you?"

21

Fang gave me the address of a coffee shop on the outskirts of Stanford's campus and suggested we meet there around four, which was in about half an hour. Palo Alto's architecture was a mix of California mission and tech-company glass. The coffee shop Fang suggested was in a row of buildings that was more of the former—white stucco walls and red-orange Mediterranean roofs.

He texted me to say that he was inside and could he get me anything. I was keyed up enough from worrying about Robert and didn't want to spike my heart rate any further, so I told him a bottle of water and would meet him outside. Now at least I knew what to look for.

A man in khaki pants, a gray jacket, and blue shirt emerged from the cafe carrying a coffee in one hand and a water in the other. Though middle-aged, his hair was thick and jet black to the point it carried a sheen. We locked eyes, and I nodded. He acknowledged the gesture, and I closed the distance between us, extending my hand for the water. I took it and switched it to my left hand so I could shake his.

"Professor Fang, thanks for meeting me on short notice," I said.

"Of course. Johnnie's death was tragic and unexpected. I am still coming to grips with it," he said.

"Would you care to take a walk?"

"That would be nice."

"How long have you taught at the university?"

Fang said, "Two years. I'm visiting faculty on loan from Peking University. I'm here as part of an exchange program."

"Were you and Johnnie close?" I asked once we were moving.

"We hadn't known each other long, though I'd known him by reputation for some time. May I ask what your interest is?"

"I'm a freelance investigator. A news organization is looking into his death."

Those statements were all technically true, even if I was stretching it in context.

"Why is this group interested in Johnnie's death?" he asked. I noted a subtle quizzical skepticism in Fang's voice.

"There's some speculation that it may have been intentional."

"I see," Fang said. "And what do the police think about this theory?"

"Have you spoken with them?"

"I have not. And I have no desire to," he said in a warning tone. "I've nothing to offer them, I'm afraid."

"You didn't contact them after you learned of Zhou's death? May I ask why?"

"As I said, Mr. Gage, I had nothing to offer them. My relationship with Johnnie was cordial, though not particularly deep. I would characterize us more as acquaintances than friends."

"How did you first meet Mr. Zhou?"

"I teach a course on the history of Chinese-American relations. As a successful entrepreneur, I'd hoped I could get him to deliver a guest lecture on his experiences starting a business as an immigrant." We stopped at a corner, and Fang pointed to the north. "There's a nice park up this way," he said, then continued his train of thought. "We met a few times to discuss the possibility of his lecture. Naturally, we discussed China, Chinese-American relations, history, that sort of thing. It was just a few times. I learned about his death in the news."

"I must have been misinformed. I was led to believe you met with him more frequently." An image of Johnnie's notes flashed in my mind, and I could clearly see the ledger-like entries describing monthly contacts going back almost a year.

"Indeed, you must have been."

"You mentioned you discussed Chinese-American relations. Did you ever discuss politics?"

"What a curious question," Fang said.

"Seems like something a professor of Chinese-American relations would talk about, no? Particularly since the tensions between the US and China are about as tense now as they were since the mid-nineties."

"As I said, our relationship was not particularly close. I wanted him to speak on business matters, rather than political ones. I didn't know Mr. Zhou's politics and didn't know him well enough to ask."

We reached the small park and found welcome shade beneath a large, leafy tree.

"Surely, Mr. Zhou would have mentioned his activism to you. Would this not be a major part of his lecture? It certainly informed his experience as an immigrant and how he chose to spend his time here in the United States. Our reporting tells us that he was involved in the Tiananmen movement in 1989 and that he stayed committed to the pro-democracy movement in China."

I was entering dangerous territory here. The Chinese government controlled nearly everything, and one had to assume that university professors were required to be CCP members just to get a job. CIA knew Chinese intelligence agencies used connected professors as talent spotters—just as we did. All that to say, I had to assume Fang's loyalty lay with the state, unless and until he proved otherwise. The only reason I was having this conversation was I wanted to understand why he and Johnnie had met monthly up until his death, and why he felt that was worth documenting.

"I knew he was involved in the student protests," Fang said softly. "You must appreciate, Mr. Gage, that is a highly sensitive and polarizing event in our culture. It might be the same as asking someone their opinion on the Million Man March or the January 6th insurrection. Even now, it is something discussed only among close friends and relatives."

"I can appreciate that." I knew from Robert how charged these conversations could get and how paranoid people could be. You didn't need to spend much time in oppressive regimes to understand why. If people feared their government enough to constantly fear for their safety, the calculus of ratting out a friend or even a family member out of self-preservation got a hell of a lot easier. "During those times that you met, was it always just the two of you or had you ever met with a larger group? I know you are both active in the Chinese-American community. Curious if he'd ever introduced you to some colleagues."

"Unfortunately, no. That would have been nice. I'd hoped to get Mr. Zhou to speak with my students because I believed his successes in business served as an example of how someone can bridge the political divide between our countries. Perhaps, given time, we could have established the kind of relationship you are describing." Fang slowed his pace and turned to face me. "Now I have a question for you, if you'd indulge me."

"Seems fair," I said.

"You said you are a freelance investigator for a news organization. I'm curious, perhaps in an academic sense, how they learned of Mr. Zhou's death and what their interest is in it."

He'd asked me a version of this earlier, and I thought I'd deflected it well enough. Apparently not.

"The police are calling his death a suicide, but they've had his home tied up for three weeks and are still calling it a crime scene. Our understanding is that they haven't even released the body back to his daughter so she can bury him."

"Have you spoken with his daughter?"

"I have, though I'm trying to be respectful by keeping my distance."

"What do you think of the police's efforts into this matter?"

"Seems strange to me they're calling his home a crime scene for three weeks. These kinds of things are usually cleared in a few days. Feels like there's a question to be asked there."

"Indeed, there does. You asked me about his associations. Have you spoken with any of them?"

"A few. He was well known, as you know. There have also been a few deaths in the Chinese-American community lately. Probably unrelated, though I think it bears asking."

Fang offered a slightly sad smile, one which I could see him giving to students who perhaps wasn't living up to their potential. He extended a hand. "Unfortunately, I'm due back at the university for a staff meeting. Mr. Gage, thank you for contacting me and giving me the opportunity to share what I know. I don't know that I was much help, but as you say in this country, every little bit helps, yes?"

I took his hand and shook it. "Thank you for your time, Mr. Fang."

I watched the professor fade into the distance and then turned to head back to my car.

Nate texted me back and said he had time to meet for a fast drink after work if I was nearby. I told him I was, just not in Palo Alto. Nate suggested a place called the British Banker's Club in Menlo Park.

The bar, true to its name, was a converted bank. Tech-bro happy hour was in full swing, and I was grateful to quickly find Nate inside. We shook hands. "I got us a table on the roof," he said. I followed him upstairs to the deck. We put in our drink order—a themed cocktail for him, some joke about offshore banking, and a local hazy IPA for me. I didn't say anything until the drinks arrived.

"So, what's going on?" Nate asked. "You look... Matt, I've seen you in every situation our profession can throw at a person. This is the first time I've seen you look scared."

"Well, in the span of about twelve hours, two men tried to kill me and Elizabeth fired me. Then she threatened to sue me if I persisted with the case."

Nate held an unbroken gaze, took a sip of his drink, and said, "I think I'm going to need some backstory."

"I don't even know where to start. I stumbled on something much bigger than I thought would be there. And worse. Maybe its best if I just reconstruct this for you chronologically."

"Okay," Nate said, drawing the word out with his skepticism.

"I told you Johnnie was funding a network of activists and dissidents. A lot of those guys are journalists. I tried contacting them, and no one would return my call. Eventually, I forced a meeting with one; his name is Robert

Li. I'm telling you this in the strictest confidence. You cannot let his name get out."

"I know how to protect a source, Matthew. Li...he was the one who discovered the operation?"

"Correct. I went to check it out. I couldn't get anywhere, so I recruited Robert to help." I walked Nate through Robert's research into the community outreach center and their program of coercing suspected dissidents into forced repatriation to stand trial for crimes against the state. How they'd tried to get Robert to come in already and about the others. I also told him about the oddly coincidental meeting with David Hu.

"Our counterintelligence people have suspected the Chinese had something going on here for some time, but they couldn't say exactly what. Just indicators," Nate said.

"Leaving Chinatown, I picked up a tail. Robert admitted to being coerced into downloading an app at the center, so he could leave. I'm certain they got on his phone and were tracking us. I ditched the tail, got Robert to safety, but kept the phone. Eventually, they forced a confrontation with me."

"Any idea who they were?"

"Not sure. My guess is they're Chinese special ops attached to the PLA's intelligence division. Like we do with the Army SF guys in the Special Activities Center. I was poking around the operation Johnnie discovered, they followed me, and we tangled a bit. I think they'd have killed me if they had the chance."

"What happened to them?" Nate asked tentatively.

"I got the drop on them. One probably needs back surgery. I shot the other in the leg. The next morning, I went to check on Robert. His house was a crime scene. I couldn't get anything out of the cops there. Robert left me some material with the clerk at my hotel, notes of Johnnie's that he'd translated, but I don't know *when* he left them. I haven't heard from him since. And I destroyed his phone."

"These notes...what were they?"

I realized the corner I'd backed myself into.

"I wasn't getting answers from the police, so I broke into Johnnie's house to look around. Elizabeth okayed it. Wrote up a limited POA."

"For breaking-and-entering?" Nate deadpanned.

"Not exactly," I said. "She did tell me she didn't care if I had to bend the rules to get answers. The police had her father's house locked up and wouldn't tell her why. I knew I could be in and out without disturbing the crime scene, so I went in."

Nate didn't blow a cork, or even glower. He just nodded as though I were debriefing him, which, in a way, I suppose I was. Perhaps it was a show of solidarity since he'd violated some sacred Agency rules by disclosing his identity to a former agent, Zhou. Or maybe he was just as angry as I was that the officials didn't seem to be doing anything to solve his friend's killing.

"I didn't want to tell you before, in case things broke badly."

"I understand."

"Police removed what you'd expect as evidence. I reasoned that if they were still considering his home a crime scene, there had to be something else there that maybe they hadn't yet found. I found a concealed safe in his bedroom, built into the floorboards. I figured out the cipher and opened it. Inside, he had two notebooks, a burner phone, and a key. The notebooks were written mostly in Mandarin, except for the American names of his contacts. I researched all of them and found that two died just before Johnnie did. The third was killed two days ago. I called two, but no one would speak to me except Robert Li. He and Johnnie went back to the Tiananmen days. There was one more name in the notes, and the weird thing is it was listed separately from the rest of his contacts. Lawrence Fang. I looked him up; he's a Stanford professor. Johnnie documented that he'd met up with Fang about ten times over the last year. I set up a meet with Fang, and he lied about how many times he and Johnnie had connected. Claimed the only conversations he'd had with Johnnie were about doing a guest lecture for his class in Chinese-American studies."

"That sounds bogus to me," Nate said.

"I thought so too. My gut is Johnnie wanted to recruit him, but Fang got spooked when Johnnie died. Given the number of people in Johnnie's orbit who have died, that's not an injudicious call to make."

Nate nodded and was quiet for a time. I'd given him a lot to process.

"Talk to me about Elizabeth," he said.

"Seems me asking questions about her inheritance got her dad's part-ner, Benjamin Blake, to reconsider the payout and that suicide clause. He's decided to give Elizabeth everything Johnnie's estate would've had he died in any other way."

"So, why'd she fire you?"

"I don't know. She got really mad, really fast. There's a couple state police involved in the investigation. They tried to scare me off. Then, to convince me, they decided to make trouble for the bar I work out of in Santa Monica. There's an office upstairs they let me use. Then they called her and threatened her with a bunch of bullshit. She got scared, said she was worried they'd get her disbarred. I reminded her that she hired me because she thought the police were covering something up and that I was close to uncovering the what. She kind of lost her shit then. I don't know, Nate. It feels a bit like what she wanted me to do was scare Blake into settling for the full amount."

"That doesn't sound like her, though I don't know anything about her financial situation. And it is a lot of money. For what it's worth, when she first talked to me, she was genuinely distressed. If it was an act, she's in the wrong line of work."

"Nate, we can't quit this now. I can't look at everything I've learned and conclude anything other than your friend, Johnnie Zhou, uncovered a Chinese espionage operation. They found out and killed him to keep it quiet. And there are three other people they've silenced. *And* I don't know where Robert is."

"Matt, I'm going to ask you a hard question, and I want you to think on this before you answer me."

"Okay."

"Why is this your problem to solve?"

"I understand what you're saying. You have to—"

"Matthew."

"Because people are dying, damn it. There's no reason to think that's going to stop if I quit. I've tried to contact some, but they won't take my calls —there's no reason to believe I'm not part of it. What should I do, Nate? Walk away? Let people get murdered?" An especially dark and bitter Irish writer once said, *There are no prayers for the dying and only tears for the dead.*

I'd done most of the talking to this point, and I drained half my beer in one go.

"This is...complicated," Nate said. "I can talk with our CI guys, see what they think."

"No, that's not fast enough. I think we need to involve the FBI." That was a hard conclusion for me to come to. I didn't like the Feds, and I trusted them even less, given our history. This was also their job. The FBI had the legal responsibility for domestic counterintelligence. The Agency could advise, but they could not act. "I can't contact them, so I was hoping you might."

"We don't want to do that," Nate said.

"Someone tried to kill me, Nate. Your CI team has to involve the Feebs at some point," I said, using CIA slang for the FBI. "There's nothing you can do here."

Nate held his drink up and contemplated its contents, but he didn't drink. Instead, he was quiet.

He didn't meet my gaze when he finally spoke. His eyes were on the table, then they went to the skyline. Anywhere but me.

"I hadn't wanted to tell you this, for reasons that'll be obvious in a minute. I don't see how I can avoid it though. I know you, and if you don't get the answer you want, you'll just go and do it. Hopefully, this encourages some discretion. Johnnie Zhou wasn't just a former agent," Nate said. "He was an active one." He held up his hands before I could object, like he was pushing the words back down my throat before I got them out. "I already know everything you're going to say. You're absolutely right. We've both skirted the line here, so let's just call it even."

I didn't know about *even*, though this wasn't the time to bring it up.

"Johnnie hadn't been an active agent in a decade, and anyway, he'd moved his family to the States and become a citizen. Then, about two years ago, someone from the China Mission Center wanted to reactivate him. They were reviewing old case files and got the idea he might be perfect for something they had in mind. He'd already had his network going before I tapped him for this. What we were using him for was to leverage contacts back in China to organize a resistance movement. Many of the protests you've seen in recent years...that's his organization. The journalists he's running, many of them wrote for anti-communist, underground websites or to help support the uprisings."

"Stop," I said. I'd been so caught up in Nate's telling that I'd missed the most important part of it. Now, warning lights were going off like a klaxon behind my eyes. "You told me you were running an Agency-backed VC firm."

"I am."

"But that's not all you're doing. What the actual fuck, Nate?"

Part of that CIA/FBI separation of powers I'd mentioned earlier? Well, that also forbade the Agency from conducting intelligence operations within the United States.

"Calm down, Matt. We've got an agreement with the Bureau. We're not running the operations here; we're just running them *from* here."

I tried to dial myself back from a hard boil to an angry simmer. I knew why Nate couldn't tell me. Operational details were highly classified and compartmented. Even if I'd have still been in CIA, he couldn't tell me about this unless I was part of it. That he made me part of it, tangentially, without telling me, was what pissed me off. Even though I'd have done the same thing in his place.

"Let's see if I've got this right," I said, my voice low. "Johnnie dies. You don't know if it was suicide or not. You're worried that if it's not, your operation might be compromised. If that happens, it probably comes out that Johnnie knew your real name and you had a personal relationship. Either Elizabeth came to you with concerns, or you planted the seed. The cops ruled his death a suicide but wouldn't release the body or turn the house over to next-of-kin, and you were worried they found something. What you hoped I could do was figure out how he died and whether or not you were exposed. You couldn't go to the FBI or even the Agency's CI division, so you called me. How am I doing so far?"

"You're off the mark on a couple of minor points, but that's basically it, yes. If you couldn't connect the dots, I was sure no one else could. The fact that you put all this together is a testament to your skills as a case officer."

"I don't like being manipulated, Nate. And, I don't like being deceived." Obvious statements, those. Still, I felt like I needed to voice them. "I appreciate you have an operation to protect, but four men are dead. And it might have been five. That's on top of the attendant national fucking security concerns. So, you need to speak with the FBI, and you need to do it now. You told me you guys had a memo with the FBI, right?"

"Their head of counterintelligence, yes."

"Okay, then use it."

"The reason I don't want to just up and call the Bureau is they'll come in guns blazing and blow up our operation, one we've spent three years planning. I will talk with our head of CI, who will talk with his counterpart at the Bureau, and we'll get someone detailed who can act discreetly. That will take time."

"We don't have any time."

"Just be patient."

Says the guy no one is shooting at.

"What am I supposed to do while I'm waiting to see if the CIA is going to do the right thing?"

"Let me talk to Elizabeth. I'll see if I can smooth things over."

"That's not the point, Nate. People are getting killed. I was almost one of them."

"It's part of the point, Matt. You need the money. And Elizabeth still needs the thing she hired you to do."

"How do we know I didn't do that for her already? From where I sit, it sure seems like she got what she was after."

"Just let me talk to her, and we'll see. Okay?"

Maybe I was jumping at shadows, or maybe I just thought everyone in this thing had some kind of agenda. This felt like a blatant play to keep me engaged in the case so I wouldn't go to the authorities and just hand over everything I knew.

I pushed my chair back, needing to get away from that place. Be by myself for a bit before I said something I couldn't take back.

"Matt," he said after me.

I just left and drove a twisted route to the hotel. I wasn't any calmer when I got there.

A man I'd trusted more than anyone else had lied to me and used me, and he'd done it because he'd fucked up and was worried he was going to get caught. He wanted me to save his career—when no one had stood by to save mine.

The phone rang around seven.

Another number I didn't recognize.

"Gage," I said.

"It's David Hu," he said. This was a different number than he'd used last time.

"Now's not the best time."

"I'm calling to give you a heads-up. My guy at Los Altos PD said they're naming Robert Li a suspect in Johnnie Zhou's murder. If you know where he is, you need to tell him to come forward before this gets any worse."

22

"We need to meet," Hu said. "Now."

"Hold on, chief. I asked you for details on this before, and you gave me shit. I'm not jumping in my car and hauling off to wherever you say without something better than a *trust me*."

"Do you know how much trouble you're in, Gage?"

"Why? I haven't done anything." That *you* know of. "Anyway, who is this Robert Li person?"

That gave me pause. I'd never mentioned knowing Robert to Hu before, so it struck me as off that he'd bring it up now.

"Cut the shit, Gage," he pressed. "Robert Li is a reporter and a friend of Johnnie Zhou. And if you don't know him, maybe you can explain why there's a paper with your name on it in his house. He's in the wind, so we can't ask him. I don't need to be a detective to put that together."

"Look, David, I don't know where Li is, and that's the truth. If you want to share information, I'm happy to do it. But you don't get to push me around just because you're a cop. I haven't done anything. Now, what have you got?"

"Not over the phone." He gave me an address in South San Francisco and a "gracious" forty-five minutes to get there.

So much for a low-key evening of drinking and self-pity.

Hopefully, this meant that Robert was still alive. Maybe Hu could tell me what the hell happened at Robert's house.

Or how he knew about Robert to begin with.

If this case had any more angles, it'd be an Escher painting.

I packed up my computer and brought it out to my Defender, locking it in one of the storage boxes. Seemed like a fair number of break-ins in my orbit lately, and I was better off not leaving things around.

I didn't want to meet Hu. However, I was more concerned with what would happen if I blew him off. Maybe I could've gotten away with lying to him, saying I'd already gone home to LA, but that was easy enough to disprove for a cop who could run plates.

Forty-five minutes wasn't particularly generous, especially in evening traffic to go the thirty-five miles from my hotel to South SF, but I did my best. I reasoned that if I got pulled over, I'd just tell the cop I was going to meet another cop, and they'd just cancel each other out.

Located just before the airport, South San Francisco was the grittier, industrial twin to the dying robber baron to the north. I met Sergeant Hu, outside of his jurisdiction, in a business park off Railroad Avenue. There were four low-slung, white buildings with blue trim and the minimum number of windows allowed by the fire code. Hu told me to meet him at building 432. The businesses were all shuttered for the day, and the parking lot was bathed in a yellow-orange glow from the streetlights. Hu, somewhat stereotypically of a cop, drove a purple Dodge Challenger R/T with silver racing stripes on the hood, roof, and trunk.

That car was loud, even when the engine was off.

I didn't bother with a parking space, just pulled up near Hu's car and got out.

"Okay, I'm here. Maybe now you can explain why."

Hu wasn't in uniform. Like the last time I'd met him, he was in jeans and a zip-up hoodie that looked a little small by an order of magnitude.

"Where is Robert Li?"

"I already told you, I don't know. I really hope I didn't drive all the way out here just to answer that question again." It occurred to me that Hu didn't know where I was staying, so I decided to keep it vague. "You told me on the phone that a paper was found in Li's house with my name on it."

"Yeah," he said.

"Was this connected to the break-in?"

When someone isn't good at lying or concealing information, it was fairly easy to tell. Other than undercovers, I assumed most cops were only good at this when the power dynamic was in their favor. Hu didn't realize yet that it wasn't. The subtle change in his expression told me he hadn't anticipated I'd known about the break-in.

Unfortunately, he covered for it aggressively well.

"If you know about that, you know where he is," Hu reasoned.

"Not necessarily. Anyone can drive by a house on a city street. Yes, I do know Robert. Not well, but we're acquainted. I asked him a few questions about Johnnie Zhou." Again, not *un*true, just not the whole truth.

"Are you hiding him?"

"No. But what if I was?"

"Then you'd need to stop it immediately and turn him over. For his good as much as your own."

"Turn him over to who?"

"To the Los Altos PD. I can broker that. It's probably better that I do."

"Why?"

"Because I can massage it to say you're helping out with the investigation. It'll go better for you."

"You keep saying stuff like that, but again, I'm not involved here. If the Los Altos police are looking for Robert Li, good on them. I can't help them, and I'm happy to explain that to your friend. I don't understand, at all, why you keep telling me I need to cooperate. I haven't committed any crime. And why am I even talking to *you*? Where is this friend of yours? Why am I not talking to him?"

"We can have this conversation in an interview room, if you'd rather, Gage."

"Oh, let's do that. Then my lawyer can have a chance to ask some interesting questions, like why you're involved in an investigation way the hell outside your jurisdiction. Or why you keep mentioning some phantom cop but won't give me a name. Or saying I need to cooperate so it'll 'go better' for me."

Hu uncrossed his arms, placing his hands on his hips. Still aggressive, but a little less guarded. His expression softened slightly, though it still looked as malleable as granite and as friendly as battery acid.

"No bullshit, Gage, do you have a way to get in touch with Li?"

"Why is he, all of a sudden, a person of interest in Zhou's murder?"

"Because they think Li was one of the last people to see him alive. Please, this is important."

And that was when I knew he was lying.

The Los Altos Police hadn't been involved in this thing for weeks, as near as I could tell. And officially, this was still a suicide investigation. Hu never once mentioned the state investigators who'd taken this thing over. When we spoke before, I mentioned in passing that the state was involved, but not that they'd swooped in and yanked it from the Los Altos department. Hu not bringing that up at the time didn't seem too out of place; it was believable that a cop might try to work around it. But Hu saying nothing now was definitely conspicuous. If he really did have a buddy in a local department feeding him information, this all would be top of mind.

So, the first question was, what does a San Francisco gang cop want with Robert Li?

"I'm surprised your friend is still getting information," I said.

"Why?"

"Well, my understanding is the CBI has taken this over entirely. I've spoken to them."

"Yeah, but the local PD is still helping out. Eyes on the ground. That sort of thing happens." He covered well enough, but not to a trained eye.

"So...look, David, I don't know where he is, but if I hear from him I'll contact you. That cool?"

"I hope you do. This can be a lonely place without friends."

I wanted out of there fast.

I backed up to the Defender and was gone.

Hu's story clawed at me as I was leaving the business park. There was a clue I was missing. Unable to shake the feeling, I turned right off Railroad Avenue, taking one of the boundary roads on the office park's outer edge. I was waiting for the light to change, the Defender's outline hidden in the shadow of a building, when I saw Hu's car turn right onto my street, heading south. The light changed, and I decided to follow him.

It wasn't easy. He drove like someone inoculated against tickets.

Still, following someone who doesn't know they're being followed isn't that hard. We wound our way through the industrial parks to pick up the 101 southbound. I trailed Hu to San Mateo and a residential neighborhood not far from downtown. Modest, single family homes, nothing ostentatious. Hu pulled into a driveway on Twelfth Avenue.

I stopped several homes down and turned off the car.

Keeping tabs on Sergeant Hu seemed like a good idea.

I'd mentioned before that despite California's rather extensive privacy protection laws, I kept AirTags with magnetic cases in my car. No, they aren't registered to me, and I only tracked them on a burner phone with a dummy account.

Taking one of them, I removed the jacket I'd worn when meeting Hu, put on a ball cap and glasses. There wasn't anyone on the street, most of the shades were closed. I walked past what I presumed was Hu's house. It had a stubby driveway and the long Challenger practically hung over the sidewalk. When I was behind it, I bent down to tie my shoe and, as I did, slipped the AirTag under the bumper. I walked to the end of the block, looped around to my car, and drove back to the hotel.

———————

It was about nine thirty when I finally got back to the hotel. I poured a drink, thought about my next steps. Robert still hadn't returned my call, and I was long past being officially worried about him. I didn't want to leave messages on his phone in case someone was monitoring it, so that meant I just had to wait.

Which I was really good at.

I couldn't figure Hu's angle.

He was a bad liar, but that didn't tell me anything. When I first met him, my instinct was that the state cops had planted him to see what I knew. That made less sense as time wore on. I couldn't see them viewing me as a threat, just an irritant. And one they believed they'd squashed by virtue of threatening Elizabeth with charges. Or going after my friends at Ray's.

That left the question of who was David Hu and what was he to this?

I'd confirmed he was a cop. Or, at least, there was an officer assigned to the Chinatown bureau named David Hu. The ID he'd shown me looked real. I didn't think Hu was lying to me about who he was.

I couldn't see the connection between Hu and Li. In researching Li, I couldn't find any evidence he'd ever written a story about the SFPD. Li certainly didn't have any connection to Chinese organized crime. So, what was it?

Sleep didn't come easy that night. I couldn't turn my mind off, continually searching for linkages between Hu and Li. Eventually, I nodded off. It was a fitful sleep that barely qualified as rest, the kind where you're dimly aware that you're sleeping.

The next morning, I had notifications of missed calls and voicemails.

These were from Kim, my targeting officer colleague.

I scanned the voicemail transcript and saw she was just asking me to call back. My heart rate spiked, and I was fully awake in an instant. I called back, but then realized Kim would be at the office until roughly lunchtime for me. I showered, and my stomach reminded me that I'd only had scotch for dinner, so I went out to stretch my legs and search for an egg sandwich. Walking back to the hotel, I got a call and nearly dropped my coffee reaching for the phone.

Kim returned my call much earlier than I'd expected.

"Hey, Matt, is now a good time?"

"Yeah, of course. Thanks for calling. Are you still at work?"

"I ran out to my car, so I just have a few minutes."

The Agency's parking lot was bigger than some cities I'd been in, and it was a long walk to the building. I was not going to waste her time.

"So, I looked at that picture you sent me," she said. "It wasn't a code. Well, it was, but not like you think."

"I don't follow."

"It's GPS coordinates. It just took me a minute to realize that's what I was looking at. I looked them up, and they're all places in the San Francisco metro area."

Dead drops.

"If you've got something to write with, I can give them to you." She read them off, and I wrote them down. "There's a phrase after each one, which

seems like a physical description to me. Like, 'loose brick' or 'tree hole.'"
She gave me those as well, and I matched them up to the correct locations.

"Kim, this is amazing. Thank you. I can't tell you how much I appreciate this."

"I hope it helps."

I paused a moment. "Can I ask why you're helping me? When we spoke last time, you seemed like you wanted to keep me at arm's length."

"Yeah, that was a little rude, and I'm sorry. You got shafted, and it wasn't right. I'm glad I could help out."

"I hope to never be in Washington again, but if I am, I owe you a drink."

Kim laughed and wished me luck.

I had several hours to kill, and it was time to do some digging.

With the benefit of hindsight, what I should have been doing at that moment was calling the remaining members of Johnnie's network and warning them. My first attempts had failed, though how hard did I really try? I bounced off a few hangups and pivoted to what I knew. Setting up a collection target, which got me Robert. These people, knowingly or not, risked their lives, and someone had to tell them.

They would get no other warning.

What I did do was...not that.

Instead, I drove to the first of the locations that Kim identified for me.

The four locations were spread throughout the Bay Area. One was in Silicon Valley, one on the San Francisco State University campus, another in Golden Gate State Park, and the last one on the UC Berkley campus. The valley and SFSU sites were both busts. Whatever had been there, if anything, was gone. However, what I found in a hollowed-out tree in Golden Gate State Park was worth the time and then some.

Zhou's tradecraft again impressed me. Nate taught him well, and Zhou had obviously taken those lessons to heart. He'd put a thumb drive inside a zip-lock bag and set it under a rock in a little hole in a tree.

I grabbed the baggie, ran back to the Defender, and fired up my laptop. It was a collection of document files and pictures. Scanning through these,

I could puzzle out that Ryan Tan, their now-deceased creator, was a hacker on top of being a computer engineer. Not only had Tan gotten into the community center's servers, but he'd traced them back to their origin.

The Ministry of Public Security.

The "community center" was, effectively, a clandestine site for the Chinese secret police.

I called Nate and told him we needed to meet immediately. He suggested the Stanford Shopping Center, and I went there straight away.

To be honest, exposing a Chinese intelligence operation outside a Stanford Pottery Barn was not my bingo card for that day.

"I need to vet these," Nate said.

"Figured you might. I made copies for you." We already knew it was the Chinese, so having the exact agency narrowed down didn't fundamentally change the case. Knowing that would help us plan our response, however. You could expect a different style of operation from the PLA's Intelligence Department as you could from the Ministry of State Security. "What do you make of MPS being behind this?"

Nate's mouth twisted into a concerned pucker. "I don't know yet. It's troubling, for sure. They aren't normally expeditionary. Inside China, they handle counterintelligence the way our FBI does, but there's so much distrust between MSS, MPS, and the PLA, each of them has some facility for it. The thing that really bothers me is what your source is reporting about them being in multiple cities worldwide. Do you think he'd be willing to talk to us?"

"If I could find him," I said, warily. "Nate, I still don't know if he's in the wind or he's dead."

"Damn it. And you can't go to the police. He's the only living connection we have to Johnnie."

"I know," I said, more angrily than I meant to.

Nate put up some defensive hands. "If he turns up, let me know. Meantime, I'm going to run this down."

"Johnnie never said anything to you?"

Nate shook a negative. "I told him if he was going to organize dissidents outside of our work together, I didn't want to know about it. I had to wall him off from our activities for exactly this reason. I told you before, *our* CI guys and the China Mission Center had inklings there was something going on here, but it was vague. We certainly didn't know it was as active as this seems to be. We were worried about crossing the line into running a domestic intelligence operation. In retrospect, maybe I should've been a little more keyed into what he was doing."

"There's one more thing," I said.

"There usually seems to be," Nate quipped dryly.

"Remember that cop I told you about, David Hu? The one whose story wasn't adding up? I think he might actually be an asset."

"You have proof?"

"As much as we ever do. He's got knowledge of Johnnie's death, claiming it came from a Los Altos cop whom he won't name. Now he's trying to pressure me into giving up Robert's location, saying he's wanted in connection with Johnnie's death."

"That might actually be true, if the police knew about him," Nate said.

"I don't see how they would."

"You can't know what was in Johnnie's files that they might've removed. Don't assume you're the only one capable of finding valuable intelligence in his house."

Valid point.

It was hard to convey a gut feeling in conversation. Knowing someone was dirty was a lot like being in love. You just *know*.

I also couldn't be sure Nate urging caution here wasn't to keep me from provoking the police.

"Are we at the point where we involve the Feebs?"

"Matt, I'm working on it," he said.

This was putting Nate up against a wall, even if it was his own doing. Local cops were one thing; he could hide from that. Even the state guys, I had no doubts Nate could outmaneuver them. The Feds were a different matter. Even I would admit, grudgingly, that their counterintelligence guys were pretty good. Once they started digging into this, it was nearly a certainty they'd make the links between Johnnie Zhou, his network, the MPS station, and Nate's op. Since Johnnie was dead, it was *possible* they wouldn't figure out that Nate revealed his true name to his once and future asset.

"How we came by this is problematic," Nate said, hedging.

"You can tell them it's original source HUMINT. Technically true. That should keep them from pushing into the provenance too much. Slap a cryptonym on it and call it day."

"You know it's not that simple. We can't manufacture sources. I'm also not sure that holds up if this turns into a criminal investigation. Which it undoubtedly will if what you say is true about this cop."

I regarded Nate for the span of a few quiet breaths. His expression was unreadable. He still wanted to handle this inhouse. Perhaps even within the confines of the team he had here. Nate was balancing on a dangerous edge.

I said nothing else.

Tacitly, it meant I agreed to play it his way, for now.

We shook hands, and I passed the palmed flash drive with Ryan Tan's files over to Nate.

I returned to my hotel and started collecting the phone numbers for Johnnie's contacts so I could begin reaching out to them. Those who were local, I'd go see personally. Those in LA, I could also handle. The couple of people who were farther flung might be a bit more of a challenge, and I'd just have to figure that out. The money I'd burn on plane tickets was worth it.

My phone rang.

It was Elizabeth.

I answered professionally, "Good morning."

"Hey, Matt," she said and then let it hang.

Obviously, this would require some prompting. "What can I do for you?"

"Right, sorry. This is a little awkward for me. Um. Shit. Sorry."

"Take your time," I said.

"Can we just meet for a drink and dinner, so I can apologize for being an asshole?"

It's a rare woman who can pull that phrase off and still sound dignified, but Elizabeth did. I laughed.

"That's not necessary. You're the client, and I work at your discretion.

You've got a right to cancel my contract at any point. I also understand your reasons and the position they put you in."

"Can we meet anyway? I'd like to have this conversation in person."

"I suppose," I said, hesitant.

"Okay. Great. Thank you. I'll text you my hotel, and you can pick me up."

We hung up.

How did you know if your judgment was clouded?

Usually not until it was too late.

23

Elizabeth was staying at a boutique hotel in downtown Palo Alto called El Prado. I felt and looked completely underdressed, even for tech-casual Silicon Valley. My only saving grace was that I'd had my blazer custom made in Florence on an R&R trip.

Elizabeth looked like she belonged. She was elegant and beautiful. The pain was still there, just pushing at the borders—lines at the corners of her eyes, instead of the consuming sadness I'd seen when we first met.

When you lost a parent, the grief never really went away. However, there came a point when it was overcome by survivor's logistics, and that had a way of pushing the pain to the background.

Elizabeth was also apprehensive, which was understandable. She met me in the hotel bar with a smile that seemed genuine, if a little hollow. She gave me a brief hug and suggested we dine in the hotel's restaurant, which was Italian. Fine by me. I was dressed for it, after all.

She ordered a martini, and I opted for a Negroni, while we waited for our table.

The bar was a gold, blue, and white carpet, the way most Americans think Tuscany looks.

"I am sorry for the way I treated you, Matt," she said once we had our drinks and the perfunctory toast.

"All is forgiven. You're under a lot of stress, and police have a way of being unnecessarily persuasive when they aren't getting their way."

Nate must have spoken to her.

"That's nice of you to say, but I'm still embarrassed."

"Don't be. For the record, these guys have nothing on the Egyptian secret police."

That got a snort, which, on her, was kind of cute.

A server showed us to our table. I deferred to her for the wine.

"I need to say, at the risk of ruining our evening, that your call was surprising and...unexpected. In our last conversation, you were pretty convincing," I said.

Her face darkened, and she looked anywhere but me.

"Matt, this isn't easy for me, and I'm very sorry for how I acted. I was scared and hurt. I also thought that you were losing sight of what I'd hired you to do. I wanted to know if someone killed my father, and you're talking about spy rings and police conspiracies and..." Her voice trembled a little, then trailed off.

I knew I was risking the slight opening I had to get her back on my side. I also had to know if this was real.

Call me skeptical, but when everyone seemed to be lying to you, the truth was a valuable thing.

"My father and I had some unresolved issues, which unfortunately, you saw. When I blew up at you, I think I was looking for somewhere to put that anger. The last conversation I'd ever had with my dad was an argument, and I can't ever take back what I said. He was scared, told me someone was following him. I told him he was crazy—who could possibly be interested enough in him to do that? That's when he told me about his work."

The wine arrived, and the sommelier went through the ceremony, which Elizabeth dutifully participated in. I noted that she dropped her angst when she had to perform and picked it back up immediately when the sommelier departed.

"I guess I shouldn't have been surprised that my father was still involved. He never could leave well enough alone," she said, shaking her head slowly and with some regret. "The police have finished their investigation now. They're officially ruling it suicide."

"I'm sorry. What do you think about it?"

"I don't want to believe them. I also don't know if I have the strength to keep the fight up, or if it would even matter if I did. It's not like this is a civil case where I present evidence for someone to rule on."

That was the final piece I needed to convince myself that David Hu had been lying. If he really did have someone on the inside, they'd have known this before she did.

I said, "That's not entirely true. If I can pass the reasonable-doubt test, that should get your father's case reopened."

"Maybe," she said in a noncommittal way.

"Does this mean they're going to let you back into the house to settle things?"

She nodded. And another opportunity presented itself.

That cautious part of my brain, the one I tended to ignore, urged me tread carefully.

"Elizabeth, I want to share some information with you. I've uncovered a few things that might inform your decision."

"You kept after this, even after I asked you to stop?"

"Investigations don't stop on a dime. I had feelers out, and some of those came back. When you asked me to stop looking into your father's death, I did. I also have some...call them obligations here, above and beyond your father."

"I don't understand," she said, hesitant. "What obligations could you have that aren't part of what I hired you to do?"

"That'll all make sense in a moment. I just need your word that you won't take any action without talking to me first. There could be consequences for others, possibly serious ones."

"Consequences for whom? You're not talking about anything illegal, are you?"

I wasn't going to tell her about Nate. So, I deflected that and instead said, "People your father worked with. And no, nothing illegal. I have reason to believe they're in danger, and if I'm right, I don't want to tip off the bad guys."

"I see. Tell me what's going on, please."

"I told you before that I believed your father uncovered a plot by the

Chinese government to kill activists and political dissidents right here in the Bay Area. And that I believed agents of the Chinese government discovered this, and they killed him for it. Well, now I have proof of that, and I also have a list of names of the people your father worked with. Three of them have died in the last month."

"My God," she said after a time. "We have to go to the police."

"Not...yet."

"Jesus, Matt, why not? We have to tell *some*one. You can't give me that national security, bullshit. Not you. You're outside of all that. I thought that was the point of this. I thought that's why Nate told me to hire you."

Well, that and Nate didn't want anyone with statutory authority digging into this too deeply, and he wanted to make sure his questionable decision didn't come back to bite him, but...yeah.

"We can't take this to the police, or even the state cops, who'd just fuck it up anyway—you've met them. The FBI is responsible for counterintelligence. This is their job. I hadn't wanted to involve them. The FBI and I have a history, and it's not a particularly good one. I was worried if I brought something forward, they'd just dismiss it."

"What—"

"I promise I will explain that later. Let me tell you what I have and what I think we should do with it. I met one of your father's colleagues, someone he'd known since the Tiananmen days. He's the one who uncovered this Chinese spy ring. That's what he and your father were after. He's now missing too. We were followed one night. I told you about how some men tried to kill me. We didn't get to talk much about it because of our argument. Well, that was after Robert visited this outpost the Chinese state police are running. I went to see him at his house yesterday, and there was police tape across his door. The cops won't tell me anything. Given what has happened to some of the others, I'm very worried about him."

"Oh my God," she said.

"The other piece of evidence I have is a little more complicated, though I think you can help me here."

"All right," Elizabeth said warily.

I took a drink, fortifying myself against what was coming next. When you were backed into a corner, there was usually only one way out. I wanted to protect Nate and I told myself that I could accomplish that while still protecting the others. It sounded good. Might have even helped me sleep at night. I didn't see a way I could do both inside the law. To be fair, I'd stalled this a lot to give Nate a chance to do...anything, and it still felt like he was slow-rolling it. Now that the state police were turning the house back over to Elizabeth, there was an opening, but it also forced my hand. We couldn't ethically delay any longer. "Do you remember the night I texted you asking about your parent's anniversary?"

"Yes. That was odd."

"Right, so your father had a safe hidden in the bedroom. I cracked the code and accessed it. There was a lot of intel in there. That's how I figured out he was running a network of people and got connected with them."

I braced for impact. If it was going to end, it would be here.

Elizabeth picked up her wineglass and considered it, probably formulating her response. Her tone was dead even. "How did you find out my father had a safe in his bedroom? I didn't even know that."

"Because I went into the house and looked for it."

"You broke in, you mean."

"I suppose the law is a little gray there. You *did* give me a power of attorney."

The words burst out of her mouth, "Not to..." and they died away just as quickly. Instead, she replaced it with a terse bark of a laugh. "You know what, Matt? You're the only person in all of this who's been straight with me. Somehow, you breaking into dad's house to get some answers on my behalf seems like the least of a host of sins." She drained her wineglass and refilled it before the waiter could touch it. "I don't even think I'm going to get angry about it." Elizabeth stared at the flickering candle on the table between us. Maybe there were answers there, I didn't know. She said, "The fact that you care enough about the truth to put yourself at risk tells me everything I need to know."

"I don't like the rules when the rules are stupid," I said.

"What did you find?"

"The names of the members in your father's network. There were also GPS coordinates for places to stash information, what we call dead drops. One of those dead drops had some hacked emails confirming this community center they were investigating was actually run by the Ministry of Public Security. That's China's,"

"I know what it is. How do you know the police don't also have this information?"

"Because they search like cops."

"You're awfully sure of yourself."

"I've been at this a long time. If they'd found the safe, they'd have emptied it. It wouldn't be there for me to find."

"So, what is your plan?"

"I couldn't come forward before now with any of this because of how I'd gotten it. However, now we have a reason to get at it. We go in and 'find' it. Then we can turn that over to the FBI, and they can act on it. They can follow the breadcrumbs your father left back to the police outpost and, hopefully, prove they killed him to keep this thing quiet."

"Wow. That's...a lot. It's a lot of everything. Dominos that have to fall just right."

"It is. It's also our best shot. I don't understand why the state police are being so cagey, why they kept you at arm's length, or why they kept this a crime scene for so long. That still doesn't make sense to me. And I agree with you that a lot of things have to fall just right, as you say. I hope, now, you understand why I don't want to run to the local police."

"I do. I also...I truly appreciate what you've done. You've risked your life for me, and I treated you horribly."

"You're under a lot of strain."

"That doesn't excuse it."

"It's fine."

"Thank you," she said. "Where do we go from here?"

"In the morning, let's go to your father's house and open up the safe. Then we'll call the FBI."

Nate was not going to be happy with me.

Still, I'd given him a chance, and he slow-rolled it. He had his reasons, whether I agreed with them or not. I just wasn't willing to sit around and wait for more people to die because the bureaucracy was trying to figure out its next ass-covering move.

"One thing. It would be a good idea if you told the hotel staff not to disclose that you're staying here. It's just an extra precaution. You can tell them it's for privacy, or you can tell them it's because there's a police investigation surrounding your father's death. Either way, I think it's important that you keep some anonymity."

We ordered, and the conversation shifted as our food arrived. We shared a first course of a scratch-made ravioli that was quite good and a bistecca alla fiorentina for the main. Neither of us had room for dessert, but we enjoyed a cappuccino after we'd finished the wine.

Elizabeth's expression turned serious again as she asked, "Matt, am I safe?"

I genuinely didn't know how to answer that question.

"You weren't involved in your father's extracurricular activism," I said, which I believed, and she didn't refute it. I didn't think the Chinese had a history of punishing family members for the sins of their relatives, particularly when the offender was dead. However, I'd never worked there. I had gone up against Chinese intelligence, but always in other countries. "Since you had nothing to do with his work and don't have any information that's of value to the people trying to silence him, I can't think of a reason they'd come after you."

"Okay," she said.

Elizabeth picked up the check before I could grab it. I supposed she would've one way or the other.

She reached a hand across the table.

"Matt, would you like to come up to my room for a drink?"

The next morning, I ordered Elizabeth a pot of coffee from room service and stayed for a cup before leaving. I kissed her on the forehead and left. We'd agreed to go to her father's place around noon, so I was going to go back to my hotel to shower, change, and take care of a few things.

The morning's warm comfort disintegrated as I hit the daylight and reality came screaming back at me.

I hadn't heard from Robert—phone, email, nothing. I'd been concerned before; now I was officially worried for his safety. The San Jose detective hadn't returned my call either, which I couldn't figure out. I'd have assumed he'd follow up on any lead he got, unless the state cops got to him first. They *shouldn't* be able to do that, however. There wasn't a documented connection between Johnnie Zhou and Robert Li anywhere that I could think of for them to find. Unless there'd been something in Robert's house. Or, to Nate's point, Johnnie's.

I assumed Hu's line about finding my name on a piece of paper in Robert's house was bullshit. If that were true, the police would be all over me like Albanian cigarette smoke. That reference might be a little inside baseball, but if you'd ever smelled it, you'd know. That shit doesn't come out. Ever.

I was back at the hotel by noon to pick her up. Elizabeth walked briskly out and got into the car.

I didn't make a habit of sleeping with my clients. To her credit, Elizabeth handled the day after well and didn't make it awkward—or act overly affectionate, for that matter. There was no kiss when she got in the car, just a hello and a knowing smile. That disarmed whatever preemptive tension there might've been.

We drove to her father's place, speaking little.

I could tell she was apprehensive about being there.

"The state inspectors were real assholes about this," she said after we'd been driving for a bit.

"I can imagine. I've met them. Not sure they have another setting."

"They said, 'Well, you can go in now. They're through with the place.' There was no 'Oh, sorry for your loss, Ms. Zhou. Thanks for your cooperation.' They gave me the name of a remediation company to...clean up."

I shook my head but said nothing. Their actions were unfathomable to me. There was no reason to torment her like that. The woman had suffered enough.

They "knew" Elizabeth was the last person to see her father alive and that the two of them had a blow-up fight. They assumed she was the catalyst for this case that they'd spent the last few weeks on and, for whatever reason, couldn't close until now. Still, that was shallow justification to treat a survivor that way.

The Los Altos prowl car was gone from the driveway when we'd arrived at her father's house, but they hadn't bothered removing the crime scene tape from the door. At least they'd bothered to lock the damn thing. I cleared the tape for her while she opened the door.

"We don't have to stay long," I said.

"It's fine," she said, in a way that meant it was anything but.

We stepped into the entryway and turned on lights. The place looked decidedly different in daylight and without the tension of felony burglary.

"It happened in the office, right?"

"That's right," she said.

"Let's avoid that."

"Thank you. I don't want to go in there."

Once we were inside, Elizabeth went to the kitchen first. I assumed it was for the feeling and familiarity of home, even though this place never would be again.

She spent some time just taking it in. After a few moments, I said, "We should head upstairs."

Together, we walked to the master suite. Seeing it in the daylight, I was actually amazed I'd found it that night in the dark. The safe was expertly hidden, the hatch perfectly flush with the floor. Standing back and just looking at that space, it was nearly invisible, and I was looking right at it.

I got down and felt along the floor for the seams between the boards. Finding them, I put pressure on the panel to open it, revealing the keypad.

I tapped in the correct code. "My first guess was your parents' anniversary. The second would've been the date your father got his citizenship, though I didn't have an easy way to guess that at the moment. The date hit me as I thought about everything I knew about him."

"Tiananmen Square," she said softly.

"6-4-1989," I acknowledged. I hit "enter," and the safe door opened.

It was empty.

24

Oh fuck.

"Matt?"

I was staring into the empty steel box that felt like it was turning into a bottomless pit right in front of me. It was just sinking deeper and deeper into the floor. I couldn't even move, couldn't process what was happening. It was just...gone. Everything was *gone*.

It was gone, and I was fucked. Purely, cleanly, molecularly fucked.

Like there was no tomorrow.

I stood, dimly aware of my surroundings, that I was even in a room.

There was a voice, like an echo in an airplane hangar. I didn't hear the words.

My mind couldn't grasp the impossibility of it.

No one knew about the safe. At least, no one was supposed to. If they had, the police would've brought in a locksmith and opened it up. But it was gone. The day after the police ended the crime scene.

Someone had been in here after me, and they'd cleaned.

Removed all trace.

"Matt, what is it? What's going on?"

I pointed at the floor, as though that were an answer.

"Someone has been in here. Someone knew about your father's safe and knew the combination. Or had some way to crack it without damaging the door."

"What was in there again?"

"There were two notebooks. They had the names of your father's collaborators. There was a phone, and there was a key. My guess was he had a safe deposit box." I'd neglected to mention the other two items the night before.

"He never mentioned anything about it to me," she said.

"Do you know who he banked with?"

"Yeah. The estate lawyer has all of that."

"We need to call them right away to see if your father had a deposit box. Whoever was in here... That'll be their next move."

Elizabeth pulled her phone out. "Okay. I'll get on it." She stepped out to make the call.

I closed the safe and replaced the carpet, then left the room. *Think. Focus on the facts.*

Who could've known about the safe?

Who benefitted from getting the contents?

Literally everyone involved.

I imagined the only one who truly wanted anything in this to see daylight was Elizabeth Zhou.

Since I'd never met Johnnie, it was impossible to truly telegraph his moves. He had good tradecraft for a civilian, which suggested he wouldn't disclose the fact he had the safe, unless it was to someone he implicitly trusted to keep the secret. Or even as a way to convince one of his people to give him something they otherwise wouldn't, proof that it was secure. Something like GPS coordinates to a dead drop where hacked emails were stashed.

Would he tell Nate about it?

Would Nate tell *him* to put the safe somewhere he could be sure about it?

I know from hard experience that when you're in a dark place, the mind has a way of making the worst of things. Nate had just admitted to me that the CIA reactivated Johnnie Zhou and he hadn't disclosed to the Agency that Johnnie knew his true name. The risk being, if Johnnie knew Nate's real identity, who else did too? Nate brought me in to investigate Johnnie's death, yes, but to do it quietly and to make sure that he, Nate, was protected. If it ever got out that he revealed his true identity to Zhou, the best outcome was that his career was over.

The possibility that a member of Johnnie's network was a double agent had always been there. The rate this case was accelerating, I had to consider that more likely.

And Robert Li was still in the wind.

He might be dead. Or he might be on the run…for a couple of reasons.

I left the room, completely unsure of what my next steps were.

The only thing I was sure of was that I couldn't trust anyone.

Elizabeth was in the kitchen. The first time I'd seen the house it was pitch black and I'd crept through it like a burglar. Seeing the house and the safe in the light was strange. There was a voyeuristic quality to it. The lights a little too bright, glaring on the white paint. Too much contrast with the dark-brown wood cupboards and gray granite counters. It looked like the life had been drained out.

"I spoke with dad's bank," Elizabeth said. "They don't have safe deposit boxes at any of their local branches. The manager did say there are several secure deposit companies in the valley and in the city. That's all they do: secure storage. From boxes to vaults."

"We should try for those. From what I gather, your father was too smart for something like a post office box. I don't know what that key might unlock, but it's important enough that he wanted to store it in a hidden safe in his home."

Elizabeth got on her phone, and I could see she was looking up secure storage companies. I left her to it. For something to do, I moved into the other parts of the house that I hadn't been in that first night. Elizabeth had mentioned her father collected wine, and I found an impressive walk-in cellar beneath the stairs. Maybe he'd hidden something else in here. I worked quickly, but somewhat absently, as I was also thinking through my next move. At the same time, trying to run down who could possibly have known about the safe *and* be able to open it. I didn't like the places that line of thinking took me.

I stood from the crouched position I'd been in, searching the floorboards. Something creaked and something else popped and I probably winced. I heard Elizabeth step into the cramped space behind me.

"I hadn't checked this room for hidden storage, and I suspect the police avoided it. It doesn't scream 'evidence,' and these bottles are fragile, many of them expensive."

"I guess I'll need to inventory them," she said, mostly to herself. "If he was as bad off as it seems, I might need to sell this too. Do you think he might have hidden anything here?"

"Doesn't look like it. Was worth checking though. My advice, don't sell this. People have attachments to their collections, whatever they are, and wine is something you know something about. I bet your father would want you to have it."

Elizabeth offered a thin smile. "It's going to be hilarious moving a few hundred boxes of wine into my condo." I recognized the joke for a what it was, an attempt to find something seemingly normal in some insane circumstances.

There was nothing left to do, for me at least. When I made to leave, though, Elizabeth hung back. "Matt, I've got about a million things to do here. Would it be okay if I stayed? You don't need me for anything, do you?"

"I don't, but would it be okay if I drove you back to your hotel anyway? Someone has been in here, and I don't like the idea of you being in the house alone."

She shuddered as the realization hit, though she tried to hide it. She grabbed her things.

We drove back to her hotel in silence. I let her out and walked her to the door, said to call me if she needed anything.

I made it back to my hotel as quickly as I could, parked, and rushed inside, intending to make a pass by the front desk to see if Robert left anything for me.

The suits saw me before I saw them, because they'd detached themselves from the wall and glided to cover my flank before I could react.

Hands went into pockets, withdrew leather bi-folds, and then flipped with practiced ease.

I knew that motion as surely as I knew the badge behind it.

Remember when I said earlier that I was fucked?

That wasn't even the half of it.

"Mr. Gage, I'm Special Agent Katrina Danzig of the Federal Bureau of Investigation. I'd like to ask you a few questions."

I'd said I wanted to involve the FBI, but it seemed I'd forgotten that old line about being careful what you wished for.

25

I knew immediately these weren't the special counterintelligence squad Nate said he'd try to get deployed here. It was too soon. The government didn't move that fast, even when it was in their interest to do so.

I said before that I didn't like the Feds, and they felt the same way. On my last assignment with the Agency, one of theirs tried to manufacture some evidence to make me look incompetent, corrupt, evil, or all three. It was because I'd caught him screwing someone who wasn't his wife, and he thought piling on to whatever accusations Langley was making would save his ass. The Bureau wasn't interested in my side of things.

I'd enjoyed good cooperation with the FBI before then. Their actions tainted it forever.

That made it hard to come forward before and difficult to trust them now.

"Agent Danzig, how can I help you?"

"We'd like to talk to you about Johnnie Zhou. Come with us please."

"Sure thing. Where are we going, exactly?"

"We've got an office in the area."

"Okay, great. I'll follow you."

"You can ride with us," her partner said. He was about my height,

Korean-American, and had about twenty pounds more muscle on him. Danzig was a little shorter than me, dark hair cut short, in a navy suit.

"This is my partner, Special Agent Daniel Choi," she said.

They were being decidedly frosty.

Danzig and Choi walked me out to their car.

"Are you based out of the San Francisco Field Office, or did you come through DC?" I made it conversational, though what I really wanted to know was if they were a counterintelligence team or a criminal investigation team.

"We're sort of a flying squad," Danzig said. "We're not based here."

Huh.

We reached their car, a standard issue G-ride.

"We'll need your phone. You can't have it with you inside the building," Choi said.

This was where my association with Jennie Burkhardt really helped. She coached me on what to do in these situations. I was well versed in what other nations' police forces could do to civilians—usually whatever the hell they wanted—less so on what ours could get away with. When I started working for her, Jennie helped me understand what to do if I got braced. She'd been worried that I would get jammed up researching something controversial for her against a subject that may have ties to the cops, such as a bent LA city council member.

"Before I go anywhere, I'm telling someone where I'll be," I said and dialed Jennie.

Unfortunately, I got voicemail, but the Feds didn't have to know that.

"Jennie, I'm about to be taken in for questioning by the FBI. If you don't hear from me in about five hours, get a lawyer. I'll be at the FBI office in Palo Alto."

"Okay, you've made your point. Now, hand it over," Choi said and held his hand out for my phone.

"Are you kidding me right now? If I hand this over to you, I'm tacitly giving you permission to snoop it. Forget that."

"Don't be an asshole, Gage," he said. "We can't get into the phone without your permission or a warrant, and the manufacturer won't let us jailbreak it. It's just for safekeeping." He said the jailbreaking part with some remorse. It tickled the dark corners of my heart, the place deep down where I *really* hated these guys.

I remembered the line Jennie coached me to say. "I do not give you consent to search my device and do not give you permission to access any of my electronic data." I added the last part because it sounded official. This wasn't on the record yet, and I wasn't sure that statement would hold up in court. It was also the only thing I had right now.

Choi shook his head, and lines formed along his jaw where he was clamping his teeth down to bite back whatever words he had for me.

"I'm going to search you now," he said, then patted me down. Even though my pistol is licensed, I didn't have a concealed-carry permit in California. That required a DoJ investigation, which these assholes denied. This time, it worked out in my favor, because I didn't usually have a gun on me unless I was going to be in a situation where I thought I'd need it—and that hadn't been the case here. Things would've gone south for me fast if I had.

Satisfied I was neither a danger to them or myself, we got into their car. Danzig drove.

The ride over to Palo Alto was ice cold and silent, save for some partner banter between Danzig and Choi that I wasn't invited to participate in.

"What's this about?" I asked, finally.

Danzig's eyes flicked up to the rearview mirror, and she didn't answer my question.

"Ahh, the old mushroom treatment." *So that's what this feels like.* "Should I have a lawyer present?" I asked.

Choi responded with the old chestnut, "You guilty of something, Gage?"

"No. Though I obviously can't tell you what I'm not guilty of since you won't tell me why I'm in the back of your car on our way to an FBI office. And as for my lawyer, I don't trust you, so that's reason enough to want one."

"I suppose with your history you'd have reason not to," Danzig said flatly. There were any number of ways I could take that statement.

The interview room bullshit was exactly that.

They wanted me on their turf to tilt the power dynamic immovably in their favor. My entrance into the Federal Building was less than a full on perp walk, but only because I wasn't in handcuffs. I still had two federal agents flanking me and did everything I could to wash the scared rabbit look off my face. I felt a little better when I saw the destination. Yes, it was still a looming gray-concrete structure with tinted windows so dark they looked like soulless eyes, but much smaller than the Federal Building in San Francisco. It probably didn't have a detention facility. Choi told me they had to confiscate my phone for security reasons, so I powered it off and handed it to him. I signed a government form, and Choi said they'd return it to me when I left.

They led me inside and to a small conference room, rather than an interview room. The distinction was important because it telegraphed how they viewed me at the moment.

Danzig activated a recording device on the table. She identified herself and her partner, then identified me, punctuating it with today's date and time. Being on the other side of it had the feeling of holding up a copy of the day's newspaper for a proof-of-life photo.

"You've got quite the file, Mr. Gage," Danzig said.

"I'm surprised you have the clearance for it."

"Oh, there isn't a lot that gets by me. I was granted authorization to look at it once we knew you were involved here. Former Chief of Station in Managua, responsible for a hastily planned, poorly executed operation that got an asset killed by a foreign intelligence service." Danzig looked over at her partner as though this was coffee talk. "And exposed America's operations in the region to the Russian SVR."

So, it's going to be like that.

"That wasn't my plan. It was some half-assed desk officer at Langley who wanted to play cowboy. I told the division chief it was stupid and refused to do it. They ordered us to go anyway. I wouldn't risk my people getting hurt, so I went."

"And got someone killed in the process, I understand."

"That's out of line, and you goddamn know it. Tell me why I'm here, or I walk."

Choi leaned his bulk forward. "We can make it more official, if you prefer."

"Mr. Gage, what is your interest in Johnnie Zhou?" Danzig asked.

"His daughter suspected he was murdered. She didn't feel like she was getting straight answers from the police, so she asked me to look into it. Ask some questions."

"Are you licensed to do that, Mr. Gage?" Danzig held a flat expression. This wasn't her first time interviewing a suspect, and she masked her intention well. I could read, though, that she felt like she'd just maneuvered me into a trap. I was prepared for it. *Note to self: stop referring to myself as a 'suspect.'*

"You and I have both been at this game for a long time, Agent Danzig. I think we can skip to the part where you ask me the questions you don't already know the answers to."

"So, you admit you're not a licensed private investigator?"

"I'm an independent contractor and security consultant," I said with a slightly superior smirk. "Most of my work is for an investigative journalism and open-source intelligence group. I agreed to look into Ms. Zhou's case. If, in my estimation, it appeared the police were not being truthful, then we were prepared to start a journalistic investigation."

Danzig kept her tone convivial, yet snide. It was an amazing feat of verbal gymnastics. "Not being a law enforcement officer, or a licensed private investigator, it may surprise you to learn that sometimes the police are not able to fully disclose every aspect of an ongoing investigation. Even to next of kin."

"They called Zhou's death a suicide and stuck by that, yet they kept his house locked up as a crime scene for over two weeks. The whole time, they kept Elizabeth at arm's length and gave her no hint as to what their real motives were, whether they were looking for a killer or were just lazy cops. She reached the end of her patience and asked someone for help. They didn't even have the courtesy to return her phone calls. Under the circumstances, I don't see that as unreasonable, do you?"

"I can certainly understand why she'd think that," Danzig said, softening her tone. It sounded like acting though, and my guard stayed up.

Choi broke in now with a new line of questioning to throw me off. "Mr. Gage, what do you know about Johnnie Zhou?"

"What his daughter told me and then my own research. Chinese immigrant. Moved to the US in the mid-'90s. He was a student activist. I understand that he was involved in the Tiananmen Square protest in '89. Computer engineer by training. Did well in the first tech boom in the '90s and early 2000s. Spun that into a successful venture capital fund."

"Do you know anything about his politics?"

"I never met him," I said.

"What about his activism?"

"Same answer."

"Do you think he was murdered?" Choi asked.

"Well, your partner keeps reminding me that I'm not qualified to make those kinds of judgments, so I'll just say that the police haven't given his daughter anything that convinces her he was or wasn't. Look, guys, you want to tell me what this is about? So far, we're just trampling the same ground I already covered with those two state cops. They tried to scare me off too. Which has me wondering why. What are they afraid of me finding out?"

"Maybe they're not afraid of you finding out about something so much as getting involved where you don't belong," Choi said. "A civilian playing Phillip Marlowe doesn't help anyone out."

"Except Elizabeth Zhou, perhaps."

"Especially not her."

Danzig took over. "I think what we're wondering, Mr. Gage, is how is it that Elizabeth Zhou, an entertainment lawyer in Hollywood, came to hire a disgraced ex-CIA case officer." My eyes narrowed at the "disgraced" line, and I bit the rising bile back in my throat.

Choi maneuvered something on the table in front of him, which I now saw was a tablet. He flipped it open and unlocked it. They showed me a black-and-white video, clearly from a surveillance camera. It took me a moment to orient myself as to what I was seeing.

Johnnie Zhou's home office.

The person on camera was larger than me, and I hadn't worn a hoodie the night that I'd been there, so I knew it wasn't me. Of course, I had no idea when this camera was installed, and it was entirely possible they had me on film. If I'd ever been grateful for the Agency's training on how to handle yourself when the light comes on and your hand is in the cookie jar, it was now.

The figure entered from the sliding glass door and immediately set to work, moving throughout the room, clearly searching for something. He wore a hoodie with the hood up and glasses with the same deflective treatment mine had. He kept his head down, never looked up, and moved professionally. He quickly searched the desk, the drawers and the shelves in efficient, organized patterns. Finding nothing, he lifted the pictures on the walls to see if there was a safe behind them.

Choi turned the tablet back to face him, typed something, then flipped it back around. There was a new image. We were now in Zhou's bedroom.

I watched the scene play out. The person moved through the room with the same practiced efficiency, searching and finding nothing, using the same basic method that I had. They must've had some clue that Zhou had a floor safe, because I saw him methodically testing the floorboards until he came to it. The camera's angle on the room didn't give me a line of sight to the safe itself, though his haul was unmistakable. I could follow along with the motion as he lifted the items and moved them to his backpack. And then he was gone.

Danzig spoke when the video ended.

"Whomever broke into Mr. Zhou's house had some solid tradecraft," she said. "Notice how he knew to keep his head down, wore a dark hoodie to break up the silhouette."

Choi piped in with another helpful comment. "Probably wore a sweatshirt underneath it to add some bulk."

Danzig nodded. "Seems like he's had some training."

"Agreed," Choi said. "I like how he knew to treat the glasses so they blocked his eyes from the camera."

"Oh, any hacker or privacy nut knows how to do that," I snapped.

I said nothing else, not wanting to cede any more advantage than I already had just by being in the room. Asking, again, what we were doing here would just make me look nervous.

Finally, Danzig picked it up. "We have two theories, and perhaps you can help us fill in the blanks, Gage. How much do you know about Chinese intelligence operations?"

"Well, I'm sure I have a different perspective on them than you do."

"We're still curious what an ex-spy is doing here. You haven't gone over to the other side, have you? Wouldn't be the first time. Agency fires someone, and they're angry, maybe a little bitter, decide they'd like some getback," Danzig said.

I cut in. She was trying to get under my skin and had succeeded, I'd give her that point. I was a lot of things, but I was no traitor, and it'd be a cold day in hell before I let some Feeb puke accuse me of it.

"Stop. There's no way, no *fucking* way that I'm betraying my country. Not for money, not for revenge, not even to spite you, Agent Danzig. And I'll tell you, that's a mighty tempting offer. If you actually did read my file, unless they doctored it, you'd see *when* some bureaucrat at Langley directed me to do something I thought was ill advised, possibly illegal. *Your* Legal Attaché at the embassy should've been the one person I could trust. Except I caught him screwing a State Department employee who didn't look like his wife. He threw me under the bus so I wouldn't expose him. Next."

"Sounds bitter to me," Choi said.

"You can see, though, Gage, how we'd—"

"Next."

Danzig nodded and punctuated it with a smug smile, just to underscore that she'd racked up another one. "Okay. Since you're already familiar with China's intelligence operations, you're no doubt aware they target people years, even decades, in advance. They have hundreds, possibly thousands, of potential sleeper agents in our country."

I could already see where this was going, and I didn't like it.

More than that, these were not people I could go out on a limb with. Any hope I had of sharing what we knew about Johnnie Zhou's safe was gone. If I told them we found an empty safe, they'd say, "So what?", and when I told them how I found it, they'd simply accuse me of being the guy in the video and arrest me.

"So, our second theory is this. Perhaps Mr. Zhou was working for them. Both the Ministry of State Security and the PLA's intel division actively recruit immigrants. You mentioned he was involved in the Tiananmen protests. None of us really know the man, right? What's to say he wasn't recruited back then? He could've been an agent for them all this time."

It was possible Danzig was laying a trap for me, forcing me to disprove her statement, thereby acknowledging that Johnnie Zhou was a CIA asset.

"Like you said, none of us met the man," I told her.

"Chinese intelligence tends to play on heritage, legacy to the mother-land. You might be an American citizen, but you're *Chinese* to the core. That sort of thing. They also go hard on familial responsibility. I wonder if Elizabeth was working for her father?"

"It's an interesting question," Choi added. "You have to wonder why she'd be so keen to have someone running interference, messing up the official investigation into her father's death. Possibly even breaking into his home."

"You also have to question what might've been in her father's house that she wouldn't want anyone else to find," Danzig said.

I had to restrain myself from saying, *Wouldn't you love to know?*

"You think Elizabeth Zhou is spying for the Chinese?" I asked, incredulous.

"I mean, she did hire an out-of-work, ex-CIA officer as a 'private investigator' when no one else would take her case. She didn't tell you *that* part, did she?" My expression gave nothing away, though my silence may have. "Word is, she called about ten different detective agencies in the area before she settled on you. No one would touch this, and with good reason. Licensed detectives are trained to smell 'illegal.'"

I didn't know exactly what Danzig's angle was here. I was certain of one thing, however.

Elizabeth was no spy.

The Feds indicated her father was, and what they believed their video showed was someone going in as a cleaner. My opinion, they had it flipped. This was a Chinese agent wanting to eliminate evidence and get the rest of Johnnie Zhou's book of names.

Elizabeth just wanted answers.

At least I now knew why the police had been so tight-lipped about everything. They had the Feebs whispering in their ear that my client was a suspect—not in her father's murder, but in the broader espionage operation. Normally, I'd be ecstatic that they were so far off the mark. Just not when it involved my client.

In all honesty, Danzig, Choi, and I should be on the same team. Whatever I thought about the FBI, whatever they thought of me...we should have been able to put cards on the table and address a glaring threat.

And maybe solve four murders.

It was probably our collective failure as humans to not see past our shared mistrust of each other that got in the way of actually solving the case.

I knew, unequivocally, that the Chinese secret police had an outpost in San Francisco and were using it to round up enemies of the state. I couldn't tell the Feds that, though, because I'd broken the law to get that information and my reputation with them was such they weren't going out on any limbs. Maybe there was a way to broker an immunity deal; I just didn't trust them to honor it.

And I wasn't going to jail for anyone. Not Nate, not Elizabeth, and sure as hell not for the Agency that threw me out when it was convenient for them.

Jesus Christ, I wasn't finding my way out of this maze without a map.

Instead of all that, I said, "Tell me something. Do you know a Sergeant David Hu with the SFPD?"

"No," Danzig said and looked over to her partner. That was the tell that I'd finally come up with a point they didn't have yet.

"That's a pity."

"Who is he?" Choi asked.

"He's a cop on their gang detail. Mostly handles the Triads, based out of their Chinatown station. You guys are right to be looking for Chinese agents," I said, and what started with a low chuckle to emphasize the point turned into a full throated laugh. "But, man, are you looking in the wrong place."

"That's enough of that, Gage," Choi said.

"Why do you bring up this Sergeant Hu? How do you know him?" Danzig asked.

"He approached me after I started asking questions. Claimed to represent a friend in the Los Altos PD that resented you guys taking Zhou's case over." I considered telling them about Robert—maybe the Bureau could marshal some resources to help find him. Maybe. The problem was I already didn't trust them, and they'd done nothing here to convince me otherwise. "Anyway, Hu came to me again two days ago. Pressed a little harder this time. He thought I knew who Johnnie Zhou's contacts were and tried throwing his weight around when I didn't give him anything. He backed down when I suggested bringing my lawyer into it."

"And that makes him a Chinese spy?" Choi said in the kind of tone you'd expect.

"No. But I find it curious that a cop is pressing me for information on a case thirty miles outside his jurisdiction that he's got no connection to. More than that, he had information the police didn't."

There were times when you wished you could pull words back into your mouth.

God the trouble I'd have saved myself if I could do that.

"How would you know?" Danzig said.

"I can guess what the police know by the moves they're making," I said. It wasn't a great cover.

"Gage, I already know from your file that you're not terribly conversant with the law, so I'll remind you that it's a crime to lie to a federal agent."

"You know what, forget I said anything. You aren't going to do anything anyway."

"How exactly do you know Sergeant Hu is a foreign agent?" Choi said.

Goddamn it.

Because I broke into Zhou's house and found a notebook with cyphered GPS coordinates in it that took me to a dead drop. There I found a thumb drive that one of Zhou's agents had stashed containing files hacked from the Ministry of Public Security.

Sounded kind of farfetched as I said it back in my head.

"I'm waiting."

"I'm not giving up my sources until I know they're safe, and my experience with the FBI so far says I can't trust you to do that."

"Well, you're not leaving us a lot of options, Gage," Danzig said. She and Choi stood. She tapped a finger on the table, which was clearly a preset signal. "Let's go."

"You've pulled that one already."

I might not have been willing to go to jail for Nate, or Elizabeth, or the CIA...but *apparently* I would for my own big mouth.

This office was too small for a holding facility, so they drove me all the way across the valley to the Santa Clara County Jail, and they booked me into a solitary holding cell.

Danzig's last words to me were, "When you get tired of being in here, tell the guard you're ready to talk. I'll leave him my card."

"You cannot hold me without suspicion of something."

"Well, we'll start with suspicion of breaking-and-entering and obstruction of justice. I'm not moving to espionage yet, but if you piss me off, I just might."

Choi looked at me and smirked. "Have a nice night."

I'd never wanted to hit a person as much as I did right then.

There were any number of ways I could prove that wasn't me on camera, and the FBI wouldn't believe a one.

26

Long hours burned slowly.

They had me in a solitary holding cell. I assumed to let me know they could wall me off from the world if they wanted to.

Getting out of there cost me.

My one phone call went to Jennie to see if I could get a lawyer that the Orpheus Foundation had on retainer. They had access to them, but because I wasn't working on a case for the foundation, I had to pay out of pocket. Which was money I didn't have. The FBI could hold me up to seventy-two hours without a charge, though they could easily make something up and hold me longer. While espionage was nearly impossible to prove in court, given my background, it wouldn't a tough sell to a judge. Then I could be here indefinitely while whomever was murdering Johnnie's people would just keep working down the list.

I made Jennie a deal, one I had absolutely no authorization to make.

I'd give her everything I had so Orpheus could justify an investigation and put me on contract...and, thereby, under their legal umbrella.

And then wait for everyone I was associated with here to blow their absolute shit.

By the time everything got worked out, I'd still spent the night in jail.

The attorney called the lockup and scared the shit out of the sergeant on duty. The city, wanting to avoid a massive public relations scandal that they were taking on behalf of the FBI, sprang me. I presumed Danzig didn't fight them on it. She'd made her point.

The thing about walking out of jail was, no matter what time of day, no matter what the circumstances were that put you there, you were walking out of jail.

It didn't matter what it was for.

Guilty or innocent.

Right or wrong.

You were now one of *them*.

The first thing you noticed walking out of the building was the line of cabs out front because they knew you didn't have a ride. The second thing you noticed was the looks you got from people on the street.

Feds probably did this on purpose just so I'd have to look my fellow citizens in the eye.

It was a subtle "fuck you" from Agent Danzig and a reminder of what she could do with the full weight of the federal government behind her. I hadn't even been arrested, just spent the night in holding to make a point. The people walking to work didn't know that. They'd just assume I was some asshole that just made bail. Did it matter? Not really. I'd never see any of these people again. I still hated them thinking I was a criminal.

I walked a few blocks just to put distance between me and where I was, eventually finding a coffee shop serving breakfast. Knowing I smelled like jail, I got a breakfast sandwich and coffee to go. I ate and walked. The morning was cold, and I was grateful for the hot food. My phone was dead. I'd shut it off before handing it over to Choi, so they must have tried to get onto it. Or left it on to spite me. I couldn't call anyone for a ride and obviously wasn't walking to Cupertino.

The jail complex wasn't far from San Jose's airport, so I walked in that direction, knowing I could find a cab there. Forty-five minutes later, I was at the hotel and behind a locked door, which I braced with a chair. The phone charged while I showered, and I spent a good thirty minutes underneath the nearly scorching torrent, letting the heat work its way into my muscles.

Now I had some decisions to make.

Agent Danzig planted a few seeds in my head, which I'd tried unsuccessfully to claw out. Namely, questioning Elizabeth's intentions and her rapid turnaround. We'd gone from "you're fired" to "come up to my room" in a pretty short span, and as I thought on it more, I was surprised I didn't get whiplash from the reversal. It was probably just bad timing, just that our sleeping together came so close to Danzig dropping hints they thought Elizabeth might be a spy. I cautioned myself against jumping at shadows. But it remained a chill I couldn't quite shake.

I'd told her absolutely everything about what was in her father's safe but Robert's last name.

Nate was another angle forcing me to rethink my assumptions.

He was a mentor, and he was my friend. Nate had handpicked me for the most impactful and meaningful work I would ever do. We took the worst of the bad guys off the board, we got the secrets that satellites couldn't see, that even our regular case officers couldn't get to. I could say with confidence we stopped the US from getting involved in another war that we had no business being in. Nate had also gone to bat for me when the Agency brass cashiered me. When they questioned my judgment, Nate said I had integrity when it counted—not when the bullets were flying, but when no one would know but me and my agent in the dead of night. That was a direct quote. It hadn't mattered to the brass. It did matter to me.

Walking these streets alone, though, I forced myself to consider the question on whether I'd wanted to believe that about Nate just a little too much.

I knew I was jumping at shadows.

I also felt like they were jumping back.

The FBI had surveillance of someone breaking into Zhou's home and that person wasn't me. I assumed it was Hu.

Could it be a contract CIA cleaner?

That wasn't impossible.

Dark thought swirled then. Christ, what if it was Hu and he was both? Someone the Agency used to make problems go away, and he was probing me to see what I knew. That'd absolve him of the murders, but little else.

I'd just spent the night in jail because I wouldn't tell the FBI everything I knew about this case.

How far was I willing to push that point?

Was I really willing to risk that again to protect an operation run by the Agency that had thrown me out?

No good answers.

When I'd had enough of the shower, I toweled off, dressed, and went to check my phone.

It had proverbially blown up, and looking at the number of messages and calls, I'd almost wished it had literally done it too.

There were the expected missives from Jennie, each with an increasing level of panic and urgency. There were several from Elizabeth, first asking me if I could talk, did I want to meet for a drink, and finally asking if everything was okay. God, I hoped she didn't think I was ghosting her now. There was a message from Benjamin Blake. And two from Nate.

And an alert from my AI news aggregator.

I knew what it was before I even clicked on the summary.

I clicked anyway, and a terrible hole opened in my stomach. I thought I was going to lose my breakfast.

Jia "Jessica" Chen was found dead two days ago at her home in Berkley. The police were calling it a "home invasion gone tragically wrong." Chen was described as an author, public speaker, and community organizer. The article described her as active in the Chinese-American community and an outspoken critic of the Chinese communist government.

I sank to the floor and just sat there for a long, long while.

Her death was on my head. Yes, I'd called, and she hadn't answered. What I should've done was bang down her door, said I knew she'd worked with Johnnie Zhou and that her life was in danger. If she wouldn't have listened to me, she might've listened to Robert. Even though he hadn't wanted to get involved, maybe I could've convinced him to for just this bit.

I wanted to scream, for all the good it would do.

The FBI presumed I was a suspect until I could prove otherwise, which I couldn't do without either Robert or the contents of Johnnie's safe. I couldn't give them the names on the list without putting myself in jeopardy because of how I'd obtained them. That would convince them I was the guy in the video, and they'd arrest me, and Johnnie's people would get killed anyway.

I had to find out who was in that house and what they'd done with the documents. Or find Robert and get him to come forward.

Once I'd collected myself, I called Jennie to tell her I was out of jail and that I owed her. She was furious with the FBI and wanted blood. I knew that lawyer wasn't cheap and that I probably couldn't afford them anyway. So, the only way I was going to pay that back was to give the foundation everything I had for a story. I told Jennie I needed a few days to wrap things up, and then I'd tell her what I knew.

Offering sounded better than them asking to collect.

Then I called Elizabeth.

"Oh my God," she said when I told her where I'd been.

"I think the FBI just wanted to scare me into talking. There's an old score they're trying to settle. It had as much to do with that as it did your case. However, that group of journalists I told you I work for?"

"Yeah?"

"Well, they put a civil rights attorney on this. That's who got me out."

"Matt, we can't keep this up. Not now. I don't want you to get into trouble."

"Trouble, as the famous line goes, is my business."

"This is serious."

"I know. I'm not being flippant. The Chinese government is murdering the people who worked with your father. They just got away with another one."

"That's exactly why we have to involve the FBI."

And there were a hundred reasons why I couldn't do that, none of which I was going to get into on an open line.

Instead, I deflected. "I've got a couple of phone calls to make. Let's catch up later today."

"Matt, I'm scared. People are dying." The line went quiet.

We agreed to meet up later. I messaged Nate in Signal and told him what had happened.

He gave me an address and a time.

Two hours. I'd spend every second of that on a surveillance detection route.

Against my better judgment and general paranoia, I kept my phone.

I didn't think the FBI could get a wiretap up in the time they had, and phone manufacturers generally resisted the law enforcement agencies trying to get onto devices. They'll snoop you themselves for data and ads targeting, but they weren't allowing the cops on the platform for anything.

I also checked my Land Rover for tracking devices. It hadn't been moved from its spot in the hotel parking lot, so they wouldn't have been able to do any real damage to her. After about thirty minutes, I was satisfied they hadn't planted anything on it.

We met at the Foothills College Observatory, which had a commanding view of Silicon Valley. I parked in a covered lot beneath the observatory with solar panels on the roof. I followed a zigzagging path up a hill with golden grass and intermittent trees. Nate leaned against the large, circular, redbrick building, watching. Not watching me necessarily, just anyone paying attention to me. He wore a safari jacket and an LL Bean felt Panama hat, looking every bit the quirky university professor.

"What'd they haul you in for?" Nate asked. He did a good job of hiding his nerves.

"A bunch of made-up shit. They just did it because they could. And because I wouldn't tell them what I knew about Johnnie. I did tell them I thought the Chinese had an asset on SFPD but wouldn't tell them how I knew. Before you ask, I didn't tell them about you."

"I wasn't worried that you would, Matt," he said, kind of peevishly.

"I need you to get them called off, Nate."

"You know I can't do that."

"Can't you? You told me the FBI approved whatever you're doing."

"There's a memorandum of understanding between the FBI's head of counterintelligence and the DNCS, that's it." Under other circumstances, I'd have snorted at his intentionally snide pronunciation of the director of the National Clandestine Service as "Dinkus." Nate knew him personally and had little respect for him, though he hid it well when he was back at headquarters.

"So, tell them."

"It doesn't work like that, Matt. He signed it and said if we got into trouble, we were on our own. We're all worried that if this got pushed to lower levels, the Chinese would find out."

"We can't even trust ourselves. That's perfect."

Every time I talked to him, we seemed to peel a different layer of the rotten onion back. It still felt like I was a few layers from the truth.

"You know the game, Matt. You know they've penetrated nearly every bureaucracy at some level. Jesus, they even flipped a case officer ten years ago."

"Nate, you have to do better than that. One night in jail is all I'm willing to do."

"It's not that simple."

"I don't owe the CIA *anything*," I said, angrier than I'd intended to be. After a couple calming breaths, I said, "I can't tell the Feds where I got the intel on this police outpost because that will blow up your operation and I'll be admitting to burglary. Which then convinces them of their theory that I'm a Chinese agent."

"You shouldn't have gone into Johnnie's house, Matt."

"No. You don't get to distance yourself from me now, Nate. That better not be what this is. And if I didn't, we wouldn't know any of this. We wouldn't know about the MPS operation, we wouldn't know about Johnnie's people, and they'd all be dead before anyone put anything together. Oh, and speaking of that, another one of his network was murdered. You need to get off your ass."

"What are you doing here, Matt?"

"Exactly what *you* told Elizabeth to hire me to do. She didn't think her father killed himself, and nobody believed her. I think there's some pretty damned convincing evidence that the Chinese government did. Now I find out the FBI in their cosmic stupidity somehow came to the conclusion that Johnnie was a Chinese agent and maybe his daughter is too. They're going to ruin a dead man's reputation and legacy because there's no one to speak up against it, and probably his daughter's while they're at it. You can't go to bat for her, because it exposes your op and your—" I bit off the words, not wanting to vocalize it. "As for what I'm doing here, Nate, I'm trying to save some people's lives. People who don't even know they're in danger!"

"I know," Nate said. "I made a mistake, Matt. It's one of those things that's harmless at the time. You bend the rules because it doesn't matter. Johnnie was settled back here in the States; he'd been deactivated for a decade. Made a good life for himself. I figured there was no possible chance he could be brought into service again now that he was out of China. He'd passed all the polys before, so we knew he wasn't compromised."

"How'd you get by them the second time?"

"I didn't have to. I always used my cover legend around him, and that's not the kind of thing the polygrapher ever asked about. Matt, this thing we have running, it's important. We're trying to destabilize a behemoth. More than that, it's the first time we've had a real offensive capability in that country in decades. If we get burned because of some overzealous Fed looking to score career points, years of work goes up in smoke. Given the state of things, we may never get that back. I know you don't owe the Agency any favors, and I don't blame you for wanting to burn it all down. I'm asking you to hold the line, for me."

The "I quit" refrain was on the tip of my goddamn tongue. I could almost taste the words and the seething bile behind them.

I'd always wonder what might've been different if I had walked away at that moment. I assumed it would have resulted in my eventual arrest. And if I took the easy way out, so would everyone else.

Nate and the Agency's involvement here would vanish so fast it'd make a mirage look like a brick wall.

I didn't know Elizabeth would be protected.

I *did* know that eleven brave people would remain in danger and that their lives may be counted in days. If I took the easy way out, people died. I hadn't lost my sense of right and wrong just because the CIA burned me. If anything, that only made the dividing line more acute.

And that was why I stayed the course.

And, to be honest, because the FBI threw me in jail for a night just because they could, and I wanted to hit them back.

Also, because of the doubts Special Agent Danzig put in my head about Elizabeth and Nate.

I'd never walk away from this until I knew Elizabeth or Nate weren't involved in some way other than what they said. God help either of them if they were. I'd burn them to the ground.

"I don't know what 'holding the line' means, Nate. If you want me to stay involved, here's what needs to happen. Number one, I want to know who I'm going up against. What can you tell me about Special Agents Danzig and Choi. Number two, you get your CI people on this MPS outpost, and you do it now. Number three, get Zhou's network secured. Those people are in jeopardy."

"Matt, I don't need a list. What I need is for the FBI not to detonate an operation I've been planning for the last three years. I need you to keep Elizabeth safe until we can shut the Chinese operation down."

Left unsaid: *What I need is for you to be a moving target.*

"Not good enough. Either those people get protected, or I become a problem. For everybody."

Deciding I hadn't received enough positive reinforcement today, I returned Ben Blake's call from the voicemail he'd left while I was in jail.

"Matt, thanks for getting back to me. Hope I didn't catch you at a bad time."

If you only knew, pal. "It's fine. What can I do for you?"

"So, look, we haven't heard anything from Betty yet."

I'd never heard anyone call her that. She certainly didn't.

"I don't really control her calendar," I said.

"You're in touch though, yeah?"

"I am."

"We're about to close a...well, it's a significant deal with a foreign investor. There's been some rumbling that Elizabeth is going to the press over this. Something about wanting to clear her father's name. Listen, Matt, we can't have that. This deal is worth a lot of money to the firm, and it'd be good for Betty, too. We close this, and we're prepared to put another two million on top of what we've already offered. All told, that should wipe out her father's debts and give her a good nest egg. We just need her to shut this investigation down and get back to living her life."

"You need to tell her that, Ben. Why do you keep asking me to be your go-between?"

"Because she'll listen to you. She's...well, she's sort of ducking my calls."

"I told you before, I'm not doing your legwork for you."

Blake paused. "What if I triple your fee?"

What *if* he tripled my fee? Elizabeth hadn't specifically said she'd rehired me, I'd just sort of assumed it. The kind of money Blake was talking probably would keep me in my house another six months.

My phone buzzed with another call. While Blake was waiting for a response, I looked down at the screen.

It was Robert Li.

Or it was his phone.

"Ben, I need to take this. I'll get back to you."

"Okay, but listen, Matt—I mean this. We can't have any more publicity on this, or it'll tank the whole deal. Discretion, please."

And hopefully by then I'd have figured out a good story for why the press was already involved.

27

"Robert?"

"Hello, Matt. I'm sorry I haven't called you. I—"

"Robert, where are you?"

"I'm staying at a hotel."

"Don't go anywhere."

"Hold on, I need to give you the latest one. I've changed it a few times."

He was in San Mateo now, at the SFO Hyatt. I raced to him and met him in his room, my laptop bag in tow. Ironically, his window practically overlooked the bar where we'd first talked.

"Where have you been?" I tried to hold in my temper. Robert and I had only known each other about a week, and though we shared a common mission, he owed me nothing, and I deserved no demands on his time.

"I was scared, Matt."

It hit me that he'd been incommunicado that whole time and didn't know what I'd learned about our mission.

"Why didn't you contact me to let me know you were okay?"

"I didn't know what to do. These people at the community center tried to force me back to Beijing. Then they followed us and broke into my home. And it all started after I met you. This is the reason I didn't speak up when Johnnie died and why I tried to burn everything I'd left at that dead drop when you found me. And the whole time you're telling me I can't talk to the police. You promised you'd protect me!"

Robert's fear was as visceral as it was justified. This also couldn't go forward without him. I wanted to drop everything that had happened in the last few days—the FBI, Elizabeth. If I overwhelmed him with information, he could panic and rabbit again. There was another, darker possibility. Until I could prove to myself Robert wasn't involved in Johnnie's death, as much as it pained to think it, I couldn't rule him out as a suspect.

"I understand, Robert. For whatever it's worth, you were right about the center. It's the Ministry of Public Security. I also think they've turned an SFPD officer named David Hu."

"So, what do we do now?"

"How about we get a drink."

Robert and I relocated to the airport bar. It was in the center of the hotel, lots of metal framework that, for some reason, reminded me of building girders, which I suspected was not what they were going for. I wanted to see if I'd been followed, and I couldn't do that from the hotel room. I didn't like meeting in hotel rooms because it usually meant being cornered. Also, I was starving. I got a burger and a beer, and Robert ordered a sandwich.

"Did Johnnie ever mention a Stanford professor named Lawrence Fang. Yìchén is his given name."

"No, why?"

"His name was in some of Johnnie's documents but listed separately than everyone else."

Robert shrugged and took a pull off his beer. "Johnnie was always trying to recruit someone, so it wouldn't surprise me. What's he a professor of?"

"Asian-American studies," I said. "He's a visiting professor from a university in Beijing."

"Now I'm not surprised. He'd be a perfect person for Johnnie to recruit. A great source of information on what's happening back home, and he's in a position to cultivate sources. Given that much of our protest begins with student movements, this is a logical move."

"I met him. Fang was evasive, and he lied about how often he met with Johnnie," I said

"I imagine he would be concerned, as I am. Likely, he knows more than he's letting on. And you must remember that we're used to omnipresent government surveillance. If he doesn't trust you, he won't speak to you."

When I started this, I'd assumed I could simply apply tradecraft to being a detective. After all, the two jobs dealt with similar problems, right? What I was learning—the hard way—was that in the private sector, the timescales are so compressed. I'd also assumed I'd be relying on traditional HUMINT models to get questions answered and facts uncovered. Turned out, that wasn't always true. Professor Fang was certainly proving that to me —though, in intelligence, there were always dead ends and recruitment targets that never materialized. Still, I couldn't help but feel I'd missed an opportunity with him.

"Do you think he would talk to you?" I said.

Robert considered this. "Possibly. He may be willing to admit things to a fellow countryman that he wouldn't to a foreigner. I may be able to gain his trust. And I knew Johnnie in life."

Our food arrived, and I didn't speak again until I'd plowed through half of the burger. I'd also need to sleep soon. The night in jail was catching up to me.

"It's worth a shot," I told him. I finished my food in another couple bites and washed it down with the beer. The speed and voracity with which I'd ripped through that meal astonished my companion. I didn't tell him I'd been locked up last night, fearing that might send him over the edge. Thinking you couldn't trust anyone or anything was terrible knowledge. "You were asking about our next steps. If you're willing, I would greatly appreciate you contacting the rest of Johnnie's network to warn them their lives are in danger. I've tried. No one will take my calls. I assume Johnnie had some sort of instruction in place about what to do if he died."

"I can't do that, Matt. I told you, I don't want to know names."

"You know where I spent last night, Robert?"

"No."

"Jail. Two FBI agents pulled me in for questioning. *They* believe there's a Chinese intelligence operation here and that Johnnie might have been involved in it."

"That's insane. He'd never..." and his voice trailed off. Not because

Robert didn't believe what he was saying about his friend, but because his words were crushed under the weight of it.

"It gets better. Someone broke into Johnnie's house, found a hidden safe, and got into it. The Bureau has all this on video. At some point, they went in there and hid some cameras, believing somebody was going to enter the home." I'd never told Robert where my information on him and the network had come from. "Based on what Elizabeth tells me, it's a good bet everything Johnnie had on his network and its operations would be in that safe. So the opposition has it now. The FBI thinks it was me on that camera, and they accused me of playing for the other side."

"But that's...that's just not right. Why would they think that?"

"The FBI and I don't have a great history. I'm not going to get into it now, just know that we've got some bad blood, and it's not deserved. I need you to come forward with everything you know about Johnnie. We have to assume the Chinese have the names now. It's only a matter of time before this gets wrapped up." I didn't tell him the other possibility—that the break-in was the CIA covering their tracks. Why muddy the waters?

And maybe I didn't want to believe it myself.

"I know them," Robert said softly.

"Know who?"

"Johnnie's network. Most of them, anyway. We worked together. Once I brought the information about the community center forward, Ryan Tan said he could hack into their network. I don't know what came of it, though."

Now things were starting to make sense. Ryan was one of the first to be killed. He must have been successful hacking into the community center's network and proved Robert's suspicions were correct. Then Ryan put the data on a thumb drive and placed it at a dead drop for Robert or Johnnie to retrieve—the only guaranteed way not to leave a digital footprint. Since both Johnnie and Ryan were killed, Robert never knew for certain what Ryan had discovered, which was probably why he'd agreed to go in for me.

"I'll speak to them. Warn the others. I owe them that much, owe Johnnie that much."

"Will you talk to the FBI as well?"

He nodded.

I didn't discount the possibility that Johnnie had a double agent inside his network. If true, it explained how the secret police had found Johnnie and murdered him. Robert convinced me that he hadn't done it. His disappearing act was strange, but understandable. I trusted Robert was who he said he was. Perhaps he was the only person in this whole affair I could say that about.

Robert didn't make eye contact with me for some time. "The police have said I can go back home. That's what I'm going to do."

Not for the first time since meeting him, Robert's bravery and quiet nobility struck me.

I was reminded of the man who stood before the People's Liberation Army tanks at Tiananmen. It seemed the most suitable visual metaphor for the struggle against that regime. One noble person standing before unstoppable forces, regardless of the consequences. Perhaps, in spite of them.

We returned to Robert's room, and I gave him the remaining names in Johnnie's network, so we could bounce that list off the ones Robert already knew. Their lives depended on us having them all. Given what happened at Robert's house, I knew this was risky, and he recognized my concern immediately.

"I have a few safe places yet," he said with a sly grin. Under different circumstances, he'd have made a hell of a spy.

I gave him Fang's contact information as well.

He asked, "What will you do about this police officer?"

"I need to catch him in the act."

"In the act of what, exactly? You can't arrest him. What good does catching him in the act do us?"

"I've got so many police following me around," I said, "all I have to do is stand still and wait for them to catch up. If I can lead them to Hu and show that Hu is a foreign agent, we can expose this whole thing."

It was a good line, and mostly true, though I wasn't sure that it was actually an actionable strategy. I just needed to project confidence in my plan to Robert. We agreed to check in again in a few hours. He promised to start making calls and in-person visits, just as soon as he had the crime scene cleaned up.

Midafternoon, I drove back to my hotel. I set an alarm to go off in a few hours and disappeared.

———————

I woke before I wanted to—and worse, to the sound of someone hammering on my door.

Only cops knocked that way.

Shit.

I growled out a drowsy, "Hold on," and rolled off the bed.

I opened the door.

Danzig and Choi.

I folded my arms, creating a visual block in the doorway.

"Sorry, I was just catching a nap. Had trouble sleeping last night."

"You want to let us in?" Danzig said.

"Not particularly."

"I'm not sure you want to do this in front of your neighbors."

"First of all, I don't know what *this* is, and second, I don't know any of these people. I don't care that they know I'm talking to you."

"Where's Robert Li?" Danzig asked.

"Have you checked with the San Jose PD?"

"Yes. They don't know either."

"Well, neither do I," I said. In the purely existential sense, that was true. I knew where he *had been,* but not where he currently was at that precise moment. I felt I was covered from the standpoint of not lying to a federal agent. "You made your point last night. Several of them. I have a civil rights attorney representing me in this matter, by the way. I imagine he'll have a few points to make of his own. And, I'm sure, some choice words for the US Attorney about overreach." I let that simmer a moment. "Why do you keep harassing me?"

"Because you're interfering with an investigation," Choi said.

Danzig said, "You've got no legal standing here, Gage. No reason to be involved. Yet, here you are. If you have information regarding Johnnie Zhou's death, this Chinese intelligence operation you claim to know so much about, or anything else, you need to tell us."

"Unless you're complicit in a crime," Choi added. "In which case, you should probably tell us that too. Better now than later."

Admittedly still groggy from my nap and needing to stall for time, I stepped back to allow them inside while I busied myself at the room's coffeemaker. It was one of those one-shot makers. I did not offer them a cup. Then, once I tasted it, I realized it probably would've been a bigger insult if I had.

"Robert Li," Danzig said again.

"What's your interest in him?"

"You don't get to ask questions, Gage."

"Jesus, it's a wonder you people catch anybody. Let me tell you how to elicit information from a potential recruitment target."

"Cut the crap. It's not funny, and we're not interested," Choi said.

"I can't figure you two out. You treat me like I'm the suspect of a crime and throw me in jail for a night, just to remind me that you're willing to abuse your badge. So, if I'm not a suspect, one would think I could help you in whatever the fuck your investigation actually is. Which I *still* don't know, because you haven't told me. You're perfectly willing to threaten me, just not bring me into the tent and ask for my help. Are you trying to root out a Chinese intelligence operation? If that's it, as an American, I have a vested interest in solving that problem and would be glad to help. I already gave you David Hu's name, and you don't seem be doing shit with it."

"Are you about done?"

"What side of this are you on, Danzig?"

Danzig's eyes bored into me. Suddenly, I did not want to be on the other side of the table in an interview room with her. She was formidable, sure, though there was something else that I couldn't quite place. And it scared me.

She reminded me of an Egyptian state security officer I'd had the misfortune of crossing once.

That was a person who'd left bodies in his wake.

Then she surprised me. "Okay. Robert Li was one of the last people to see Johnnie Zhou alive. We want to talk to him."

"So, you don't think it was a suicide?"

"You haven't earned the right to ask any questions, Gage. I'm giving you that one for free."

Ignoring this, I asked, "Is Robert's life in danger?"

"At this point, we can't rule anything out."

The information itself was valuable, but not necessarily revealing, and I decided I wasn't going to trust her. Not until she'd earned it.

"I don't know where he is. That's the truth. My guess is he probably goes home soon."

"You're playing a dangerous game, Gage. I want you to know that. You think you know what's going on here, but you don't."

"I'm not playing games, Danzig. If you actually did read my file, you know damned well why I don't trust you. And you're not doing a very good job convincing me you're any better."

Danzig's eyes narrowed to dangerous slits, and I realized I'd probably pushed it too far.

"That's a convenient excuse, Gage. If I were you, I would give a lot of thought to how far you're willing to go to protect certain interests."

"And what would those be?"

"I think you know what I mean," she said.

"What—do you think if you say 'CIA' three times, a case officer appears?"

"The next time I see you, I'm arresting you."

"For what?"

"Either you have information about this case and are withholding it," Danzig started.

"In which case, that's obstruction of justice," Choi added.

"Or you're involved."

"In which case, that's a lot worse."

I was really getting tired of Choi's sidekick/straight-man act.

"The third possibility is that you're playing to type," Danzig said.

"What the hell does that mean?"

"You're a dirty ex-CIA officer, and now you're playing for the other side."

"What's funny about this is that we should be sharing information. Instead, you're going out of your way to make sure I don't tell you anything. So, if I *did* know where Robert Li was or how to get in touch with him, you're giving me absolutely zero reasons to share that with you. Meanwhile, people connected to Johnnie Zhou are dying. And you're not doing anything about it because you don't know shit about what's actually happening here."

"If you have information on Robert Li, you need to tell me right now."

"No, I don't. Remember that lawyer I mentioned? If you threaten me again, without evidence, we'll hit you with an injunction that'll stop this case cold. I'll launch a civil suit against the Bureau alleging you're coming after me personally to settle some Bureau grudge. And you and your whole case are going to be on the front page of every news organization in the world. Based on what you did here today, you've all but ensured I won't say a damn thing to you without a lawyer present."

It'd be more impressive if I thought I could actually do any of those things, though the bluff was solid.

Danzig didn't call it.

"Solving one murder doesn't take another off your conscience, Gage. Think on that." She nodded to Choi, who shouldered past me and went out into the hall. Danzig followed, stopped and turned her head. "You've been given all of the chances you're going to get."

She left.

Her last words did not.

Danzig had indeed read my file. When she'd told me yesterday, I'd assumed she was bluffing. She wasn't.

She knew I was involved with a woman at my last posting in Managua and that woman had died for it. It was a cheap shot by Danzig, and one intended to get at me because she could. To throw me off balance. It was a more visceral version of locking me up for a night.

I could see Danzig and Choi's strategy now. Bucking them like I did might not have been smart, and it sure as hell didn't do me any favors, but I'd be damned if someone was going to accuse me of betraying my country. Turning Robert over to them might be a way to protect the others in the network, might actually get the Feebs to move on the Chinese. It just wouldn't protect me. It seemed like they were attributing Hu's moves to me. The Bureau was using my poor reputation with them and drawing some shitty conclusions with it.

I had to serve him up to clear my name. Or I had to lawyer up and walk away. Which I wasn't going to do.

As I played the conversation back in my head, it was clear they wanted to isolate me. If I was alone, they reasoned, I'd have nowhere else to turn but them.

The good news was I saw it coming.

The bad news was, to greater or lesser degrees, I suspected everyone.

28

Time to move.

I'd slept enough that I could keep going the next few hours.

I walked out to the Defender and powered up the burner phone I used to track the AirTag on Hu's car. It wasn't until I'd done the mental inventory of things that I realized I hadn't checked the tracker since I'd placed it.

Unfortunately, David Hu was smarter than I'd given him credit for.

He took his car to the usual places, work, errands, that sort of thing. What I didn't see was trips into Los Altos.

I'd made the dangerous assumption that the only ones capable of tradecraft were spooks. That was foolish. Plus, if Hu was what I thought he was, he'd have similar training as what Nate had given Zhou. That meant he'd have a drop car—which I assumed was a short order for a cop.

First, I messaged Nate in Signal, asking for updates, then I drove to Elizabeth's hotel.

As I drove, I counted my blessings Danzig hadn't called my bluff about the attorney and the Orpheus Foundation. Jennie and I talked while I was driving to meet Nate. She'd spoken with the attorney and debriefed them on my situation. The FBI was clearly exceeding its authority in holding me, and there might be grounds for a civil rights complaint, though she didn't think it would actually make it to trial. That was the good news. The not-so-good news was the Orpheus Foundation didn't want anything to do with me if I was supporting the Central Intelligence Agency. Jennie didn't ask and explicitly stated that she didn't want to know. If I'd uncovered a Chinese intelligence operation silencing dissidents, they were interested. If I'd uncovered evidence that the state police were abusing their authority to scare off a private investigator, they were interested.

If I was protecting my old employer, they couldn't come within a hundred miles of it.

That was a hard question to answer because, at this moment, I couldn't look Jennie in the face and tell her I wasn't. I owed her something for bailing me out. The question was how to do that without exposing Nate.

Man, I needed to stop trying to thread so many needles.

If I got jammed up again, I was on my own.

Unless I was willing to sell Nate out. Or, at least, to stop covering for him.

I knocked on Elizabeth's hotel door, and there was no answer, so I called and heard the phone ring inside the room. After another handful of seconds, she opened the door. Elizabeth was not in a good place. There was a haunted look in her eyes. She was tired. She let me inside. There was a bottle of wine open on the suite's table, and she'd worked through half of it. Elizabeth returned to her spot on the bed, hugging her knees and cupping the glass of wine between her hands.

"Something happened," I said. "Do you want to talk about it?"

"I spent all day with the FBI is what happened." Her voice was thick and strained. "You could have warned me they thought I was involved."

So that was Danzig's play. Drive a wedge between Elizabeth and me, make it look like I was hiding something from her. Isolate me from everyone until I had nowhere left to turn, no one left to protect.

"I didn't know they thought you were."

"Special Agent Danzig told me she asked you that exact question."

"She would say that," I said.

"So, now we can't trust the FBI either?"

Shit.

"They danced around the subject, Elizabeth. They don't know what to make of me so—"

"Lot of that going around."

"—so they won't tell me what their investigation is actually about. I offered to help, and they refused to clue me in. Instead, they threw me in jail for a night."

"Why do that?"

"They think I'm hiding something, and the only way to get to it is if they scare it out of me. It never occurred to them, apparently, to just be honest. I told her that given my history with the FBI, I don't trust them. They did nothing to change my mind. Look, I'm not telling *you* not to trust the Feds. You should cooperate with whatever they ask. I do think the Chinese have flipped a local cop. I do not think the FBI are comprised, I just think they're assholes. Fair?"

"I guess," she mumbled.

"What did they say to you?"

"First, they wanted to know if I knew anything about my father's activism. Was I involved? Did he ever talk about it with me? A lot of the questions you asked when we first started. Then they wanted to know what my father and I fought about, since I was the last person to see him alive. It was so awful reliving that with them. Like I haven't been over that a million times in my head already. Then they asked me how much I stood to gain if he was murdered. Can you imagine how callous you'd have to be to ask that?"

"I can," I said. Nothing Danzig did at this point would surprise me.

"They didn't know about the deal Benjamin Blake offered me. It doesn't matter, since it didn't exist when my father died. I threw it at her anyway, just to watch the embarrassment on that snide bitch's face when I told her something she didn't already know." Elizabeth took a healthy swallow from her wineglass and returned her eyes to their transfixed, forward-staring position.

After a few beats of silence, she added, "They wanted to know why I hired you."

I exhaled some anger. More remained. "I told them all that," I said.

"No, Matt, they wanted to know why I hired *you*. She wanted to know where I got the name of a 'disgraced ex-CIA officer.' Her words. She said you were fired for cause. Is that true?"

"According to my personnel record. That doesn't make it fact."

"You told me you quit. If you lied about that, what else haven't you been honest with me about?"

Why am I always getting in trouble over someone else's secrets?

"I never lied to you. I just didn't tell you all of the truth."

"That's the same thing."

"No, Elizabeth, it isn't," I said with hard words. "There are things I can't share with you. Just because my work with the government ended, doesn't mean I can unburden myself of what I know. It's part of the job. I've had to learn to live with a lot of horrible things. I don't get to just spill the secrets I learned throughout my career because I'm pissed off they shit-canned me."

"That's really very interesting," she said snidely.

Telling someone who didn't understand, "You don't understand!" was a terrible defense.

"I could get thrown against a wall for sharing this much, but here goes. I was the Chief of Station in Nicaragua. It was a small post, and we had just a few officers. A lot of our work—along with the other posts in Central America—is figuring out how we can stabilize the region to help reduce the flow of illegal immigrants coming across the US border. The Nicaraguans and the Russians have had a long history of collaboration. The SVR—that's the Russian's foreign intelligence service—had operatives all over Managua. The SVR has been losing ground for years, and the Russians have had to cut back on 'security cooperation' ever since they overextended in Ukraine. My team hatched a plan that would've gotten the Russians out of there for good.

"Unfortunately, that plan relied on an asset we learned the SVR may have compromised. I told Langley we needed to back off until we knew for certain. They denied it and told me to proceed. The person at headquarters responsible for Nicaragua—we call them desk officers—came up with what he thought was a bold plan to expose the Russian agent and still accomplish our original objective. However, it relied on us doing some things that were highly questionable, if not illegal. I pushed back and got overruled. I wasn't going to send my people in to do this, so I went. This was risky because as a Chief of Station, I was in a declared position, meaning it was the one role at the station that the CIA acknowledges. Station chiefs generally don't do operational work for that reason. I hoped this would get Langley to reconsider. They did not.

"I told the asset, Oscar, we knew the Russians had bought him off, and if he screwed me, I was going to dime him out to his bosses in Nicaraguan intelligence. He agreed. The op went forward, but the guy must've panicked, and he told the Russians everything. They exposed it, and it blew up in our faces. We lost multiple agents, including the double, and that all fell on me. Langley can be very bureaucratic and very petty, especially regarding failure."

"But it wasn't your fault."

"That doesn't matter. Nearly any sin is excusable in the CIA so long as they can keep it quiet. You want to see some Old Testament retribution, wait'll the press gets a hold of an intelligence operation. And I was Chief of Station. It was ultimately my responsibility. I'd stated for the record in a cable that I thought it was a bad idea and we should cancel the mission. That ended up counting for less than I thought. It's bad enough when we lose agents—that can often result in what we call a tour curtailment and someone getting yanked home.

"It gets worse. Because I was the Chief of Station, the Russians knew me and had me followed to and from work most nights. In order to meet with this double agent, I decided I needed a cover, something that would throw the Russians off. I'd been seeing someone at the embassy. She was Diplomatic Security Service, so she wasn't a spook and knew how to handle herself. My thinking at the time was that my people were all potentially compromised, and Angel wasn't an undercover. We'd been seen out together, I'd assumed, so it wouldn't raise any suspicion. She wasn't supposed to do anything in the field, just drive the car and help me not look like who I was. We still don't know how the Russians figured it out. They grabbed her from the car while I was meeting with Oscar."

My voice broke.

I couldn't speak for a while.

"Local police found her body the next morning. We don't think they tortured her. They weren't after information, they just wanted to send a message to us not to get involved. Oscar's body turned up later that week. I got yanked back to headquarters and relieved of command. It created a major international incident, which the State Department worked very hard to keep under wraps."

"Oh my God," Elizabeth said.

"Yeah," I said, and poured myself a glass. "Angel and I were serious. The relationship made sense to us, I suppose. We didn't make a lot of plans—that had seemed strange to do, given our careers and situation. But I loved her. So, the reason I'm not getting any help from our friends in the FBI is that at every embassy, there's a senior special agent called a Legal Attaché. Their job is to be the representative of US law enforcement in that country. I used to have great relationships with these guys, and I'd seek their advice all the time. Except Special Agent Bradford Keane. Managua is a considered a hardship post, so a lot of people don't or can't bring their families. Keane didn't. He did, however, have a string of affairs with State Department officers and at least two foreign diplomats that I knew about. It was starting to get around, and I told him, as a counterintelligence matter, to keep it in his pants. If the opposition found out, this was something that could get him compromised. Rather than take my advice, once I got jammed up, he added some extracurricular details, like I was running shoddy operations, was drinking on the job, using operational funds to support a girlfriend, shit like that. Anything to undermine my credibility so that if I exposed him, no one would believe me."

"I'm so sorry, Matt."

I shook it off, hid my reaction behind the wineglass. "Did you tell Danzig how you got my name?"

"I told them I looked you up online. Which, from a strictly legal standpoint, I did do. I just left out the part where I'd found out where to look." A dry, dark smile formed at the corner of her mouth. Elizabeth was a shrewd attorney. "Nate was my father's friend for thirty years, and he was good to me. I'm not making any trouble for him."

I sat down in one of the suite's chairs.

"So, look, I'm not going to tell you not to trust the FBI, but I want you to understand why I can't. In spite of everything, I gave them a chance to cooperate, and they told me to F off."

"Did you?"

"As far as I'm concerned, I made a good faith effort." A grim smile broke my lips. "Though it may have come across like a grenade in a punchbowl." I shrugged and took a drink. "Did you have any luck with the safe deposit box?"

"I did, actually. There were four in the area and dad had an account with one. It was the first one I called. Los Altos Secure Trust."

Sometimes there was the obvious answer that slaps you in the face, and it was embarrassing that you hadn't figured that one out.

"The good news is that dad has a box there. The bad news is that I need a probate court to authorize them to release it to me because my name isn't on the account. That's a thirty-day process. I've got my estate attorney on it." She purged the air in her lungs. "We should not hold our breath."

"Knowing it's there is a huge help. We should tell them someone stole your dad's key; that way, they don't let anyone in who isn't you."

"I imagine someone like you could forge a power of attorney," she said.

"Yep. Or a court order. You can believe they'll use every dirty trick in the book. And, if I'm right, they've got a cop at their disposal."

"And you told the FBI all this?" Elizabeth said.

"More or less. If they believed me, they don't seem to be acting on it."

"This is stupid," she said, mostly to herself. "Well, I'll get my estate guy on the probate court, try to shake that loose. God, they don't make this easy." She cradled her wineglass and drank deep, finishing it in one gulp, then slid off the bed and refilled. As she did, she held the bottle for a moment, considering. Then, "Matt, the FBI scared me."

"I know. That's how they operate."

"No, it's not that. Well, it *was* that, but not all... I don't know. Was my father involved in something illegal? You've got more insight into this than anyone. You don't think he could've... He wasn't a spy, was he?"

I didn't respond immediately. Though I knew the answer, I thought she needed to know I was being deliberate. "I've told you this before, Elizabeth, and I still believe it. Your father risked his life to organize people to speak out against an oppressive government in Beijing. He wanted the world to know what was happening there."

"Was he working for the CIA? Special Agent Danzig really tried to make an issue of that. She didn't see how I'd come in contact with an ex-CIA officer." Elizabeth was bringing this up again, so, clearly, my first deflection hadn't done the trick. Though a federal agent can be quite persuasive.

"I think Danzig is trying anything she can to connect me here. The Bureau has had it out for me ever since Nicaragua, and it's coloring her judgment. Your father did righteous work. I know that took a toll on you and on your family." Unfortunately, that's also why I can't go to them with what I have. Since I'd already suspected them of attributing Hu's moves to me, there was nothing I could do to convince them otherwise unless and until I could serve Hu up on a platter.

Elizabeth hid her face behind her glass. "I think I was just angry and looking for somewhere to put it."

"Maybe, maybe not. I've seen this sort of thing play out before in families with agents I've run. I recognize the burden this can be. You aren't wrong in feeling this way. I just wanted you to know that. But I also wanted you to know what your father was doing was brave and important."

"Thank you for saying that. It helps." Elizabeth turned to look at me for the first time in several minutes, her face drawn and serious. "I'm just not sure I should keep this up," she said. "I'm scared, Matt. What the hell do I even do?"

In the back of my mind, there was Benjamin Blake's offer, circling like a surveillance drone keeping its dirty eye on me. I had to tell her. She'd find out if I didn't, and Blake would spin it to make it look like I'd kept it from her on purpose. Which wouldn't be technically untrue, Blake would just be wrong about the motive. And there was the FBI to consider. Danzig could also spin this in her favor. She could make it look like I'd hidden Blake's offer as a way of manipulating things in my favor.

"I want to know who killed your father. Or rather, I believe I *know* now, but I want to be able to prove it. I won't lie to you. The only part of this I don't have an answer for is how I convince the FBI to look in the right place. I guess that's what I'm hoping is in your father's safe deposit box. I want to keep going. But...there is something else to consider."

A terse, bitter laugh issued from her mouth. "There's a shock."

I couldn't avoid it any longer. "I didn't want to put anything else on your shoulders, but ethically, I can't keep it from you. Ben Blake called me earlier today."

"Christ, what now? I haven't returned any of his calls. I just don't have the energy."

"He's upping his ante. Apparently, the company is about to sign a major deal with some foreign investors. He didn't come out and say it, but I got the sense they were selling the firm and that the buyers were Asian. He said they cannot afford any bad publicity, and by that, I think he means anything that suggests your father might've been involved in 'something.' He's increasing his offer to you by two million as long as everything with your father stays quiet." I thought on how to message the part about his paying me a triple fee above what Elizabeth was doing. That would amount to almost a half-year's salary for me. "He tried to buy me off. I'm only telling you because it would look bad on me if I didn't. I can't blame you if you want to take his offer. It's a lot of money, probably squares your father's debts, and gives you a lot left."

"Would you keep doing this if I took that money?"

"What do you mean?"

"Exposing this Chinese spy ring, or whatever you'd call it. This is important to you. I can tell," Elizabeth said.

"Would you be angry if I did?"

"Yes," she said. "If it's a condition of the deal with Blake, and I asked you to stop."

Well, that's good to know.

"There isn't much I can do without your approval. However, I now have the additional complication of having to clear my name with the FBI. And there are the people your father worked with. They need to be protected. If you asked me to stop, I could walk away from your end of it and do my best to keep your name out of it. You have my word on that. I cannot allow a foreign spy ring to operate on US soil and not do something about it. What are you going to do?" I asked. Lurking in the background, though unspoken, was my commitment to Jennie and the Orpheus Foundation for getting me out of jail and buying me a couple of days. I had to give them something. If I didn't, Jennie would always think it was because I was covering for the Agency.

"I'm not there yet. Two million dollars more is a lot of money, but Blake has to pay me my father's shares if this turns out to be a murder. I also have a verbal offer from him to forgive the suicide clause. Which, now, seems like a way to clear the sale of the company. If the sale valuation is higher than what they're offering, I'm better off not cashing out. And I get his point about publicity. He's worried that this case torpedoes his deal."

"I don't like Blake very much, but I see his side. He's got nothing to do with your father's activism, and he says he tried to help. I don't want to see them lose the deal over this."

Elizabeth nodded. "I need to know what Dad had in this safe deposit box. For me. Something doesn't add up here, and I want to know what it is. Whoever stole that out of dad's safe must've had an idea what it was. We need to get it before they do."

"Now you're thinking like a spy," I said, darkly. I stood and set my half-empty glass of wine on the table.

"What are you going to do now?"

"Do I have your permission to keep going?"

"For now."

"Then I'm going to try to convince the FBI they're looking in the wrong spot," I said and moved to leave.

"Be careful, Matt."

I acknowledged with a nod.

That wasn't actually what I was going to do. Given the circumstances, I felt better knowing I was the only one who knew what my next moves were.

I stopped in that empty space between the room and the door and turned back to face her.

"Elizabeth, this case is important to me in ways I can't fully explain to you."

"I think I can appreciate that now, even if I can't understand them," she said. She unwrapped her arms from her legs and slid off the bed. I walked over to her.

"You're important to me too," I said. When she didn't react, I added, "What I mean is, if it comes to that. If you ask me to stop, I will. Just know there are some things I can't walk away from."

And a choice was made.

Elizabeth walked over, and I took her up in my arms. She looked up at me, and I ran a thumb along her cheek.

Sometimes you could say a lot without saying anything.

I drove back to my hotel and noted it was darker than usual. A quick glance around confirmed that two of the parking lot lights were out. I'd let the staff know on my way in. It was long past sundown and given my large, late lunch I wasn't particularly hungry. First order would be to check in with Robert and probably a supplicant call to Jennie to see where we stood. I couldn't afford to piss Orpheus off.

Keeping my laptop locked in its hidden compartment in the Defender, I closed and locked the vehicle and headed inside.

I felt a hard stab in my kidney, followed by an explosion of bright, all-consuming pain. Like my body was being pulled apart at the seams. My last conscious thought was it was a taser. A thick, rope-like arm wrapped around my throat in a vise grip and squeeze.

I fell into a black pit.

It had no bottom.

29

I awakened to the pain first.

It felt like coming to in a lake of fire. My body radiated a dull ache in some areas and sharp, searing pain in others. The one thing my body could agree on, everything hurt like hell.

Gradually, other senses and faculties returned.

It was dark where I was, and I learned the hard way that it was a confined space. Stars erupted across my blacked-out vision as I sat up and hit something metal with my whole face. My long training as an intelligence officer concluded that I was in the trunk of a car.

Banging my head helped clear it, and now I could evaluate my situation. My hands were bound with plastic zip-ties, as were my ankles. This put the odds of David Hu being my attacker squarely in the "probable" column. He was a big dude and lifting my limp frame wouldn't be that difficult for him. It actually surprised me that he hadn't pinned my hands behind my back. While that would've made it harder to maneuver me, it would have also made it significantly more difficult for me to get out.

It also surprised me that Hu had left me alive.

There'd be a reason for that, though the time to figure it out wasn't now. First, I needed to get the hell out of the trunk.

The only thing I was certain of was that the car wasn't moving. I didn't know anything else about my surroundings and had no way to judge time. My watch, phone, wallet—all of my personal effects had been removed. Listening was certainly impaired, but I heard something rhythmic, a staticky sound, in the background.

Hu had cleared the trunk before dropping me in here. A quick scan with my limited reach confirmed there was nothing I could use to free myself.

There were a few ways to get out of plastic cuffs, though most of them required use of an improvised shim—which I didn't have—foresight to create space between the wrists when cuffed—which I hadn't had—or space to move your arms—which I didn't have much of.

Plastic ties became more rigid and, therefore, more fragile the tighter they are. This was why, when they were applied, the hands were usually placed behind the subject's back so you could leave a little flex while still keeping the person secured. In placing them in front of me, Hu had inadvertently given me a little space to work with. As a cop, I'd have expected him to know better. Of course, he may not have had much time.

I pulled my wrists up to my mouth and yanked on the end with my teeth, tightening it until there was no slack left. The plastic bit painfully into my skin. Then I rolled onto my back to get some space. First, I thrust my elbows out as wide as they'd go, which put pressure on the cuffs. I snap-twisted my wrists as hard as I could. I repeated the process several more times, violently winging my elbows out and then twisting my wrists in opposite directions.

There was a "pop" and an immediate release of pressure, followed by a lessening of sharp pain...followed by a flooding of fresh pain of a different sort. I was fine with that.

Once my hands were free, the feet were small trouble. Hu had cinched the cuffs around my ankles, but over my pants. I removed my shoes and socks, yanked my pants free and then just worked with the gap to slide the zip-tie under one heel and then the other. Borrowing moves from Houdini, I managed to get my shoes and socks back on. The trunk had an emergency release lever. But would popping it alert anyone?

I pulled the release with one hand, holding onto the trunk lid with the other to control its ascent. I lifted it a crack and saw a sliver of light. Clearly daytime. The sound I'd heard earlier was the crashing of waves. Pungent salt air flooded the trunk, and the roar of the waves ground out any other noise, so I knew I had to be close to the water.

Time to test my luck. I slowly lifted the trunk lid about six inches. If someone was watching, they'd see the movement for sure. If not, I might be able to slip out and catch them off guard. My muscles ached like hell from being bound for what was probably hours and were slow to respond. That could be a problem if I needed to move quickly or defend myself. Both highly likely. Then there was the more holistic trauma to my nervous system from some rather aggressive tasering.

I rolled onto my side, still holding the lid as steady as I could, knowing the motion would draw attention. I thrust a leg through the gap and lifted my midsection, inching my way over. I hadn't attracted any notice that I could tell. Or, if I had, they were just watching for amusement. My left foot touched the ground and gave me enough purchase to shift my weight and slide the rest of my body through the gap. Holding onto the license plate, I closed the trunk as gently as I could. Crouching behind the car, a light-colored Ford Taurus, I peered over the trunk. The car was empty. Clouds hid the sun. My guess was midmorning, eight, maybe nine.

I stood and stretched my legs, which brought some fresh pain, which I welcomed in a way. I checked the doors and found them locked. There was a small bag in the back seat. Time to get a check on my surroundings. Hu had ditched the car on a dirt road on a low cliff above the water, shielded from the main road by a pair of large, leafy trees. I could make out the dark silhouette of mountains to the north and south. There were a few lights visible in the bluffs above and directly below me.

I smashed the back window glass with a rock and opened the door. The bag contained my personal effects, though not all of them. Curiously, he'd left some things—my watch and wallet, but had taken my phone and car keys. Interesting that he'd want me to be found with identification. My guess had been pretty close: it was eight forty-five.

Part of my Agency training included identifying the effects of chemical agents and intoxicants. While not as common as it was during the Cold War, it wasn't unheard of for spies to be captured and incapacitated with drugs. I couldn't deduce the specific agent Hu had used, just that I felt the effects of something. My reflexes would be sluggish for some time.

My regular phone was missing, and the burner that I'd used to track the AirTag was hopefully still locked in the Defender along with my laptop and pistol. First order of business, figure out where in the hell I was.

We didn't live in a time when I was willing to knock on a stranger's door and count on their humanity, especially not after seeing my face in the car's sideview mirror. I looked, rightly, like I'd lost a fight. Or was strung out. So that left finding a gas station.

A quick search of the car revealed the keys were long gone. While I'd been trained to hotwire, it was harder on newer model cars, and I didn't have any tools. With no better options, I'd walk. I found a rather steep trail leading up to an affluent neighborhood atop the bluff. Surely a disheveled man in dark clothes wandering among these posh homes wouldn't attract attention. Normally, I'd welcome the police's assistance, except that I had to assume Hu left me alive for a reason and that probably meant making me a target. It was reasonable to assume there was an APB out on me. Until I could prove otherwise, I'd need to stay away from anything official. I could see some shopping centers up ahead, maybe a half mile away.

Moving inland, I passed a string of beachside restaurants and shops, mostly still closed. I was in a beach town that looked mostly asleep. The shopping center was on the far side of the highway that separated the beach from the mainland. I spotted a grocery store and some coffee shops that were open. I picked one, ordered a large coffee and breakfast burrito. The kid behind the counter gave me a curious look, so I simply said, "Rough night," and flashed a crooked smile.

Sustenance in hand, I spotted a commuter lot and a Park and Ride across from the shopping center. And it had a twenty-four hour gas station. Signage told me I was in Linda Mar. Of course, not being familiar with the Bay Area, I had no idea where that was. Now, to figure out how to get out of here. One of the downsides of ubiquitous cell phone ownership was that most municipalities had stripped out their pay phones. I walked into the Chevron station.

"Hey," I said.

"Help you," the guy behind the counter said.

"This is pretty embarrassing. Um, my wife and I just had a huge fight, and she threw me out of the house." I closed my eyes and exhaled, as if exhuming recent trauma. "She even threw my phone into the woods. I just need to call a cab so I can get a hotel. Any chance I can borrow your phone? I didn't see a payphone out front. I'll buy some stuff for the trouble."

"It's no trouble at all. I got a wife too, man," he said. He googled the cab companies nearest the gas station, then turned the screen so I could see. I got a cab dispatcher to send one out to me, and they said it'd be about thirty minutes.

The fiction might not be necessary, but I worried that my not having a phone and not knowing where I was would raise too many questions. Fearing that Hu might have tipped off the local police—to what, I had no idea—the last thing I needed was this guy deciding to call the cops.

"So, we're separated, as you can probably guess. I actually live in the southland and came up here to patch stuff up. So much for that. Anyway, I'm not from here, and I don't really know the area well. How long would it take me to get to the airport from here this time of day? I think I'm just going to head home early."

"Man that must've been some fight. Well, SFO is just over the mountains there, about twenty minutes. I think it's eleven, twelve miles."

I thanked him for his time and bought a Gatorade, then headed outside to wait for my cab, which only took about fifteen minutes.

Even at this hour, it took forty minutes to get back to Cupertino. My head was still foggy from the stun gun, the beating, and the drug-induced trunk nap. One thing was clear—I'd need a few hours of legitimate sleep if I was going to be functional today. The question was how to get it. My hotel had to be burned. I had the cabbie drop me at the Safeway on the other side of the parking lot, paid and thanked him, left a decent tip. There was a Santa Clara County Sheriff cruiser parked in front of the hotel, confirming my suspicions that Hu was the one who mugged me and that he'd scorched me with the local cops. That meant he was doing something that he needed me out of action for, but still alive.

I'd parked my Defender on the side of the hotel, and it was still where I'd left it. There didn't appear to be dedicated surveillance on my vehicle, just the one deputy in front of the hotel. If they had a dragnet on me, they were just getting going.

In addition to the hidden panels inside, one of the mods Miguel had done for me was to add a small, concealed box in the undercarriage. It was designed so that it wouldn't accidentally open if I was off-roading and was a place to store a spare key. At the time, he said, "If you're asking me to build in somewhere to hide a gun, might as well hide a spare key."

Sound logic.

I opened the Defender and found my phone and main set of keys. The phone was dead. Best guess, Hu assumed the locations services were active —no way in hell of that—and wanted anyone looking for me to look here rather than forty minutes away on the coast. That confirmed my suspicion that Hu's plan called for me to be alive but unreachable for several hours. I also don't think he expected I'd get out of the car as quickly as I did. Maybe time was still on my side.

Sleep would have to wait.

I plugged the phone into the Defender, another of the aftermarket mods. I was desperate to check messages, but I wasn't going to do it here. It would take a few minutes to charge it enough to turn it on.

Time to move. Time to find answers. By now, I was familiar enough with Cupertino that I could improvise a surveillance detection route. I wound a curving path through the city, doubling back at random intervals. I had no idea whether I was black or not—Agency parlance for being unde-tected, in the clear. If I was being followed, they'd have multiple radio-coor-dinated cars.

The phone had enough charge that it'd gone through its booting cycle.

I almost wish it hadn't.

I pulled off the main street to check messages.

Several calls from Elizabeth, including one that was less than five minutes ago. Several from Nate. A few unlisted numbers. I scrolled through the voicemail transcripts. The translations weren't perfect, but I got the gist. Everyone wanted to talk to me, immediately. One of the unlisted messages was from Special Agent Danzig.

About the only person I hadn't heard from was Robert.

I pulled out of the parking lot, picked up I-280 eastbound, and raced to

San Jose. I could assume that Elizabeth was up from the time stamp, but I didn't want to call her just yet. Not until I knew what was going on. Even with my exhausted mind, that case-officer sixth sense began connecting disparate pieces of information, and I started forming what I thought was a reasonable hypothesis about the last few hours.

It was confirmed when I neared Robert's house.

There were multiple police vehicles out front.

And a coroner van.

——————

Idling on the corner, half a block from his house and staring, utterly incapable of movement. Every case-officer instinct screamed *get moving!* The setup was obvious, achingly transparent, and flawlessly executed. Knowing their operation was exposed, Hu's handler had him knock me out and hide me somewhere for a string of dark hours. Then they murdered Robert while I was out. It could've been Hu or, God forbid, they had another agent.

Because they'd broken into Zhou's home and accessed the safe, the Chinese now had the names of all of Johnnie's people. But Robert was the one who could identify them, because he'd been to the center.

And I was one of the last to see Robert alive.

Killing him while I was nowhere to be found and without an alibi meant I'd be the chief suspect.

Worse, the FBI had pressed me on his location, and I'd refused to tell them. I could only imagine how that made me look to authorities now. To say nothing of the fact that if I'd cooperated, Robert might've been safe.

Spying was a dangerous and potentially deadly business.

We risked our lives to steal our enemies' secrets, to get inside their decision loop.

Worse, we manipulated others to take risks on behalf of America's national interests. We went to sleep at night knowing this, and we told ourselves versions of the lies we told our agents—*this risk will make us safer.*

We lost agents.

Case officers—the good and righteous ones—would move heaven and earth to protect their assets. Often times these assets were dark and dirty souls, people with blood on their hands. But you would risk everything to protect them because that responsibility was a sacred trust. Losing an agent was a terrible, awful, catastrophic thing.

Robert Li didn't die in pursuit of America's interests.

He died because I'd talked him into making himself a target.

That was never the intent. It was just the outcome.

Robert had discovered a Chinese covert police operation that was punishing people for speaking out against oppression. He wanted to hide. I pushed him into the open. And it cost him his life.

Tears welled in my eyes, and I fought back a surge of anger I hadn't thought myself capable of. It was a pure and raw thing, a roiling fury threatening to explode. People sometimes talked about "seeing red" before they lost all self-control and got violent.

I finally understood what that meant.

I backed up, turning around in someone's driveway so as not to expose myself further on Robert's street.

My first call went to Nate.

"Matt, what the hell is going on? Elizabeth just called me in a complete panic."

"They killed him," I growled out. "Robert Li. The Chinese, or their agent, that cop—they killed him last night. And I think they framed me for it."

"I'm going to send you an address and time in Signal. Assume DISCUS is in effect."

He hung up.

I found a commuter parking lot in downtown San Jose and pulled into a spot.

DISCUS was a codeword we used in Nate's unit. It was a randomly generated cryptonym that didn't mean anything on its own. We used it to say that an operation was burned and that our unit's version of the "Moscow Rules" were in effect. Essentially, assume everyone outside the unit was potentially compromised. Use extreme surveillance detection practices. Assume the opposition was using any and all means to surveil you. Assume your life was in danger.

The location Nate sent was the parking garage of San Jose's Norman Mineta Airport. That was dangerously close to Robert's house, which Nate couldn't know. I understood why he'd chosen that spot—an airport parking garage would have constant vehicle traffic we could blend in with, and not even the FBI could use surveillance drones or aircraft over an airport. The meeting time was in thirty minutes.

Invoking DISCUS meant a few things and not just that I should assume there was an APB out on me.

One of our dictums was that everyone outside the unit could potentially have been turned by the opposition. That meant, I wasn't supposed to trust Elizabeth either.

I grabbed a tactical flashlight that I kept in the glove box and got out. The flash was twice as bright as the one on my phone.

It didn't take long.

I found it on the inside of the wheel well, a small GPS tracker. The good news was I'd found it before I went on my SDR to meet Nate. The bad news was I hadn't looked before now.

It meant that whoever put it there knew I'd escaped the trunk and was on the move.

Whatever they were planning was going to pick up speed now, and I had to burn half an hour just to have a meeting.

I tried to focus on driving and surveillance detection, mostly so I could avoid the crushing guilt that I'd gotten Robert killed. It was inescapable, however.

The man's sad, knowing smile was burned into my mind, and I couldn't unsee it.

"I'm sorry, Robert," I said aloud.

30

I got to the garage with ten minutes to spare so I took time for a field shower with one of the packets of body wipes I kept in my go bag. Cleaning off the sweat and grime of the last few hours helped revive me a little. I put on a fresh t-shirt and pulled the Glock out of its secure storage slot in the door, clipping the holster to my waistband.

Nate arrived exactly on time driving a blue Tesla Model X. He wore a jacket and pants that I knew had been altered to add about ten pounds to his appearance. He also wore a pair of aviator-style eyeglasses.

"What happened, Matt?"

I gave a timeline of last night, including my conversation with Elizabeth. If he had reason to suspect her, there might be a clue in her words. Invoking DISCUS spun me in a bunch of different directions regarding her, and none of them were good. If she was involved, it certainly made it easier to believe I'd been set up. They'd known where I was and where I'd be going, which did most of Hu's work for him.

Nate said nothing, just nodded and mostly looked at the pavement.

"Hu was waiting for me in the parking lot. I was already tired from being up all night in jail, and I didn't see him. Hit me with a stun gun and then a choke hold for good measure. When I came to, I felt effects of a toxin, so I assumed he injected something while I was out. I woke up in a trunk in some abandoned car on the coast about a half hour from here. Freed myself and then figured out how to get back to my hotel. Hu left my phone and car keys in the vehicle, and my vehicle in the parking lot, so anyone tracking me would think I was still there."

"Why didn't he kill you? Why bother with kidnapping and leaving a potential witness?"

"By putting me out of commission, they could take Robert out without much of a fight. Which they did. Remember, they came at me with a couple of their goons before, and I fought them off. More than that, they can also frame me for his murder. I have a shit alibi for where I was. I tell that story to the cops, and they'll think I made it up."

"What does framing you accomplish that killing you doesn't?"

"Arresting me ends the investigation. If the police think I'm a crooked ex-spy who's playing for the other team, they can hang all of those murders on me, and the MPS skates. At least long enough that they can roll up the rest of the network and extract their operatives. If they kill me, it means the murderer is still out there, and the police keep looking. And now the Chinese have the entire list of names of Johnnie's network and the locations of all his dead drops."

"How'd they get that?" Nate asked.

"Hu broke into Johnnie's house and got into his safe. The FBI had the place up on surveillance. They showed me the video, and they think it was me. There was also a key in there to a safe deposit box that Johnnie had, and that was gone too. Elizabeth tracked the box down. The vault company won't let her access it without a court order because she wasn't listed on the account."

"The Chinese don't know you're ex-Agency though, right?"

"No, that's my bad luck," I said. Anger bubbled up at the question, and I tried to let it go. I understood why he asked, but it still felt self-serving. "As far as Hu knows, I'm just a private detective. He doesn't know anything about the Agency, and I didn't tip him to it. There's no reason for him, or them, to make that connection."

"So, right now, the Chinese have everything from Johnnie's house—the names of all of his operatives. Though some of those they must already have because they knew Robert, and you said, what, four others have been killed?"

"That's right. We knew they had an incomplete list. Now they've got everything. Assuming it was Hu."

"What's that supposed to mean?" Nate asked, picking up on the question within my tone.

"Tell me it wasn't one of your guys in there that night."

"Watch yourself, Matt."

"No, you don't get to duck this. My ass is on the line here. Tell me that wasn't you. It wasn't an operative or a contractor or someone to whom you vaguely expressed a desired outcome, so you could have deniability. Look me in the eyes and tell me you aren't covering your tracks."

I expected Zeusian fury. Thunderbolts and cursing.

Instead, Nate looked at me, his face somber, almost sad. "It wasn't us, Matt." He paused, probably to see if I'd argue further. I didn't. "For what it's worth, I think your reasoning on the MPS's plan is sound. Though, if I'm being honest, I think you're giving them more credit than I would. They aren't nearly as savvy as State Security and have no track record of operating abroad. You think Elizabeth is trying to get into Johnnie's box at the vault? That's the next move? Any idea what's in it?"

"Not entirely. Considering what was in his house, I'm guessing it's the last piece that ties all this together. If not, I'm in some deep shit."

"I don't like the idea of you pinning all your hopes on a black box."

"What other choice do I have? At this point, I have to assume I'm a suspect in Robert Li's murder, and the FBI already thinks I'm working for the Chinese. The only hope I've got is by finding the contents of the safe and the deposit box and giving that over to Special Agent Danzig. God willing, I can lead them to David Hu." That was the plan, just not *all* of it.

There wasn't a lot to suggest Danzig was going to act on any information I gave her. Even if it came straight from Johnnie Zhou. I was going to have to use the foundation as leverage. Basically, she could either act on the intel or I would give the whole thing to Orpheus and let them blow it all the way up.

It was paper thin.

"What about your next moves? And what do you need from me?"

"I don't know," I said. The beating and the drugs and the night in a trunk...it was catching up with me. My brain felt like it was trudging through four feet of snow. "Now would be a great time for you to pull whatever levers you have with the Bureau in Washington."

"I'll see what I can do."

That wasn't nearly good enough.

"Hu is going to make a play for that deposit box. I need to get what's in there or lead the FBI to him."

"How are you going to do that?"

"Right now, the less you know, the better. Let's just say I have an idea. You invoked DISCUS for a reason. Why?"

"I've known Elizabeth her whole life, though I'm more of a distant relative than a close confidant. People change. We've seen good men betray their countries, their friends, even their families over and over. We've convinced them to do it. I'm not saying she has. I'm not even suggesting it's possible. I am saying you need to be absolutely certain of her before we proceed. We don't know what her financial situation is, and we don't know what her politics are. I was worried before that Johnnie had a mole inside his group." Nate let the words hang awkwardly in the air. He didn't know how to finish the sentence so he just stopped the words.

Righteous indignation boiled up inside me, and I couldn't believe he was talking about my client like that. The daughter of his friend of thirty-some years. His goddaughter. My...

And that was it.

I knew that any pure objectivity regarding Elizabeth and her involvement in this had ended a few nights ago. I'd known her as a person and a client for about two weeks. I couldn't answer any of the questions Nate just implied. He didn't say it, though I think he suspected.

"We still need her, though. The answer to this is in her father's safe deposit box. I'm certain of it. I can't get at it without her. And we have to be there when she opens it."

"If she's compromised, she'll push back on you being there. That's how you'll know."

I nodded, saying nothing. Then, "I'll call you as soon as I have something."

Or the FBI grants me my one phone call.

"Matt, this is not the time to make it up as you go."

"I know that, Nate. I need to get to Hu and then figure out how to get Danzig there so she can brace him. I just haven't figured that part out yet. I'm still a little groggy."

"All right. I'll see what I can do on my end. Keep in touch."

"I will."

"Good luck."

"*Vaya con dios*," I said.

Once I was back in the Defender, I unlocked the secure box where I stashed my laptop and the burner phone I used to track the AirTag on Hu's car. The alert popped up immediately. He was moving. I secured the phone on the dash so I could follow along and raced out of the garage. There wasn't time for an SDR, so I just had to hope the Bureau hadn't loaded anything on my phone that would allow them to track me. I picked up the 101 coming out of the airport and slammed into a wall of morning traffic.

I've driven through Istanbul and Delhi and places where traffic laws are handed down like oral tradition. They don't hold a candle to Californians at rush hour.

A thought hit me. There was no way Robert had finished making all those phone calls, or even one. So, Johnnie's people and Lawrence Fang were all in danger. I had to find a way and time to warn them as soon as possible.

Hu was still in San Mateo, so I reasoned he was stuck in the same morass as I was. If the laws of commuter physics applied, it would be faster on the tail end, allowing me to gain ground while he trudged along. I weaved through lanes, cut people off, and split lanes. Basically using every dirty trick from the Agency's combat driving school and the post-graduate courses we took in Nate's unit, short of bumping and running. I'd leave that one out. For now.

My eyes flicked from the phone screen to the road and back with the regularity of an outgunned herbivore, and I was able to keep reasonable track of Hu's progress.

Believe it or not, I was making good time. Relative to him, anyway. He was still meandering his way through San Mateo. If it weren't his hometown, I'd swear he was lost. Meanwhile, I'd passed through Sunnyvale and Mountain View and was nearing Palo Alto, having made zero friends along the way. Hu looked like he was bound for the airport. Then he reversed direction and started going south.

I hadn't paid much attention to his route because I'd been focusing on my own driving. I'd just checked in periodically to gauge his current vectoring. "What the...,"

I made a sharp turn across the lane next to me, narrowly avoiding another car, to pull into a gas station. I needed to focus on the screen, and I couldn't do that while I was driving. Using my finger to zoom out, I could see Hu's full route, which the AirTag captured like breadcrumbs. I confirmed my suspicion. Hu had driven in an ever-widening loop, like an expanding corkscrew, while gradually moving to the southwest.

Hu was running a surveillance detection route. It was shitty and amateurish, but there was no denying what it was.

That was why he was taking so long.

He was going to meet his handler.

There was a chance to wrap this up, if I could convince Danzig and Choi to meet me there.

The problem was I had to be absolutely certain. I had no traction with them, and they weren't going to arrest people on my say-so.

No, I had to catch Hu doing something illegal. Which made signaling the FBI problematic. His handler, if they were worth anything, would have a solid cover.

Hu was heading south now toward Palo Alto and was moving in, more or less, a straight line. This was the breakdown in his tradecraft, and a sign that he was an amateur with a short course in how to be a handled agent. He'd given the bare minimum to trying to shake a tail and now appeared to be heading straight to his destination.

Since I was now in Palo Alto, I ditched the slogging freeway in favor of local streets. On the screen, I could see Hu had stopped. I was also stopped at a light, so I could zoom out my map a little. He was in Redwood City, a small bayside community between Palo Alto and San Mateo.

The dot wasn't moving, so I assumed that was his destination.

Ten minutes later, I found Hu's unmissable car in a shopping center parking lot. There was a grocery store, a coffee shop, and a few small restaurants that catered to the breakfast and commuter crowd so there was a constant flow in and out of the parking lot. Smart.

I kept my distance because he'd seen me in the Defender. The lot was a rhombus shape on my map, running northwest to southeast. I found a spot in the southern tip outside a restaurant with several landscaped medians between me and Hu.

Conducting covert surveillance in the open was tricky because you needed to maintain a constant line of sight on the target. In public spaces, that tended to draw attention. A good camera with a telephoto lens was great for this, assuming you were close enough. You could usually watch as long as you needed to under the guise of lining up the right shot. Failing that, a rifle scope was a good backup, which is what I had currently. Without a weapon attached, most people assumed it was a surveying tool. I'd done this before, watching a target, pretending to be a survey crew. Of course, I'd had the benefit of a reflective vest and creatively acquired badges from the local government.

I sighted Hu and zeroed in the scope. My angle on him wasn't great, of course he wasn't who I really needed to see. I wanted to confirm that his handler was Huang from the community center. A white Tesla Model 3 pulled up next to Hu's car in the opposite direction, cop style, so they could speak to each other through the driver's-side windows. Smart. Minimal exposure.

The problem was, I couldn't see the other person.

I got out of the Defender and took a couple steps to the right and then crouched. A passing car drove through and blocked my sight line. It passed, and I saw clearly again.

Hu was angry. Waving his hands. I could see the lines of tension in his jaw. He was either shouting or, at least, speaking loudly. I slid over a few inches. *Lean back, asshole, you're blocking my shot.*

He didn't. Hu kept his tirade flowing another few seconds before he collapsed back in his seat, his fury apparently exhausted. For now, at least. I had a feeling this guy could summon it on command.

I could see through the car to the other driver now.
My blood iced.
It was Lawrence Fang.

31

Everything coalesced for me in that one terrible moment.

Johnnie had Fang listed separately because he knew he was a spy. That was why his meetings with the professor were all documented. Nate said he didn't want to know about any of Johnnie's extracurricular activities. Perhaps Johnnie had tried to convince him there was a problem, but the Chinese silenced him before he could bring Nate into the loop. Or maybe he just got in over his head, thinking he was more spy than agent.

My conversation with Fang came crashing back at me in horrible clarity as I realized how much of that was a reverse interrogation. I'd told him I'd been in contact with members of Zhou's network and his daughter, which might explain why they'd kept me alive—beyond my theory of keeping me alive to give the police a shiny object to chase, there might have been an intent to interrogate me about who else I'd been in contact with. They'd want to know if there were any names that weren't on the list.

I had enough facility in lip-reading to know Hu and Fang were not speaking English. I could also pick up a lot from nonverbal context. The conversation began with Fang's frosty disdain and boiled up quickly. Hu reacted as I expected he would—bowing up his large frame, pressing against the seatbelt, and leaning forward aggressively. Fang was nonplussed. He was in complete command, unintimidated and unimpressed with the other's physical presence. The old case officer in me had to wonder what Fang had on Hu that he could act with such impunity.

Their argument kept on for another minute or so, and then Hu reached down to the seat next to him. For a panicked instant, I thought Hu was going to shoot him in the face.

Instead, he handed Fang something in a zip-lock bag. I recognized it immediately. It was one of Johnnie's notebooks. So, it *was* Hu who'd broken in after me.

It took every iota of self-control not to blast my Defender across the parking lot, crash into their cars, and rip that bag out of their fingers.

The tension I felt a second ago transformed into a roiling anger at yet another fact I couldn't share with the FBI. I wasn't sure what I'd do with this knowledge, other than know that I was *right*. Even if Danzig and Choi hadn't wanted to arrest me, for everything, immediately, none of this was admissible in court since I wasn't a law enforcement officer or even acting as an informant for them.

I couldn't do anything but watch.

The feeling of frustration and righteous indignation was as maddening as it was overwhelming. Everything I needed to clear myself with the Feds was right here, and I couldn't do anything with it.

Fang appeared to have regained his composure. To his credit, I could tell by watching his face as he spoke that he delivered whatever the reprimand was in a harsh, yet still conversational volume. I could see why he chose "college professor" as a cover.

That was the part that didn't track for me.

Fang lived and worked as a Stanford professor.

Ministry of Public Security officers didn't live under cover.

Granted, American intelligence agencies had poor penetration of their Chinese rivals, and what networks we did have had been rolled up in a sweeping counterintelligence campaign in 2016. That meant we knew far less about them than we did, say, the Russians. Still, there was no evidence that MPS officers ever operated abroad—until Robert uncovered this covert police station—and no indication they'd ever lived as sleeper agents.

This didn't add up.

Fang drove off, and Hu pulled away in the opposite direction a moment later. I now had a choice to make. Which one do I follow? Hypothetically, since Hu had a tracker on his car, I could tail both of them. Since Hu would be the operational arm of whatever Fang was planning, I decided to tail him.

I followed him out of the lot, giving him a three-block head start since I could track his movements anyway.

I called Nate.

"It's starting to come together," I said. "Something is going to happen, and it's going to happen fast."

"What's going on?"

"I followed David Hu to a meet after we left. It's Lawrence Fang, that Stanford professor I told you about." I'd thought he was someone Zhou wanted to recruit, so I'd sent Robert to talk to him. And it had cost Robert his life.

"Something about that seems off. MPS doesn't usually run agents like that. Nor do they run illegals," Nate said. An "illegal" was a term for a foreign spy living in a country without an official cover, like a sleeper agent.

"That's what I'm starting to think."

"Do you have any conclusive proof that this Fang is an intelligence officer?"

"I just watched Hu hand him one of the notebooks that he took from Johnnie's safe. So, no, I didn't see him wearing an MSS ID badge, but I think it's fairly clear at this point."

"Okay, okay. What are you doing now?"

"Following Hu."

"The information on MPS and the...what'd you call it, outreach center? Where'd you get that from?"

"Johnnie's team. One of his guys, now dead, had hacked into their email system and found messages between the Ministry of Public Security and the center. From the context of the messages, they were clearly directing actions and had knowledge of the operation."

"So, you think we have State Security *and* Public Security operating in the same area? Both of them silencing dissidents? That doesn't sound right to me, Matt. We've got no evidence that those two work and play well with each other."

"I don't know that they are. Is it possible there are two separate operations here? Maybe Johnnie learned about the MPS effort and got targeted by the MSS somehow?"

"Possibly," Nate said. "Seems coincidental."

"How certain are you that MSS never figured out who Johnnie was? Or that one of his sub-sources wasn't a double agent?"

Hu turned north, and so did I, heading toward the Bay.

"You know this game, Matt. You can't be certain of anything. I don't believe Johnnie was turned, and we never had any indication he'd been targeted by MSS, or was even known to them. And I've told you, I don't know how many times, that I had no knowledge of his sub-sources."

I didn't necessarily believe Nate, though I wasn't going to press the point right now.

"Well, I think we have two concurrent espionage operations happening right here by two services that don't historically work together. You, or someone at Langley, needs to get the Bureau off their ass and do something about this."

"You know I can't do that."

"Goddamn it, yes, you can. Someone signed a memo authorizing your op. Call them."

"Matt—"

"Nate, don't. Call them, and do it now. Those idiots are so busy chasing *me* they're missing the actual Chinese spies right here."

I hung up and continued following Hu. He'd stopped again, and I found him at an auto repair shop on Broadway. This was an industrial section of town, and there was an electronics factory across the street with a wide employee parking lot in between two buildings. I circled the block once and pulled into the employee lot, disregarding the "employees only" signs and admonishments that violators will be towed with extreme prejudice.

I couldn't see Hu's car from the road. The repair shop occupied a quarter-block lot with the building in the center and vehicles parked around it in varying degrees of order. I was on the opposite side of a main road and half a block down. I couldn't actually see the garage from my spot because the factory blocked it on this side of the street, and a long, low building adjacent to the garage blocked it on the other side. I settled in to watch. Ten minutes melted into twenty.

The AirTag hadn't moved.

In my head, I envisioned a handler-to-agent conversation about their pre-meet SDR and whether it had been diligently executed. Hu would say it was, and Fang would demand to know how. Describe the steps. When Hu confessed to the abbreviated run, Fang would admonish it as insufficient and maybe demand he check for surveillance devices. It was possible, if not probable.

What was neither possible nor probable was that David Hu would schedule an auto service ten minutes after meeting with Fang.

I got out of the car and, finding a lull in traffic, dashed across to the neighboring building. I rounded it on the northern side and came to the repair shop's rear. There was a government building beyond it, separated by lowest-bidder landscaping and concrete, then a large lot for school buses. Squeezing between a building and a tree, I maneuvered around to look at the repair shop from the north. There was Hu's car tucked securely next to the building. Okay, he hadn't found and discarded the AirTag.

He'd switched cars.

One of the many things cops and spooks had in common was cultivating a network of support assets. It wasn't a stretch to imagine a bent cop having someone that could hook him up with a clean car if he needed it. Hu was gone, and I had no idea where.

Or maybe I did.

And that only meant one thing.

Elizabeth was in real danger.

32

Elizabeth wasn't picking up.

I left a voicemail asking her to call me back immediately. All the AI voice assistants on my phone were disabled for security, so I had to look up Elizabeth's hotel number while driving. That meant waiting until I hit a stoplight to find her phone number, and was I already getting angry honks from behind me by the time I found it. Rolling forward, I dialed.

I said, "This is Detective Hanley with the Los Altos Police. Can you get me Elizabeth Zhou's room, please?"

Impersonating a local cop would be the least of my sins today.

There was a pause. "Please hold."

"Hello, this is Armand, I'm the guest services manager."

"Armand, this is Detective Hanley with Los Altos PD. I need you to connect me to Elizabeth Zhou's room immediately. This is an emergency."

"Right away, detective," he said.

The phone rang about a million times.

"I'm sorry, detective. It appears Ms. Zhou isn't answering. May we leave a number?" I left mine and repeated that it was an emergency. If Elizabeth got the message, as soon as she tried to dial the number, my name would pop up, and hopefully, she'd understand the ruse.

I crossed the valley to pick up the 280 southbound while I raced with a mostly open road, going against traffic.

I called Nate.

"Hu switched cars at a service station and slipped past me. I think he's going to get Elizabeth," I said. "I tried calling her, but she isn't picking up. On her cell or on her hotel phone."

"What does he want with her?"

"He's got the key to her father's safe deposit box, but he doesn't know where the box is. And he'd need her to get past security, which he can probably do with his badge. I keep thinking, though... I think what's in that box is proof that Fang is a spy."

"Why do you say that?"

"Because Johnnie had everything else in his home safe. Whatever he's got locked up in some vault is probably damning enough he wouldn't want it in his house. That's explosive, and I'm assuming you didn't know about this."

"I did not," Nate said. "Where are you now?"

"I'm leaving Redwood City. Hu's got about a twenty-minute head start."

"That's about all he'd need."

"I'm going straight for the vault. Try to get Elizabeth on the phone, then get there as fast as you can."

"Me?"

"Hu doesn't know what you look like. You can recon where I can't. If you're inside and can spot him, I can try to ambush him outside. We only get one shot at this, Nate."

"Matt, you're saying he's got her as a hostage."

"She might not know it. Hu is a cop. The easiest way to do this is to convince her that whatever is in that safe is part of an investigation. Hu isn't going to risk an actual hostage situation." I racked my brain to remember if I'd ever told her Hu's name, though he could easily use an alias and had all the tools he'd need to make an expert fake ID.

"I'm still not sure what you're asking me to do," Nate said.

"Get inside. Talk your way in. See if you can get a tour of the vault—that's where they'll be. You can message me once you're inside. You confirm she's there, and I get Special Agent Danzig to roll in. That'll expose Hu. If

Danzig won't bite, then I'll try to get the drop on Hu outside, get the box contents from him. I can turn that over to the FBI and, hopefully, work an immunity deal."

"Matt," Nate said warningly.

"We don't have a choice, Nate."

"You want me to go into the vault and confirm Elizabeth is there with Hu so that you can call in the FB goddamned I? What happens when they do field interviews of everyone there?"

"Don't you have a cover?"

"Yes, but if they push too deep into it, it won't hold up," Nate snapped. "Then what? You haven't thought this through."

"We can't let Hu get whatever is in that box."

"You don't even know what's in it. You also don't know that he's there."

I couldn't believe what I was hearing. Not from him.

I left the interstate and took El Monte through Old Los Altos to the Foothills Expressway. That would take me almost directly to the vault. Traffic on the expressway slowed my progress considerably. Time ticked off the clock, and I could only pray that Hu was in similar situation.

Out of instinct, my eyes flicked to the rearview. One of those feelings scratching at the back of my mind.

And I saw the prowl car behind me.

Shit. I needed the police...just not at this exact moment.

Lights weren't on yet, but he was close enough that he was running my plates.

"Nate, we've got a problem. I think there's already an APB out on me for Robert Li. Now, Hu is using them to run interference. You've got to get her. I'm not sure how much longer I'm going to be out in the open."

"What's going on?"

"There's a police car behind me."

I hung up the phone and ditched the expressway at Edith Street at the last moment, a block away from the Los Altos Deposit Corporation. The only turn I could make without a protected arrow was a hard right; anything else would've caused an accident or triggered lights and sirens from the cop. Unfortunately, now I had no idea where I was or how to get back. I put the accelerator down and checked the rearview. The cop hadn't turned yet. On the right side of the street, I saw a house with a wrought-iron fence wrapped around the yard and a lot of trees. It had a large carport with several vehicles parked inside. A dumpster and a portable storage unit were next to the carport—apparently, some sort of construction project was going on. I turned onto the driveway, screeching the tires slightly, and braked, then pulled into a space in front of the garage. It looked like that would be blocked from the street courtesy of a redwood in the front yard.

Agonizing seconds crawled by as I waited for the cop to pass.

My rapid ingress drew the attention of the work crew doing what looked like a major remodel. Most of them just went back to work, except the one guy with a clipboard and a radio. Hoping I'd burned enough time, I gave an apologetic wave to the foreman and pulled back out onto Edith Avenue. There were no signs of the cop. The light at the intersection was long because I was trying to cross a major road during morning rush, and I was three cars deep in the line.

Sitting there at the light, I tried once again to connect the disparate dots and guess Hu's plan. My mind was fried—sleep deprived, exhausted, and still feeling the aftereffects of the drug. Dull aches from where Hu had beaten me while unconscious punched my muscles every time I moved them.

It had been eleven when I'd found him at that mechanic's parking lot. Figure, twenty minutes to drive to Elizabeth. She'd be at the hotel or her father's house. Hu would assume I'd warned her about him, so he'd use a different name. Give him between five and fifteen minutes to convince her to come with him—unless he just did it at gunpoint, though that seemed unlikely. It left Hu without an exit strategy. Another ten minutes to get to the vault from the house, fifteen from her hotel. It was almost noon now. Assuming no delays, they should be here shortly.

I called Special Agent Danzig.

Danzig picked up immediately.

"Whatever you're doing, Gage, you need to stop it and turn yourself in now. That's the only favor you're going to get."

"I have—"

"You don't have shit. You have one chance before this gets unfathomably worse for you. I'm only giving you the courtesy of turning yourself in because of your service to the country. Such as it was," She really couldn't help herself.

"Goddamnit, Danzig, will you shut up and listen to me? I've just uncovered a Chinese espionage operation going on right under your nose. Now, we can sit here and threaten each other, or we can try to stop this."

"The only thing I'm going to stop is you. You're wanted for murder, Gage."

"I was unconscious and tied up in a trunk when Robert Li was killed. And that's a state charge, not a federal one, so it's not even your problem. And what possible motive would I have? If I'm trying to expose a spy ring, the last thing I'm going to do is silence the one person who can testify to it. Robert was my friend."

"And I'm sure someone can attest to your being in a trunk last night," Danzig said.

"The man you're looking for is an SF cop named David Hu. I've told you this. He's an asset for a Chinese intelligence officer operating under the alias Lawrence Fang. Hu killed at least Robert Li and possibly four others in Johnnie Zhou's network. I have their names. I believe he's taken Zhou's daughter, Elizabeth, hostage. If you want him, or me, go to the Los Altos Deposit Corporation. That's where they're headed."

I disconnected the call and gunned it across the intersection.

Well, somebody was going to jail today. I just hoped it was the right guy.

I didn't see any police vehicles in front of the deposit building. That made sense. If Hu called in some local support, he wouldn't want them hanging around the vault company. Even if he convinced Elizabeth that he was legitimate, having other cops out front would be far too risky for him. Rather, he'd want to create a perimeter or bubble around Los Altos, a dragnet to sweep me up.

I crossed the expressway and looped around back so Hu wouldn't see my Defender if he was already here. I found a public parking lot at the end of the block. No sign of police.

The holster was still clipped to my belt, and I covered it with my jacket.

If Danzig was going to bite, it would take her ten to fifteen minutes to get here, *if* they rolled immediately.

The Los Altos Deposit Company occupied an unattached, two-story space on a block of First Street. There was a gated garage on the side. There were three exits—one on First Street, one out the garage, and a third to the parking lot in back. That was a lot to cover. The building's facade was a golden-brown brick with darkly tinted windows and a style of lettering intended to evoke something from California's frontier past. Upon entering the double doors, visitors were greeted by a quaint lobby with a large, cherrywood desk on the far wall. A receptionist and armed security guard manned the desk. There was a bar, of all things, immediately to the left of the front door, with an impressive selection of whiskey, tequila, and California wine. Entertaining high-value clients while they waited, I supposed. The vault door was on the same side as the bar, at the opposite end of the wall. It was currently open, which I suspected they did during business hours. There was a secondary metal gate behind it that was closed. On the other side of the entryway, there were glass-encased offices. There was a long, leather couch with a pair of Manhattan chairs opposite flanking the wall across from the bar.

A young woman in pinstripes and a tight tail greeted me as I entered. Her countenance shifted slightly as she took in my appearance, though she still managed a friendly, "How may I help you?"

This was the hyper-casual Silicon Valley, after all, and the rich didn't necessarily dress like it.

This time, we were going to try the truth. "Hello. My name is Matt Gage. I'm a private investigator, and I was to meet my client here. Her name is Elizabeth Zhou. Her father, Mr. Johnnie Zhou, had an account with you, and we were going to access his deposit box."

Okay, a version of the truth.

"Oh, Ms. Zhou and her guest have already arrived," the woman said, somewhat skeptical of me.

"Is it a police officer? A Detective David Hu, perhaps?"

"No," she said. "Hu wasn't the name, and he was with the FBI, I believe." She looked over to the security guard, who nodded.

"Could you show me where they are?" I asked.

"I'm afraid I can't, sir. I can't take you into the vault if you're not a customer, or escorted by one. I'm sure they'll be out in just a moment. If you'd care to have a seat over there, I'd be happy to bring you a beverage while you wait."

"I'll take a water, if it's not too much trouble," I said and walked over to the bar so that I wasn't in the line of sight from the vault. "It's a bit early for me. Impressive selection though."

"Thank you. I didn't get it at first, a bar in a bank. The idea kind of grew on me. I'm Brenda, by the way. Sorry I didn't introduce myself earlier."

Brenda continued talking about how they'd designed a social aspect into the secure storage business, and I largely tuned it out, listening for movement from the vault.

A booming chuckle issued from the vault, bouncing off the walls.

"That would be Mr. Donnelly, the manager," Brenda said. "He's... exuberant."

A big man in a dark suit opened the inner gate, which I could partially see from my vantage point. He stepped through first, walking backward to carry on a mostly one-sided conversation with the party behind him.

Elizabeth was next, followed by David Hu wearing an FBI windbreaker.

Hu and I locked eyes immediately, and under other circumstances, I'd have wished I could package the look of total shock and astonishment washing over his face. I assumed he knew my vehicle had moved because of the GPS device planted on it. What he didn't know until now was that I'd gotten out of the trunk.

"It's over, David," I said. My hand dropped to my side. "The actual FBI is on their way here right now. I'm sure they'll wonder how you got one of their snappy jackets. Among other things. Like how you know Lawrence Fang. Or why you drugged me and stuck me in a trunk overnight. Though, I guess that one kind of explains itself, doesn't it?"

"Matt?" Elizabeth said.

"What's the meaning of this?" Donnelly, the bank manager, asked.

"I've had enough of your shit, Gage," Hu said and drew his piece. "You're under arrest."

"You can't arrest me, asshole. You're a San Francisco police officer thirty miles outside of your jurisdiction, impersonating a federal agent." That one got a lot of uncomfortable and confused looks from everyone else in the room.

"I don't know what you're talking about. My name is Thomas Xie, and you're under arrest." He turned to the security guard. "Sir, I'd like your assistance detaining this individual while I call for backup."

A moment of terror welled up and overtook me. I'd never considered the possibility that Hu was an FBI undercover. That he could've wormed his way into Zhou's network to figure out Fang's identity, then get close to him. That'd be right out of the CI playbook. Having him pose as a local cop would be a way to convince me to talk without showing the FBI's hand, knowing what I already thought of the Bureau. He could easily get into Zhou's house and break into the safe; a warrant would cover that.

The only thing that theory couldn't explain was who'd jumped me last night.

My one option was to push all the chips in, double down, and find out.

"Matt, what's going on?" Elizabeth asked.

"That's David Hu. He's a dirty cop and a Chinese agent. Your father identified his handler. I suspect that's what he's doing here. Your dad didn't trust that information in his home safe, so he stored it here. Hu broke into your father's house and removed it. The Bureau had a surveillance camera in the ceiling. They've got him dead to rights." A slight exaggeration, but a necessary push.

Hu closed the distance with an aggressive, lumbering gait. "Turn around, hands above your head."

"Soon as you show me a badge."

I leaned my head around Hu to keep talking to Elizabeth, who was holding a small drawstring bag with the vault company logo on it. "He stunned me and drugged me last night. Dropped me in a trunk and then murdered Robert Li, the only other person that could expose him."

Hu's hand came up to my shoulder to force me to turn around.

The wail of distant sirens pierced the otherwise silent room.

"Hear that, dickhead?" I said. "That's the sound of your rapidly dwindling options. Your *best* bet, at this point, is to turn state's evidence and hope to Almighty God that you can deliver Fang to the FBI. Because, otherwise, you will go to jail forever."

And I saw in Hu's eyes that he knew it too.

It *was* him.

Then he chose the hard way.

33

Hu tried to grab me, and I snapped my wrist up, blocking him.

Then, he threw a hard right cross, which I could not.

Holy shit, I hadn't been hit in the face in a long time, and Hu was a big dude. My head snapped to the side, pain exploded in my head. I feared I was going to fall over.

I staggered back into the bar and had nowhere to go. The bottles were out of reach, or I'd have hit him over the head with one.

Hu grabbed me and whipped me around to put handcuffs on. Admittedly, I was still reeling from that punch.

The sound of sirens outside intensified.

"Hands up," he grunted through anger clenched teeth.

"You've got maybe five minutes before the real FBI gets here, *Dave*. You'd better have a great story lined up for what you're doing in one of their jackets."

"I cannot wait to put you in jail, asshole," he said.

Another set of sirens joined the chorus. Police would be here soon, and in force.

Then it hit me. He didn't have handcuffs or zip-ties. He'd have left his SFPD-issued gear at home, and he hadn't expected me to be here.

Hu let go, and I turned to see him stalking over to Elizabeth. He grabbed her by the arm, then turned to the rent-a-cop. "I need to get Ms. Zhou and this evidence to a safe location. Keep him here until backup arrives. You're legally authorized to use force if you have to. I'm deputizing you."

Elizabeth looked to Hu and then to me.

And then she went with him.

"Elizabeth, what are you doing?"

"Matt, he said you killed Robert Li. He said you killed the others and that you used me to get to them."

"And you believe that? You know me."

"Do I?" she asked, though I could hear the confusion cracking her voice.

"He's lying to you."

David Hu, wearing a stolen FBI windbreaker, led my client out of the building through the side entrance with her thinking I was the cause of all this.

"Did he ever show you a badge? How about credentials? *Anything* to prove he's a federal officer beyond a jacket?"

Elizabeth's gaze went to Hu.

Hu didn't meet it, instead turned to the security guard and said, "I'm deputizing you."

That was when I knew for absolutely certain this was all a bluff. Feds couldn't deputize rent-a-cops. This wasn't a Western.

My hand was inches from my Glock.

Hu murdered Robert, probably the others, and maybe even Johnnie. And he was about to walk off with my client as a human shield, and, presumably, the proof that Fang was a Chinese spy.

If I drew down on him, I might get a shot off, but that stupid rent-a-cop would fire back at me, and I had no cover. It'd be a chip shot.

Hu stared me down.

"I need to get you to safety, miss," he said to Elizabeth, and his big hand went to the small of her back. Hu pushed her toward the side door. I couldn't read Elizabeth's expression because I only saw her in profile. I didn't know what she was thinking, what she believed in that moment, but she went with him.

If there was any justice in this world I could shoot him in the back and get a medal for it.

I took a step to follow.

"I'm going to have to ask you to freeze until the police get here, sir," the rent-a-cop said. He'd sidestepped away from the desk to put himself between me and the side door.

"No," I said.

"That FBI man said to keep you here until the police arrived, and that's what I mean to do."

"FBI man?" I asked, incredulous. I repeated my question to Elizabeth from a moment ago. "I'll ask you again, did he show you *any* proof that he's a Fed?"

Stammering, "Well, not exactly."

"He had no proof, except a jacket. And you didn't question him because you watch TV, right? So, you know that's how FBI agents dress."

"Um. So."

I stormed past him.

"Sir, you need to stop."

"Next time, ask to see a badge." And I left.

There were two ways out, one to a gated garage and the other along a brick corridor leading to the back parking lot. He wouldn't lock himself in, so I chose the latter. My phone buzzed, It was Nate.

Ignoring the call, I ran to the end of the corridor just in time to see a nondescript sedan speeding out of the parking lot.

I answered the phone. Red and blue lights were clearly visible on the adjacent streets.

"Where are you?" Nate said. "I just got here and—"

Cutting him off, I said, "Around back. I need you to get me."

Not two seconds later, Nate's blue Tesla Model X ripped into the back lot.

Nate rolled the window down. "Get in back. The rear seat folds down." Immediately, I knew where he was going with this. Nate didn't stop, though he slowed down enough that I could get in while still moving. I pulled the rear seat down and rolled into the trunk.

"What the hell is going on?" Nate asked, and I could feel his right turn out of the parking lot, which would lead down the side street toward the public parking lot. He hammed the brakes and stopped fast. Sensing what was about to happen, I rolled back into the trunk and pulled up the seat.

A few seconds later, I heard the window drop.

"Hello, officer," Nate said.

"May I ask where you're coming from, sir?"

"The office. I have a meeting here in Los Altos. I was trying to cut through some side streets because of traffic."

There were no other sounds for a long string of seconds except for the muffled sound of the officer's radio.

"May I see your identification, sir?"

"Of course," Nate said. Briefly, I considered a riff on the move I'd done earlier this morning—popping the trunk and sliding out the back.

Another inexorable string of seconds ticked off the clock. Hu would be clear of any dragnet now. Danzig would arrive soon—these local cops had to be the initial response to secure the crime scene for the Feds. Going back and confronting Danzig was an option. Tell her everything that happened —the people at the vault company would attest that Hu never showed them credentials.

Did I trust her to act on that information? She could prove quickly that the Bureau hadn't had anyone here.

That wasn't a chance I was willing to take. Not without proof.

"Thank you, sir. You're free to go," the cop said.

A few seconds later, we were moving.

A few seconds after that, I started breathing again.

I dropped the back seat but didn't leave the trunk in case we needed to pull this disappearing act again.

"David Hu has everything from Johnnie's safe and the deposit box. He's also got Elizabeth as a hostage, whether she's aware of that or not."

"Well, Hu has what he wants, so he'll just let her go, right?"

"I honestly don't know," I said.

Nate asked, "What's the next move?"

"Hu is going to hand that stuff over to Fang. Or he's going to destroy it. I don't think he'll do either in front of Elizabeth because that breaks the illusion that he's a Fed."

"You don't think he'll hurt her, do you?"

"Depends on how backed into a corner he is. He's an American citizen. I don't think he's going to want to flee to Beijing as an asylum seeker. And he's a cop. He knows he's in deep shit and wants to play Elizabeth off as a way of getting out of it. Setting me up for Robert's murder was a way to take out the only one who could prove he's an asset. He tries to convince her he's a Fed and draws that out until he's in the clear."

"You know that only holds up for a few days though. Imagine you get arrested and you accuse Hu of espionage. The FBI would bring him in and depose him, at least."

"I don't think he'd have a problem lying under oath at this point."

"That's not what I mean. This stunt with framing you is just to buy them time. They're going to kill you, Matt."

That ended the conversation for a while.

We drove around for a few hours, which accomplished little more than burning the battery in Nate's car. Neither of us heard from Elizabeth.

Then again, we didn't hear from the cops or the Feds either, so we could assume we were clear. My car was burned. Even if it wasn't stuck outside the vault company, both the Feds and every law enforcement activity in the valley would have my plates.

We kept our roving patrol of this corner of Silicon Valley, stopping for food, coffee, and bio breaks.

As the afternoon dragged on, my hopes diminished.

I liked to believe Hu was still, at his core, police and that there were certain lines he wouldn't cross. Right now, hope was all I had to go on that one of those lines wasn't disappearing the body of someone who could identify him. Too many people saw her leave with him—he couldn't hope to get away with such a thing.

Unless they buried me in a hole so deep no one would ever find me.

The burner phone pinged a little after five.

Hu was back in his Charger.

Or this was one big bait-and-switch.

Only one way to find out.

"He's moving," I said.

Hu's car was headed south from the mechanic's garage in Redwood City.

There was no word from Elizabeth.

My instinct that Fang had ripped into him for a sloppy SDR earlier seemed validated as I watched the corkscrew pattern he drove. He'd take the 101 for a few miles before ditching it for city streets, where he'd periodically double back to check for tails. Twice, the AirTag sent a "location last reported at..." message as Hu went into a parking garage.

I'd stayed in the back seat of Nate's car that afternoon, in case I needed to drop into the trunk again. After watching these maneuvers play out for fifteen minutes, we decided not to follow. Rather, we'd hang back like a free safety watching for a break in the coverage. One thing was clear—which the app underscored by having a line mark the AirTag's progress—Hu was ultimately moving southeast.

He then made a hard hook due east from Palo Alto.

"Could be he's going to the airport," Nate said.

"Palo Alto has an airport?" I asked.

"It's a general aviation terminal. If you wanted to get out of here fast without anyone noticing, that'd be the place to do it. Fang could be at the Los Angeles Consulate or out of the state within a few hours, and we'd never know. If he's smart, he'll assume the FBI has a team on the Chinese consulate here."

"Let's roll."

"Hu drives a purple Charger with a racing stripe on it."

"Goddamn amateurs," was all Nate said.

We made fast time for the airport and spared no red lights.

I'd kept my phone off, except for brief periods to check if Elizabeth had tried to call. Even if they didn't bug it, the Feds could triangulate my location by seeing which cell towers my phone connected to. Any time we sat idle with it active was an invitation for arrest. So, I powered it up once an hour, checked, and then shut it off. Considering her last words to me, it was far more likely she'd call Nate anyway.

It took us twenty minutes to get to the airport. Hu's car had just pulled into a lot across the road from us. Palo Alto's small municipal airfield abutted a salt marsh at the bottom of the San Francisco Bay. Embarcadero Road ran along the airport's eastern perimeter and serviced the main gate. There was a nature preserve and park beyond the airport at the tail end of Embarcadero. Hu parked in a lot that serviced the sprawling wetland park.

"Don't pull in," I said. "We'll do a rolling drop next to that tree." I pointed to a large cypress between the road and the parking lot.

"Why would Hu park here, across the street?" Nate asked. "Why not just go in and meet Fang?"

"Maybe Fang isn't flying out of here. What if this is just a dead drop?"

"Yeah, it could be that. Same reason as why we met at the airport this morning," he said. No surveillance overflight, though I assumed the FBI could square that circle if they had to with a general aviation terminal. It wasn't the same thing as telling the FAA to pound sand. I turned on my phone. One way or another, it was time to end this, and to do that, I'd need a cop. Or at least one who wasn't bent like a U-turn. I checked to make sure my pistol was secured in the holster and that the holster was clamped tight on my belt. Nate slowed to a few miles an hour. There was no one behind us.

"Get ready," Nate said. "I'll set up an OP up there by that pond."

"No. You get out of here. The FBI will already have a warrant to track my phone by watching the cell towers." I assumed they still needed warrants for that sort of thing, but who knew anymore. "I need them here to arrest Hu. If you're here, they'll know you were hiding me in the trunk."

"All right," Nate said. "Be safe."

"Yeah, we're past that, I think."

"It's just something you say," Nate quipped.

I opened the door, stepped out just as Nate cleared the cable-and-pylon fencing around the parking lot. I hit the ground and dropped into a tuck-and-roll through two-foot-tall grass to slow my momentum. This was a time-honored maneuver case officers and their agents used in opposition-heavy environments to ditch tails. I have jumped into and out of more moving cars than I care to remember. With me out, Nate accelerated and disappeared around the bend. Could I have driven with him and gotten out farther up the road? Absolutely. The problem was, the approach was a long walkway without cover.

And, to be honest, I missed the spy game.

My roll turned into a crouch, and then I was beneath a leafy cypress tree, surrounded in inky shadows. Hu parked in the first spot, backed in. Light was draining from the sky, though we still had two hours before sunset. The parking lot was unlit.

I had a clear view of him.

He was the only one in the car.

34

I crouched next to the tree in the tall grass, unseen.

Hu got out of his car carrying a coyote-brown pouch, probably ballistic nylon. It was the exact color of the grass. The trailhead was in the middle of the parking lot, maybe six spaces from where Hu's car was.

"It's over, David," I called out.

There were no other cars in the lot, so I drew my Glock.

He turned halfway around to see it leveled at him.

"Where's Elizabeth?"

"What do you hope to accomplish, here, Gage?"

"You're not very bright, are you, Dave?"

Hu wasn't very good with words, so instead he just tried to shoot me.

I had to give him credit, he was a fast draw.

Admittedly, having been days away from a decent night's sleep and hungover from whatever drugs he mickeyed me with last night, I wasn't as quick as I should've been. Instead of firing back, I threw myself to the ground, out of the way. I landed hard on my shoulder, sending a fiery shock of pain all the way through the right side of my body and reawakening some remembered hurt from his beating last night. I fired back. It was a one-handed wing shot lying on my side.

I hadn't expected to hit him. It was just for spite.

Hu turned and bolted down the dirt trail into the marsh. I got up, sighted his car, and put a round in the rear tire. Then I put a second in the front one. Shooting out a tire wouldn't make it explode. Instead, it was a leak like any other, just a little faster than hitting a nail. Still, that car wasn't going anywhere. I ran after him. Grassy wetlands unfolded before us beneath a reddening sky. Beyond the marsh, the mountains rose on the far side of the bay. From this distance, they were a blue-gray line above the horizon. The tinny buzz of a single engine plane drowned out everything else as it flew overhead on final.

There were no trees here, just a large, wide row of bushes about my height that ran along the back side of the parking lot. Hu would be on the far side of that now, and he'd be waiting for me. Crouching, I orbited the bushes, maneuvering around the opposite side, careful not to give away my position by crunching a stick or grass beneath my feet.

I had exactly one chance at this, and if my guess was off, I was dead.

Slinking around the bushes and keeping to the shadows, I listened. All I heard was a harsh, brief rustling of leaves and then silence. Movement. Shoes on a dirt path, gaining momentum.

I rotated around, brought the gun up and...

Nothing.

Hu was gone. I watched his dark form disappear down the trail in the opposite direction.

There was no time to search the bushes for what Hu dropped if I wanted to catch him, so I took off down the trail in pursuit. My plan was so far off the rails now I didn't even know where the track was. Chasing after a dirty cop in fading light.

I'd stopped worrying about what I would do if I caught him hours ago.

The trail rose slightly after the parking lot, following the land's low, rolling contour. More bushes and a random scatter of trees on the left side, and on the right was marsh. If he decided to make for the marsh, he'd be nearly impossible to find. He'd just need to tolerate hiding in waist-deep, brackish water behind some sea grass until I gave up.

Except hiding might not be his primary goal.

Instinct told me Hu still had a handoff to make, and having seen him get yelled at by his handler for sloppy tradecraft earlier, he wasn't going to repeat that mistake. And this site was burned. He'd probably be moving to the backup drop once he evaded or killed me.

Adjusting course, I ran over the small rise and landed back in the parking lot, then vectored to the far side. By the time I reached Hu's car at the end of the row—with two flat tires, I noted triumphantly—I was going full tilt. Picking up a minor dirt trail that led to a maze of bushes beyond, I slowed, skidding in the dirt.

The sky above was an angry, glowing red.

Fitting.

The contrast of red yet darkening sky against the leafy corridors between the bushes only deepened the contrast. It was like wading through ink.

It was hard to hear with my heart pounding in my ears, and I fought to control my breathing so I didn't give my own position away.

I heard the sound of shoes on dirt and dropped to a crouch, pistol ready.

A shape materialized in the murk, big, though I couldn't be certain it was Hu. Odds on favorite it was him. Not enough that I was going to risk a shot. Crab-walking to the left, I stayed low to make use of the cover, trying to get closer for visual proof. This was a leafy labyrinth, and I immediately regretted charging in here.

The form disappeared behind a man-sized shrub. I crossed the dirt path in a single long, quiet stride and hugged the bushes on the far side, slinking around their perimeter.

Two shots rang out, and I dropped to the ground.

Son of a bitch shot through the shrubs.

I didn't see a muzzle flash or anything else to give away his exact position. The environment made sound direction hard to judge.

There was a gap of about fifteen feet between the bush I was currently using as cover and the next one—the only problem was it was slightly behind me. This meant I'd be exposed a little longer if I went for it and would have more ground to cover. Still, without knowing whether Hu was shooting at random or had somehow seen me, I needed to move.

Picking myself off the ground and settling into a running stance, I first looked for signs of my target. The bush in front of me was incredibly dense, and I couldn't see through it. Conversely, I was reasonably sure he couldn't see where I was right now. But leaves didn't stop bullets.

I launched into the open space and sprinted for the cover on the opposite side. A shot cracked the silence, and dirt exploded at my heel, just missing my foot. I skidded behind cover. I sighted what I gauged Hu's location to be and fired, just to keep him occupied. Then I crept around the far side of the bush I'd ducked behind. Couldn't stay here long.

There was no better move than short dash, maybe twenty feet, to the next shrub, though that put me farther away from Hu. I ran with everything I had. I made the next bush and dove behind it, no shots fired. This stand of shrubbery was U-shaped, and I found there was a small gap between the bushes.

Distant sirens.

"You hear that, Gage? That's the sound of you running out of time," Hu called out, parroting back my line from the vault company.

I had a rough idea of where he was. Not enough that I was willing to waste bullets on it though.

Four shots had been fired by now. People would be calling police, if they hadn't already. Hopefully, they just thought it was some asshole doing target practice in the marsh and not a couple of guys trying to kill each other.

I crept through the narrow gap between the two bushes that made this copse and, using them as cover, tried to sight Hu. I spotted movement about fifty feet from me. The line of sight was obstructed, and there wasn't a clear shot. I couldn't tell what direction he was looking. It didn't seem to be mine. I crouched and moved as quickly as possible for the next stand of shrubs.

"These are my pals I've called, Gage," he shouted.

He didn't know where I was.

I had a long, dark line of greenery to hide behind and used every bit of it to clear the distance. I had him in sight now.

Hu turned.

I fired.

He dove to the ground, squeezing off a return shot, errant and wild, as he hit the ground.

I rolled into cover.

Hu was on his feet and running for me.

Shit.

It took me a second to free myself from the tangle of clawing branches I'd landed in. By that time, he was halfway to the street.

I low-crawled through the bushes, getting a multitude of scratches for my troubles. Once on the other side, I found myself in the clearing in the center of this dark-green maze.

Hu's thundering footsteps got closer.

Picking a straight line, I just sprinted for my life, hurdling a small shrub, another fervent dash, and then cutting a sharp left into a narrow line between bushes.

I made the street and blasted across it, heading for the small airport. There wasn't a clear strategy in mind here; mostly I was looking for cover and to have a second to plan out my next move.

"Freeze, police!" I heard Hu shout, and I figured that was for the benefit of anyone who might be watching us shoot it out.

Asshole.

I hit a dirt trail on the far side of the road and looked over my shoulder to see Hu lumbering after me. I stopped, dropped to a kneeling shooting stance, and fired.

This time, my aim was good, and I drilled that son of a bitch right in center mass.

Hu's momentum shifted violently in the opposite direction, and he went down. His head bounced off the pavement as he landed, and that made me happy, because Hu deserved the concussion.

I fell back into the dirt, chest heaving. Adrenaline can only take you so far.

Hu rolled onto his side, and in the failing light, I saw his gun arm come up. It took my fogged, sleep-deprived mind too long to process that I needed to move. Hu was kneeling, moving to stand by the time I did.

I had hit him.

I had *hit him*.

What the hell?

Hu was on his feet now, staggering but recovering quickly.

Kevlar tactical vest under his clothes.

I had a newfound dislike for dirty cops.

That primal part of your brain that only thinks about survival shouted, *Gage, you need to be moving!*

I rolled over, got to my feet, and took off. There was a chain-link fence separating the airport property from the trail, though it stopped a few feet short of the brackish pond next to it, so I could easily move around. Drawing whatever minor reserves I had left, I dialed up some speed and bolted along the fence line.

I ran, hugging the fence as closely as I could without kissing it. It was a dark-metal chain-link, and while the airfield itself was lit, the light was focused inward rather than along the perimeter. We were still in the hours creeping on sunset, so there was a heavy contrast between light and dark. I kept to the shadows and ran for my life.

Hu shouted behind me, having cleared the fence and now taken off. It was too dark for a clean shot, and not even he would risk firing at the airfield. Wasn't sure how long I'd gone. It was a long while, though I knew from experience the mind had trouble marking time while under stress from physical exertion. I couldn't keep this pace for much longer. I'd been running all out on a completely empty and exhausted tank. Hu was fresh, nearly ten years younger, and in better shape.

And hadn't been beaten up, stunned, and drugged the night before.

Not far ahead, the path turned sharply to the right, marking the end of the runway.

And that wasn't all.

There were huge landing lights bathing the entire area in a bright glow. I'd be a painted target.

If I made it that far. My legs were slowing. There wasn't anything left to push.

Up ahead, on the right side where the trail sloped into the marsh, I saw a long, caterpillar-like drainage tube. I just needed to make it another dozen feet or so. It was the only thing even close to cover I was going to find.

Once I reached the drainage tube, I jumped laterally across the trail and then dove for the ground. Carrying the momentum, I hit the slope and rolled, crashing over the heavy, black corrugated pipe. A bullet cracked out, and I heard the soft thud as it hit the dirt nearby.

I rolled right into the pond. Marsh grass, mud, and water cushioned the fall.

I got my legs under me and whipped around, staying next to the pipe for cover. Crouching, I was up to my waist in marsh water.

Hu was looking for me with his pistol. Probably no more than thirty feet away. Whoever shot first at this distance was going to take it.

Behind me, I heard the increasing whirr of a twin-engine aircraft taxiing.

I couldn't see the aircraft because it was behind me, but I saw its bright running lights as they tracked from right to left, lighting up the dusk. The beams hit the fence and kept moving as the aircraft turned.

They lit David Hu up in daytime brightness for a split second. He turned his head to shield himself from the glare.

I fired.

I didn't know how many times.

Hu made a weird pantomime of someone jerking a marionette before cutting its strings.

He collapsed to the dirt. I climbed over the hard plastic drain, scrambled up the bank, and ran over to him. I punted his gun into the darkness. It bounced off the fence somewhere in the distance.

He was still alive, rolling back and forth, one hand on his neck, the hand covered in blood. Looked like I'd hit him multiple times At least three rounds hit the vest, and one struck him in the neck. I couldn't tell how bad with his hand covering it.

Sirens were close now.

I wasn't sure he had that long.

Choices.

If anybody deserved to die in the dirt, it was him. David Hu was a traitor and a murderer. Not only did he betray his country, he betrayed his badge. He traded on the sacred trust his city placed in him.

But it wasn't going to be me who did it.

Okay, I *had* shot him. That was self-defense though. Now that he was still alive, I had to keep him that way.

"I need to make a field dressing for your neck. Do you have a knife I can use to cut a strip of cloth?"

Probably good to know if he had one anyway, seeing as how I'd just shot him.

"Fffffuck yyyyooouu," he grunted out.

Some people made doing the right thing really hard.

I'd read that drop guns were a myth that Hollywood perpetuated and wasn't something cops had done regularly since at least the '60s. I checked him anyway. There was no second gun. I did find a folding tactical knife, pen light, multitool, and lock pick set in a ballistic nylon pouch attached to his tactical vest with velcro. "I'm cutting your sleeve off, nothing more," I said. "Try not to move."

He stared raw hate back at me but, otherwise, let me work.

My phone buzzed, and I saw it was Nate. I awkwardly thumbed the speaker button and got a smudge of blood on my screen.

"I'm still here. Just outside the airport. I took a spin through the inside, looking for anyone matching Fang's description. He's not there."

"Nate," I said.

"Let's go."

I looked down at Hu bleeding out. If I left, he was done.

If I did go with Nate, there was a chance we could get Fang before he fled town.

"Hu is down and bleeding. If I don't stay with him, he dies. I have to see this through," I said. "Go."

And he was gone.

The cavalry arrived in force just as I was finishing the field dressing.

Ten minutes later, I was in handcuffs, sitting with my back against the fence.

Special Agent Katrina Danzig stood over me, a superior, smug look on her face. The kind of "we always get our man" bullshit they put on pamphlets. Choi and the two state detectives, Nugent and Montoya, were with her too.

An ambulance had rolled up, and they were loading Hu onto it now. Unclear whether he'd live or not. The EMT didn't like his chances. They think my shot clipped an artery. Nugent informed me if he didn't make it, they'd be charging me with murder.

Which would make two.

Nugent walked over to me. "Mr. Gage, it is my distinct pleasure to inform you that you are under arrest for the murder of Robert Li."

35

"I didn't kill anyone," I said.

"Said every murderer ever," Nugent replied.

"Fang Yìchén," I said. "He goes by 'Lawrence.' He's a Chinese State Security officer and David Hu's handler. Hu was trying to stash the evidence he got out of that Los Altos vault today for Fang to pick up. You need to get him before he gets away."

"We'll get right on that," Nugent mocked.

I ignored him and turned to Danzig. "Agent Danzig, please, you probably don't have much time. I can give you his address. His cover is that he's a visiting professor at Stanford. He knew Johnnie Zhou. He's the key to this whole thing. You have to get him, and you have to do it now. He knows his cover is blown."

Nugent kicked me in the ribs. I grunted with the impact but wasn't giving him the satisfaction of a bigger response. "You just shot a cop, you son of a bitch!" Nugent yelled. "You better pray he makes it through the night. You don't wanna know what happens to cop killers in jail."

"Hu was wearing one of your FBI jackets at the bank. That's how he convinced them to let him back there. How he got Elizabeth to go along with him." I said to Danzig, still ignoring Nugent. "I bet it's still in his car." I motioned toward the parking lot with my chin, the one part of my body I could actually move without help. "Ask anyone at the bank."

Nugent grabbed me by the collar and tried to haul me to my feet, except he wasn't in good enough shape to do it, and I wasn't helping.

Danzig pulled him back. "Jack, let us handle this."

"No. He's a prime suspect in a murder and the attempted murder of a police officer."

"And we have an *active* counterintelligence operation underway, and time is a factor. Please give us some space," Danzig said.

Nugent tried to protest, but Choi interposed himself between the two. Choi was a big guy, and he moved like he knew how to handle himself.

Once Nugent and Montoya were out of earshot, Danzig asked, "Now, what's this about a Fang Yìchén?"

"I learned about him through Robert Li. I didn't put it together until much later. Hu mugged me last night, drugged me, and stuck me in the trunk of a car. I think he did that so I'd be out of the picture and he could take out Li. I think they also wanted to press me and see if I knew the location and identities of any remaining members in Zhou's network. When I met with Fang, before I knew he was MSS, I told him I'd met some of them. The only reason I think I'm alive is he wanted to frame me for Li's murder. Once I got out, I found Hu and followed him. I watched—"

"Wait, how'd you find him?" Danzig asked.

"Have you seen his car?"

Danzig's eyes narrowed.

"I put an AirTag on it. I thought it a little strange that a cop would be so aggressive pressing me for information about a case he had nothing to do with and outside his jurisdiction. It didn't seem right, and I didn't want him getting the jump on me. So, I tagged his car."

"Which is a violation of Sergeant Hu's civil rights, among other things. And if you bugged his car, how'd he ambush you?"

"Switched cars," I said. "I watched him do it again today."

"Mr. Gage, here's what I know. I have a dead man and a police officer who may not make it to the hospital. I have a young woman with potentially compromising national security information. And in the middle of all of that, I have *you*, a disgraced ex-spy who seems to have little, if any, regard for the law. Let's go."

We went.

And the precious minutes to take action burned away.

We drove in silence to the FBI Field Office in downtown San Francisco so they could, apparently, separate me from the rest of the world.

The US Attorney couldn't charge me for Robert's murder. That was a state crime, which was why those two assholes from the California Bureau of Investigation had been present. When I asked what we were doing there, Danzig gruffly explained, before tossing me in a holding cell, that the FBI was keeping me because, as a former CIA officer, I was a "higher class of criminal and required special handling."

They probably just didn't want me scaring the local cops into letting me out again.

My guess was I'd been held for about an hour before they came back to get me. That put it around ten.

God only knew what had happened in that time.

"Let's go," Choi said. There was a uniformed FBI officer with him who put bracelets on me and led me out of the room.

We wandered the dark and silent halls of the Federal Building until we got to an interview room. The officer cuffed me to the table. Danzig was already there, and Choi took up a seat next to her. Danzig identified herself and Agent Choi to the room, then gave the date and time, so I assumed this was being recorded.

"Let's start with the last twenty-four hours. Walk me through your movements starting at eight p.m. yesterday."

"How about we start with not letting a goddamn foreign intelligence officer get away. What are you doing about Lawrence Fang? And where is Elizabeth Zhou?" I said.

"She's not your concern."

"Did Hu hurt her?"

They exchanged a look. Choi said, "No."

"What about Fang?"

"He's no concern of yours."

"You're going to let him escape to spite me?"

Danzig flipped a page on her legal pad.

"Gage, we need to know about your whereabouts over the last twenty-four hours."

"You can't be serious! He's going to get away, and you're sitting here asking me jerk-off questions about what I was doing last night?"

"You are currently under arrest for the murder of Robert Li and the attempted murder of a police officer. If you want me to consider absolutely anything else, you need to give me a damned compelling explanation for where you were last night. Now, I've got two state police officers who would very much like to string you up, and I've got half a mind to let them. So, last time, where were you last night?"

"I was with Elizabeth Zhou. She'd just come from your questioning session, and she was upset and confused. She'd heard things about her father that bothered her. She asked me to meet her."

"We understand she'd terminated your employment. Is that correct?" Danzig said.

"That's right."

"But you did not quit?"

"I did not."

Danzig made a note.

I continued. "After leaving my meeting with Ms. Zhou, I returned to my hotel in Cupertino. I believe this was approximately ten p.m. As I was exiting my vehicle, someone approached me from behind and hit me with what I believe was a stun gun. He then put me in a choke hold, which incapacitated me. I lost consciousness. I awoke several hours later, groggy and displaying signs of having also been drugged." Choi opened his mouth to object, so I said, "As a former CIA operations officer, I have been trained to recognize the presence of chemical agents in my system based on their aftereffects. I came to in a trunk. My hands and feet were bound with zip-ties. With some effort, I was able to extract myself from these. I have been trained to do that as well. I used the interior release from the trunk to get out. It was morning. The car was parked off-road in what I would later discover was the community of Linda Mar. I had no phone, so I walked approximately two miles to a Chevron station in town The attendant will attest to seeing me."

"Did you tell him you'd been assaulted?"

"No. I assumed that whoever knocked me out wanted me out of the picture but not dead. That meant they were doing something during those hours. I feared Robert Li or Elizabeth Zhou or both were in danger."

"If they were in danger, why not go to the police?"

"Since I had reason to believe that I'd been abducted by a police officer, I thought it best not to involve any more of them. I didn't contact you for reasons which should be obvious by now."

"What did you do then?" Danzig asked.

"I took a cab to my hotel where I accessed my vehicle and found my phone. I went to check on Robert Li and found police vehicles out front. Once I saw the coroner van, I figured what happened."

"Can anyone confirm your whereabouts for those hours?"

"No," I said. "I was alone in the trunk."

"When was the last time you saw Robert Li?" Choi asked.

"That afternoon. I think about two hours before you came to my hotel. He'd gone into hiding after someone broke into his home. This was the first time I'd seen him since the break-in."

"Why didn't you tell us you'd seen him?"

"You didn't ask," I said. "You asked if I knew where he was, which I answered. I'd actually intended to tell you, but you two came off so aggressive, threatening me with jail and accusing me of working for the Chinese, I decided I couldn't help you."

Danzig stared me down, an explosive remark just behind her lips. Her mouth twitched like she was trying to hold back bile.

"Do you know who broke into his home?"

"No, not for certain. My guess is it was Chinese operatives working out of a clandestine site in Chinatown. Robert, through his reporting, found that the Ministry of Public Security had covert outposts in cities all over the world. They were using those to target political dissidents, agitators, anyone deemed an enemy of the state."

"What did Mr. Li think the Chinese government did with these people?"

"Tried to convince them to go back to China, and usually it was over some made up passport or tax problem. Once they were on Chinese soil, they'd be arrested, tried, and tossed in prison. Since they'd already been harassing Robert over some imaginary problem with his citizenship, we agreed he'd go in and see what he could learn. They followed us on the way out, and I think they were tracking his phone. He said they'd made him download an app. I got Robert to safety, and two men with some training caught up with me, still following the phone and thinking I was Li. It got a little violent when I didn't tell them where he was."

Danzig and Choi traded a look.

"What were you and Mr. Li planning to do with that information?"

"We had the names of what we believed was the network Johnnie Zhou built. People like Robert. Four of them are dead—two prior to Johnnie's death, two after. Their names are Kevin Wei, Jessica Chen, Ethan Jian, and Ryan Tan. They all lived in the Bay Area. Chen was the last to die; she was shot. The rest...they at least tried to make them look like accidents. Robert wanted to keep his head down, but I convinced him to contact the other six and warn them. We hoped they'd take him seriously. I'd tried before, and no one would talk to me. He was also going to talk to Lawrence Fang. We didn't know...," the words failed me. They crumbled in my mouth and turned to dust.

"At the airport, you admitted to putting a tracking device on David Hu's vehicle. Why?"

"I already told you," I said.

"Tell us again," Choi replied.

Right, so it's on the record.

"The first time Hu contacted me, it was right after Robert went into the police outpost. That struck me as curious timing. Told me he had a friend in the Los Altos PD who wanted to share information to keep the investigation going. The next time we spoke, he was more aggressive. He wouldn't tell me who this other cop was, just that I needed to share what *I* knew so I could prove I was serious. Say what you will about me, I know deception when I see it. This morning, when I'd freed myself from the trunk and got back here, I followed Hu and saw him meeting with Fang."

"Why would Hu want you dead?" Danzig asked. "Before, you told us they wanted you alive to frame you for Li's murder. Now they want to kill you. Which is it?"

"Both. Once I blew his plan up, Hu didn't have a choice. I'd seen him with Fang and knew what they both were. If that hadn't happened, they'd have preferred me to get arrested to buy them time to get rid of the rest of Johnnie's people."

"Why? What do the Chinese get out of it?"

"You're looking at it." I said.

"For someone facing one to many murder raps," Choi said in a loaded tone, "you sure don't try to do yourself any favors."

"*You're* the spy hunters. If you're questioning *me*, you're not out looking for *them*."

"What did Hu want with Mr. Zhou's safe deposit box?"

"I admit, I don't know exactly what the contents were. I believe it contained information that Mr. Zhou didn't trust to leave in his home safe. Which seemed to prove prescient since you showed me footage of someone breaking into his house and accessing that safe. I think Zhou figured out Fang was a spy, and the vault was where he kept that information."

Danzig scribbled something on her notepad, which she showed to Choi. He nodded and then got up to leave.

Danzig placed her hands on the table and gave me an enigmatic stare. "Who are you protecting?"

"I'm only working for my client," I said.

"I don't believe you."

Typically, when interrogating a subject you'd ask them the same questions with slight variations in the technique, the tone, and the aggressiveness. Or you'd change up which of the interrogators was asking particular questions. The intent was to break down the subject's resistance, trip them up, and force them to reveal the truth. Danzig only asked me the one round of questions. By now, she'd known I'd been through some of the most rigorous interrogation and counter-interrogation training our country has to offer and perhaps decided it wasn't worth the effort. Whatever the reason, she only asked once.

When she decided she was done, Danzig had a pair of uniformed FBI police take me back to the holding cell.

Long hours marched on. At some point, they cut the lights.

I knew then that Fang was going to get away.

I'd made my choice and would have to live it with it.

There was only ever a slim chance I could've gotten to Fang in time, but I'd burned it saving Hu's life. Maybe there was an even slimmer hope I could've convinced the Bureau to act, but I'd failed in that too.

The dead would not be avenged.

As I sat there in that cell, my mind crawled into the dark places. Danzig asked who I was protecting and didn't believe me when I'd told her I was only working for my client, Elizabeth. How far was I willing to push this? I could tell myself all the lies and the half-truths that I was protecting Nate.

I knew now I wasn't.

Nate, like me, was a cog in a wheel. That was all we were to them—replaceable parts. If it wasn't Nate running this operation, it would be someone else. And if he was exposed and scandalized for running something of dubious legal standing, they'd fold it up, repackage it, and launch it anew from somewhere else.

I could get out of here right now if I'd just knocked on the door and told Special Agent Danzig what she wanted to hear, that I was purposefully obfuscating a CIA operation.

All I had to do was admit it.

Time took on an elastic quality when you were alone in the dark. I didn't realize I'd nodded off until the lights came on and the door opened. I found myself staring, bleary eyed, at Special Agent Danzig. She hadn't changed clothes. There were no windows or clocks near me so I could only conclude she was in the middle of a long night. There were a pair of uniformed officers behind her.

"On your feet, Gage. Let's go."

I didn't move. "Either you're letting me go or you're taking me to my lawyer."

"It's neither, and I don't have time for your bullshit. Elizabeth Zhou's life is in danger, and God help me, we need you."

"Then let's not waste time here," I said, and I was on my feet, moving for the door.

36

"What's going on?" I said.

Danzig made fast steps down the hall, making for elevators. I finally found a wall clock and saw it was one thirty.

"A lot. I'll see if I can summarize. We confronted Hu with what you told us. I told him I was going to charge him with five murders."

It struck me that she'd said five and not six.

Danzig continued. "We also said we'd charge him with impersonating a federal officer, two counts of kidnapping, and conspiracy to commit espionage."

I whistled.

"Yeah, it's like a million years in prison," Danzig said, not breaking her stride. We reached the elevator. "I'll take it from here," she told the uniforms. We got in, and she hit the garage button. "Hu copped to murdering Mr. Li, in exchange for information about Fang and maybe pleading off the other charges. For what it's worth, he said the other four murders weren't him. He said that he thought Fang had some kind of hit squad."

"Those would be the guys I tangled with."

"Right. The state is going to formally dismiss the murder charge against you in the morning."

"Tell me about Elizabeth."

The doors opened, and we were in a garage. We walked quickly through the cold, dark concrete cavern to Danzig's ride.

"We don't know where she is."

"You told me she was safe."

"I lied," Danzig said flatly. "At that point, we didn't know if you were working with Hu and had a fallout, if *you* were working for the other side, or—"

"Are you fucking kidding me?"

"Gage, if you were me, what conclusions would you draw about someone with your record? Hu said they were holding Elizabeth in case they needed collateral. He convinced her he was an FBI agent, and you were right about the jacket. It's a fake, he got it online at a costume shop."

Danzig pulled out of the space and didn't spare the rubber getting out of the garage. She slowed only to let the massive security gate lower into the floor before blasting out onto the empty streets of San Francisco.

"We used Hu to call Fang and set up an exchange. Fang doesn't know Hu is compromised but does know he's burned. That's why you're here. Hu said you could make the exchange. He told Fang he's too scared to move but that he'll give you the material from Johnnie Zhou's safe deposit box and you'll give that to Fang in exchange for Elizabeth's safe release."

"What aren't you telling me?"

"We're convinced it's a setup. Fang will have that hit squad waiting for you. As soon as you make the exchange, we think they'll try to kill you—and most likely her as well."

"Let me see if I've got this straight. David Hu, who has admitted to being an agent for a Chinese intelligence officer we know as Lawrence Fang, forces Elizabeth to open her father's safe deposit box, which we believe contains information confirming Fang is a spy. Hu hides her somewhere to keep her quiet instead of killing her. Either he thinks she could be of use to him, or—"

"Fang wanted her as a bargaining chip. Hu admitted that to us."

"Right. Hu is supposed to stash the material from the safe at a dead drop—I'm assuming so Fang can get it without being seen. Then he intended to disappear. Except I caught Hu in the act and shot him." Then I added, "Purely in self-defense. Not because he deserved it."

Danzig sighed heavily and said nothing.

"So now, you've used Hu and set up the exchange of documents for Elizabeth?"

"That's right."

"And you're certain it's a trap."

"We have high confidence that it is, yes."

"Sweet. What are we waiting for?"

"I wish there was a better way, Gage. We all do."

"Where is your partner?" I asked, looking around.

"Dan joined the FBI after serving in the Army as a ranger. His first ten years in the Bureau was with the Hostage Rescue Team."

"Oh," I said, in a knowing way. HRT was the Bureau's elite counterterrorism unit, modeled after the US Army's Delta Force. The Agency occasionally worked with them in the field, and I knew from experience they were top-tier operators. "He'll be doing overwatch and looking for their kill team."

"What do I do?"

"Exactly what I tell you. You're going to be on a tactical radio with Dan and me. He's already getting in position. You're to take this bag," Danzig reached behind her and handed me a black, ballistic nylon pouch about a foot in length. "You'll meet at the designated spot and wait for Fang's signal. You'll make the exchange, the pouch for Elizabeth Zhou."

"What's in it?"

"A lot of evidence you're not cleared for. What I will tell you is it confirms what you said about Fang."

"And you're giving it to him?" I knew how this stuff worked, the unpalatable choices people had to make in situations like this. I still needed to hear her confirm it.

"There's a chance that Ms. Zhou isn't there, or that she's already dead. If the former, the Chinese will suspect we've pulled a switch. We've copied everything in here already, but should they attempt to take it without releasing the hostage...well, that's part of what we've got Dan for."

"Where are we going?"

"The meet is a place called Warm Water Cove Park. It's in the Central Waterfront District, next to Pier 80."

"I'm not that familiar with the city," I said.

"West side, facing the bay. Pier 80 is one of the main commercial cargo terminals. It's actually not far from our field office, which is about the only break we're going to catch tonight. Gage, I need to ask you one last time if you're sure you're up for this. I know you're going a few days without sleep, and Hu admitted what he did to you last night. I know you're not at your sharpest right now." Danzig let her invitation for me to back out hang in the air a moment. "I also know you guys have trained for that."

"Do I get a gun?"

"You do not. I have a tactical vest. That's as much as I can do. I need to warn you that your life will be in immediate, mortal danger, and I cannot guarantee your safety. I understand what I'm asking you to do."

"Well, if I don't make it, that's one less thorn in your side."

"It's not like that. At least not anymore. And whatever my personal feelings might be, I don't want anything to happen to you."

"Thank you," I said. "I'm in."

"I figured you would be."

"Then let's get this son of a bitch."

We drove the rest of the way in silence. We passed SFPD cars—some crouched and ready for action. One other roared down a cross street, lights and sirens. There were times I saw almost formless shapes moving through the tent communities and the black spaces between buildings.

This time of night, there were only predators.

———————

We staged out of an empty parking lot on the corner of Illinois and Twenty-Third, a few blocks from the park.

"Have you thought about whether this is a ruse?" I asked. "Does Fang actually know what was in the safe? What if he gets away?"

"We've got an APB out with Homeland Security, and every TSA checkpoint on this side of the country knows to look for someone matching his description traveling on a Chinese-issued passport. We've got them looking for Singaporean and Malaysian ones as well. We'll get his photo from Stanford first thing tomorrow. The airports have shut down for the night, but we've got people at SFO and Mineta working with airport police to do sweeps. If we don't get Fang tonight, we'll widen our sweep to include Portland, Seattle, LA, Phoenix, and Las Vegas."

Good enough.

Danzig opened the trunk and handed me the tactical vest. The night was cold and damp. I had on only the light jacket I'd been wearing when Hu ambushed me. I was thankful for the extra layer. She fitted me with a tactical radio and an earpiece. The radio was small enough that I could hide it under my jacket, which I couldn't close because of the vest. Though, in the dark, I doubted Fang would see it.

We did a mic check.

Special Agent Choi's voice came on, smooth as a cold glass.

"I'm in position, and I have LOS on the park. I count five total." He gave us a moment to process that. "Don't worry, Gage. I've got your back."

I wondered at what point my life had turned into a Dali painting. Hours ago, I was looking at a fabricated murder wrap, and now I was going undercover for the FBI.

"Copy that," I said, huskily.

Danzig walked me through the plan a final time. I'd approach the park with the bag clearly visible. Fang would call me with instructions, Hu having given him my number. Choi would take out anyone who tried to get the drop on me. Meanwhile, Danzig was maneuvering around the opposite side of the park to cut off any escape. The goal was no shots fired. Though it went unsaid, none of us believed we'd get that lucky. Seemed like a lot to cover with two agents and me, who was unarmed.

But what do I know.

Danzig asked me if I had any questions.

I did. Like, a lot. Now didn't seem to be the time.

"Good luck, Gage. You putting yourself at risk like this...it says a lot about you."

Yeah, like I'm a fucking idiot.

Instead, I said, "Thanks." And I left.

Down these dark streets go I.

Central Waterfront was an industrial district, supporting commercial ports and cargo handling, warehouses. The streets were dark and quiet. It was an eerie feeling, being alone in such a massive city.

I crossed the three blocks quickly, as much to get warmth into my muscles as to get this moving. I approached from the north, cutting over from Twenty-Third Street in between a fenced-in lot and a warehouse over-looking the black water of the bay. The air was thick with the pungent reek of marine life and industry. I passed from shadow into light as I crossed through a single lonely lamp illuminating a narrow wedge in front of the warehouse before stepping back into darkness. The park was ahead of me, an inverted L of grass and trees, likely the only patch of land they couldn't put a structure on.

I approached a long, low building at the end of a cargo ramp that lay between me and the park. I guessed that was where Choi was camped out. He'd have an unobstructed view of the park and could easily descend the single story.

There was a wall of corrugated metal, rusted and heavily tagged with graffiti, separating this lot from the park. "There's a pass-through next to the water, Gage. It's open," Choi said over the radio, all but confirming my suspicion about where he was hiding. I realized then that the building he sat upon was less a building and more a three-sided truck shelter. I found the chain-link gate with a picked lock, opened it, and stepped through. I padded softly on the dead grass moving to the park.

"Park" was, perhaps, a generous term. It was a patchy slope that rolled down to broken rocks and the bay. There was a high fence on the right forming the other border. The warehouses and factories surrounding the park were lit, giving this the impression of a black hole.

My phone buzzed as soon as my foot hit the concrete path.

"Good morning, Mr. Gage" Fang's voice was both syrupy and venomous. "Do you have the contents of Mr. Zhou's safe?"

"I do. Prove Elizabeth is alive, or I walk."

There was shuffling and muffled instructions.

"I'm here, Matt," she said, her voice small and scared.

"Where are you?"

"I'm in the park. Next to the wat—"

Fang yanked the phone back. "Satisfied?"

"Not hardly, but it'll do," I said.

"Good. Walk forward until I tell you to stop."

Choi said softly over the radio, "Gage, I've got three tangos converging on your position. Two at two o'clock and one at three."

I couldn't roger him because I was still on the phone with Fang. I said, "I understand," into the phone, intending to answer both of them.

"Okay, Mr. Gage, that is far enough," Fang said over the phone. I was about halfway into the park next to the shadowy, nebulous shape of a tree and the equally dark and nebulous San Francisco Bay to my left.

"Let me see Elizabeth."

"All in due time," Fang said icily. "Place the bag at your feet and put your hands above your head."

And I knew it was a setup.

I heard a dull thud in the distance and a grunt. Then another.

"Two tangos down," Choi said calmly.

I couldn't see Fang or Elizabeth.

"Tango three down," Choi said.

I dashed into the trees.

"Gage, what are you doing?" Choi said, warningly.

It wasn't hard to find a body. The guy was alive and writhing on the ground. I stepped on his wrist, and he let go of the pistol.

"What are you doing, Gage?" Fang asked over the phone.

Having simultaneous conversations in each ear was a cognitive overload I don't recommend.

The Chinese soldier—I didn't actually know if "soldier" was accurate, though at this point I wasn't splitting hairs—made a half-assed grab for me, so I kicked him in the ribs, and he went back to crying in the dirt.

"I'll kill the girl, Gage."

"No, you won't because that's the only leverage you've got. By the way, the three hard boys you sent to ambush me, they're all down. Cheaters never win, Fang," I said and hung up. I needed the free hand. I got low and crept beneath the cover of trees.

"Danzig, if you were going to show yourself, now would be a great time," I said quietly over the radio.

"Gage, I don't have eyes on Fang or Zhou," Choi said.

That meant I was on my own. "They must be around the corner," I said.

I ran over the wall that formed the park's other border and crept along it, pistol in a two-handed grip. The pouch had a velcro patch on it, and I'd secured that to my tactical vest.

"Moving position," Choi said.

I slid out from around the corner. There was Fang and Elizabeth, maybe thirty feet away and just a few feet up from the rocky bank.

A chorus of sirens broke the night. They were immediately joined by others.

Oh shit.

A lot of cops were about to crash in on this place in a matter of minutes.

Then I heard something else. A high-pitched, mechanical whine from an outboard motor. *That's why Fang picked this park. Son of a bitch had a boat.* Well, that about nullified Danzig's dragnet.

"Give me the bag," Fang shouted. His voice sounded strange, different in a way I couldn't place.

I stepped out of cover, pistol out. "Let her go first, then you can have it," I said. Fang whipped around, yanking her closer to use her as a shield.

"I think not. Drop your weapon and then toss the bag to me. Do it now or she dies."

"No. You're out of options, Fang. I'll make the trade, but we do it up close."

The outboard motor got louder, and while I couldn't see it exactly, I could roughly judge where the shape of the black Zodiac-style boat was pulling up to the bank. That was a smart play on Fang's part. The Chinese military probably had any number of fishing trawlers or small cargo craft that covertly housed electronic surveillance in these waters. They could easily re-task one to pick up Fang.

The sirens were getting closer.

And he was going to slide right by them.

I closed the distance between me and Fang.

"Choi, where are you?" I said quietly and before I got too close.

"Coming around the park's northern end. I don't have LOS yet."

The boat pulled up next to shore.

"Give me the bag," Fang said hurriedly.

"Let her go."

"Obviously, you don't know how this works. I get the bag and get in the boat with Ms. Zhou. I probably dump her somewhere in the bay so you'll be tied up looking for her rather than chasing after me."

He was nothing if not transparent.

"We have two guns on you, Fang. Even if you get to the boat, you won't get ten feet from shore."

"Not as long as I have the girl. Now, give me the goddamn bag!"

"I have no shot," Choi said in my ear.

There was a flash of movement. I couldn't see exactly what had happened; it was too dark. Elizabeth must have hit or elbowed Fang, because he grunted in pain and staggered back, losing his balance on the slick rocks. His arm shot out, grabbed her collar, and I watched them fall backward in slow motion.

Then I heard the shot.

37

Dropping the bag, I exploded into movement.

Fang scrambled to his feet among the rocks.

Elizabeth was in the water. She did not move.

Fang turned and leapt for the boat. I sighted and fired.

I talked a lot about honor, but I wasn't above shooting someone deserving in the back. Fang's body snapped, and he collapsed into the water. The motor kicked up, and the boat roared off. I heard the muffled, staccato thuds of suppressed rounds, and several shots hit the side of the raft.

I ran over to Elizabeth. She was lying face up in the water, eyes glassy. I pulled her to the rocky bank and felt something warm and wet beneath my hand. Fang's bullet had hit her.

"Elizabeth has been shot," I shouted into the radio.

Choi was next to me now.

He trudged into thigh-deep water, grabbed Fang, and hauled him up onto shore. The raft looked like they'd made it about twenty, thirty yards before they realized it was rapidly deflating. I assumed they could swim.

Choi secured Fang while I triaged Elizabeth.

"Come on, stay with me," I said. I had nothing but my jacket to make an improvised bandage with, so I used that. I kept talking to her, pressing my jacket over the wound. She did not regain consciousness, and I only knew of her shallow breaths because I could feel her abdomen lift slightly.

Seconds later, the whole place erupted into artificial daytime as a multitude of police vehicles converged on us from two directions.

I didn't know that my eyes had filled with tears until I saw the refracted kaleidoscope of multicolored lights.

Fang was maybe five feet from me, with Choi hovering over him, inspecting the wound.

There was just enough light now that I could see Fang in profile.

A shock ran through me, something primal and profound, an earth-shattering awareness.

It wasn't him.

One of the cops took over and worked on Elizabeth with a first aid kit until paramedics arrived. The bullet went through her back near the ribs. It was too dark to see anything, and they couldn't tell how bad it was.

I begged her again to stay with me.

Then she was in an ambulance and making best speed to a trauma center within minutes.

I didn't pay much attention to the operative I thought was Fang. Beyond knowing that I'd hit him, I didn't know what his condition was. Nor did I care. I'd stayed with Elizabeth until they put her in the ambulance and would've gone with them if Choi hadn't pulled me back.

Choi and I stood on the bank, kind of just processing. Danzig spent a few minutes with the SFPD's on-scene commander and then walked over to us. By then, the SFPD's Marine Unit fished the three-person boat crew out of the bay.

We had seven Chinese operatives, which we suspected were PLA Special Forces, in custody, and if any of them spoke English they were pretending not to. Between the Bureau and SFPD, they would have a Mandarin speaker on site within ninety minutes. So much for the theory of the MSS and PLA not playing nicely with each other.

"Well," Danzig said in a loaded tone. "That happened."

"He was never here, was he?" I asked.

"Doubt it," Danzig said. "We'll run some traces on your phone, though I doubt anything will come of it. He could've been calling from anywhere. They probably had a conference call set up so you could talk to Elizabeth. Let's say, for argument's sake, Fang bugged out the second we arrested you at the airport. Even traveling over land, he could've made the consulate in Los Angeles by now. We're going to try to throw a net up, though I don't want you to get your hopes up."

"What was in the bag?" I asked her again.

"Everything," was all she said.

Danzig returned to the on-scene commander for a bit. Choi had grabbed the bag as soon as the police arrived so it didn't end up trampled or in some SFPD evidence locker.

Choi and I drove back to the Federal Building while Danzig finished up with the police.

"You probably saved her life, Matt," he finally said. "I never had a clean shot."

"Thanks, man. I appreciate that."

I didn't know if he believed it or if it was just something to say.

The question that would plague me for a long time to come was whether or not I was the one who pushed that first domino over that eventually put Elizabeth on that rocky beach tonight.

There would be time to think on that once I was done worrying whether she'd live through the night.

Not long after, Choi guided me into a conference room with a window overlooking downtown. Well, it wasn't an interview room, so that was a step up. Maybe that meant I wasn't getting arrested after all. He stepped out and returned with a pair of styrofoam cups. I numbly accepted one of them. It tasted like hours-old, government-flavored coffee. Presumably, there was caffeine in it, and it was warmer than room temperature. Good enough, under the circumstances.

He took one call from Danzig, looked at me, and said, "When's the last time you ate?"

"I don't even know," I said.

We wouldn't do the formal debriefing until Danzig got there, and I wasn't much in the mood to talk anyway. Not until I knew what Elizabeth's condition was.

And there was the simmering anger that Fang had escaped. I tried to push that to the background. I was not successful.

Danzig rolled in maybe a half hour after she spoke to Choi. She had a tray of fresh coffees and an aromatic bag of food from the Pinecrest Diner, which advertised being open twenty-four hours on the bag. Danzig sat and passed out containers. "I didn't know what you liked, so I just got us all breakfast sandwiches. There's some hashbrowns in there too."

I took a coffee.

"How is Elizabeth?"

"She's in surgery now. The bullet was a clean exit. It perforated the bottom part of her lung and nicked a rib. They're listing her as critical. The one you hit, who we'd assumed was Fang, he's got a collapsed lung and a lot of internal bleeding. We think he will survive. Dan shot the three who were going to ambush you, none of them fatally. With the three we pulled out of the drink, that's seven we have to interrogate. None of them are Fang, of course, but we should get solid intel out of them. We'll be talking with the State Department in a few days to discuss how to handle this."

I reached for the food. I wasn't hungry, actually felt nauseous. Still, I had to eat. I'd need the strength. We would be here a while. The sandwich and the coffee were both good, and I was grateful for them.

"What was in the bag?" I asked.

Danzig cradled her coffee cup and pushed the food aside. "That's where things get a little complicated." She took a deep drink, and the expression on her face said she wished it was something stronger. "I'm going to tell you what we know, and then I hope you can fill in some blanks."

"Okay," I said.

"First, there were two passports with Johnnie Zhou's photo but names that were not his. One Malaysian, one Chinese."

That can't be good.

"There were two small notebooks. One had ledger entries depicting a record of payment in ten monthly increments of ten thousand dollars each."

I closed my eyes, as if to brace myself against what I knew was coming.

"The payments were from Fang to Zhou," Danzig said, finally. "Mr. Zhou kept detailed notes of their meetings, what they discussed and when. We don't know exactly when they'd originally met, but the first payment was ten months ago. Mr. Zhou believed Fang was, in addition to being a university professor, a representative of a Chinese-American civic organization that offered to help him pay off his rather substantial debts. He never says for certain in the journal that he knew Fang was an intelligence officer, but it seems unlikely that he wouldn't know. By the fourth month, it seems clear in his journal that he realized what he'd done. There's never anything like an actual acknowledgment; this is more of a factual accounting of what happened."

Documenting events exactly the way Nate would've taught him all those years ago when he was Nate's asset.

I said, "So, Johnnie is running this private network of political agitators, activists, and dissident journalists. He's bootstrapped the whole thing and paying for it out of pocket. Which eventually bankrupts him. At some point, one of his people uncovers evidence that the Ministry of Public Security has a secret police outpost in Chinatown and they're going after people like Zhou."

"That's right," Danzig said.

"Only now Johnnie is broke. He gets contacted by Fang, probably because he was an attractive recruitment target. Once Fang finds out Zhou is in financial trouble, he offers to help him out. That sets the hook. Johnnie agrees and, too late, realizes Fang is an MSS officer."

"That is our assessment, yes."

"Fang didn't know about the MPS angle, did he?"

"We don't think so," Choi said. "I interrogated Hu in the hospital. They didn't learn about that until they broke into Robert Li's house. It would appear you've got two separate state security organizations not knowing what the other was doing."

That was the most ironic statement I'd ever heard. I almost wanted to spill my guts on the CIA angle just to see the look on their faces. What a twisted shit circus this was.

"By all accounts, David Hu was a good cop. Fang used cultural ties to loop him in and offered him intel on the Asian gangs that Hu was policing, which helped him rise through the ranks quickly. Fang convinced Hu that Mr. Zhou and the people like him were terrorists."

Danzig said, "We think the MSS learned about Zhou's efforts through a double agent in his network. That allowed Fang to target and eventually turn him."

At this point in a case, I should be feeling relieved. Instead, I was over-burdened with terrible knowledge that I knew I could never forget.

Johnnie Zhou was a double agent and a Chinese spy. He'd betrayed the cause, betrayed Nate, his adopted country. His family. Everything. I could almost see the thought process, the justification. He was in so deep trying to do what he thought was righteous, he traded on all of that just to keep playing. Maybe he thought he could outsmart Fang. Maybe he thought he could leverage Nate somehow.

We'll never know now.

Other dark tumblers fell into their bitter places.

"Hu got the names of Johnnie's network from his house when he broke in that night. But four people had already been killed before then…" I lost steam, and my voice died out.

Danzig's response finished the thought I couldn't bring myself to give word to. "Mr. Zhou gave up the names. At least some of them. Once Fang had a hook in him, Mr. Zhou didn't have a choice. At least, that's the way it looks. I guess we'll never know for certain. We assess that he hadn't given them all, which was why Hu broke in. We don't know why Zhou didn't give them all the names before he died. Though, that is ultimately what started this whole thing."

"CI investigations take a long time. How is it that you found out about this?" I asked.

"We've been looking at Mr. Zhou for about eighteen months. His busi-ness partner, Benjamin Blake, first reached out through his attorney with a concern that Zhou was embezzling and possibly selling proprietary infor-mation to cover his financial losses. Within a few months, the Bureau deter-mined it was an espionage case, and my team was brought in. We were working on a way to approach him when he killed himself."

"No," I said flatly. "There's no way."

Danzig nodded slowly. "I'm sorry," she said.

I thought about all of the ways to fake a murder. Especially now that I knew the Chinese security services were involved.

"The forensics confirm this," she went on. "The reason for all of the secrecy after the death was that we needed to get surveillance equipment inside the house. That took a warrant."

My blood iced. I knew they had a camera because they'd shown me footage, but I didn't know when it went in there. If they had me on camera, that would complicate things.

"Zhou died before he could give them all the names. We believe Fang sent Hu in to get them and to clean up. Hu used police connections to convince someone over the phone he was a distant part of the operation, using an alias, and confirmed they didn't find anything of use, so he went in looking for a hidden safe. He admitted to being given some electronic cracking tools that let him bypass the lock. It took longer than we anticipated to get the warrant and then get the surveillance equipment in place, but it was still enough time to catch Hu on camera." Danzig paused to sip coffee. "We think the suicide was a combination of guilt and not seeing another way out. Though it's possible Zhou wanted to protect the ones who were left. Elizabeth helped us reconstruct their last argument. It's likely that pushed him over the edge. She's carrying the weight of it."

"Then why didn't you tell her? Why all the bullshit secrecy?" Anger bubbled up in me, and I didn't even try to contain it. "No one told her this was an investigation. No one told her *anything*. That's why she hired me in the first place. Because she felt like the police were lying to her, or at least intentionally keeping things from her."

"They handled that badly, Matt. The state inspectors were not good cops. Which I think you can attest to. However, given the Chinese's long history of recruiting family members—and I urge you to look at this objectively—we could not involve her in the investigation until we could rule out that she wasn't part of the operation."

Danzig's argument infuriated and offended me for all of the wrong reasons.

It was because of my feelings for Elizabeth, not because of its inherent logic. Ironically, I could see that perfectly clear because everything else had been stripped away.

"When did you know she was in the clear?"

"When we spoke to her...I guess it was two days ago," Danzig said.

"Does she know he was a spy?"

Danzig shook her head. "Not from us."

Danzig and Choi exchanged a look, the kind of unspoken communication that passes between partners. Then Danzig said, "Matt, we're going to need to do a more thorough debriefing with you over the next several days. Right now, though, I suspect you'll want some sleep."

"Does this mean...I'm not being charged with anything?"

"That's correct. Matt, I need to say..." Danzig's tone was heavy. "You were the only one who put all this together. We had no idea about the police outpost. Without you, I doubt we'd ever have found out about it. Also, if it hadn't been for you, Fang and his hit squad would have silently removed each member of Zhou's network, and no one would know a thing."

Would Robert still be alive? Would he have been able to expose that police outpost, or would the kill team have gotten to him first? I'd never know the answer to that.

The only answer I did have was I'd talked Robert into coming out of hiding and that got him killed.

We got up to leave. As I was walking over to the door, I stopped, turned, and walked back to Choi, offering my hand. He took it. "Thanks for having my back," I said.

He offered a small smile. "You got it."

Danzig said she'd drive me back to my hotel.

As we walked through the darkened Federal Building, she said, "I did read your file. There was one part I left out."

"What's that?"

"Brad Keane, our LEGAT in Nicaragua who ratted you out? The brass found out about what he did. The affairs. He got his tour curtailed and yanked back to the States. Then they pressed him on the information he offered on your investigation and he admitted to making it up. He was fired for professional misconduct two months ago and had his pension yanked. His wife found out what happened through the spouse's network. I'm told it's...ugly. The Bureau never came forward about what they'd learned because—and this is unofficial, mind you—they didn't want to acknowledge that to your agency." Danzig stopped and turned to face me. "You shouldn't have had that woman in Managua in the field. That part is on you. That doesn't mean either of you deserved what happened, and I cannot fathom the weight you carry. I was wrong for what I said, and I am sorry. I also apologize for what Keane did. We are better than that."

We rode the elevator in silence.

It was close to four when we got back to the parking lot outside the vault company where I'd parked my Defender.

"Nickel's worth of free advice, Matt. If you're going to keep this up, you need to get a license."

"Yeah, well, you people made that a little difficult."

"I can have that removed. It was spiteful and petty, and the Bureau should be above that."

"I appreciate that," I said and meant it.

I got out. Danzig handed me a card and asked me to come in and debrief after I'd had some sleep.

"Johnnie Zhou's network...please do whatever you can for them, and quickly. Just in case we didn't get everyone."

"I'll get it on it immediately. Stay out of trouble."

I told her I'd try. The day was young.

38

I slept for eighteen hours.

After showering any last semblance of incarceration or trunk imprisonment away, I found a diner and ate two breakfasts.

Once the sun was up, I texted Danzig and asked what time she wanted me in for the debriefing. We agreed on ten. There was something I had to do first.

Danzig told me Elizabeth was still in critical but stable condition and was expected to survive. She was awake and under guard. I was grateful for that. For all of it.

I was not allowed to see her.

I went to see Nate.

It was a calm, sunny morning in late September, crisp air with notes of autumn. Nate greeted me with a mug of coffee, and we went to his office.

"I'm so relieved you're okay," he said.

Nate looked worn, older somehow than the last time I'd seen him.

I said, "I'm sorry I didn't call. By the time I finished up with the FBI, I crashed. I'd been going for a few days at that point."

I told Nate everything that happened with Hu and Fang and the switch. I did not tell him what I'd learned about Johnnie Zhou.

"And they think Elizabeth will be okay?"

I'd already given him Danzig's report. I think he just needed to hear me say it. "That's what they tell me. Nate, there are two things I have to talk to you about. And they're important."

"All right," he said.

"Johnnie was an agent. He was one of theirs. Fang flipped him. He found out Johnnie was heavily in debt from running his own spy game, and he used that to turn him. The Bureau guys don't think Johnnie knew at first. Apparently, Fang was masquerading as a member of a civic organization helping Chinese-American citizens in need. And it was Johnnie who gave them the names of his network, at least some of them."

I paused there, to let Nate process what he'd heard.

It was a lot to take in.

No, it was overwhelming.

To learn that your own agent and close friend had been turned.

It hit him about as hard as it would've hit me.

"Does Elizabeth know?" he finally said.

"I don't think so."

"And they murdered him? To keep him from talking?"

"He killed himself," I said.

"I see," he said.

"I have to go have a formal debriefing with the FBI today. I don't know if it's just questions or a formal deposition. If it's the latter, I can't hide the CIA's involvement. I don't know what all they'll ask me about, but you need to be prepared for the possibility that when do they do a full counterintelligence investigation on this, they may find the links between Johnnie and the Agency. I don't want you to be blindsided."

"I understand," he said. "Thank you. What will you tell Elizabeth about her father?"

"About his being a spy? I don't know that accomplishes anything good. As to how he died, I think she deserves to know. It's what she hired me for."

"Be careful with the truth, Matthew. It doesn't always do what you intend."

An interesting sentiment, coming from him. I wasn't sure if it was advice or a warning.

The debrief was on the record but not sworn testimony. And it was just Danzig, Choi, and me. We reviewed the events again from the time I was released from the Santa Rosa County Jail to the exchange at Warm Water Cove.

When they'd first questioned me after the showdown with Hu, Danzig asked if I was protecting anyone, and I'd told her I was only working for my client. It was the strictest interpretation of the truth. We both knew then that it wasn't the whole truth.

She did not ask me that question again.

Maybe it was professional courtesy.

Danzig turned off the recording device signaling the end of the interview. Danzig said, "You mentioned before that you worked for an investigative outfit. The Orpheus Foundation, was it?"

"That's right."

"And they get a story out of this?"

"Yeah. That was to cover bailing me out of jail. I'm afraid I can't spike it."

"I'm not asking you to. Just the opposite."

"Maybe it's the two days without sleep, but I'm not following you."

"I'd appreciate it if you could keep the active parts of our investigation out of the spotlight. But everything else is fair game, as far as I'm concerned."

"That's...surprising," I said.

"Matt, we've got seven Chinese special forces operatives that were a covert kill squad on US soil. Our government is probably going to trade them for some concession. People like Robert Li in all these other cities need to know what the threat is. Light the bastards up," she said. "Off the record."

I checked out of my hotel and packed up the Defender. I called Elizabeth from the road. I knew I couldn't get in to see her, and I didn't want to put the pressure on her by asking if she wanted me to stay around. I told her we could catch up when she got home, and I would have a final case file prepared for her.

I left, wondering if I'd ever see my old friend, Nate, again.

The revelation that Johnnie Zhou was a spy for the other side, a corrupted angel, was something that would haunt me for some time.

I drove home taking the Pacific Coast Highway and couldn't help but feel that I'd lost something.

"And that's everything," I said.

It wasn't, not even close. I'd made no mention of Nate or his operation and had entirely hidden the Agency's hand in any of this.

Jennie and I sat on her balcony in a downtown Los Angeles skyscraper, watching the sun dive into the Pacific. This was the kind of view people wrote stories about.

The advance from her book about having a role in breaking the Panama Papers paid for it.

We had a pair of martinis, and something told me they wouldn't be the only ones.

She said, "You want my advice?"

"No."

"Don't fall for your clients."

"I didn't," I started…and stopped because I knew she was right.

"There's definitely a story there," she said. "I mean, the secret police station, then the espionage ring. Damn. Major exposé potential. The fact that the FBI didn't know anything about it…" Jennie shook her head and reached for her drink.

"I've got a favor to ask."

She barked out a laugh. "You're all out of those, Matty."

"I'm serious, J. Run with the secret police. We know from Robert Li's investigation they've likely got outposts in dozens of cities across the world. Probably more. Focus on that. I want you to leave Johnnie Zhou out of this. The FBI still has a counterintelligence investigation to run, and we don't want to tip the CHICOMMs anymore than they are."

"That's the story," she protested.

"No, that's a part of the story. It's not the whole thing. And it's not even the most important part. The police outpost thing is a global operation. When you boil it down, Lawrence Fang is one spy in one city."

I looked over at her and saw another debate forming on her lips.

"Don't touch it," I said. "For me. Please."

"Okay." Again, Jennie shook her head. "If you'd didn't want me to write about the FBI angle, why the hell did you even tell me?"

"I had to tell somebody. I gave Agent Danzig my word that I wouldn't compromise her operation. I trust you to put it together in a way that makes sense."

I had a feeling the Chinese secret police attacking dissidents globally would keep her busy for a long time.

I was right.

The series Jennie went on to write didn't have nearly the impact that the Panama Papers did. Maybe because this was something people just assumed the Chinese government was already doing. It did, however, get picked up by the *New York Times*, the *Washington Post,* the *Guardian*, *Le Monde*, and others. Jennie then was invited to write a longer-form story for the *Atlantic*. It brought significant public attention to the issue. It shined a light on something someone tried to hide, which was what good journalism did. We liked to think that the security services in these countries were already aware, though certainly in many of the smaller nations in Africa, Asia, and South America, they weren't. By the Foundation's estimate, they'd exposed seventy-three police outposts in nations across the world and six continents.

I'd made good on my promise to Robert to bring this thing to light. However, I didn't, I couldn't feel good about any of this. I just hoped wherever he was, Robert was satisfied that his work was finished.

Jennie agreed that my getting a PI license made it easier for the Foundation to keep working with me.

Days faded together, and I spent a few of them trying poorly to surf, much to the chagrin of the staff of Cosmic Ray's, who berated my technique, or lack thereof. They informed me in no uncertain terms that I was a kook (the most derisive term in surfer ergot) and as much a danger to myself as I was to others. They eventually welcomed me back and appreciated that I'd caused trouble and embarrassment for those cops who'd threatened them. Word on the street was Nugent got a formal reprimand and was reassigned to something more suited to his "talents." I assumed that meant parking enforcement.

Nate quietly retired from the CIA. Told them it was time. I hoped he could dodge the bullet that was probably coming, though I wasn't so sure.

It was three weeks after I'd returned from the Bay Area that Elizabeth Zhou walked into Cosmic Ray's. She was dressed for business.

I was at my usual table. I stood as she approached the table, unsure if I should hug her, shake her hand, or smile awkwardly. She may as well have had a force field. I offered her a chair, and she sat.

"How are you feeling?" I asked.

"I'm okay. Fine," she said, and I knew it meant she was anything but and wanted to avoid the question.

I knew from Nate that the funeral had been the week after I left. I did not attend. She didn't ask me to be there, so I assumed she wanted space.

"I hope a check is okay," she said and removed a heavy envelope from her purse. She set it on the table. I didn't look at the amount.

"I've typed up a case file for you. It details everything that I did and what I discovered." Pretty much. "I also have a final invoice for you. I thought you might need that for the IRS."

"Thank you. I don't...I don't think I need to see the file. Keep it. If I decide I need it, I'll ask."

"I understand."

"Special Agent Danzig told me everything you did. They also told me what that cop, Hu, did to you. I'm so sorry. You could've been killed."

"I'm far too stubborn for that," I said, and she finally smiled.

She reached across the table and covered my hand with hers. She held it there a moment and then drew it back.

"How did everything work out with Ben Blake?" I asked.

"They lost the sale. A local reporter found out that the FBI was involved and that it was Blake who called them. That scared off his buyers. Blake and team still agreed to settle for my father's original share of the company. I can settle dad's obligations, and I'll have a lot left over."

"Any plans for what you'll do with the money?"

"Dad would want me to do something with it, something that matters. I just need time to figure out what that is. I took a leave of absence from the firm. Not sure I'll go back. I'll probably travel a bit, try to heal."

My pulse surged a bit, and I half expected, or maybe just hoped, she'd finish the sentence with, "And I'd like you to come with me."

She didn't.

I realized at that moment that what we'd shared was time. The night we spent together meant more to me than it did her. That wasn't to say it hadn't been anything to Elizabeth, just that we were in very different places that night.

Did I love her?

I can't answer that question. I hadn't allowed feelings for anyone after Angel.

However fleeting, our relationship meant something profound to me. This wasn't the time, I supposed, and certainly not for her.

Maybe things would change in the future.

"Matt, I need to ask you something." She looked away when she said it, and I knew it was because she hid tears. "Did my father kill himself?"

There was no easy way to have the conversation that ended in, "And your father was a Chinese spy who killed himself."

There was a quote from scripture at the entrance to CIA Headquarters. It's the Agency's unofficial motto, though one I feel they fall short of too often. "And the truth shall set you free."

The woman across from me was barely holding on. She held a rigid and professional mask that she maintained through discipline and sheer force of will.

If it were me, I'd want to know.

It wasn't me.

"A Chinese spy named Fang Yìchén killed him," I said. It was a kind of truth.

The promise to find him, at the ends of the earth if I had to, floated in my mouth but I didn't say them aloud. I wonder if it would've changed things if I had.

"Thank you for everything you did," Elizabeth Zhou said, and she left while she had the composure to do so.

I looked at the check. It was a hundred thousand dollars. Orders of magnitude more than what we'd agreed to.

Was I wrong in not telling her the truth about her father? Probably.

Would there be long nights ahead when I questioned this decision? Where the guilt of taking the easy way out might consume me? Certainly.

I'd still do it again. She'd suffered enough, and this would do her no true good.

The truth might set you free, but it was worth asking, *Free from what?*

One Bullet Away
Book 2 in The Gage Files

For some, loyalty is a game played with loaded dice.

In Miami's deceptive calm, private investigator Matt Gage is pulled into a case that cuts to the core of the city's athletic empire. Hired by sports agent Jimmy Lawson, Gage is tasked with infiltrating the shadowy Sunshine Sports Collective and unraveling a dark conspiracy that spans the recesses of Miami's underbelly to the pulsing heart of its illustrious arenas.

As an ex-CIA operative, Gage is familiar with danger. But the Collective is a new breed of enemy. Behind the glamorous facade of endorsements and celebrity athletes lies the prospect of grim machinations. And when a shocking act of violence turns the case personal, Gage finds himself alone in the Magic City, a place as dangerous as any he survived in his years as a spy. With no one to trust and nothing as it seems, Gage learns that death is only one bullet away.

Get your copy today at
severnriverbooks.com

AUTHOR'S NOTE

I believe any good spy story should have an element of truth to it. Unfortunately, for this story, that's the secret police outposts the Chinese government have set up in cities throughout the world. I first read about this in April 2023, when the *Guardian* broke a story about one of these covert stations in New York City. The reporting suggested they may be in as many as fifty-three countries worldwide and have existed since at least 2016. Reporting by other news agencies speculate these stations may have existed as early as 2002. The intent, as described in this book, is to silence Chinese citizens—activists, journalists, and dissidents—who are speaking out against the communist government in Beijing. One report stated as many as 210,000 Chinese citizens had been "forcibly returned" to China because of this activity.

The intelligence practices used by the Chinese government depicted in this book are consistent with the methods and tradecraft described by intelligence and law enforcement personnel. The Central Intelligence Agency's former head of counterintelligence, James M. Olson's book, *To Catch A Spy*, was particularly useful. *Chinese Communist Espionage* by Peter Mattis and Mathew Brazil was especially instructive in describing how the communist government has used espionage and pervasive domestic surveillance since the earliest days of its existence, and how it informs the culture today. Any factual errors are my own.

As a fiction writer, my job is to give you a good story that entertains you for a few hours. I hope I've done that here. I don't advocate a specific political position in any of my fiction, rather I present facts as I understand and observe them and construct a story from it. However, one thing I hope we can all agree on is that governments using secret police to silence their detractors is vile and must be combatted. For a nation to establish clandestine operations in other countries to further this end is a violation of international law and national sovereignty, and it's something I hope our own government is doing its utmost to thwart.

Dale M. Nelson
    Washington, DC, December 2023

ABOUT THE AUTHOR

Dale M. Nelson grew up outside of Tampa, Florida. He graduated from the University of Florida's College of Journalism and Communications and went on to serve as an officer in the United States Air Force. Following his military service, Dale worked in the defense, technology and telecommunications sectors before starting his writing career. He currently lives in Washington D.C. with his wife and daughters.

Sign up for Dale M. Nelson's reader list at
severnriverbooks.com

Printed in the United States
by Baker & Taylor Publisher Services